TAMER OF HORSES

Other books by Amalia Carosella

Helen of Sparta
By Helen's Hand

Writing as Amalia Dillin

Forged by Fate
Tempting Fate
Fate Forgotten
Taming Fate
Beyond Fate

Honor Among Orcs
Blood of the Queen

Postcards from Asgard

TAMER OF HORSES

Amalia Carosella

Tamer of Horses

ISBN: 1535240490
ISBN-13: 978-1535240499

Cover art created by Lane Brown
www.lanebrownart.com

Edited by Elayne Morgan

For Adam.
And for everyone who read *Helen of Sparta* and said to me:
"Pirithous should have his own book."

Contents

"Now brave Pirithous, bold Ixion's son,
The love of fair Hippodamia had won.
The cloud-begotten race, half men, half beast,
Invited, came to grace the nuptial feast"
—Ovid, *Metamorphoses*, 12.

CHAPTER ONE

HIPPODAMIA

"If the queen of the Lapiths is dead, I do not see why we should not let this foolishness die with her," Eurytion said, not for the first time, as they traveled down the mountain. Since word of the queen's passing had reached the centaurs, he had done nothing but grumble.

Not that Hippodamia blamed him. By all accounts Pirithous, named king of the Lapiths upon his mother's death, was more pirate than hero—and he had certainly proven he was in no hurry to take a wife, even if he'd agreed to the match his mother had made for him. Once, perhaps, Hippodamia had found the idea of marriage to Pirithous attractive, but after five years spent waiting for him to claim her as his bride, the shining prize of such a husband had tarnished. Son of Zeus he might be, but she was beginning to think she would be better off dedicating herself to Artemis and following the goddess to the hunt. As a woman, she had no true future among the centaurs as anything but a maiden, besides—which was precisely why she had been so pleased by the thought of marriage to Pirithous, even beyond its promise of peace for her people… until Pirithous had never come.

"With Queen Dia's death, it is more important than ever to reinforce the bonds of kinship between centaur and man,"

Centaurus said, his tail flicking with irritation, though Hippodamia could hear none of it in his tone. "The Lapiths are our best hope for peace and protection, and King Pirithous would make a powerful friend. Perhaps he is not as wise or reasonable as his mother, but he has always treated us with respect."

Eurytion snorted, kicking up an excess of dust with his clomping. "That does not mean this pirate deserves the hand of your daughter!"

"It is my choice," Hippodamia said, bumping against the younger centaur's flank with her shoulder as she walked beside him. This high up the mountain, the trees were thinner and the path wide enough that they could travel all three abreast. "And I go willingly if it means peace for our people. No matter what Pirithous is, the bargain is worth striking to keep our people from being hunted like beasts again, but if the king of Athens calls him friend, he cannot be all bad. King Theseus is the Horse Lord's son, after all, and it is said they are like brothers."

"He should have come to us long before now," Eurytion growled.

She shook her head. Though she had been raised among the centaurs, there were times she did not understand her friend. Eurytion had watched over her from the moment she had begun to crawl, protecting her from being trod upon by careless hooves, and keeping her from losing herself in the caves where she had played as a child. He had taught her to love her own strangeness as a girl, and had seen her arrival as a gift from the gods, as their salvation. But now, when she reached out with both hands to embrace her fate, he refused to accept her choice. Refused to believe that any man could be worthy of her. Though how he thought she could save her people otherwise, she could not imagine.

"Whether he had come earlier or not, you would have found him just as irksome," Hippodamia said. "If the choice were left to you I would live the rest of my life as a maiden, for no man would ever be worthy."

"No man *is* worthy," Eurytion said. "Among the centaurs at least you would be loved and honored. Among these Lapiths—"

"What is done is done," Centaurus said, and her father's voice was firm. "But I will not have the Lapiths say we centaurs did not honor our oaths, nor will I give them cause to find insult." His eyes narrowed as his gaze fell upon Eurytion. "Am I understood?"

Eurytion's tail switched, and his broad nostrils flared in his dark face. "Of course, Lord Centaurus."

Her father nodded, pushing aside a branch and holding it back that she might pass. It was not so long a journey down the mountain to the lands belonging to the Lapiths, and now she looked out over the valley, the sun gilding the walled palace with gold and fire. It was beautiful and terrifying, witnessing the dawn of her fate.

"They live differently, of course, but I do not think you will be unhappy, Mia. Not so long as you do not look for love. By all accounts, Pirithous is rich enough that you will want for nothing once you are his queen."

"If he will have her," Eurytion said, coming to a stop beside them. It was the last clear view before they descended into the trees below, to follow the fainter deer trails as they approached the border between their lands. "And have you thought at all what you will do if he refuses us?"

"He will not refuse," Centaurus said. "He will not wish to begin his rule as king with a war."

"We hardly have the strength to do him much in the way of harm. We would not make it past the palace walls!"

Centaurus sniffed. "War with men, you fool foal. Dia's death breaks the peace between the Lapiths and the Myrmidons just as it has ours. He will not risk the gift of our friendship offered elsewhere."

"If the Myrmidons would have us as allies, why do we bother with the Lapiths at all?" Eurytion demanded.

"Because Pirithous is kin, son of Zeus and Ixion by Dia, and half-brother to Centaurus," Hippodamia said, tearing her eyes from the palace to elbow him back. The way he pranced and pawed so near to her, she risked losing a toe. His hide shivered beneath her touch and he sidled away with another snort. "Really, Eurytion, it's as if you've forgotten everything we were taught. The Lapiths might believe we're capable of going to war against them, but as long as Centaurus is king, sacred laws bind him. Do you wish so much to see our blood spilled? Our people cursed?"

"I wish only to see you happy, Mia. And though your father might believe it possible, I do not see how you will find any joy among men. And the things I have heard of Pirithous—he will not honor you as he should."

"As a centaur might, you mean?" she asked. "And what good will that do me, to have honor and nothing else? I cannot stay, even if I wished to, and no matter where I go, everything must change. Why should it not be in service to my people? Let Pirithous be a fool, or a pirate, or a hero-king, I care not. We will have peace for ourselves and our foals, and that is all that matters."

"Your *children*, you mean." His black eyes burned, and she looked away, her face flushing. He knew too much of her desires, her hopes. "And like as not, Pirithous will take your sons from you to be weaned by another, or given up to some other king to raise."

"If he truly is so cruel as that, I will ask Chiron to tutor my sons," she said, pleased her voice stayed steady. "The old centaur would not deny my request, nor would Pirithous refuse the honor. And I will have the raising of any daughters, besides."

"Enough," Centaurus said, when Eurytion drew breath to argue. "If you cannot hold your tongue, you will remain behind. I will not stand by while you shame my daughter for doing her duty. And it is a good thing she desires children, or there would be little purpose to any of it. We should all pray that Hippodamia bears Pirithous a strong son, that he might inherit his father's kingship and grant us peace for that much longer." His tail switched, snapping against his flank. "Gryneus awaits us below. Hippodamia, you will ride upon my back. I do not trust Eurytion not to run off if you sit upon his."

Her father smiled, but from the wariness in his eyes, she knew he was only half-jesting. When he held out his hand to her, she took it, then leapt up onto his bare back, as she had a hundred-hundred times before. But this ride would be one of her last, for once her father gave her to Pirithous, she was unlikely to see much of him, nor would it be proper for her to sit upon his back like a child once she was made queen.

If she was made queen.

She glanced sidelong at Eurytion, trotting beside her father as he picked his way down the mountain trail. Centaurus was rarely wrong, but if he was now, what then? She would be dishonored among the Lapiths, and none were likely to want a girl raised by centaurs as a bride even if they did not think her shamed. Nor could she stay among the Lapiths if they insulted her people by refusing the friendship of the centaurs. Still, there was nothing left for her upon the mountain but sorrow and fantasy. Returning would only encourage Eurytion, and she could not bear for him to look upon her with hope in his eyes. Not when she knew in her heart what he offered would never be enough. She could not spend another season watching the females foal, knowing she could never share in their joy.

Pirithous *would* accept her, she decided. And whether she cared for him or not, she would know, at least, that her people were protected. If it was as Eurytion said, and Pirithous took her sons, she would still have her daughters to love. Daughters that no centaur could give her.

And if nothing else, there were the horses. Perhaps that was the opportunity which tempted her most of all, for the Lapiths were well known to have the finest beasts in all Achaea. If Pirithous only allowed her to spend her days in his stables and granted her nothing else, she would be very happy indeed.

After all, if he was truly a pirate, he would hardly be at home.

CHAPTER TWO

PIRITHOUS

Today, he was king.

Pirithous stared at the draped canopy of linen above his head, dyed the richest of deep violets. Apollo's chariot had only just begun its journey in the east, turning the mountains a matching shade of purple, and still he had not slept, knowing what morning would bring.

One of the women beside him stirred, her fingers weaving through the hair on his chest. The second woman had rolled away from him, curled into a ball on the opposite side of the wide bed. He'd had each of them twice in the hope of exhausting himself, but he ought to have known it would not serve. He was a true son of Zeus, after all. Pleasure of that kind would never tire him properly.

A knock on the door was followed by the steward's dark head. "Forgive me, my lord, but you wished to know when King Theseus arrived."

"So soon?" Pirithous slid out from beneath the first woman and rose from the bed. Even if he could not sleep, it did not mean the women should be kept from their rest; they were useless to him if they could not keep awake at night, besides.

The steward entered, a pitcher of water in hand and a towel over his arm. "Poseidon saw fit to speed him on his journey. He came by sea, with the tide."

"Of course." He leaned over the silver washbasin and stared into the water as the steward poured. Gold flickered off the surface, reflecting sunlight. Theseus would have made all haste the moment the messenger arrived with news of Dia's illness and Poseidon would not have refused his son's prayers.

While Pirithous's mother had lived, he had not needed to take on the true burden of kingship. She had ruled well and long after Ixion's madness, and Pirithous had made his name and his fortune as a pirate and a hero with Theseus, refilling the coffers Ixion had emptied. But now, everything was changed. Now he must settle, and prove himself king enough to protect the Lapiths, his people. All the more important now, with Peleus and his Myrmidons free to make war upon them. The bonds of peace had been broken with his mother's passing.

"There is one other matter, my lord," the steward said. "The centaurs have come to pay their respects."

Pirithous grunted, splashing the clear, fresh water on his face and neck. Ixion's madness had bred the centaurs, his lust for Hera driving him to mate with her false form, made of nothing more than clouds. As they were his kin—even so strangely related—he could not turn from them. But even when they stayed upon their mountain they were inclined to cause trouble for his people, and the Lapiths were in turn inclined to resent them, their very existence a reminder of all else the Lapiths had suffered under Ixion's rule, which was why his mother had gone to the trouble of arranging things as she had. And, he had no doubt, why the centaurs had come so quickly—they would press for a decision, and he had not yet made one. They must have peace, of course, and he could not risk sending the centaurs to the Myrmidons for protection and alliance, but a marriage? No matter what he decided, it was bound to cause trouble.

"Offer them our hospitality," he commanded. "I will give them audience after the morning meal. They are to be treated with all proper respect."

"Of course, my lord." The steward bowed. "And King Theseus?"

"He, at least, I need not fear offending. Send him up. We will share a private meal."

He had much to discuss with his friend.

***

They clasped arms, and Pirithous smiled beneath Theseus's searching gaze. "I am well, my friend. Truly. Apollo gave my mother time enough to say goodbye, and her shade flies, free at last from the pain of her sickness."

"We all grieve with you, Pirithous," Theseus said, clapping him on the shoulder. "Even the centaurs have come to honor her."

"Ixion may have been mad, but Dia loved him—and his children, no matter how ill-gotten. Though I confess, I am not certain I will ever know how she found the strength." Pirithous guided Theseus toward the low table, set with fresh bread and cheeses, grapes and figs and honeyed nuts. A pitcher of water, mountain-cold and flavored with crushed mint leaves, waited to be poured.

Theseus seated himself on the cushions provided, and they watched the serving girl fill their cups. Pirithous dismissed her with a lift of his chin. She smiled shyly, her gaze flitting over Theseus in invitation, but when he did not respond she bowed and left them to their meal.

Since Theseus had married, he barely noticed the women around him, no matter how comely. Pirithous had made a game of it, asking for the most beautiful of the palace women to serve him, with a prize of gemstones to the girl able to catch the Athenian king's eye. Thus far, the gems had gone unclaimed, and with every visit the wagering grew more intense.

"You intend to take Centaurus's daughter as your bride, then?" Theseus asked, once the servant had gone.

"I intend to keep the peace my mother forged," Pirithous replied, pushing the bread toward his friend. Theseus had not so much as glanced at the girl as she left, though Pirithous had seen no reason not to appreciate the enticing sway of her hips. No doubt she would reappear at the funeral banquet to try again, once Theseus had drunk his fill of the wine. "If it means I must marry the girl, it makes little difference. I have women enough to please myself, and I need only plant her until I get an heir. At least it will quiet the old mothers, and I need not dance around offers from kings I do not dare offend."

Theseus snorted as he smeared a large wedge of bread with honey. "You take this marriage too lightly. She will not only be your wife, Pirithous, she will be queen."

"As long as she sees to the weaving and the kitchens, she need not be bothered with the rest." He shrugged, taking a handful of nuts and passing the dish along. "You have your Amazon, Theseus, and I am happy for you if you have found some kind of love in your bed, but not every man desires a wife who thinks herself equal to a man."

"If the Lapiths were not already in the habit of obeying their queen, perhaps it would not matter what wild woman you married," Theseus said. "Surely you must have considered this? Or if you did not, tell me at least Dia made some arrangement."

"I think you worry overmuch, my friend." He leaned back with his cup. The mint water had cleared his mind, despite his lack of sleep. "I have yet to meet a woman I could not tame, and the Lapiths know me as their king, besides. I am chosen by Zeus himself."

"Then I shall have to content myself with letting Antiope speak to your new bride. At least then we will know if she means to poison you or slit your throat in your sleep."

"I had not realized you had brought your wife," Pirithous said, frowning. "You did not leave her in the megaron, I hope?"

"Surely you do not believe Antiope would stand for it if I did?"

The thought of the Amazon queen running wild among his people did nothing to reassure him. Better to have Antiope sneering at him across the table than causing trouble among the men. Pirithous may have made his peace with Theseus's choice of bride, but she still presented certain challenges as a guest. His men did not yet know what to make of her, and were liable to insult her without meaning to. He'd lost more than one good spear-man in such a way.

"Tell me at least she will not challenge the centaurs to combat over some slight."

Theseus threw his head back and laughed. "The look on your face—oh, Pirithous. You need not fear. She is only in the kitchens, doing what she may for Dia's final banquet."

He allowed himself to smile at his own expense, any irritation at the jest overwhelmed by relief—and gratitude. Antiope would not humble herself for just any woman. "I can think of no greater honor to my mother, Theseus. My thanks to both of you."

Theseus's lips twitched. "Call off your women and we shall call it an exchange of kindnesses."

Pirithous grinned. The wagering would be even more intense when the women learned Theseus knew of the game. It would make them all the more determined to claim the victory.

"For Antiope's sake," Pirithous agreed. "But only as long as she remains at your side."

***

Perhaps he would turn one of the larger storerooms into a small megaron for private audience, Pirithous thought as he took his seat in the heavy carved chair that served as his throne. He did not trust the servants not to eavesdrop from the balcony overlooking the main hall, where feasts, rituals, and gatherings were held and justice dispensed.

Pirithous lifted his eyes to the open square above the main hearth, catching sight of several of the palace women leaning over the rail. Sun streamed down so brightly they had no need for a fire, but the hearth was always tended, its flame a symbol of the health of his lands.

Theseus settled himself upon a high-backed chair in the place of honor at Pirithous's right, looking kingly in his blue linen tunic, embroidered with silver and gold horses at the hem and sleeves. Theseus had always looked the king, even without his crown, and Pirithous could not recall a time that the burden of kingship had weighed at all heavily upon his friend's shoulders. For all Theseus's advice that Pirithous approach this betrothal with caution, the king of Athens had always done as he wished—and Antiope was the proof of it. Theseus had risked even the curse of the gods by taking the Amazon queen as his wife, and there were times when Pirithous wondered how much *persuasion* had been required to keep her.

He smiled at the thought. The gods gave wonderful gifts with their ichor. Since he had discovered his own powers of persuasion and perception, he had never taken an unwilling woman to bed, and the difference it made to his own pleasure was marked. All it took was a hint of his own lust to light a spark in the hearts of his bedmates, which he then carefully nurtured with mouth and hands into flame. No woman left his bed dissatisfied, and soon enough, they needed no encouragement at all. Yes, his father had given him a very fine gift indeed, and if Theseus did not make use of those same divine gifts with his wife, he was as great a fool as he was a king.

"My lord," the steward said, bowing low before him. "Centaurus and his party await."

"Show them in," he said, leaning forward in his seat. The better to catch sight, among the centaurs' large hairy bodies and clopping hooves, of the woman he would soon make his wife.

Centaurus entered first, of course. Although Pirithous had met Ixion's son a handful of times before, the appearance of the centaur king never failed to disturb him. He was a large, well-muscled man at first glimpse, naked save for a loincloth and sandals—but from his back extended the hindquarters of a horse, dappled gray and beautifully proportioned. The other three centaurs were not so alarming—more horse than man, for Centaurus had mated with true mares to breed them—with only the head and torso betraying what was left of their humanity. Pirithous had often wondered what might have resulted had Centaurus found a willing woman. But perhaps a woman could not have survived the birth of such a beast, for Centaurus's children had all been born as large as foals.

Pirithous rose, one king to another, as Centaurus and his people approached the dais. He would not have anyone say he did not grant the centaurs all proper respect, nor would he give his people any excuse to treat them poorly. Not when he meant to take Centaurus's adopted daughter as his wife. And where was the girl? Surely they had not come so far empty-handed.

Centaurus stopped, and though he did not bow, he nodded. "Son of Zeus and Dia, King of the Lapiths, of the valley and the mountain where we roam, we come to see your mother's pledge fulfilled. In exchange for peace, we offer you our only daughter, blessed by the gods themselves."

"Peace with the sons of Ixion was my mother's last wish," Pirithous said, his voice raised to carry into the balcony above the hearth. The megaron was full enough that word would travel swiftly throughout his lands. "As such, it has become mine as well, by this means or another. Let me meet this daughter, then pray to Zeus. If my father offers his sign and the augurs and omens agree, I will make her my queen."

One of the centaurs beside Centaurus snorted, his hide a shining black and his well-muscled chest a rich brown from the sun. He scraped his feathered hoof across the tiled floor, nostrils flaring, and glared at Pirithous with eyes like coals.

"And no doubt the omens will prove ill if our Lady does not please your eyes?"

Theseus stirred behind him, and Pirithous felt his cousin's amusement, though he did not dare turn to look. Instead of addressing the insolent centaur, he kept his gaze upon Centaurus. "If the sons of Ixion have no faith in me, I fear there is no purpose to any truce."

"I swear to you, King Pirithous, it is not mistrust which provokes Eurytion, but love for our daughter. He has had the guarding of her from her earliest days, and protects her as he would his own foal." Centaurus's back hoof kicked out, catching the black centaur's flank with a meaty thud. Eurytion stumbled, dancing sideways with a grunt and a clatter. "He allows his affection to cloud his judgment, that is all."

"My mother, too, inspired great loyalty in those around her," Pirithous said. He did not care for the way Eurytion's eyes flashed. No matter what Centaurus said, there would be trouble there. "In a woman who might be queen, it is a blessing and a strength."

Centaurus stretched out his arm, and a girl stepped forward, hidden until that moment by the centaur's bulk. She was not so young as Pirithous had feared, though her brown eyes were wide and clear with an innocence belying her years. Dirt smeared her cheeks and the beds of her nails were darkened with mud and filth, but beneath the dirt and stained gown, her skin was clear and healthy and her body lithesome, with strong, shapely legs and wide hips. For all of that, he knew he could not be sure of the true color of her dark hair or her sun-darkened skin until she was properly bathed. Her bare feet alone were nearly black.

"King Pirithous." She lifted her chin and met his eyes. "I am Hippodamia, daughter of Centaurus, and Tamer of Horses. In honor of your mother, I have come to forge a lasting peace between our peoples."

Zeus help him. She looked as though it pained her to say the words, and the way Eurytion's tail whipped against his flanks, eyes dark and lips parted, he feared he understood the reason why. That Eurytion wanted her for his own, Pirithous had no doubt. Whether the centaur had taken her already, and claimed her heart besides, he must yet discover. It was one thing to marry a girl, an innocent, to get an heir and strengthen the bonds of an alliance, but another thing altogether to take a bride who had already given herself up to a beast. She was as likely to slit his throat in their marriage bed as do her duty, and then there would be no peace at all.

Theseus had not been wrong in the slightest about the trouble she might bring him, though he hated to admit as much. Pirithous narrowed his eyes at the girl, refusing to turn his head to see his friend's knowing smile.

One king to another, he would never hear the end of it.

CHAPTER THREE

HIPPODAMIA

She had expected darker hair and an older face. Out of everything she had heard of Pirithous, nothing had led her to believe he would be so engaging. Even Eurytion's outburst had not ruffled him. Without so much as a blink, he had turned the centaur's insult to his own advantage. But after so long at sea, could he not at least have had a worn look about his face? Some hint of salt-scoured lines instead of an expression that spoke of laughter and good humor? No wonder Eurytion had bridled. After seeing Pirithous, she could hardly blame the centaur for his anxiety.

"You honor me, Hippodamia." Pirithous certainly looked like a king as he bowed over her hand. Worse than that, he had the grace of one, pressing his lips to her fingers without any hesitation for the grime that coated them. Eurytion had worried what it would mean if she married Pirithous, feared she would fall in love with a man who would never return her affections, but it was not until that moment that she understood why.

Hippodamia did not so much as glance at her friend, shifting her gaze instead to the man who had risen to stand beside Pirithous. Tall and broad-shouldered, just like the king, with darker hair and bluer eyes. He took her hand when Pirithous let it go, and smiled.

"My lady queen has come to give you welcome to this hall, though she has been made busy preparing Dia's banquet. It is our hope you will accept my welcome in her place. I am Theseus, King of Athens and son of Poseidon Earth-Shaker."

"Son of the Horse Lord," Gryneus murmured, behind her. She knew without looking that he had bowed his head, touching his fist to his silver-furred chest. Poseidon of the Horses was their most honored god, for without the mares of Magnesia, Centaurus would have had no offspring at all. It was a great shame Theseus already had a queen; not even Eurytion could have objected to a marriage to Poseidon's son, and she could see in his face Theseus possessed a humility Pirithous had yet to discover.

She dropped to one knee before him, pressing his hand to her forehead. "I beg your blessing for my people, King Theseus, and upon my union with King Pirithous."

"I dare not speak for my father, Princess," he said gently, the pressure of his hand around hers urging her to rise. "Please, girl. You need not kneel to me."

She rose obediently and met his eyes, the color of the sea. "It is enough that you speak for yourself, my lord, if you will give your blessing to our marriage."

Theseus pressed his mouth into a thin line, his eyes dancing, and exchanged a strange look with Pirithous. "For whatever worth it might hold, you have it, Hippodamia. I can think of no better way to honor Dia than with this peace. But the decision belongs to the gods, not to me."

"I am certain the gods will give a favorable sign," Centaurus said. "Let us go to the shrine directly, that we might know their answer and see this matter concluded at last."

Pirithous nodded, and it seemed to her as if he swallowed a smile. "I would not dream of delay."

***

Pirithous insisted upon escorting her personally, expressing concern for her on the rough track to the shrine. Hippodamia did not think it appropriate to remind him she had spent her whole life on the mountain, tripping and traipsing after the centaurs on paths much rougher than the well-trod climb through the trees to Zeus's altar. But when he reached to steady her unnecessarily, cupping her elbow or pressing his hand flat against the small of her back to guide her forward, her skin prickled and her cheeks flushed.

"It is not much farther," he said, his voice low enough that it would not carry over the hoofbeats of her kinsmen. "But I do not think Eurytion will be so pleased to arrive."

She nearly tripped over a tree root then, staring at Pirithous instead of where she placed her feet. "My lord?"

"It is clear he does not favor our marriage," he went on, his gaze fixed on the path ahead.

She let out a breath, her stomach unknotting. "It is only as Centaurus said—he would not see me slighted. Perhaps if he were allowed to remain as my guard it would ease his fears."

Pirithous's hand tightened on her arm and he glanced at her sidelong. "As your husband, it is my duty to guard you. I hope you do not mean to imply I am incapable."

"No, of course not! It is only—" She bit her lip, stopping herself. She must trust her father. Centaurus would never give her to a man who would abuse her, no matter what Eurytion believed of Pirithous. And it was not his fears which twisted her heart, besides. "Forgive me, please."

Pirithous studied her openly for a moment, his hand gentling on her arm. "It is only what? If you fear me, I would know it now, that I might find some way to prove myself."

"No," she assured him, quickly. "It is not that. If you took me to wife only to treat me poorly, there would be no purpose to marrying at all. You would not dishonor your mother in such a way."

His lips twitched. "I am relieved to hear it."

She flushed at the dryness of his tone. "It is unkind of you to mock me."

"Forgive me," he said. "If I mock anyone, it is only myself. But go on, please. You still have not said what you fear, if it is not me."

He gazed at her so earnestly, his storm-gray eyes searching and kind. If she had needed some proof of his nature, he could not have given her better. She had not expected his concern, or even his attention. No doubt Pirithous had more women than he could count, beautiful and practiced and happy in his bed. Taking another for his wife should have been nothing to him.

She should have been nothing to him.

"I have lived my whole life among centaurs, my lord," she said. "And though my father has done his best to teach me, your people and customs are strange. Is it so odd that I might want to keep one friend at my side?"

"If he were only your friend, Hippodamia, I would not hesitate." His hand fell away from her elbow and he glanced back at the others before going on. "But I am not so great a fool as to believe it is only friendship Eurytion wants of you. If peace is your purpose, surely it is not your intention to begin this marriage with betrayal?"

She stiffened and stopped, staring at him. That he could believe her so dishonorable, when she had given him every benefit, every consideration— "How dare you!"

"What's this?" Theseus asked, appearing at her side. His expression was fixed with a smile, but it did not reach his eyes. "A lovers' quarrel already?"

"There are no better words to describe it," Pirithous agreed, his lips curving. He looked as though he might laugh, and it only outraged her more to see it. "But I believe we understand one another better now."

Her nails bit into her palm, she had fisted her hands so tightly. To think she had believed him kind a moment earlier! But it had not been kindness that had prompted his interest, only his pride.

She *was* nothing to him, after all, and the realization stung her all the more for having believed otherwise even so briefly.

"Yes," she said, lifting her chin. "We understand one another much better now. And in fact, the mistake was mine. I will never be so foolish as to think you capable of consideration or kindness in the future."

The laughter faded from Pirithous's face, his eyes hardening to stone. "You might yet be spared a future at my side, Hippodamia, if the thought is so offensive to you."

"Come," Theseus interrupted, shooting Pirithous a warning look. "The shrine is only beyond those trees, and the gods will settle it soon enough. There is no worth in arguing at all until then."

She let Theseus guide her the rest of the way, and for the first time since she had learned of the agreement and the part she must play to fulfill it, she prayed the omens would be ill.

***

Pirithous offered a kid to the old priest for sacrifice, but Hippodamia did not watch as the stooped man sorted through the entrails for some sign from the gods. Instead, she watched Eurytion, noting every stamp of his hoof, every shiver of his glossy black hide, every undisguised glare and insolent look when his gaze fell upon Pirithous. No matter the truth of his feelings or hers, she could see clearly why the king would not suffer Eurytion as her guard. At every turn he offered insult, and though Pirithous refused to take offense, it still wore upon what little patience and forgiveness the Lapiths had granted them.

"Even now you delay," Eurytion sneered. "The auguries are clear. I saw the eagle myself as we traveled, but of course you would not trust the word of a centaur. And when the entrails do not give you the answer you seek, what then? Will there be another ritual that must be performed, another way in which you might slither free of our agreement?"

The priest had stiffened, glancing up at his king, but Pirithous, jaw set, nodded once, and the old man went back to his work. Eurytion's tail switched, his hide shuddering as if plagued with flies.

"There will be no other reading of any omens, unless your lady requests it," Pirithous said. She looked up sharply, finding Pirithous's cool gaze upon her, his arms crossed over his broad chest. "It is her right to demand the same satisfaction I have claimed, after all, if she is unhappy with the outcome."

"Our marriage secures peace for my people and yours," she said, careful not to let him see her confusion. She had known for some time that women among the Lapiths had few rights. Her father had made it clear to her what role she must play, even as a queen. "If it requires a trade of my happiness in exchange, I will give it gladly."

"I do not believe in taking women unwilling, Hippodamia. Least of all a bride. Oaths sworn before the gods are just as binding as marriage vows, and the peace you desire will be made between our people all the same."

"Until your death, only," Centaurus said. "But if Hippodamia provides you with an heir, a child born and raised as our kinsman, our peoples will be united behind him, and his children after. This is why Dia wished for your marriage to my daughter, and why it is my wish as well."

But Pirithous did not look to Centaurus when her father spoke. He kept his eyes upon her. "And what do you wish for?"

"Centaurus raised me as his own, saved me when I would have been left to die upon the mountain. I owe him my life, and it is his to spend as he sees fit."

"Already you speak as a queen," Pirithous said. "But you do not answer me. I would know if you have given your heart elsewhere before we go forward, before the priest gives us the blessing of Zeus. For it will be a blessing, Hippodamia. The gods cannot want less than peace and my father will be glad to see me wed, hoping it might reconcile me to the task of kingship I am set."

She swallowed, unable to turn from his gaze. This was his pride again, she was certain. It was not enough that he had insulted her, suggesting she had come to him already tarnished by another's use. He would shame her now, too, before her father and her friends. Whether it was for her own benefit, that she might know her place, or for Eurytion's, that he might learn his, she did not know, but it was clear she would not escape the lesson.

"Hippodamia?" Centaurus prompted, his eyes narrowing at her hesitation.

"And if the answer does not please you, will you punish my people?" she asked.

"I have sworn already that I wish for nothing but peace, my lady. But I will not marry you against your will, nor will I be the cause of your misery. No lasting peace can be built upon strife."

"Then I must admit I do not believe myself capable of love for you, though for a moment in your megaron, I feared otherwise. My heart and my affections are my own, unclaimed, but the longer I know you, the more certain I am they will never be yours."

CHAPTER FOUR

PIRITHOUS

"You misjudge me, Hippodamia." Pirithous smiled, slow and satisfied. "There is no answer you might have given that would have pleased me more."

As long as she did not love the centaur, the situation was not beyond repair, even if she did not know it yet. And after having his way so easily for so long, the challenge in her words, in the lift of her chin and the flash of anger in her eyes, only served to fire his blood. Once she sipped from the cup of pleasure he would serve her in their marriage bed, she would feel differently. She would be his, then, heart and body and mind, and would surely flush with embarrassment to remember this day.

Indeed, she flushed already, her face flaming red beneath all its grime, but Pirithous behaved as if he did not notice, nodding again to the priest. "And what sign does my father give?"

The priest stared, opening his mouth, then shutting it, as his gaze slid from Pirithous to the centaurs to the girl, and back again. Pirithous could not blame the man. No matter what answer he gave, there would be some of his audience who would be displeased by it, and certainly Eurytion's behavior offered no assurance of their supposedly peaceful natures, even if Centaurus had been all politeness.

"My king," he finally managed. "It is as you said, a blessing. But—"

"But?" Pirithous arched an eyebrow. A *but* could only serve to give Hippodamia and Centaurus an excuse to change their minds, and he had not the patience for it now that he knew her free of Eurytion's influence.

The priest cleared his throat, glancing again toward the centaurs. Whatever he had been about to say, Pirithous had dealt with him often enough that he knew to think better of it.

"I fear it is not yet an auspicious time to wed," the man said, bowing his head. "It must wait until the summer solstice if you wish your bride to bear you fruit."

Pirithous exchanged a glance with Theseus. Seven days, then. A sevenday until he could take Hippodamia to bed and ensure himself an heir. But that did not mean he could not spend the time well. By the solstice she would be eager for him. And no doubt, Antiope would encourage her to change her mind, even if she only offered her assistance at Theseus's request, without any care for his needs. Even if it was only for Hippodamia's own good, for that matter.

"We would be honored if you would remain as our guest until the solstice," he told her.

She looked to her father, who nodded, and then pressed her lips together in what was clearly unspoken irritation. "Might I keep a companion of my own kind until the wedding?"

If she asked for Eurytion, after everything they had discussed, he would lock the centaur in the stable and Hades's curse upon the peace they were meant to build. Still, he had no grounds to deny her such a small request, and if she was to become his queen, he must trust her at least this far. And yet…

"Antiope, Queen of Athens, will make you welcome, but if you require another companion, I must warn you she does not suffer men of any race gladly. She was the Amazon queen before she consented to marry Theseus."

Hippodamia's eyes widened. Word of Theseus's wedding to the Amazon queen had spread far, but not, it seemed, to the mountains—or if it had, Centaurus had not seen fit to share the story with his daughter.

"Of course," she said. "And I would not wish to give offense to the wife of Theseus. But there are females among my people. Father, will you send word to Hylonome? Perhaps she would be willing, though I know she does not care to leave the mountain."

The old centaur smiled, no doubt relieved now that the day had been named. "I will ask it of her myself."

"Then it is settled," Pirithous said, for Eurytion stirred, his black gaze locked upon Hippodamia with a possessiveness he had no wish to tempt with opportunity. "We will feast tonight to celebrate. You and your people are welcome to remain, Centaurus."

"Better if we go," he said, shaking his head. "The sooner we reach the mountain, the sooner I might send Hylonome back for Hippodamia. A delay will serve nothing, and I think we have already worn your patience thin this day." One hind-hoof scraped the packed earth floor, kicking dust at Eurytion. "We will return upon the solstice, but know that while our daughter is housed within your walls, we consider the Lapiths bound to Dia's peace."

"And so we shall be," Pirithous agreed. "You have my word as king."

Centaurus stretched out his hand, and Hippodamia clasped it, pressing it to her cheek. He drew his daughter into his arms and Pirithous stepped away to grant them a moment for their farewell. The priest and Theseus came with him of course, though Theseus did not turn his back completely upon the centaurs, and Pirithous trusted he would keep sidelong watch upon Eurytion, even now. He was not so foolish as to think his betrothal to Hippodamia brought an end to the trouble that centaur might cause, peace or no peace.

"You goad your young bride unkindly," Theseus murmured. "If you continue this way, it will only serve to make her wilder."

"I have no objection to wildness in my bed." He smiled broadly, now that Hippodamia would not see it, though he kept his voice low. "She has such spirit, Theseus! It is no wonder Dia chose her."

Theseus grimaced in return. "I wonder very much if your mother chose her in a fit of rage after you despoiled her maid. Already this girl is determined not to love you, and you only look pleased by the challenge. Have you considered at all what it will mean if she never softens?"

"You speak as if you did not win the heart of an Amazon." Pirithous clapped him on the back. "Do not worry so, Theseus. She is still a woman, and Centaurus did not even raise her to hate men."

Theseus shook his head, his mouth a sour line. "If you speak so before Antiope, I will not blame her if she responds with violence against you, king or not. And worse, you antagonize Hippodamia's companions. You said yourself that strife is no way to begin this peace. Eurytion looks as though he will not be happy until he has your head at the end of a spear."

"Eurytion leaves with Centaurus. When next he meets Hippodamia, he will see a woman well-loved and know himself defeated." Pirithous shrugged, casting a glance over his shoulder at the black-furred beast. "It hardly matters. Whatever trouble he brings, it will be nothing I cannot finish."

"And you will give your bride another reason to resent you when you have cut down her kinsman," Theseus replied.

"King Pirithous," Hippodamia called, sorrow softening her tone. When he turned back to her, her eyes were downcast, her hands knotted tightly before her. "My father would return with us to the palace, that he might place my hand in yours before your people."

"Perhaps Theseus would go ahead of us to spread word that the announcement will be made?" When he looked to his cousin, Theseus nodded, and left them with a bow. The king of Athens never hesitated to humble himself, though Pirithous could not understand the practice. Perhaps that was the difference between a son of Zeus and a son of Poseidon. Certainly Theseus did not share his appetite for women, if he could spend so long with only Antiope in his bed.

Pirithous offered his arm to Hippodamia and grim-faced, she took it.

"You cannot think me so repulsive, surely," he said gently, for she reminded him now of the young girl he had feared she would be, all the fight having drained from her body. "And you will be queen soon, among a people where that title carries great meaning."

"Your people will surely honor me for bringing them peace, if nothing else. But as for being queen—I am more concerned with what naming me queen means to their king."

"Nothing awful," he assured her. And he ought to have realized it would concern her. Raised among the centaurs, how could she know anything at all about how a husband might treat his wife? "Antiope would hardly tolerate me were I to answer otherwise."

"And is it her opinion you value, or the respect and friendship of her husband, who would not tolerate any insult to his wife?"

Pirithous laughed. "Is that all you fear? That I will treat you as nothing more than a prize?"

"Am I not a prize, King Pirithous? Another woman for your bed and little else."

"If that were your only value, my mother would not have chosen you as my bride. And we have already agreed there is no sense in this if I mistreat you. Any slight I give you before my people will serve only as an example to them of how they might ignore the spirit of our peace. It would be worse than dishonorable. Now, I ask you, what purpose would that serve either one of us?"

Her forehead creased and she fell silent, but Pirithous did not for a moment believe he had won. If it was not the answer she had expected him to give, neither was it the one she had wanted. He was not Theseus, willing to tie himself to one woman and one woman alone, but that did not mean he would not grant her all proper honor and respect.

She would simply have to understand.

***

Antiope stood at Theseus's side when Pirithous returned from the shrine ahead of the centaurs. The king and queen of Athens waited with the Lapiths nobles at the palace gate. If the charcoal patterns drawn upon her skin did not set her enough apart, as always, Antiope wore a man's tunic, the same blue as Theseus's own, stopping just above her knee and girdled at the waist with a knot of golden snakes. Though she had given up her axe and bow, the knife sheathed at her waist was deadly enough in her hands, and Pirithous had no doubt she had already found and assessed his store of weaponry in case of need.

He greeted her warmly, taking both her hands in his and lifting them to his lips to kiss her fingers. She laughed at his exuberance, flicking her fingers free of his grasp. In private they might disagree, even argue, but before his people, Antiope would not shame him. Her grace was one of the many reasons Theseus had not hesitated to take her as his queen. It was Pirithous's hope that Hippodamia possessed some measure of the same or, if she did not, that Antiope would train her to be queen enough.

"It is fortunate you were at home when your mother took ill," Antiope said. "I can only imagine what trouble it would have caused had you been at sea."

"Dia was stubborn enough to linger until I returned," Pirithous said, half-smiling at the thought. Even the gods would have been forced to wait until she was ready to leave this earth. "But I fear I will not have opportunity to raid as I would like this summer. Theseus must go alone if he wishes to fill his coffers."

Antiope's amber eyes lit. "Once I have seen your bride settled, I shall accompany him myself."

Pirithous laughed, for Theseus's expression had lost its humor at her words, his attention caught completely by the suggestion. "With Pirithous's wedding to disrupt the season, it would be better if I remained in Athens," he said quickly. "Besides, he is new to kingship, and I would not abandon him so soon."

"You are a true friend, cousin," Pirithous said, clasping his arm. And though he tried to keep his expression sober, he could not quite stop himself from grinning. "May the gods reward you for your sacrifice."

"I pray to them nightly," he said, glancing sidelong at Antiope. "Athens is in need of an heir as well."

"Centaurus comes." Antiope's eyes narrowed against the sun. Theseus often teased her for having the eyes of a falcon—a fine compliment to any archer, but not usually meant to describe color as well as sight. "The girl rides upon her father's back."

Pirithous turned to look, conscious of the murmuring that had broken out among the nobles. They had hardly seen Hippodamia, hidden as she had been by the horse bodies of the centaurs while they stood in the megaron, and again as they marched out to the shrine. But now she was clearly displayed, and dressed as strangely as Antiope, with her legs bared below the knee. All the better to ride upon a centaur's back, he assumed, though she did not sit astride now.

"They say she has only to whisper and even the wildest stallion will obey," Antiope said, behind him. "Imagine the lines she might breed! Already your people are known for their horses, but with her skill, you will have animals even the gods will envy."

"A worthy bride for a king of the Lapiths," Theseus agreed. "If you can win her."

"Has he not already?" Antiope asked. "She has agreed to the marriage, or surely Pirithous would not accept her?"

"She has agreed for the sake of her people," Theseus said. "Not for love of Pirithous or a desire to be queen. And I fear my cousin has not helped the matter."

"She will have no cause for complaint as long as she is mine," Pirithous said, keeping his eyes upon Hippodamia.

Her dark hair was crowned with a wreath of white wildflowers, but even so, she had not lost the stray bits of leaf and stick, the disarray a reminder of her upbringing. A wild creature, born of the mountain and the wood, only waiting to be tamed by her king.

He stepped forward to meet them, and Centaurus stopped, angling his body so that Hippodamia might be seen clearly by all those who waited at the wall. Her father reached back, and Hippodamia took his hand, her head bowed demurely and her gaze seeming to fall upon Pirithous's sandals.

"Pirithous, King of the Lapiths and son of Ixion and Zeus, in honor of Dia and in the name of the peace she forged between our peoples, I give you my daughter, Hippodamia, Tamer of Horses, to become your wife upon the summer solstice."

Centaurus held out her hand, and Pirithous took it.

"For as long as Hippodamia remains among the Lapiths, we are bound by this pledge of peace." Pirithous caught her about the waist, lifting her down from her father's back and setting her gently to her still-bare feet. When she did not look at him even then, he tipped up her chin, meeting her eyes, the color of rich, fertile earth. "Let this peace begin between us, my lady."

"As you are to be my husband, my guardian, and my king, I can hardly disobey."

He searched her face for some hint of warmth or affection and found nothing but cool regard. For the first time, he allowed himself to dip beneath the surface of her body, tasting the flavor of her emotions. Sorrow, first and foremost, for everything she would leave behind, and resignation after, for the fate she had chosen and accepted in sacrifice. But there was no sweetness there, no desire, no love but that which she held for her kinsmen and her father.

Pirithous leaned down, brushing his lips over hers. To seal their vows, he told himself, even as his body lurched at the softness of her mouth, the caress of her breath upon his face. To make his intentions clear.

She stiffened in his arms, her lips pressed firmly closed against his, with indignation flaring bright and hot between them. He sighed, releasing her chin, and forced a smile he did not feel. By all rights, she ought to have softened, some spark of want flaring that he might fan it into flame, but at least she'd had sense enough not to reject him openly before both their peoples. At least she did not shame him so publically as that.

Perhaps he would make a queen of her yet.

Chapter Five

Hippodamia

It took all her will not to turn her face away. Every part of her mind screamed for her to free herself and slip from his grasp. But though she had braced herself for his imposition, Pirithous's kiss had been gentle, the merest whisper of his lips across hers. Nothing more than a chaste token of their betrothal. It would have been easier if it had been more. Easier to remember how he had shamed her at the shrine just to satisfy his pride.

Pirithous turned away, lifting their clasped hands for all his nobles to see, and looking quite pleased with himself as he did so. The Lapiths cheered their king, but Hippodamia barely heard their shouts. Behind her, her father had turned, hooves thudding against the earth as the centaurs took their leave. She closed her eyes, listening to the cadence of their strides, straining to hear every step even as the sounds faded. Her heart ached with loss, but she dared not look back. She must be strong now, if ever, and meet her fate.

"Come, my lady." Hippodamia opened her eyes. A tall woman, her arms and legs marked in strange tattoos, with warm, golden eyes and hair as dark as midnight, stood before her, hands outstretched. "Dia's own rooms have been made ready for you, and we've time to bathe and dress before the banquet."

Antiope, she realized, for Theseus stood beside her, his hand resting on her back and adoration in his eyes. What would it be like to have Pirithous look on her in the same way? But if Pirithous were capable of love, of a true bond of marriage, she had yet to see any sign of it. So preoccupied with his pride, he even seemed pleased to know she could not love him.

Hippodamia took the queen's hands and returned her smile. "Thank you, my lady."

"We will both be queens soon enough, my dear, and we will see much of one another in the coming years. Pirithous and Theseus behave like brothers, always traipsing back and forth from Thessaly to Athens. You must call me Antiope, and it will be my honor to know the woman so brave even wild stallions do not give her pause."

"Compared to the daughters of Ares, I am but a foolish girl, undeserving of the blessing given by the Earth Shaker."

"We shall see," Antiope said, drawing her away from Pirithous's side. "But whether or not you are deserving of the gift you have been given, it is a talent that will serve you well among the Lapiths. They will look on you with awe and wonder, and kneel before you, begging for your blessing upon their beasts. Only wait, Hippodamia. Before long, you will be queen in your own right among these people, and they will see you as a true daughter of Dia, fit to rule in her place."

"I am not certain Dia's son will be pleased if that is so." As they passed beneath the palace gate, she glanced back at Pirithous, distracted by some exchange with Theseus. Even he had said Dia would not have chosen her without some greater purpose in mind than giving her son an heir, but surely he had not meant she was to take his mother's place so completely.

Antiope squeezed her hand. "His pleasure is easy enough to ensure once you are in his bed. True son of Zeus or not, he will kneel before you along with all the others, tamed as easily as any other rutting stallion. And you will have my help to see it is so."

***

Antiope herself helped her bathe, shooing away the maids who would have washed and oiled her hair and skin. The Amazon's fingers plucked each leaf and twig from her curls, then combed and pinned them carefully.

"My sisters and I used to serve one another this way," Antiope said softly, replacing the wreath of wildflowers on Hippodamia's head. "None of the women in Athens are worthy of such attention, and the nobles are too afraid I will poison their wives and daughters with my strange ways to allow me their company, besides." Her lips curved in a satisfied smile. "I cannot promise Theseus I will not, of course, and so he has despaired of finding me any fit companion."

"Does King Pirithous not fear the same?" She had promised to oil Antiope's dark hair in return, but centaurs did not bother with pins and combs. She stared at the long, crimped tresses and frowned, unsure of what Antiope might expect.

"A simple braid will serve me," Antiope said, as if she knew her thoughts. "Theseus does not have much patience for pulling pins from my hair, and one is always forgotten no matter how carefully we try to find them."

Braids she knew well, for the centaurs favored them to keep manes and tails from being caught by branches in the forest. Hippodamia began the style at the crown of Antiope's head, weaving delicate white flowers into her hair as she went. If one was forgotten when she undressed, at least it would not cause her any discomfort.

"As for Pirithous—and you need not always refer to him by his title, Hippodamia, when he is arrogant enough without the reminder of his power—he is accustomed to me by now, and doubtless he believes there is nothing I might say that he should fear. He is too confident by half, but that is as much to do with his blood as anything, and he believes himself capable of winning any challenge. Including the affections of a most reluctant bride." She laughed, and Hippodamia had no trouble imagining her sly smile, though she could not see her face. "He thinks because Theseus tamed an Amazon, he will have no trouble with the daughter of Centaurus."

"As long as he sees me as only a challenge, another woman to seduce into his bed, he has no hope of winning anything of mine," she said, her tone much sharper than she had intended. She sighed, finishing the braid and tying it off with a bit of string. "But I fear his confidence is not completely misplaced. For this peace to last, I must give him a son, and until that is done, there is no helping the rest. Nor would I do him harm. I am as bound by Dia's peace as my people, and if he were betrayed by my hand, it would mean a terrible war."

Antiope tilted her head, turning to look at her. "Do you hate him so much that you would consider it? Why did you not simply refuse to marry him if that is so? You must know it would not have stopped this peace."

"I do not wish to hate him," she said, then pressed her lips together in remembered irritation. "But he does not make it easy to feel anything kinder. I had barely given him my name when he accused me of taking Eurytion as my lover and insisted I renounce him before everyone in the shrine. As if Centaurus would offer him such an insult. As if any affection I had for another mattered at all! I have been promised to him for years, though he could not be bothered to take me to wife before now."

Tears burned behind her eyes, and she blinked them back. For one blinding moment in the megaron, she had seen a future she might love, with a man worthy of her affection. She had seen Pirithous upon his throne, proud and kingly and laughing, with their son upon his knee. If they could never truly love one another, at least he might have offered her some kindness, even consideration. Like a stumbling foal, she had hoped he would look upon her with pleasure, impressed with her manner and her courtesy, and declare her his queen. Instead he had treated her as if she were some foolish, faithless country girl, willing to betray even her king. All because he thought Eurytion looked on her with lust.

Antiope rose, opening her arms, and Hippodamia was not too proud to take what comfort she offered. "He is only a man, my dear. You cannot expect him to think reasonably in matters such as these. But if there is one thing you can always trust in Pirithous, it is that he cannot stand to take a woman unwilling. It is a matter of honor in his mind. Had your affections belonged to another, he could not be certain you would ever want him—and that is near enough to force to hurt his pride."

"And what of *my* honor? *My* pride? Am I to sacrifice it all to him?" she demanded, her eyes blurring again. She turned her face against the soft wool of Antiope's tunic, hiding her tears. Perhaps she was a fool after all, to think Pirithous was anything more than any other man—the same men who had hunted her people for sport, who raped women in the forest and left them lost and dazed to find their own way home. More often than not, the centaurs were blamed. "Is it not enough he will have my body, my children, my life bound to his, but he must have that too?"

Antiope sighed, her arms tightening. "It is the nature of men to take what they have no right to hold, but Pirithous is not so great a fool as most. I do not think he will overreach so boldly again, and if there is some sliver of your honor he has stolen, we will take it back, Hippodamia. On that, you have my oath."

***

"My lady," Pirithous said, rising at once from his place at the long table. The megaron fell silent, and Hippodamia hesitated at the entrance to the hall. Every head had turned to look at the woman who had captured their king's attention. Her face, already flushed from the tears she had only just wiped away, went hot.

Antiope had offered her a choice of gowns and tunics, long and short, with girdles in gold, silver, and bronze, and armbands in every style to match. She had chosen a simple gown in purple, the square cut of the bodice barely covering her breasts, and a wide girdle embroidered with silver horses, racing against the wind.

Horses were everywhere in the palace, drawn upon the floor and painted upon the walls, reflecting their importance to the Lapiths. And where there were not horses alone, there were images of men upon them, riding to the hunt or into war. Even the tables in the megaron were set in the shape of a horse's hoof around the large central hearth. She should not have been surprised to find horses upon her gowns as well, for they had come from Dia's things in part, and from Antiope's belongings brought from Athens, where the son of the Horse Lord ruled as king, but somehow she had expected eagles and lightning bolts, storm clouds and great white bulls. Perhaps it was only that Pirithous had not long been king, and he had not yet ordered the palace repainted with symbols of his father.

Whatever the reason, the imagery gave her some small comfort, and as she stood before Pirithous and his nobles, she touched one of the silver horses at her waist, reminding herself of what Antiope said: Pirithous was nothing more than another wild stallion to be tamed by her hand. And why should she not think him so, when he saw her the same way?

She lifted her chin and stepped forward into the hall, taking in the large room with one sweeping glance. Even the realization that more men and women stood above the hearth, peering down at her from an open gallery, did not break her stride. She passed the servants refilling pitchers from the kraters set in the corners of the room, and at least ten men at another table. Pirithous held out his hand to her, and she took it, determined to meet his eyes unflinching.

But when their gazes locked, her breath caught. His eyes were gray-blue and warm, like sunlight breaking through clouds, and in his expression there was no laughter, no mockery. He looked on her with appreciation. His fingers tightened around hers and he lifted her hand, brushing his lips against her knuckles without so much as glancing away from her face.

She shivered, her thoughts going at once to his kiss and the warmth of his breath against her lips. Hippodamia swallowed against the rising thickness in her throat, for when he looked at her that way, she saw the king she had once imagined. The man who would honor her above all others as his bride.

Of course her father had told her it was different among men. Kings kept women as prizes to take their pleasure, and though they married, they did not limit themselves to a single mate. But Hippodamia had dreamed of love, once. And as she had grown older, she had dreamed of children of her own, when the females foaled.

Among her people, she might have found love. But time and again, she had faced another truth. The same truth which had driven Centaurus to offer her hand in marriage to Pirithous when Dia had negotiated her peace. The same truth which had prompted the dream of a man who might hold her child in his arms, and look on her with love—a dream Pirithous had shattered with his pride.

Centaurus knew as well as she did that no woman mated with a centaur, no matter how in love, had ever survived the birth of a foal.

CHAPTER SIX

PIRITHOUS

He would have to thank Antiope later. Bathed and dressed and no longer smeared with dirt and mud, Hippodamia was as glorious as Aphrodite. Her hair, he could be certain now, shone a brilliant dark chestnut in the firelight, and her skin, smooth and oiled, gleamed a deep bronze from too much sun, paling only slightly just above her breasts where her body had been covered by her tunic.

"Your beauty leaves me speechless, Princess."

"Yet your lips still move," she replied, the beginning of a smile in her eyes.

More than anything, he wanted to caress the softness of her skin, tangle his fingers in her curls, but he dared not do more than kiss her hand. And when she stiffened after a moment, her eyes darkening with a swell of some remembered pain, he released her carefully, and helped her take her seat beside him.

Seven days before they were wedded, and if he wished for a fruitful marriage, he could not risk her maidenhead before the solstice. But there were other ways to find pleasure, and if the rest of her mouth was as clever as her tongue, she would take to the arts of love and lust as easily as a fish swam through water. He smiled at the thought. No doubt she would surprise him, and he was eager to learn what precisely the centaurs taught their women.

Antiope had joined them as well, taking her place beside Theseus. When Pirithous dragged his gaze away from Hippodamia, the Amazon was already murmuring in her husband's ear. As ever, Theseus's brow furrowed, his expression growing grimmer with every word spoken. How Theseus could frown with such frequency without headache, Pirithous did not understand, but the King of Athens had always tended toward excessive concern—all the more so in matters Pirithous refused to consider seriously.

To distract himself from Theseus's poor mood, Pirithous served Hippodamia the choicest portions of roast boar from his own plate, and filled her cup to the brim.

Her eyes widened slightly after her first sip. "But this is wine!"

"Attican wine from the King of Athens, to honor Dia. Theseus always brought it for her when he came, knowing she preferred it."

She frowned into her cup before taking another cautious sip. "I am not certain I care for it overmuch."

He laughed. "Do not let Theseus hear you say so. He takes great pride in his wines."

"I meant no insult to King Theseus, only that I do not care for wine at all, if it all tastes this way." Her nose wrinkled. "It smells so sour, and the flavor is too thick upon my tongue."

Pirithous put down his cup, studying her face. "You cannot mean to say you have never tasted it before now?"

"The centaurs do not grow grapes upon the mountain, and there is little for us to trade that your people desire. When the opportunity arises, we ask for pottery, for the most part, and finely woven cloth for the few of your women who live among us. Our own wool is harsh on bare skin."

"Did Dia know this?" he asked, wondering at his own ignorance. "What do your people drink if not wine?"

"Water, my lord, and milk at times." She was looking at him as though he had two heads. "What else is there?"

What else, indeed. He poured half the wine from her cup into his, and though it was already mixed with water, he gestured for one of the servants to bring more.

"I feared you were young before we met, but never did I think I would need to cut your wine as I would for a child." He smiled to let her know he was only teasing and filled her cup to the brim with water. "Perhaps that will be more to your liking."

She sipped it again, carefully, a wrinkle appearing between her brows, but it relaxed almost at once after she had tasted the new mixture in her cup. "It is much better this way, but I do not know that I will ever wish to drink it plain. Will it truly make me a child in the eyes of your people?"

"They'll hardly notice, if at all," he assured her, smiling again. "We shall keep it a secret between us, besides, and before long I am certain you will be drinking stronger wine. But tell me, what libations do the centaurs offer to the gods, if they do not have wine to pour?"

"Blood, of course." She had gone back to frowning, at her plate now, and began picking through a relish of greens. "Your people have such an odd way of preparing food. Do you not eat the vegetables raw? They would taste much better. With a bit of olive oil and some vinegar."

Blood. Of course. He was not certain he wished to know more. It was not that the Lapiths did not offer blood as well, but it was one thing to offer it with the sacrifice of a goat or a bull at the shrine, and another to keep a rhyton full of it to spill upon the ground before each meal. Perhaps they did not give libations at all except before their feasts? The thought reassured him. Centaurs would not want to be plagued by the swarms of flies a pitcher of blood would attract. For all that their hides were covered with fur, he had seen them shuddering enough in irritation with the things, and whipping their tails to shed them.

He cleared his throat. "As queen you may order the food prepared to your liking. As long as there is bread and meat enough, the rest will matter little."

She lifted her head, meeting his eyes again for the first time since he had seated her. They were bright and dark and rich, and he could not help but wonder how much darker they would appear when she lay naked in his bed beneath him, on the edge of release.

"Must I wait until the solstice?"

He laughed, for she voiced his own thoughts, if upon a different matter. "I do not believe letting you loose upon the kitchens will affect the outcome of our marriage. You may begin tomorrow if you wish, though I have never met a woman so eager to take up the task. Are you certain you would not rather begin with your rooms? Surely you will want to repaint at least one wall."

"I had not considered…" She stared blankly at one long wall, painted with a bull hunt, and he realized suddenly how much she did not know about living among men. Even the needs of a simple household would be new to her. The centaurs lived in caves.

"Whatever you desire, Hippodamia, you need only name it," he said gently. "The palace is yours now, and no doubt you will spend the greater number of days within its walls. My mother's steward will help you learn the way of managing it, though in truth he does not need much oversight. Tell him what you wish done and he will see it finished. Certainly there is gold enough, and any spent in trade will be replenished by a summer's raiding."

"But surely there are things you would want—paintings which carry some significance, or foods you prefer?"

Pirithous glanced over the walls of the megaron, but he could not think of any one image he would miss on any wall in any room. Dia had repainted much of what he had known as a youth, preferring not to remind their people of Ixion's madness, and what she had not changed was all more of the same: horses and riders and the great bull hunt.

"All I require is a warm welcome upon my return and a wide bed in which to take my pleasure. My rooms are as I wish them and the rest you may make your own." Then he smiled, and took her hand in his, caressing her knuckles with his thumb. Her skin was softer than he could have imagined beneath all that mud, and her fingers strong. It was not such a terrible thing to have a woman who did not fear dirtying her hands as queen. But he could think of better uses for them, ways in which she could bring them both pleasure.

He pressed a kiss into her palm. "I only hope you are as eager for our marriage bed."

She flushed and looked away, and though he wanted more than anything to turn her face back to his and claim the warmth of her mouth, he did not tease her further. Slowly and carefully, he decided, for auspicious or not, he was certain that once he tasted her he would not want to stop.

***

Pirithous sank into the tub, careless of the water which spilled over its sides. He tipped his head back against the wall and closed his eyes, trying not to listen to the sounds of Antiope and Hippodamia on the other side of the door. Once Dia had seen Theseus's private bath in Athens, she had been determined to have one of her own, and Pirithous was glad to benefit. The rest of the palace and its guests used a large, spring-fed pool near the kitchens, and though hauling water up the stairs by amphora or pot was hardly ideal, he would not trade the private luxury for anything.

He smiled, hearing laughter from the other side of the door. Perhaps, at that moment, he might be induced to trade it for one thing. By all rights, he should have called for Hippodamia to wash him, and just imagining the touch of her hands upon his chest, his shoulders, his back made him tighten with need. He had known she would be beautiful once properly dressed and presented, but he had not realized how badly he would want her—all the more so because she denied him.

Of course he could persuade her, give her the spark of his own desire and feed it until she bloomed, but if she found him so offensive as to claim she might never love him, his problems would be compounded by morning. And in truth, he did not want to trick her into his bed. Imposing his own need upon the woman who would be his wife was offensive in the extreme. She should want him, and the child he would give her, and until she did…

Well, he had a week to convince her of his worth as a husband. A week to soften her feelings and tease her with what they might share together. And in the meantime, he had plenty of other women to curb his own appetite.

Pirithous washed briskly, thinking of the two who waited in his bed. He might have asked them to bathe him, but he had not wanted Hippodamia to hear their laughter as he had listened to hers. However things were done among the centaurs, it was clear to him she did not wish to be one of many in his bed, and to flaunt his habits on the very first night of her arrival would have been worse than cruel.

The door swung open, and Hippodamia stood framed by firelight. The warm glow behind her burned through the thin linen of her nightdress, revealing the curves of her hips and the dip of her waist.

Pirithous stiffened, aching to reach for her. She had not seen him yet, her head turned away as she called something to Antiope over her shoulder. He held himself still, drinking in the sweet fullness of her breasts, half-bared, and the tumble of her dark hair upon her shoulders, shot through with red flame. He drew a shuddering breath and rose from the water.

Hippodamia spun at the slosh of the bath, muffling a shriek of surprise with a hand over her mouth, her eyes wide as full moons.

"You seem to have found me at a disadvantage, my lady."

Her gaze had already fallen from his face to his bare chest, and his body hardened as it dipped lower still. She stared at the evidence of his desire, her hand slipping from her mouth until only her fingers pressed against her lips. He did not dare move with every line of her body tensed as if to flee, like a mouse caught out in the middle of the room with the first light of dawn.

The silence held, and he would have traded the bathing room a hundred times to know what thought made her cheeks flush with such a charming shade of red.

"You need not tremble so, little mouse," he said softly. "But if you wished, you might do more than simply stare."

"Hippodamia?" Antiope called from behind her. "What's the matter?"

She made a strangled sound and whirled, leaving him behind.

Pirithous grinned as the door swung shut, and reached for his towel.

She would come to him soon enough.

Chapter Seven

Hippodamia

Hippodamia lay awake in her bed, staring at the ceiling and trying to count the golden stars painted upon it, winking in the moonlight. How often had she counted the stars, lying in the meadow grass and looking up into the night sky? Always it had settled her mind, allowing her to drift into sleep. But not tonight. Not when every time she closed her eyes, she saw Pirithous, proud as any stallion, his skin gleaming with drops of water from his bath.

She should not have stared. She should have turned away at once and barred the door behind her. She should have kept her eyes locked upon his face rather than follow the sprinkling of golden hair upon his muscled chest to the narrow trail below his waist, then lower still.

How many times had she seen the centaurs rutting, or the mares mounted by their stallions? Not once had the sight of such arousal caused her any confusion, but to see Pirithous standing there, to feel his gaze as hot upon her as the warmth of the hearth at her back, and the low purr of his voice…

You might do more than simply stare.

Her stomach had twisted at the words, heat blossoming from her center and tingling through her limbs. Her fingers had itched to touch him, trace the hard planes of his chest and stomach, and smooth the pale, silvery scars that marked his skin. In that moment, she had wanted nothing more than to go to him.

Until Antiope had called her name.

She closed her eyes, a flush of embarrassment flooding through her body, even in memory. An Amazon would never have been so caught by a man, even one as naked and beautiful as Pirithous. An Amazon would have smiled at the evidence of her power, turned, and left him wanting, without another thought.

Except that Antiope had married Theseus, and from the things she had said, Hippodamia was certain of her affection for her husband. Theseus, who did not have the patience to take the pins from her hair before he bedded his wife, and took no other women for his pleasure. If only Antiope had married Pirithous. If only Theseus had been king of the Lapiths. She might have trusted him, loved him without fear.

But it was not Theseus she ached for now, unable to sleep for the thought of his kiss and the memory of his body, taut with desire. And it was Pirithous, with his light hair and laughing gray eyes, who haunted her dreams when, at last, she slept.

***

She rose at dawn, as she was used to, but hesitated outside the bathing room door, listening for any sign of Pirithous beyond. Satisfied by the silence, she opened the door a crack, her stomach knotting. Empty. For the briefest moment, she was not certain if the lurch in her heart was disappointment or relief.

Better not to dwell upon it, lest she find an answer she did not like at all. Hippodamia collected her tunic from the tiled floor, damp where the water had spilled over the rim of the bathtub, and retreated back to her room. She must be more careful to remember her things, but now that she knew Pirithous bathed after supper, it would not be difficult to avoid him. Perhaps she would not need to see him at all but for mealtimes.

She dressed quickly, determined to eat her morning meal before Pirithous rose from his bed, and went in search of the kitchens. It would be easy enough to busy herself with preparing the midday and evening meals, and no one could fault her for taking on the duty. Antiope would only be pleased she need not concern herself with the task, and the Amazon had already warned her she would not rise early.

Hippodamia flushed. Watching them at the feast, she could have no doubt as to what might delay Antiope. Theseus loved his wife, honored and desired her above all else. He had stolen her from her people, risking the wrath of the gods and the Amazons themselves to have her, and she had given up even her honor to marry him. And yet, Antiope stood by her husband unashamed, considering the sacrifice itself to be honorable, that she might meet Theseus as an equal in all ways. They had returned to Athens together, unsure of their fate. For such a sin, the people of Athens would have been within their rights to turn away their king, demanding his life to appease the insult to the gods, and Theseus would have been honor-bound to grant their request. According to Antiope, each day since had been a gift, celebrated and shared together.

But Pirithous had risked nothing, sacrificed nothing even while he took from her. It did not matter now how considerate he was, how attentive, or how beautiful. She had come to him in honor and good faith, and he had dismissed it as though it were nothing. It was a slight she could not overlook.

Hippodamia took up her anger as a cloak around her heart, and left her rooms to face the day.

***

"Theseus warned me you were likely to rise before Apollo," Pirithous said, smiling up at her from the bottom of the stairs. He wore an undyed kilt of wool, his chest bare, with a wide band of spiraled gold wrapped around his arm above the elbow. He held out his hand, his gray eyes bright, it seemed to her, with challenge. "Come, let me show you the lands you will rule at my side."

"We agreed I would see to the food and observe the work in your kitchens," she said, willing herself not to stare at his chest and shoulders, or the way his arm bulged with muscle beneath the gold armband.

"The kitchens will wait until we have returned, and the rest as well." His gaze swept from her hair to her bare feet, and she wished suddenly she had worn one of the long gowns instead of this tunic which stopped mid-thigh. "Did Antiope not give you one of her maids?"

"I had thought the kitchens might be overwarm," she murmured, pulling absently at the hem. She had not failed to notice the other women wore layered skirts reaching their ankles. "Antiope assured me I should wear whatever I wished."

"I do not doubt that she did." His lips twitched and his eyes laughed, even if his voice did not. "And I find no fault in your choice of gown. It is only that I would not have you walk barefoot through the filth of the stables, but that is remedied easily enough, and I will have you on a horse soon after."

She hesitated still, halted several steps above him. "And if I would prefer the kitchens?"

He twisted a shoulder carelessly, dropping his hand and stepping back. "It seemed a morning spent riding with the wind against her face would be preferable to a woman raised with all the mountain to roam upon. If I am mistaken, I beg your forgiveness."

Easier if he had been mistaken, better if he hadn't put any thought into the matter. One moment she was certain he cared nothing for her but the purpose she might serve as a brood mare and peacemaker, and the next he seemed almost too attentive, as if he wished to impress her with his consideration. She chewed her lip. It would be foolish of her to refuse, and she *did* wish to see his horses.

"You are certain the kitchens can wait? I would not have your people think I neglect my duty."

Pirithous smiled slowly, extending his hand again. "Dia avoided the kitchens at every turn with one excuse or another. Our people will not even note your absence."

Our people.

She gave him her hand. "Then I must thank you for the opportunity."

His fingers closed gently around hers, the sunlight in his eyes winking with promise. Her stomach knotted ever tighter as she realized the danger too late. He would charm her now, even seduce her, convince her to come willingly to his bed. And once he had won his challenge she would be cast aside in favor of another girl, more practiced in the arts of pleasure. No doubt he only bothered with her now because she had admitted she did not care for him, and once she did…

Once she gave him what he wanted, he would not care if she spent all her days in the kitchen, longing to go riding with him in the woods.

"Hippodamia?" His thumb brushed over her knuckles. "Are you unwell?"

"No," she said. "Only hungry, I think. A bit of bread will make the difference, if you will excuse me—"

His hand tightened around hers when she moved to pull away. "I have bread, cheese, and fruit enough for both of us. And a skin of water for you, steeped with mint." He guided her through the central courtyard. "My physician tells me it is quite good for stomach ailments, but I find the mint clears my head if I have not slept well."

He had thought of everything, and now he held her hand, it was clear he had no intention of letting her go. Her fingers twitched, but he only threaded her arm through his, smiling down at her as if he did not hold her trapped at his side.

"I hope you had a pleasant night, my lady."

She flushed, her gaze falling to his bare shoulder, and the glint of scattered golden hairs across the expanse of his chest. "I fear I slept poorly."

"That has ever been my own experience beneath a strange roof," he said, leading her between the tall columns and down the wide porch steps. The palace walls loomed over them, but Pirithous turned away from the gates. He frowned slightly. "I much prefer to sleep upon the porch, or a balcony, where I might see the stars. As long as I can see the sky, I know myself free."

"Free of what?" she asked, in spite of herself. There was something about his expression that drew her, and a distance in his eyes she did not like. "I cannot imagine any man imprisoning a son of Zeus."

"No," he agreed. "But it is a dream which haunts me all the same. Blackness and unbreakable restraints." His frown deepened, then he shook his head and laughed, his eyes warming again when they found hers. "It is nothing, I am sure. Just a child's fear of the dark, poorly remembered. The night has ever been my friend."

She thought it best not to respond to the suggestion in his words, and looked away. It did not stop her from feeling the caress of his gaze, heating her blood, but at least he would not see her blush. She would not give him the satisfaction.

They reached the stables then, an immense stone wing attached to the palace itself. She had noticed fencing on either side of the main gate leading to the porch steps, and now she understood its purpose. It appeared all the land inside the palace walls was left open for the horses to graze.

And they were fine horses, strong-backed and well-proportioned, in every shade of brown and black and white. A few whickered softly in greeting, trotting toward Pirithous in response to his low-voiced calls. He stroked the neck of a gleaming chestnut mare, silvering around the nose.

"Fire was the first I saw foaled," he said, offering the mare a parsnip. She had not realized Pirithous had brought anything at all for the horses, but he seemed to have something to offer to every animal who approached. "And the first horse I claimed for my own. She always bred true and never threw me once."

"She's beautiful." The mare nuzzled her palm, looking for more parsnips. "Sweet girl," she murmured, pretending not to notice the kindness he showed, greeting each horse by name, stroking necks and noses and scratching their ears or backsides.

Centaurus had told her once that it said much about the character of a man, how he treated his animals. A man who kicked his dog or beat his horse would not hesitate to treat his children or his people the same way. He would make war for the love of bloodshed, and attack without cause or reason. But her father had not told her what it meant if a man was gentle with his beasts, if he knew how each liked to be rubbed and scratched.

Pirithous smiled at her over the back of one of the horses, and the snug cloak around her heart loosened. If he showed this much attention to his animals, could he truly be so cruel to his wife?

She dropped her gaze, combing her fingers through Fire's mane. Not cruel, perhaps, and maybe even kind. But it would not be love. He would never give his own heart back to her. And the kinder he was, the harder it would be to face the truth of it when it came.

"Come," Pirithous said suddenly in her ear. She spun, her heart racing. He stood much too near, his bare chest a temptation she did not want. His hands found her waist and he lifted her up, setting her on Fire's back. "Our horses wait for us in the stable, but Fire is not so old she cannot take you that far. I trust you will have no trouble guiding her?"

Bad enough his hand lingered upon her thigh though she had not so much as teetered. She narrowed her eyes at the added insult, and pressed her heel to the mare's ribs. Fire danced away obediently, and with another kick, the horse broke into a canter.

Hippodamia twined her fingers in Fire's mane and left Pirithous behind.

CHAPTER EIGHT

PIRITHOUS

Theseus had warned him that she would not soften easily, but after seeing the desire so clearly written in her eyes the previous night, Pirithous had been certain some progress had been made between them. Until Hippodamia rode off on his favorite horse and left him in a cloud of dust.

Not that she could go far inside the palace walls. Fire was too old to do more than fall back into a walk after such a burst of speed. Pirithous followed after his horse and his bride-to-be without hurry, giving them both time to tire. Fire was already circling back toward the stable, and Hippodamia leaned forward, stroking the mare's neck with obvious affection. He grinned at the sight. For all her stubbornness, if she could treat his horses with kindness and affection, she would learn to treat her husband similarly. He was, after all, twice as charming as even the best horses in his stables, and much less likely to kick, though he would not make her any promises in regard to the application of his teeth now and again. In the most pleasurable sense, of course, and wild as she was, he would not be surprised to feel the bite of her own. Nor would he complain in the slightest.

But when she saw him approach in the stable, all the warmth in her expression faded away into cool regard. She turned her back upon him, bringing Fire alongside the readied horses held in the gentle hands of the horsemaster, and leapt from the mare's back to the back of his raven-black stallion in a move so graceful he might have believed her to be a goddess, had he not known otherwise.

The stallion tossed his head, dancing back half a step before she had him in hand, her fingers coiled in his mane instead of holding the reins. And this from Podarkes, who permitted no other rider but Pirithous and the horsemaster himself. By all rights, she should have been thrown, Tamer of Horses or not.

"You should be more careful of yourself, my lady," Pirithous said, pausing beside her. "Leaping upon a strange horse so carelessly might cost you dearly one day."

She lifted her chin and Podarkes snorted, no doubt responding to her anger, though for the love of Aphrodite and Hera, he did not know what he had done to inspire such emotion. "I earned my name, *King* Pirithous."

His jaw tightened at the implied insult and a jerk of his head sent the horsemaster from the stable. "In private, you may speak to me however you desire, Princess, and I swear to you I will take any tongue-lashing you wish to give without objection, but in front of our people, you will show respect to your king."

"The same respect you show to your queen," she agreed coolly.

"And what insult have I given you, Hippodamia?"

She laughed, high and sharp, and turned the stallion away. "Better to ask what insult you have *not* given, Pirithous. And I promise you, I will not be shamed so cruelly again. Not by the man I am meant to marry or any other."

He vaulted up onto the mare, younger and spryer than Fire, and guided her after Hippodamia. This time, she would not leave him behind. A well-placed heel against the mare's ribs, and they caught the stallion before he left the stable. Pirithous leaned over and took the reins she so disdained, leashing her horse—*his* horse!

The impudent little wildling. Not that he did not admire her horsemanship, but he had hardly expected less from a girl raised by centaurs—ah! Was that what had troubled her?

"You should not mistake my teasing for insult, Princess." She had been perfectly well-behaved, if hesitant, until he'd put her on Fire's back. And after the previous night, he had counted it only for shyness, not unusual at all in a maiden.

But there was no hesitation now, just a flash of anger in her eyes and a toss of her head, echoed by the stallion between her shapely legs. If she rode a horse so well, he could only imagine how well she would ride him, and the thought made his own seat much less comfortable than it had been a moment before.

"Perhaps you should not mistake insult for teasing, my lord."

He laughed, drawing the stallion near enough that her bare leg brushed his as they rode toward the palace gate. "You are determined, aren't you?"

She slanted him a narrow glance, her body stiffening at the contact. "To win your respect, yes. I am that."

"Not that," he said, grinning. "I would not waste my day in showing you the lands we will hold if you did not have that already. But as you are absolutely determined to misunderstand me, I fear you won't trust it to be so, even when I say it plainly."

"And should I trust your word so easily, when you show no faith in me or mine?"

"No faith?" He nodded to the guards upon the gate as they passed, and the young men smiled to see their king laughing with his future wife. Or at least laughing in her company, for Hippodamia sat haughty and unforgiving beside him, her mouth a thin line and her eyes narrowed. "What greater faith might I have shown in you and yours, Princess, than by accepting the terms of this peace? Nor did I doubt your word when you claimed yourself to be free of affection for any other. What more proof would you have of me?"

"You should not have asked at all!" Podarkes jerked his head at some sign from her, dancing sideways, and the reins nearly slipped from his fingers.

He tightened his grip and clucked his tongue. The stallion settled, knowing his master's firm hand, and Hippodamia glared at him, though he was not certain if it was because of his offense or the failure of what might have been her escape had he not been quick enough to thwart her.

"You ride my horse, Hippodamia. You can hardly expect him not to obey my commands."

"It is not your horse which offends me."

"I suppose it isn't," he agreed, letting his gaze travel from her face down her body. Her legs hugged his stallion as if she had been born to ride, and the tunic did not do much to cover them. They were as sun-browned as her arms, the smooth skin marked with thin silver lines. No doubt from riding through the forest, cut and scraped by branches and thorns along the way.

His fingers itched to trace each mark, his body to be pressed between her sleek thighs. He lifted his gaze back to hers, cool as ever. Not tonight. Not until those dark eyes turned to pools of desire. And he would see them so, he promised himself. Before the solstice.

"But as you have agreed to become my bride and mother of my sons, I fear you will be offended for a very long time."

He twitched the reins and turned both their horses toward the mountain.

***

Pirithous released his hold on the stallion's reins when they reached the faint trail, too narrow to ride side by side. Podarkes knew the way well enough, and Hippodamia had settled, the flame of her anger quenched by curiosity. This part of the mountain had always belonged to the Lapiths, the forest too thick for the centaurs and missing the caves they preferred. But the hunting was good, and when the trail brought them out of the forest to the stone outcropping, the view was even better.

Hippodamia, riding in silence before him, drew in a sharp breath, and urged Podarkes forward, until the stallion stood on the very edge of the precipice. Pirithous brought his mare up beside her, though not quite so near the edge. His mare was not so steady as Podarkes. The great herd of the Lapiths grazed below them on the plain while the herdsmen watched for raiders and lions. Lapith horses were never left unguarded but, they still lost a handful each year to raiding from their Myrmidon *friends*. It was an unspoken rite of manhood among their people to sail north and follow the river inland to steal horses from the Lapiths.

"I have never seen so many," Hippodamia murmured.

"Gold and silver might be traded away, but we will always have our horses. None but the Lapiths can break them, so we let them run half-wild. The horses Peleus and his Myrmidons steal come back to us in time, useless to his people but for breeding. Even if he had the land to keep such a large herd alongside his cattle and goats and sheep, his men are such poor horsemen they are bound to lose them, one way or another. When the mares he's stolen make their way back to us again, we gain their foals as well, courtesy of Peleus's finest stallions." He watched her carefully then, and listened harder to the current of her awe as he went on. "I have sent word to my people that any foals studded by Peleus's stock are to be given up to their queen in dowry, and you will have another ten horses from the palace stable as well. Any but Fire, of course."

She stared at him, wide-eyed, so startled the stallion felt it, and threw up his head, dancing back from the ledge. Pirithous hid a smile. Put her on a horse and he need never use his power to know her feelings, she communicated them so easily to the beasts.

"A woman who earned her name taming horses ought not be kept from them, Princess. Surely you did not think me so foolish as that?"

"But so many?" she breathed. "For my own?"

"Yours to do with as you wish," he promised. "Dia would have wanted you to have some wealth of your own, and I thought you would prefer horses to gold, though I will give you cups and plates and bowls enough of that, too, if you desire it. Gold and silver halters, perhaps, to mark the horses which belong to you?"

"You would shower me with riches," she said, her gaze returning to the grazing horses, softer now, her surprise laced with confusion. "But I am already yours, King Pirithous. I am paid for by peace between our peoples."

"And you will be my wife, my queen. Even if you cannot love me, as you say, I would give you every pleasure." And if she would not accept him into her bed yet, he might at least begin with the pleasures he could offer outside of it.

He brought the mare around, guiding it back toward the trees. "You might do more than simply stare, Princess."

He smiled slowly, letting the flush of her discomfort wash over him, though he did not look back to see the blush in her cheeks. Let her think he had not noticed, and let her believe, too, that he had spoken carelessly. Better if she did not know yet that he had felt the flash of desire, quickly buried, or she was bound to find some reason to take offense, rallying anger from its ashes instead. He must go carefully now. Slowly. It had been a long time since a woman had given him such trouble, and the release he found in her body would be all the sweeter for the wait.

"There is a trail down to the plain," he went on, before she could balk. "We'll share our meal with the horses, if you wish."

***

As a boy, before he had grown old enough to spend his summers raiding, Pirithous had taken his turn as herdsman, helping to guard the horses. And even as a man, when the seas were too rough or some demand of Dia's kept him from taking ship, he had come here, riding through the half-wild herd and making himself known to them. Day after day, month after month, he had waited for them to grow used to his scent, his movements, his presence in their midst, but Hippodamia had only to laugh and instead of starting, the horses lifted their heads, ears twitching. When she reached out her hand, they stretched out their necks, touching velvet noses to her fingers and breathing her in.

Yes, she would make a very fine queen, and in truth, she was no wilder than the horses of the plain, so cherished by his people. She need only become used to his presence, trained to take food from his hand and to tolerate his touch. She need only be tamed enough to ride, and then he would set her loose again, to run wild with the herd, if she wished it. A horse queen would serve his people quite well.

They had left their own horses with one of the herdsmen, though Pirithous carried the bags packed with their meal, and more parsnips, for he had thought he might need to lure the horses. He need not have worried. A filly came nosing at her hands and Hippodamia smiled at him over her shoulder, her eyes bright with joy.

Pirithous was glad to return it. He would have gifted her the horses yesterday had he known she might forget her sworn dislike of him so easily. He only hoped her glow of pleasure would last through the day.

"Not so wild after all," she said softly, when he moved to her side. "Or is it only because they know you?"

"Most of them have known me since birth, or the winter just after." He grinned, showing her a handful of parsnips. "But more, perhaps, that they know I bring them food."

She laughed again, and the horses came nearer, crowding around them. Pirithous nudged more than one nose away from the bags he carried. Much longer and they would push their way in to steal the fruit he had promised Hippodamia.

"There is a hillock up ahead," he told her, nodding in its direction, "with a large boulder where we might sit and eat without the horses nibbling the food from our fingers."

Her eyes danced as she watched him struggle through the herd. She wove through them easily, speaking a soft word here or there so the horses would step aside—most often into Pirithous instead. If she had not taken such clear delight in his trouble, he would have found it far more unpleasant, but her joy fed his own pleasure. To see her smiling so carelessly was worth the price, and he would let her tease him all she wished if it meant the softening of her heart.

"Come," she said at last, laughter in her voice. Her hand found his, and she drew him with her through the press of horse flanks and the tickle of soft noses much more swiftly than he might have managed on his own. Her hand was so small, her touch so soft and gentle, like a bird alighting for the briefest moment.

Then they were free of the herd, and her fingers slipped from his. He flexed his hand, the loss of her touch almost an ache in his chest. She had never reached for him freely before. Never allowed him to touch her without some stiffness in her manner.

She ran ahead of him toward the hillock, fleet and graceful as a deer, tossing a grin of challenge over her shoulder. He dropped the bags he carried and gave himself to the race, his father's blood lighting fire to his veins and lightning burning in his eyes. Tamer of Horses she might be, and blessed by Poseidon, but she was no demigod. If she wished to race, she would not win, no matter how far ahead she started.

He caught her just before she reached the hillock, bringing her tumbling with him into the meadow grass. A shout of surprise turned just as quickly into laughter, and she was beneath him, all softness and warmth, her arms encircling his neck, her dark eyes smiling, and her full lips curving.

His body hardened between them, and her eyes widened. Just a taste, he promised himself. And if she did not welcome him, he would let her slip free. But with her hair wild in the grass and her body so inviting, he could not help but lower his head and claim her mouth with his own.

Chapter Nine

Hippodamia

She stilled completely, the hot flush of her cheeks spreading down into her belly until her stomach knotted tight. Then his lips brushed hers, so lightly she wondered if she'd dreamed it. Perhaps he had sent her tumbling and her head had struck the rock, and all the rest was nothing more than whispers of her dreams the night before. She sighed, disappointment mixing with hunger. None of it could be real. The horses and his kindness and his gift. It was too wonderful, and he had been too…

His lips brushed hers again, more confident now, and lingering. She clung to his neck, drawing him down. If he was only a phantom, and if it was only a dream of a kiss, a dream of a king she might love, she need not shy from it. She parted her lips, but he did not answer by delving into her mouth, only nibbled at her lip, sending sparks of desire and need into her center. She moaned, lifting her head to reach for more, to taste his mouth if he would not take hers. He was mint and honey and exultation, and when she parted his lips with her tongue all the gentleness of his beginning fled.

Pirithous pressed her down, the thickness of his desire hard between them, and even that only sent a thrill of heat and pleasure up her spine. She threaded her fingers through his hair, tasting his laughter on his tongue even before she heard it break, muffled against her mouth. The rough warmth of his palm slid up her thigh, beneath the hem of her short tunic, and when she lifted her hips in welcome, his laughter turned into a groan.

"Not this way," he gasped, tearing his mouth from hers. He dropped his forehead to her shoulder, lifting himself up, and the wind moved between them, cooling her body where it ached for his. "Zeus give me strength," he murmured against her neck.

She curled her fingers more tightly into his hair, her own laughter bubbling up. To have reduced him to this—the proud Pirithous who had stood glorious and naked in his tub, now panting at her throat and begging the gods for help. It could only be a dream.

It could only ever have been a dream.

Her laughter died with the thought, and she pushed him away. His shoulders were so solid, his body so heavy she could not have moved him had he not been willing. He rolled to his back beside her, rubbing his face with the hand that had slipped beneath her tunic and held her firm against his need.

"Forgive me," he said, his voice rough. "I never meant—I had not expected—" He made a sound, half-growl and half-groan. "Aphrodite save me. I had not realized the centaurs taught you so much."

She flushed, thinking of Eurytion, his gleaming black hide and his ebony eyes. Whatever there might have been between them had ended when Dia proposed her peace, and Centaurus had forbidden the others from touching her. Not that there had ever been more than the sweet, stolen kisses of children. Not that he had ever filled her with sparks of need and desire, flaming bright hot at his touch. Compared to Pirithous, Eurytion fumbled like a newborn colt nosing for his mother's teat.

"I wish this could be more than a dream," she said.

He rolled to his side, propping himself up on his elbow and smiling down at her. He brushed a strand of hair from her cheek with a feather touch. "Have you always dreamed of me so?"

"I dreamed of a king I could love."

His forehead creased, his gray eyes darkening. "Am I so terrible that to want my kiss you must think me a phantom?"

"Proud and selfish and caring only for your own pleasure. You would demand a bride who is untouched, unspoiled, while you take woman after woman to your bed, and men, too, when it suits you. For all you Lapiths think the centaurs beasts, we do not demand anything from another we ourselves would not willingly give."

"I have never met a woman so difficult to please," he said softly, sitting up. "Nor so determined to believe the worst in me." He sighed, then rose to his feet and extended a hand to her. "Come, Princess. I promised you a meal. Perhaps when your stomach is full you will believe yourself awake, even if you cannot think better of me for it."

***

He did not speak to her while they ate, but for offering her some food or another from the pack he had carried, and he spoke even less as they rode back to the palace. Her stomach sank and her heart twisted as the silence stretched. Not a dream, after all, and she could not help but relive her own foolishness with every breath.

She could not help but relive his kiss, either, or the way he had broken it.

Not this way…

Hippodamia closed her eyes, trusting the stallion to keep to the trail. What other way did he wish it to be? How better than upon her back in the meadow grass, with the sun to kiss their skin and the sky to blanket them?

No, she remembered suddenly. It was the words of the priest. Pirithous could not take his bride to bed until the solstice if he wished for a fruitful marriage, and they must be fruitful. As the promise would be sealed by their wedding, so must the peace itself be sealed by a child of both their peoples. The child she must give to Pirithous, and preferably a son.

She was still his brood mare, that was all. Not to be risked before her time.

The trees broke into cleared land and the walls of the palace, beyond which the village sat nestled against the bend of the river. Horses grazed here, too, with goats and cattle, and even the smallest houses had sheltered stalls beside them. But they had no need to ride through the village, and soon the palace filled her vision, hiding all signs of the people who lived on its other side. Later, perhaps, Hippodamia thought. Antiope would surely ride with her if she asked, and Pirithous could not object to her exploration of the village. Whatever else stood between them, she did not doubt his desire to make her queen in deed as well as name.

They rode through a smaller gate on the near side of the walls and Pirithous called out to the horsemaster when they came into sight of the palace stable.

"Machaon is the master of my stables," Pirithous said, his gaze trained on his man as if he could not stand to look at her. "He knows every horse by name and lineage, back to Poseidon's creation of the beasts. Anything you would know, he will tell you. When you have chosen your horses, you need only name them, and I will have halters and bridles made in silver and gold."

She twined her fingers into the stallion's mane, but the coolness of his tone was a weight against her heart, and her throat thickened. He had meant it, then, all of it. The horses and the halters, the bowls and plates and cups. Would she return to her rooms to find them filled with such prizes? And she had been so sure it must be impossible, so certain he could not be anything but selfish.

"You need not go to such lengths," she murmured. "And gold would not be comfortable for the horses, besides."

"And give you reason to believe me miserly as well as selfish and proud?" He laughed, but it was harsh and unkind. "No, Princess. You will have your gold. Melt it down again and give it as gifts to your kin, if you wish, but I would not cheat you."

"Pirithous—"

"My lady has lost her sandals," Pirithous interrupted, for Machaon had reached them. "Lead Podarkes to the porch, that she might slip from his back onto clean tile. Queen Antiope would not forgive me if any harm befell my bride."

"Of course, my lord," Machaon said, taking the reins she had ignored. "Come Podarkes, my lady. This way."

Hippodamia swallowed the words she had been about to say, for Pirithous kicked the mare into a trot as she was drawn away. The apology soured her stomach as she watched him ride off, back stiff and sunlight gleaming on his bare shoulders. She had stung his pride again, somehow. And likely it would not be the last time.

But it was the first time it had pricked her conscience, and she ached to see him go before she might make it right.

***

The rest of the day spun by with no further sign of Pirithous, though Hippodamia found herself hoping he might come in search of her. But it was Antiope who found her, and Antiope who took it upon herself to help her settle in. Pirithous did not even join them for the evening meal, and when she asked, the Amazon brushed his absence away.

"Off with Theseus, hunting a boar that's made a nuisance of itself, though why it could not wait another day, I do not know. Perhaps he wishes his people to grow used to seeing you alone at their table. He could do worse than begin as he means to go on."

But how had he begun? Had it been the insults he had delivered her before Centaurus had placed her hand in his, or did he mean for her to see the true beginning as the meal that followed, and their morning's ride? He was so different. So frustrating. And to disappear now, the way he had, without so much as a word... What manner of beginning was that?

Hippodamia forced herself to smile, murmuring agreement and focusing upon her meal. After all, she should not find fault in his absence. Not when it meant her freedom from attentions she did not want. Freedom to spend her evening precisely as she wished, without any interference from the king.

But in her bed, late in the night, she strained to hear the sounds of his bathing when she woke to the splash of water filling the tub, and found some small part of her hoping he might knock upon her door. Boars were dangerous, after all. And even for a son of Zeus, there was risk in the hunting. It was not even that she cared if he was injured badly for his own sake, she told herself, but rather what would become of the peace they were meant to forge if he died before their marriage.

But he didn't knock, and she tossed and turned the night away, growing all the more distressed when morning came and he did not stand at the bottom of the stairs to stop her on her way to the kitchens. Even after Antiope joined her much later in the morning, the sounding of each footstep in the corridor made her lift her head, only for her heart to lurch in disappointment when the man or woman—servants mostly—passed by without pausing.

"Are you certain you wish to begin this task today?" Antiope asked the second time she caught Hippodamia staring at the door. "None would fault you for waiting until tomorrow, and truly there is no reason the steward could not see it done. Men are useless for anything but passing orders along, and even in that they must be well trained, but Dia has done the work and it would be a shame to let it be wasted."

Hippodamia shook her head, tearing her gaze from the door and the hope of Pirithous. He would not chase after her like some lost puppy. His pride would prevent it even if he wished to, and she was not certain he cared for her as much as that, besides. How could he, if he would not even tell her when he went off to risk his life in the hunt?

"Thank you, my lady, but I would see for myself how it is done, that I might know if the steward fails in his duty later."

"Antiope," the Amazon said firmly. "We are equals, Hippodamia."

"And friends?" Until Hylonome arrived, she had no one else. A queen could not comport with slaves and servants, and Pirithous's people looked on her as though she had run naked and wild through their halls, besides. Perhaps she would be driven to it yet.

"Our husbands would have it so," Antiope agreed. "But if it were only Theseus and Pirithous who desired our friendship, I would not stand beside you now." The Amazon queen smiled, almost shyly. "I have missed the companionship of women sorely, though Theseus has done his best to distract me from it."

"He seems a good man." If distraction had been Pirithous's intention when he took her riding, he had succeeded. She pressed her lips together against the memory of his kiss, but her face flushed with the warmth of it all the same. Not that the warmth had lasted.

"Only wait until you have brought Pirithous to your bed, and he will be just as good to you."

But he already was. The gold and silver bridles, the horses. She traced a deep line in the olive wood table, remembering the silvered scars upon his chest. He was already good to her, and she had given him no reason to treat her kindly, no pleasure at all, for she could not seem to stand beside him for more than a moment without offering him some new insult. By the time they were married, she would be lucky if he did not seek to avoid her company altogether.

"He will not have me until the solstice, Antiope."

The Amazon smiled, slow and sly, her eyes flashing with mischief. "But that does not mean you cannot have him."

***

The splash of water being poured and the rustle of servants in the bathing room gave Hippodamia warning, now that she knew to listen for it. Antiope had left her only a few moments before, after sharing a private meal together in her room. The Amazon had brought a gown of fine, sheer fabric, lighter than anything Hippodamia had ever seen, and helped her dress. She had piled her hair atop her head, but for a few oiled curls which framed her face, and secured it with one long bone pin, for Antiope had assured her she would not want it all tumbling over her shoulders later.

Hippodamia fingered one of the oiled strands, coiling it around her finger, and waited. The servants would fill the bath, a task which took more time than Hippodamia had realized until that moment, and then leave after everything had been prepared. From what she had seen the first night, and heard the last, he did not bring his women in to bathe him, and Antiope had reassured her it was so.

"Pirithous would not be so cruel as that, and his evening bath is nothing but a soak in hot water, besides. He says it calms his mind, and perhaps that is true, but our women say he does not sleep more than a quarter of the night, and not even that much if they are willing to keep him awake longer." Antiope had snorted then, tying the girdle at Hippodamia's waist in a simple bow, easily undone. "They say the sons of Zeus never tire of pleasure, and Heracles and Pirithous are the proof. There now. And if he gets you wet with bathwater, so much the better. The fabric will cling nicely to your curves, tempting him even further."

Temptation and seduction, and Hippodamia had been instructed well over their meal, with the help of a thick parsnip when it was required. Antiope had not shied at all from demonstration, even going so far as to pinch the points of Hippodamia's breasts until they tightened and strained eagerly against the light fabric of her gown.

Just the memory hardened her nipples now, and the sound of Pirithous's voice as he dismissed his servants caused her to flush with anticipation. She need only reach him, she reminded herself, and once she held his desire in her hand, he would not deny her. She would have his forgiveness, and before they had finished, Antiope promised, he would have hers, as well.

Hippodamia cracked the door to the bathing room and peeked inside. Pirithous leaned back in the terra-cotta tub with his eyes closed, arms resting on the rim. She took a steadying breath, more ragged than she liked, and stepped inside.

Chapter Ten

Pirithous

He could sense her just beyond the door, agitation mixing with hesitation and seeping through the wood, thick in the air until it was all he could breathe. Likely she feared he would impose himself upon her after she had absented herself from the evening meal, and the whole of the rest of the day as well. Antiope ought to have known better than to hide away with her in the queen's room, but Theseus had refused to speak to his wife, and Pirithous had no interest in fighting with the woman himself. He'd done enough fighting with Hippodamia as it was, and Theseus had only laughed at his misfortune when he had spoken of it on the hunt.

He had hoped leaving the palace would do something to calm the restlessness in his heart, for it grated upon him more deeply than he liked that she found him so flawed. Proud and selfish and unkind. And perhaps he had been at the first, but had he not proven himself otherwise with such a generous gift? Could she not see the honor and respect he gave her with it? Instead, while he had bathed late last night, he had been treated to nothing more than her anxiety, itching at the back of his mind. He had not dared even look in on her, not when the mere sound of his return caused her so much unrest. Little mouse, indeed.

The shadows shifted behind his eyes with the flame of the hearth, but it was not until her hand rested upon his arm that he realized the agitation was no longer coming from outside the door.

He opened his eyes.

Hippodamia balanced carefully on the rim of the tub in a gown so sheer he could see the dark thicket nestled between her legs, and the rounded points of her breasts, so hard it made him ache.

"You said I might do more than stare," she murmured, her gaze dropping to the water and dark lashes fluttering against her cheeks. Her hand followed before he knew her intent, and her fingers wrapped around the thickness of his need.

Pirithous groaned, his body hardening even further in answer to her touch. "Merciful Zeus."

She smiled, his brave little mouse, and slid her hand up the length of his manhood with delightful ease, all hesitation forgotten now. "Isn't this what you had in mind?"

He caught her wrist before she could complete a second stroke, lest he lose his head completely. Her grip tightened, just so. Just enough that he could not bring himself to pull her hand free. "You tease me unfairly, Princess."

"Is it teasing still, if I mean to give you pleasure?"

A tug was all it took to topple her into the water, and the gown clung like spider webs to her skin, baring every curve, every dimple to his gaze. She laughed, looking up from beneath her eyelashes like a blushing maiden, all innocence in her mischief.

"This is Antiope's doing," he growled. "Her way of punishing me for whatever sins she's imagined."

"If it were Antiope's doing, would she not be here to bear witness?"

"Perhaps she is beyond your door. Waiting to see me falter, to give up my heir in exchange for a night of pleasure, taking what I desire from you."

He had lost her wrist when she fell into his lap, and she had lost her hold upon his manhood, thank all the gods in Olympus, but her body was its own temptation, and the gauze of her dress did nothing to disguise her warmth. Sweet, soft warmth, and slick with water, besides. He slid his hand from the girdle at her waist to the smoothness of her back, searching for some bare breadth of skin. His fingers curled into fists in the wet fabric, and it took all his self-control to keep from tearing the gossamer threads from her body.

"You need not take what is freely given," she said softly. "But if you will not have me yet, you might still allow me the pleasure of having you."

He growled again, for her hand had found the ache of his desire and begun to stroke once more. "Damia—"

She pressed her lips to his throat, her teeth grazing his skin between kisses. "Shh," she said. "Let me give you this."

Aphrodite knew he wanted it, wanted to bury himself deep inside her heat. But there was a part of him that fought his rising need. She was his bride, his promise of peace. "The priest," he managed to groan.

She laughed, sealing his protests with a kiss. Her mouth tasted of wine and spices, and she shifted on his lap, pressing her hip against his hardened length. But it was only a taste, for a moment later she had risen, her hand tugging at his, urging him to join her.

"Come," she said. "I would repay you fully, but I cannot do so in the bath."

He grunted, his gaze falling to her chest. Her breasts were two perfect, ripened apples. His fingers itched to trace the pink bud beneath the gauze, to roll the hard pebbled tip against his thumb until she begged for him to take her into his mouth. And then he would begin again, making her writhe.

When she tugged at him once more, he followed, careless of the water, careless of everything but the smile upon her lips and the ache of his arousal.

She moved backwards, both his hands in hers, leading him from the bathing room through the door into her chamber. He kicked the door shut behind him, and she drew him closer, guiding his hands to her waist. Her body fit against his so perfectly, but still he could not reach her skin.

The knot of her girdle unraveled beneath his searching fingers and he tossed the belt away, impatient now. If this was what she wanted, he would give it to her, and when they were through she would beg him for more. She would beg, and he would answer, until she lay exhausted, sated in body and mind.

But Hippodamia slid to her knees, kissing her way down his chest, trailing her fingers through the tract of hair leading to his need. And then her mouth found his tip, hot and soft and glorious as she took him inside. He cupped her head in his hands and groaned as she took him deeper, her tongue teasing him as she went.

Gods above, he had never thought, never imagined for a moment she might have wanted this. The centaurs could never have taught her such a skill, could never have trained her to the art. But by the way she curled her fingers around his length, stroking with her hand where she could not reach with her mouth until his blood burned hot and his eyes blazed white, someone had.

Antiope. The thought of the Amazon queen tutoring his bride, showing her the breadth of pleasure a woman could give made him tighten, deep inside. Hippodamia's mouth moving faster, her tongue applying the most exquisite pressure, did not help him to find his control. The weight of his pleasure built quickly, rushing like a mudslide down a mountain slope.

"Princess—"

It was all he could manage before the first pulse of release broke through him, spilling his seed into her mouth with a hoarse groan. But Hippodamia, his once-timid mouse of a bride, only met his gaze, her dark eyes betraying nothing but satisfaction as he shuddered with pleasure and she drank him dry.

***

He stripped the gown from her body after, laying her bare upon her bed and covering every finger-length of her skin with soft, teasing kisses until she writhed and whimpered beneath him with her own need. Even then he did not stop, exulting in each arch of her back as he suckled at her breasts, each desperate clutch of her hands upon him, nails digging for purchase upon his damp skin. When his body hardened again, her hips rose, searching for his length, and he chuckled softly against her throat.

"Not tonight, little mouse." Though his body ached for the heat of her core all the more now that he knew her desire for it, he had control of himself, the worst of his lust slaked. He slipped his hand between them, searching for the juncture of her thighs and the slick heat of her cleft. She moaned, her whole body trembling at his touch. "But you need not fear that I will leave you wanting."

Antiope had not shown her this much, he could tell, for her eyes widened further with each stroke of his fingers.

"Please," she breathed.

Pirithous lowered his head, letting his mouth follow where his hands had led, and soon after, she had no need to beg.

***

Hippodamia slept upon her stomach, her body sated at last, but Pirithous could not keep from touching her still, trailing his fingers down the length of her spine, reveling in the softness of her skin. Her dark hair had fallen from its pin long ago, tickling his stomach and thighs while she brought him to release a second time. He had loved the feel of it wound through his fingers, and the feather touch of it upon his skin. Now, it spilled across her back and shoulder to the linens, almost black in the dim, flickering light of the dying fire.

He followed the curve of her backside, cupping one plump cheek in his palm, and wondered what other lessons Antiope had given her in pleasuring a man. And had Hippodamia asked it of her? Theseus's laughter echoed in his ears, and Pirithous smiled. Antiope would have told him all, as was her habit, and no doubt Theseus would have done the same. By now they had both laughed themselves to sleep twice over at Pirithous's expense.

Not that he could blame them for it, but would it not have been kinder to warn him of Hippodamia's intent? He might have taken himself in hand if he had only known, though perhaps it was just as well that he hadn't. He leaned down to kiss Hippodamia's brow, furrowed slightly even in sleep. He should not have let her use her mouth the second time, nor would he permit her to do so again on the morrow, for she would need time to heal where her teeth had marked the soft flesh inside. And there were other things she could do, if she wished to pleasure him. Other things they might do together without risking the fruit of their marriage.

He let his fingers dip between her legs, finding the heat of her womanhood, still slick, and brought his hand back up slowly, teasing her until she stirred in her sleep. Aphrodite was cruel to him, for he was hardening again just at the thought of taking her. Still five days, yet, until the solstice, and now that he had tasted her, he could think of nothing else but her body, opened to his, hot and wet and ready.

One dark eye opened, and Hippodamia's fingers brushed over his manhood.

"Antiope was right," she murmured.

"Too often," he agreed, kissing her half-closed eyelids. "Though I dare not guess what she told you."

She smiled lazily, dragging her fingertips up with the barest of caresses. Just enough to make him stiffen even further and cause his blood to burn for more. "She said you did not sleep as long as you had a willing woman in your bed. That you never tired of pleasure."

"But did she tell you of the pleasure you'd receive in return?"

She rolled to her side, and he let his hand slide to the curve of her waist, then up, her skin soft and smooth as silk beneath his fingertips. A drag of his thumb over the point of her breast and her nipple tightened, more awake than its mistress, who still looked at him with drowsy eyes slowly darkening with desire.

"She said I would forgive you before the night was through, as you would me, but little else."

"More fool, me," he murmured. By rights, her coming to him should have meant forgiveness already given, not this game of seduction. But he had put her into Antiope's care, and he should have realized it could not be so simple with the Amazon queen advising her.

And he would not ask. He would not ask if she had forgiven him, after all. In fact, he was feeling rather unforgiving himself, though some part of him knew he should not blame her. A part he chose, in that moment, to ignore.

Pirithous turned away, rising from the bed, though his body ached with the loss of her touch, the warmth of her hand, the temptation of her mouth.

"My lord?" she called softly, and he knew without looking her forehead would be furrowed just so, for her confusion lapped at his heels.

"Go back to sleep, Princess."

And then he left her.

But for the first time in months, he spent the rest of his night alone.

***

"She came to you willingly and you left her?" Theseus said, laughter in his voice. "Surely you are not so great a fool as that!"

Theseus was not as difficult as some men to rouse in the morning, though Antiope had not bothered to hide her irritation when Pirithous had pounded on their door. No doubt they had been up late the night before, for there was no question that Antiope kept him well satisfied, and for all the teasing they gave him for the little sleep he took, they did not live on much more. Antiope was a daughter of Ares, after all, and as a son of Poseidon, Theseus was as hot-blooded as Pirithous himself, if not quite so intent upon a variety of partners.

When Theseus had opened the door, he had been stark naked, and at the sight of Pirithous he only grinned. Pirithous had waited impatiently while he returned to the bedside where Antiope lay only half-covered by the linens, kissed his wife goodbye, and dressed in the first rumpled tunic he found. They had retreated to Pirithous's rooms thereafter, with a tray of bread, cold meats, and wine.

Pirithous wasted no time in pouring his own cup, unmixed, but Theseus had refused, drinking minted water instead.

"She came to me because she wanted my forgiveness, not because she wanted me."

Theseus snorted, breaking a piece of bread from the loaf. "If you refused to sleep with the women who wanted something from you in exchange, you'd have to give up every girl you keep in the palace, and never accept another village girl into your bed. Of course she wanted your forgiveness! And how else would she have gotten it, when you said yourself you had no desire to hear anything she might say? When you left her to her own devices for more than a day without so much as a word?"

"She'd said enough to make her feelings clear, Theseus. And I do not think for a moment she would have come upon this scheme without the influence of your wife."

"And if Antiope encouraged her to spread her legs, knowing it would soften you, what of it?" He shrugged, unrepentant. "I cannot see how it hurt you in the slightest, unless she revealed some strange deformity once she undressed, but Antiope assured me she was quite comely. Breasts like ripened pomegranates and skin as sweet as honey. Or did she taste like fish instead of ambrosia? Antiope confessed she had wished for a taste, but Hippodamia was too uncertain."

His eyes burned at the thought of Antiope between Hippodamia's smooth thighs, bringing her to release before he had ever known her body. "Amazon or not, there is only so much I will tolerate from your wife, Theseus. Hippodamia is mine!"

Theseus laughed. "If Hippodamia wishes to take a lover from among her women, you'll have no say in the matter, my friend.

Were she to choose Antiope, you might at least know she is not refusing your bed for her own pleasure while we are in Athens."

"And Antiope? Has she taken some other lover?"

"Antiope believes the women of Athens beneath her notice, and I will not deny it makes things easier. But when Antiope lived among her people, she had lovers, and though I have given her all that is within my power to give, she misses the companionship she shared with those women. I can hardly blame her for it."

"Hippodamia will have no need to look to a woman for her pleasure once I bring her to my bed. As I proved to her last night." Twice over, and happily, until he had understood her reasoning. But if she thought for a moment he would let her go to Antiope for her needs—better if it had been a maid or a serving girl than Antiope, of all women. To have Theseus's wife smirk at him at his own table, knowing him cast aside so easily! No. If Hippodamia wished to take a lover, he would give her the use of any of his palace women, but Antiope had already done enough harm without giving his bride a taste for what he could not provide.

"Gods be praised!" Theseus said. "For a moment, I feared you had left her unsatisfied as well as insulted. You'll be lucky if she ever offers herself again, after this. Did it never occur to you that she simply knows no better? Living on that mountain among centaurs, and then you place her in Antiope's care. What else did you expect?"

"I suppose I expected your wife to mind herself and her manners," he grumbled, downing what was left in his wine cup. "And I trusted you to keep her from overstepping, besides."

"You wanted a queen strong enough to take Dia's place. Whether you want to see it or not, your mother had much more in common with the Amazons than she did the daughters of any of your assembly or mine. Unless you mean to entrust your kingdom to Dia's steward—and he is as like to cheat you as any other, king or not—you had better not have intended to cow Hippodamia into some meek, simpering thing. Better if she were more Amazon than less, and Antiope will see her made competent, at least."

"Competent in the arts of womanly manipulation, to be sure," he growled, tossing his wine cup against the wall. The pottery shattered, but he did not care. "And what good will it do me if my people believe me too weak even to govern my wife? I must have her respect *and* theirs, Theseus. You are king of Athens. You know what it takes to rule."

"And my wife, cousin, is an Amazon. Do you truly think my people did not question me when I took her to my bed? You think they did not whisper that King Theseus had been bespelled, that they did not say I was unfit for the crown, made weak by a wife who would surely seek to conquer me? Hippodamia is no fool. If your people do not embrace her, the peace Dia sought will not last no matter how many sons she gives you. She will not risk her people, and she cannot serve them by costing you the kingship!"

"And I am to ignore the rest? To pretend she does not seek to wrap me around her fingers and distract me with the pleasure her body might offer?"

"You stubborn ox." Theseus leaned forward, his eyes the flat blue-gray of a hurricane on the sea and all humor gone from his expression. "What she offered you last night was a gift! A peace offering by which you might begin again without strife. By all rights, you should be with her now, feeding her honeyed figs and dates between kisses and imagining the kingdom you might build together. And do not tell me you cannot match her, art for art, pleasure for pleasure, when it is Zeus's blood flowing in your veins."

"And when I cannot think straight for the want of her? What then, Theseus? When my people no longer trust me because I have spent all my days in her bed instead of seeing to my horses?"

Theseus snorted, pushing his plate away and rising to his feet. "It is a blessing to care for your wife, Pirithous, not a curse. Son of Zeus or not, you will find the balance if you would only stop fighting against the bond you might share, and your people will think no less of you for it. Provided, of course, that Hippodamia will forgive you at all. I am not certain I would, were I her."

And then he left, brushing past the steward on his way through the door. Pirithous cursed, and the steward cleared his throat, dithering just outside. His gaze darted from Pirithous to the shattered remains of the cup upon the floor.

"Regarding the bridles, my lord, you promised the smith you would send him the gold and silver this morning."

He drank the last of the mint water from Theseus's cup and filled it with what was left of his wine. The steward, of course, could not move the heavy marble which served to keep the finest of his prizes and treasures safe in their storeroom, but he had not the time now to see to it. Theseus so rarely lost his temper that he did not dare ignore his friend's words, and Hippodamia would even now be in her bath.

"Take the plates and platters from the table. It will be enough for him to begin his work, and I will send the rest later."

Later, after Hippodamia had been given her choice of his treasury. And if she would not accept gold in payment for the insult, he would find some other method of persuasion.

CHAPTER ELEVEN

HIPPODAMIA

Hippodamia lurched upright with a splash, grabbing for her discarded robe. Pirithous caught the fabric before she did and, with a jerk of his chin, sent Antiope's maid from the room. *Her* maid, now, she supposed, for Antiope had made her a wedding gift, but she would not have believed the servant of an Amazon could be so easily cowed by a man's wordless gesture, king or not.

"Surely we need not keep up a pretense of modesty any longer," he said, holding the robe just out of reach. Of course he had come dressed only in his kilt, that she might see each ripple of muscle across his chest and shoulders as he moved. "Or at least you did not seem so very shy last night."

She crossed her arms over her chest and lifted her chin. "One night of pleasure does not give you the right to impose yourself upon my bath, my lord."

He lifted one eyebrow, his gaze traveling from her face to her body, and the water which did not cover her nearly as well as she might have hoped. "But the desire to gain my forgiveness gave you the right to impose yourself upon mine?"

She flushed, cursing herself even as the warmth spread from her breasts to her cheeks, and another, second blossom of heat followed, between her legs. The things he had done with his mouth—she had not known it was possible to ache so sweetly, and when his fingers had slipped inside her, curling so perfectly, she could do nothing but buck beneath the caress, her vision bleeding white at the edges as wave after wave of pleasure washed through her body.

"You did not seem to mind."

Pirithous dropped the robe on the floor again and stepped over it. She kept her gaze upon his sandaled feet, refusing even the sight of his strong calves and well-muscled thighs. But Pirithous caught her by the chin, lifting her face, and his gray eyes searched hers, impossible to ignore.

"And was it all you had hoped for, Princess?"

She shivered, turning her face away before he saw the answer in her eyes. All she had wanted was his forgiveness, the touch of warmth in his eyes when he looked upon her. But he had given more, so much more, then torn it away again before she could even begin to understand. There was no warmth in his eyes now, either. He looked at her as though she were nothing more than a puzzle, some problem to be solved and put away again. And it was obvious she had not satisfied him as he had her, or why else would he have left?

After the pleasures of his palace women, what could she offer that he had not known already? It had been such a messy, wet business, and she had probably fumbled through the half of it, in his eyes. And even if he had hoped she might repeat her performance, she had only to press her lips together to feel the ache where her teeth had cut into her flesh, just short of drawing blood inside her mouth.

"I would have my robe, please, if you are so determined to keep me from my bath."

He snorted, straightening. "You misunderstand my intentions, Princess."

She shook her head, annoyed, and grasped hold of her courage. Perhaps she could not pleasure him the way he wished her to, but she would not shrink beneath his gaze like the maid. That did not mean, of course, she could not dart a look toward her door as she prepared to rise. She would simply stand before him, meet his gaze, and demand her robe—

His hand closed on her shoulder, holding her gently in place as she tensed. She did meet his eyes then, startled to find him kneeling beside the bath. He plucked the abandoned sponge out of the water, his fingers grazing her thigh and lighting sparks of need inside her. The sponge paused over her knee and he wrung the water from it to trickle down her bent leg.

"What are you doing?" The words came out rough and broken as he slid his other hand from her shoulder, down her arm, brushing damp strands of hair from her skin as he went.

"I should think it rather obvious." The sponge followed a trail of water down her shin. "I certainly would not stop you from bathing, but I found, suddenly, that I could not stand the thought of letting another do you such an intimate service."

Above the water, her skin prickled with the cold, gooseflesh rising. He had wanted to come to her, wanted to bathe her himself. But he had left her so easily the night before, going back to his bed and the other women he kept to provide him with the most intimate service of all. Her throat thickened, her mouth as dry as desert sand.

"Am I permitted the same privilege, my lord? If I desire that you not be served by another, will you respect my wish?"

He laughed. "I promise you, Princess, if you ever wish to bathe me, I will not refuse you the honor."

She swallowed, ignoring the tremble of her legs as he dragged the sponge up her thigh. "And if I wish to spend the night in your bed in place of another?"

He brought the sponge up from the water slowly, letting the warm water spill over her shoulder before he met her gaze. "If you wish me to promise I will have no other in my bed but you, I fear you will be disappointed."

"Then it is my right to do the same."

His eyes flared lightning-white, his jaw tightening, and for a moment she thought he might rise, leaving her alone again. She had asked too much, and stung his pride as well, no doubt. Yet she would not take it back, could not, though she had not realized until now how much it meant to her. Among the centaurs, marriage was a sacred thing, binding for life. A mated male would never betray his wife, and even though Centaurus had told her this marriage to Pirithous would be otherwise, she still longed for more, for better. Hippodamia held his white-eyed stare, and said nothing.

Pirithous's nostrils flared with one deep breath and he dropped the sponge into the water again, turning his attention to the work of bathing her instead. "You forget, Princess, you owe me a son. There can be no doubt as to his father."

But she had not forgotten her duty, not at all. She lifted her chin, though he was not looking at her face. "After I have given you a son, you can have no such objection. And until then, Antiope spoke of taking lovers from among her women."

His hand balled into a fist beneath the water. "Antiope speaks much too freely."

"She offered herself to me," Hippodamia said, conscious of the tension in his shoulders, and the cords of muscle standing out upon his arms. "I was not certain the way of it, but much that you did last night could be done by a woman, too. And Antiope cannot be without her own skill in the matter."

The water reflected the flash of white-fire in his eyes, and the ceramic cracked beneath his hand on the rim of the tub. When he lifted his gaze, she flinched at the heat of it, the fury and power all directed at her. "Do you think I cannot satisfy you? That you will be so neglected you must turn to a woman for release?"

"If you are taking your pleasure elsewhere," she managed, her voice much too thin, "how will you see to mine?"

He growled, the sound sending a tremor down her spine, and then she was thrown over his shoulder, the movement so fast she knew nothing but a blur of light before his shoulder dug into her stomach and the blood rushed to her head. She pounded against his back, clawed, scratched until blood beaded on his skin, but Pirithous only threw her down onto his bed.

"Perhaps you need more proof of what I might offer," he said, half-tearing the kilt from his hips. "A reminder of the pleasure I gave you last night. Or would you have more? The priest says we must wait, but perhaps I would prefer no son at all to being cuckolded after his birth."

She scrambled to right herself, to find purchase in the mess of bedding beneath her. The edge of the bed lay just out of reach, and she twisted toward it. Pirithous pulled her back, his body hovering over hers and she brought her leg up. Antiope had sworn he would not force her, but the savagery of his words…

Her knee connected with his groin.

"Cronus's stones, girl!" he gasped, rolling away.

She struggled upright, for he had fallen to his back, but when she glanced at his face, there was no sign of pain or discomfort, no mark of suffering. His eyes were bright gray with mirth, and when he saw her face he laughed aloud.

"Unmanning me is no way to get what you want, but you will have to strike me much harder than that to accomplish it, all the same." He tucked one hand beneath his head, and she followed his gaze to the proof of his words, for his desire had not softened at all. The twist of fear in her stomach melted with another low chuckle. "Tell me again you'd prefer a woman in your bed."

"A woman would not frighten me so," she murmured, shifting away from him. "I thought for a moment—"

"No," he said. "Though I admit, my anger got the better of me." He fell silent for another heartbeat, then two. "Forgive me, I beg of you. It is only the thought of another man between your thighs, or worse, Antiope—if you wish a woman in your bed, I would give you one of mine, but not her, Princess. I cannot stand to lose what little affection you might have for me to her."

She shook her head and looked away, for all the pain he had not shown when she struck at him now lined his mouth and eyes. "How can you not see that it is no different for me? I can never be sure of your affections when you leave my bed to return to the arms of one of your lovers. And if they give you a son before I do—if the only children I bear are girls—do you not see how difficult it would become?"

He stroked a tendril of damp hair from her face, tickling her ear as he tucked it back. "My sacrifice would be your burden, little mouse."

"I did not satisfy you." The words slipped from her lips before she could stop them, broken and heavy in the air. Tears pricked at the corners of her eyes, but she blinked them back. "That was why you left."

He barked a laugh, his hand falling away. "Is that what you think?"

"What else?" she rasped, her throat too thick. She could not cry. Would not.

He sighed. "Foolishness and pride, Princess. For I am more stubborn than a mule, and more dimwitted than an ox. But I swear to you, I slept alone, though I ached for your sweet mouth and clever hands."

"Then why…" The night was a blur of pleasure and need. His mouth lighting fire to her body, his fingers stoking the flame. And she had been near to sleep when he had left her so suddenly.

Pirithous sat up, frowning out the window. His room was much the same as hers. A large bed and low benches ringing the walls, with a round hearth in the middle, and a table nearer to the door with the remains of a meal, hastily cleared, and stools arranged for guests. Beneath the window, a golden tripod held a basin of water, and a pitcher and towels waited on the bench beside it. His linens were pale blue, and when he shifted, she caught the scent of lavender. Odd that she had not noticed the smell of it before, for it clung to his skin, mixed with his own musk, like dry earth struck suddenly with rain.

"It seems your companion has arrived at last," Pirithous said, rising to lean against the window ledge.

She frowned, jerked from her thoughts. "What?"

"Your centaur chaperone. Hylonome, wasn't it?"

"Hylonome?" Hippodamia stumbled from the bed to join him at the window, and Pirithous shifted to give her room. Had it been only three days ago that Centaurus had brought her? It felt as though a handful of moons had waxed and waned already, and the sight of Hylonome cantering up the path to the palace gates made her smile.

"Hylonome!" she called, leaning out the window to wave. If she ran, she might be able to meet her at the gate. Hylonome would help her choose the horses Pirithous had promised her. The best of his stables. She spun, intent on her goal, but Pirithous made a strange noise, like a strangled laugh.

"Wait, Princess!" He caught her elbow, pulling her back. A flick of his wrist and he had wrapped her modestly in one of the linens from the bed, his eyes laughing. "Unless you wished to run naked through the corridors? That is your choice, of course."

She flushed. Among the centaurs, she would have thought nothing of it, but she had forgotten he had pulled her from her bath, forgotten she was among a different people, with different customs, forgotten everything but Hylonome.

"Thank you," she said softly.

And then she ran.

Chapter Twelve

Pirithous

He stayed at the window, listening to the startled shouts of the servants as Hippodamia sprinted through the palace corridors, then the nobles as she burst outside, clutching the bed sheet to her chest, dark hair loose and streaming in the wind. She was light as a deer on her feet, leaping over a stray dog that threatened to trip her without so much as altering her stride.

The wind carried her voice as she called out again to her friend, full of more joy than he could ever hope to give her. She launched herself at the centaur, paying no mind to the limitations of her makeshift dress, but Hylonome caught her and reared, lifting them both into the air in a spin made all the more impressive by the centaur's size. Hippodamia laughed, clear and sweet and distinct, and the horses within the palace walls all lifted their heads, ears pricked.

He could not make out the words they exchanged, but Hylonome set her down, and they turned toward the stables. Hippodamia cast one odd glance back at the palace, her gaze sweeping up from the wide porch to the windows until she met his eyes. Her expression cleared almost at once, a smile breaking across her face instead, so brilliant his breath caught. She pointed to him, and Hylonome lifted her head, but he could not tear his gaze from Hippodamia.

This was the woman who would be his wife, his queen. And one day, he promised himself, she would run to meet him at the palace gate. One day, she would throw herself so carelessly into his arms, trusting him to catch her, full of the same excitement. And when she looked at him, it would not be with the reflection of joy for another's coming. It would all be for him.

One day, he would have her love.

***

"You did not tell me this centaur-woman was coming," Antiope said when she joined Pirithous for the mid-day meal. Hippodamia had requested her own meal sent to the stables, where she and Hylonome had spent the entirety of the morning. Choosing horses, according to Machaon. Pirithous would have preferred to help her himself, but he dared not impose himself now. Not when all he wanted was to take her back to his bed and finish what they had begun earlier.

"So Theseus does not always share everything with you, after all," he replied, leaning back to let a servant pour his wine. "It's almost reassuring to know the truth of it at last."

Antiope's eyes narrowed. "Jealousy does not suit you at all, Pirithous."

"Is it jealousy to wish my bride undisturbed by your advances?" he said, keeping his voice mild. "I suppose among the Amazons there is no precedent for a happy marriage, but I do not believe it begins by giving a man's wife the idea of taking lovers."

"I merely offered her an answer to her concerns. Did you know the centaurs mate for life? Once a male marries a female, he will mount no other. They even follow one another into death, they are so strongly bonded. The poor girl was raised to believe in marriages made for love, and then given up to you at the last, to suffer one indignity after another by your hand."

"I have treated her with nothing but generosity since she was given into my keeping," Pirithous said. But he could not quite keep from frowning, his gaze traveling toward the stables he could not see. Instead, he saw his steward making arrangements for the evening banquet. Feeding a centaur at his table was hardly ideal, but he saw no way around it, and he would not have Antiope and Hippodamia hiding themselves away again. He only hoped Hylonome was as reasonable as Centaurus.

One mate for life. It certainly gave perspective to Hippodamia's objections.

"She is as afraid of loving you as she is tired of hating you," Antiope said. "And so she should be, the way you're likely to trample over her heart. Do not think I don't know how you shamed her before the priest and her father. Even if she had taken some lover before you, or given her affections elsewhere, it is no business of yours. All that matters is that she came to you willingly as a bride. Surely a son of Zeus needs nothing more than that!"

He grunted. "Perhaps if I meant to use my father's gift to persuade her against her will that would be all I required, but what good would that do me during the months I am away raiding? Each fall when I return home, she would hate me all the more, and as queen she would have the power to destroy my people in revenge."

Antiope sneered. "Men! Always you think of force first, as if imposing your will over hers is the only answer. From the first moment she wanted to love you, and fool that you are, you punished her for your inability to see! Had you accepted her at once, with a bow and a kiss and a smile, you would not be fighting so hard to win her now."

"Perhaps you're right," he admitted softly, remembering her response to him on the plain, and the things she had said after. She had dreamed of a king she might love, and instead he had offended and insulted her. But he had needed to know she was committed to peace, to her people, to him. He had needed to be certain she would not cause more trouble, for Lapiths and centaurs both.

The cost had been high. But it was not insurmountable. She had softened, and only waited now for him to do the same. It was not as though he did not understand what it was she wanted from him in return.

"All the same, Antiope," he went on, "if you would do me the favor of not seducing my bride, I would be in your debt."

She snorted. "Then perhaps you might repay me with a horse from your stables. You never did give me a proper wedding gift, after all."

"A most expensive favor," he grumbled.

But then he smiled. A visit to the stables was just what he needed, and Antiope had given him the excuse.

***

Hippodamia sat upon Podarkes's broad back, her feet tucked up nearly beneath her bottom. The stallion's thick tail had been braided, and Pirithous sighed. Of course she had chosen his best stallion for her own.

"Pirithous!" Her smile flashed brilliant and warm, and a moment later she had vaulted from the horse's back, leaving Hylonome among the horses. "I had hoped you would come. Are there any rooms on the ground floor where Hylonome might be made comfortable? She does not need much more than a straw pallet upon the floor, but I would not have her stabled like a horse."

"Of course," he said, signaling a stable boy to deliver the message to the steward. "I confess, I feared you would insist on housing her within your own room."

"Hylonome would never be comfortable so high up in the palace, and there are far too many stairs for a centaur to climb." She frowned slightly. "Will your people think less of her for it?"

"Not at all," he assured her at once. And all the better for his own plans to have Hylonome elsewhere for the night. Centaurus could not have believed his daughter would remain untouched until her wedding night, but Hylonome was bound to take offense whether he invited Hippodamia to his bed or took another.

"I thought I might stay with her tonight," Hippodamia went on. "This is all so strange to her, even more than it is to me, I fear, and all the harder for how soon it comes after her own marriage." Her gaze slid to the mountain. "If I had known, I would not have asked it of her. I can only imagine how difficult it must have been to leave Cyllarus behind, even for these few nights. And he must be half-mad, pacing the tree line, anxious for his mate."

He glanced up in spite of himself, frowning at more than just the image she painted of Cyllarus. A half-mad centaur so near to the palace could not be ignored. Peace or no peace, he did not trust the creature to keep its wits. He ground his teeth and returned his gaze to Hippodamia, her soft brow furrowed and her eyes dark with guilt.

"Send Hylonome to fetch her husband," he said. "Better to have Cyllarus bedded down with his wife within the walls than outside them, frightening our people with his bellowing all night long."

"But Antiope—"

He smiled. "Antiope can hardly fault another female for loving her husband. And I would have you in my bed, besides."

Her head snapped back to stare at him, surprise, outrage, and pleasure all mixing together into a muddle of confusion. He spoke again before she could settle on a response, angry or otherwise.

"How else can I be certain you are not tempted to bring another to your bed? Until you have given me a son, it is clear I must keep you satisfied in mine."

"And after our son is born?" she asked.

"It is my hope we will reach some accord when that time comes, agreeable to us both."

She tilted her head, her eyes narrowing, but he did not miss the flash of relief that flooded through her body, nor the confusion that followed. "I would think upon your offer."

He bowed. "Come to me tonight and I will know you have agreed to it."

She bit her lip and turned her face away. But he already knew what she would say and he had no need to press her, to negotiate further. Not yet. And she would not press him either, too unsure, anxious that he would withdraw the offer altogether.

"Go to Hylonome, Hippodamia. Fetch her husband and return. The rest will wait."

For a breath, she hesitated still, then took one step back to Podarkes, two, three. Her fingers wound into his mane as she clutched the base of his neck, and then she stopped, glancing back.

"Among the centaurs, I was called Mia."

"Mia." The name tasted sweet as a kiss upon his tongue.

She leapt upon Podarkes's back, and rode off, calling to her friend.

Pirithous grinned. Housing two centaurs in the palace was a small price to pay, and with any luck, he would have a son before the next summer solstice—provided he kept control of himself these next few nights. Because she would come to him, he was certain of that. She would come, and he would teach her every pleasure he knew, until she dropped to sleep half-dead from exhaustion, and then he would wake her with more of the same as the sun rose. He would sate her into delirium and leave her too tired to so much as think of any other in her bed.

He went in search of Machaon and a horse fine enough to gift to Antiope that his bride had not already claimed.

His Mia.

Night would not come soon enough.

CHAPTER THIRTEEN

HIPPODAMIA

So he is not as cruel-hearted as Eurytion would have us think!" Cyllarus said, grinning down at Hippodamia after she had extended Pirithous's invitation. "I should have known the son of Dia would have more sense."

"He has sense enough," she agreed, leading Podarkes behind her as they started back down the sloping path to the palace. "But he's stubborn as a stallion scenting his first mare. And far prouder."

Hylonome snorted, nearly prancing in her joy to be with her mate. "A true son of Zeus."

"Centaurus said the Horse Lord's son stood as witness to your betrothal," Cyllarus said.

"He did," Hippodamia agreed, trying not to see the way Cyllarus looked upon his wife. She flushed to see his arousal, though it had never embarrassed her before. Centaurs hid nothing of their emotions for their mates, and lust and desire were as natural as childbirth, but she had never known quite so well what came as the result. She found her thoughts straying to Pirithous—his mouth on her body, his fingers teasing her until she cried out, aching for more.

"Mia?" Hylonome prompted, and not, she realized dimly as she shook her head to clear it, for the first time.

"Forgive me," she said. "Theseus is very noble. A true son of the Horse Lord. His wife has been very kind to me as well. An Amazon daughter of Ares, Antiope."

And kinder still, had she wished it. Hippodamia frowned slightly. Should not Pirithous have been glad that she would take a queen as her lover, and not just any woman? But it had offended him nearly as much as if she had spoken of a man. Not that she truly wished to take a lover at all. Pirithous had more than satisfied her, awakening a hunger she had never realized she possessed. And if he wanted her in his bed, and her presence there kept him from bringing his other women to it instead, perhaps by the time their son was born, he would be satisfied just as fully. But he had not promised to take his pleasure only from her. Nor had he extracted such a promise from her, in return. More and more it seemed to her his generosity did not extend beyond rich gifts, and if he believed he could simply buy her forgiveness with gold, silver, horseflesh, and pleasure…

"She's been this way all day," Hylonome said, laughter in her voice. "And if you had only seen the way she brightened when King Pirithous came at last to the stables…"

"Eurytion will be mad with jealousy," Cyllarus teased. "He was so certain you would be abused by the king, and here you walk beside us too distracted to even tell us properly of the Horse Lord's son."

"And why should I tell you when you will see him yourself at the evening meal?" Hippodamia vaulted up onto Podarkes, kicking him into a trot. "Unless you plan to dawdle the whole way down the mountain, of course."

It was enough of a challenge to send the two centaurs into a gallop, and Hippodamia had only to give Podarkes his head, for he knew his way home. Sure-footed and powerful, Podarkes broke away from the two centaurs, cutting through the trees and down a narrow path Pirithous must have used more often than the proper trail. Hippodamia leaned low over his neck to keep from being caught by branches, laughing wildly at the shouts of her friends. They burst out of the forest much lower down the mountain, Podarkes leaping the brush to rejoin the road, and Hippodamia glanced back to see Hylonome and Cyllarus left far behind.

She grinned, urging the stallion on. Down the road with the wind in her face and the beat of Podarkes's hooves in her ears, the horse's breathing as steady as his stride. She threw her arms up, lifting her face to the sun, and laughed again, giving up the joy in her heart to Poseidon Horse Lord, with a silent prayer.

Let it last!

Podarkes charged through the palace gate and Hippodamia drew her legs up, her bare toes finding purchase above his hips. She stood upon his back, steadying herself against the rhythm of his movements.

"For you, Lord Poseidon!"

She leapt backwards, throwing herself into the air and arching her back. The ground raced up to meet her but she completed the roll, her feet finding the earth without hesitation, and when she lifted her head, Pirithous himself stood with Podarkes, stroking the horse's neck and watching her with bright gray eyes, his lips curving.

Heat burned her cheeks and she dropped her gaze. "My lord Pirithous."

"My lady Mia." He murmured something else she did not catch, followed by the soft thud of hooves on grass, and then his sandaled feet appeared before her. A gentle finger touched her chin, lifting her face. "You will make an astonishing queen."

The centaurs' hooves clopped on the stonework of the road leading from the palace gate through the courtyard to the wide porch of the megaron. Pirithous let his hand fall away as he looked up over her head and smiled warmly.

"Welcome, Hylonome, Cyllarus. You must forgive me for not greeting you properly before now, but I had no wish to interrupt so intimate a reunion between friends."

"Any offense I might have taken is lost in my gratitude for the invitation you have extended to my mate," Hylonome said, bowing low.

"I would be remiss if I did not thank you, also, for your willingness to be parted from your mate so soon after your marriage. It cannot have been easy for you to make such a choice, and I would not make it harder. Cyllarus is more than welcome to remain with you for as long as you are my lady's guest. Will you honor us with your presence at the evening meal? Now we are at peace, I would have my people become used to the sight of centaurs within the palace walls."

"The honor is ours, of course," Cyllarus answered. "All the better to have them familiar with our presence before the solstice. You will have herds of us here for the wedding feast soon enough."

"Indeed. And it is my greatest hope that the gods will bless us with sun and clear skies, for I am not certain the palace will be large enough to feast so great a number, even spilled into the courtyard." Pirithous extended his arm toward the megaron in invitation. "Perhaps you can judge the truth of it for yourself?"

Cyllarus and Pirithous fell in step with one another, and Pirithous glanced just once at Hippodamia, his eyes brilliant with promise, before they continued on. She followed behind with Hylonome, who leaned down, speaking low enough that the words would not carry.

"I thought you were forbidden from joining with him until the solstice?"

She flushed, dropping her gaze from Pirithous's well-muscled back and broad shoulders. Surely it was not so obvious as that. "We are."

"And yet he looks at you as if he has already tasted delight and hungers for more."

"King Pirithous has every reason to hope for a fruitful marriage," she said, but the words came out more sharply than she had intended, and the reassurance only hollowed her own heart.

Even if he kept no other woman in his bed until she had given him a son, she had only offered him another reason not to disobey the priest. No doubt he hoped it would be no more than a year lost before he might return to the arms of his palace women, to say nothing of the prizes he might take abroad in the meantime.

"Forgive me," Hylonome murmured, drawing back. "I did not mean to imply anything other."

She mumbled something appropriate, but clouds had darkened the sun of her earlier joy. Pirithous had offered her the smallest of tokens, and she would be a fool to refuse it, even so. But their future, with all its heartache, remained unchanged.

Once their son was born, Pirithous would have his palace women, while she would spend her nights alone, lonely and cold, for she did not doubt he would forbid her from bringing any other to her bed, even while he took his pleasure elsewhere.

Unless, of course, he could not wait for the solstice after all.

***

Hippodamia excused herself from the evening meal before the final course of honeyed fruits had been served, and paced anxiously in the corridor until Antiope joined her. When Theseus's queen had risen with her own excuses, Pirithous had begun to scowl, his searching gaze nearly falling upon Hippodamia where she waited just beyond the doorway. She removed herself to her rooms before he attempted to follow.

"I had thought you would have no more need of me now that your companions have arrived," Antiope said, once they had reached the privacy of Hippodamia's room and the door was shut and barred behind them. "But I have never been more pleased to be wrong."

"It is not the same, speaking with Hylonome. It is too different for her with Cyllarus." Hippodamia forced herself to calm, clasping her hands together to keep from tugging at the loose thread she'd found on her girdle. Sitting calmly throughout the meal, her mind spinning with her plan, had been a greater challenge than she'd anticipated. "I would not have her know what marriage is to Pirithous—the centaurs would take it poorly, considering it some slight against me, against all of us. And there are some who are not so pleased with Dia's peace if it means I am taken from them."

Antiope's eyes narrowed. "Displeased enough to break it?"

She shook her head, impatient. "Centaurus would never allow such open rebellion. It is only—it is only that I would not give reason to anyone, or what good is any of it? And Pirithous does not mean to slight me. If it were otherwise, that would be something else entirely, but he wants this peace, Antiope. And…" She hesitated. To say it and be proved wrong would only make it all the more painful. The way he looked at her, though… the way he smiled at her, his eyes warm as the summer sun on her skin. Surely he would never have agreed to keep only her in his bed, even for a year, if he did not want her, too. "Pirithous has promised me a place in his bed until I give him a son. But if the priest speaks truly, the marriage will bear fruit, and then what will become of us?"

Antiope took her hands, squeezing tightly. "By then it will not matter. You will be his bedded wife, the one he has learned to share his life with, day and night, night and day. It will be his habit to turn to you, to choose you over any other."

"For a year! What is a year to the lifetime he has spent in the arms of others? All those women he keeps, a daily reminder of what he once had. A feast of pleasure, and I the woman who demanded he fast. But he has not even sworn not to have any other—only that he will keep me satisfied, that *I* will not stray!"

"The moment he has gone off to raid, you can see his favorites settled elsewhere." Antiope released her hands, guiding her to the bed. "If you cannot find husbands for them, send them to me and I will see what Athens can provide. But it will not matter, Hippodamia, I promise you. Already Pirithous is fixed upon you, determined to win your favor if not your love. He does not understand yet what it will mean, that is all. And a year from now, all you need do is speak of me. I will come for the birth, and you will see how he responds."

"And if I spoke of you now?"

She stilled, her eyes gold in the firelight. "I have sworn to Pirithous I will make no further offers. I would not break my word—for Theseus's sake, I cannot."

"But did you swear to refuse me, if I came to you?" She clutched the Amazon's hands, but Antiope was already shaking her head, pulling away. "It would drive him wild to think it, even if we exchanged nothing but these words. Wild enough to claim me before the solstice, even if it risked our son."

"Then your marriage will be for nothing, all your father's wishes, Dia's wishes, left unfulfilled." Antiope freed herself and rose, stepping back toward the door. "Is keeping yourself in Pirithous's bed worth betraying the peace you were sent to forge?"

Her blood ran cold with the thought, the realization striking her deep as an arrow to her breast. She turned her face away, hiding the tears which stung her eyes, and swallowed the answer, bitter and strangled in her throat.

Because she wanted so much to say yes.

CHAPTER FOURTEEN

PIRITHOUS

Pirithous paced his room, his gaze going from one door to the next. She was to come to him, and instead she had slunk from the megaron with Antiope on her heels. But Antiope had left her room long before the moon had risen, and still Hippodamia did not come through his door, did not so much as knock upon it or stand beyond with hesitation in her heart. From her room, all that came was sorrow, betrayal, pain—enough to make his own heart ache in sympathy, heaping grief upon the rejection she had given him by her refusal.

She should never have refused. How could she have when he had given her such a promise of pleasure? A gesture in good faith for a future they might make their own, and she had gone to Antiope instead, and spurned him!

He growled at the thought. But he dared not go to Theseus now, in the dead of night. He would not go to them and be laughed at, though it was clear Antiope had not kept her word, no doubt seeking to shame him. What else but some seduction of hers could have kept Hippodamia from his bed this night? No. He would not give Antiope the satisfaction of knowing she had succeeded. Even if Hippodamia refused him openly, Antiope would not hear it from him, would not know he had been affected at all by her choice.

Pirithous threw open the door to their shared bathing room, kicking a stray towel from his path as he crossed the room, and pounded upon Hippodamia's door.

A strangled cry sounded from the other side, followed by a hiccupping sob, smothering the fire of his anger as quickly as it had flared. He cleared his throat, swallowing the accusations he had readied on his tongue.

"Mia?" he called gently.

"Go away!" But her words were unsteady, gulped, and the wash of guilt and self-loathing that followed rooted him to the floor.

He pushed on the door, testing the bar which held it shut. If she refused him again with so tender a cry, he would break it down if he must. "If it is Antiope who has upset you, I will send her away. Theseus as well. You must only tell me what's happened, and I will give you any comfort you desire, anything at all, truly."

She made a soft sound, half-despair and half-need. "Go, please. I beg of you."

A deft thrust of his elbow against the door snapped the bar. There was not a one in the palace that could stand against the strength of a demigod, barred or otherwise, and he had broken down many a door while raiding to reach the prizes inside. To use such a skill upon his bride—he had never thought it would be needful, even in his worst moments.

"You will not be rid of me so easily, Princess."

Hippodamia moaned, hiding her face in the linens of the bed where she lay. "Why could you not simply call another to your bed?"

He narrowed his eyes but kept firm hold of his temper. Now was not the time to let her goad him. "Is that what you wished? That I would turn from you so easily, give up so quickly?"

She let out a long, shuddering breath, finished with a sob, whatever answer she gave lost in the linens. Her guilt lashed at him, but he did not understand where it could have grown from. Unless she and Antiope—but he could not think of that without his anger rising, and he dared not lose control.

Pirithous crossed to the bed, caught between frustration and concern. To leave her this way would be unforgivable, and more than that, he needed to know… "I thought we had come to some understanding."

Her hands turned to fists upon her pillow, her only answer another soft sob. He sat down on the edge of the bed and reached out, working her fingers free from the fabric, slow and gentle, and sliding his fingers through hers when he had finished. Her hand clutched his with a need he had not expected, as if she might steal some comfort from his touch.

The frenzy of her emotions whirled through his mind, but there was no anger there, no mistrust for him; only want, desire quickly stifled and buried deep, and something else, softer and more fragile beneath her pain. He nursed it with a kiss upon the back of her hand, fed it with his own strength. Her breathing hitched and her grasp upon his hand eased as the gentle glow washed against her fears, her guilt. He did not dare sweep it all away, only tried to calm her.

"Tell me now," he murmured. "Whatever has upset you, I would help."

She shook her head, her face still hidden from him, and pulled her hand away. "You can't."

He lay beside her in the bed, propped upon one elbow, watching the rise and fall of her shoulders with each breath, steady now, and even. Now was not the time to admit what he had already done to soothe her, and he feared to meddle any further. There was a guardedness to her maelstrom which had not been there before, as if in calming, she had remembered her mistrust. Perhaps he should have let her weep if this was how she would repay him.

Bitterness filled his mouth, nor could he clear it from his mind with the thought of Antiope and what conversation they might have had which would cause Hippodamia to weep.

"When I asked Antiope not to seduce you, I had not thought you would pursue the matter. Not after I had made my feelings so clear."

She sniffed, a flash of anger drowning out the soft light. "And what attention should I pay to your feelings when you care so little for mine?"

He bared his teeth. "So little that I offered you a place in my bed!"

Hippodamia lifted her head, tear-streaked face and damp eyes cutting through him. Her hands were fists again. "You offer me a taste of love without even the courtesy of true marriage, and the promise that you will take even that much away the moment you have what you desire. And I should be grateful for it? Have you even the slightest understanding of what my people would think of such an arrangement? If Hylonome knew, or Cyllarus, they would not spend another night beneath your roof! They would take me from you, enraged by the insult to my honor, and Dia's peace would be trampled beneath their hooves."

"And if you truly believed I meant to slight you, they would know already," he growled. "I have tried, Princess, to be honest with you, nor did I ever mislead you as to what this future we share will hold. Would you have me lie? Make promises to you that I cannot keep?"

"No!"

"But you reject me all the same."

Her eyes had filled with tears again. "That isn't—"

"All you had to do was come to me. If you had not wished me to touch you, I would have held myself away! Instead you turned to Antiope, knowing how the thought twists me with madness."

"Because I thought if you believed I had given myself to her, you would claim me for yourself, once and for all!"

He stared at her, tears spilling down her flushed cheeks, unsure of how to respond. Unsure, even, of his own feelings, his own understanding. Hippodamia rolled to her back, hiccupping with something half-sob, half-laughter, bitter and wild.

"All I could think was if you took me now, before the solstice, perhaps I would have that much longer in your bed. Perhaps by the time our son was born, you would be so used to me, you would not care to be rid of me in the night. Or if there was no son at all, I would still have at least the small comfort of sleeping at your side, if nothing else..."

She raked her fingers through her hair, her eyes closed against the guilt and pain that swirled inside her, so much and so thick he could barely breathe. And that glow, that fragile, soft glow, throbbing in her mind.

"And then I feared that if I went to you tonight, I would have my way. I would have my way, and everything would be ruined before it had begun. Both our peoples betrayed. For what? My own pride? After I had made so much of yours! Foolish, foolish, *foolish* girl!" Her voice broke, but she did not stop. "What worth is there in that? In love so spoiled by deceit, by jealousy? And for so little in exchange!"

"Shh." The last word had been more sob than anything, and his heart ached with it. Perhaps he should have been angry, insulted somehow, but it would have served nothing. To shout at her when she felt such self-loathing, such disgust, would be as worthless as the marriage they might have shared if she had acted so selfishly. But she had done nothing wrong. The gods had tested her, tried them both, but she had not given in. She had not given up.

He began to wonder, though, if she was not right. Perhaps he had not offered her enough in exchange for the satisfaction of his own desires. It was no hardship to him, after all, to have her in his bed, nor did it stop him from taking his pleasure elsewhere as he wished. He had thought only of what he might give her to keep her from taking lovers of her own. But she must realize why he had not promised more.

"If you knew what you asked, you would not want it," he said quietly, tucking her body carefully against his. "If we are to have a son, if you are to keep strength enough to nurture one, I would not have you wearied by my demands—nor would you find any joy in it for long. Not beyond the first nights, or perhaps as long as a season. A year from now, you would be cursing me each time I reached for you, begging me to leave you in peace, and what pleasure I might have given you at first would be soured by exhaustion and misery."

"I don't—I don't understand." Her head fit perfectly beneath his chin, and her words were muffled against his chest. "Antiope and Theseus—"

"Antiope is a daughter of Ares, little mouse, and an Amazon besides. But Theseus, too, is… more disciplined." He smoothed her hair back, that it would not tickle his jaw. "I fear it is a strength of mind and body I never mastered. And until this night, I never understood the need."

"But the women you keep do not seem…" She made a soft noise of frustration, as if she did not know what word she wanted.

"I am careful of them. And of you, I would be even more so."

She was silent, but for a soft sniffling. If he had not felt the pulse of her emotions—spinning, no doubt, with her thoughts—he might have even believed she slept. He wished she would, that in the morning she might see the reason of his argument and understand his choice.

"I wish it were otherwise, Mia," he said gently. "For both our sakes."

She stirred, drawing back from his embrace. "Even if I am nothing but the daughter of a common herdsman and a shepherd's daughter, I have the blessing of Poseidon Horse Lord, or I would not be what I am. Is it not possible that he has given me strength enough to match you in this way, as he has in others?"

He almost laughed, but even in the firelight, he could see the seriousness in her eyes. "Is that what you believe? That Poseidon has made you my equal?"

"Even your better when it comes to horsemanship," she said, and he did not doubt she meant it. Nor could he argue, though it galled him to know it. "If it is truly for my sake that you refuse me, Pirithous, you cannot object to a trial."

He rolled to his back, that he might frown at the ceiling instead of her. He could not doubt her determination. And perhaps she was right. What harm would it do to let her see what it was she asked of him, of herself? And if she could match him—he hardened at the very thought.

"It might well mean disappointment for us both," he warned.

"Perhaps," she said, and he knew she studied him. "But we cannot know until we try, and I would know one way or the other."

He snorted. "If I had known taking a wife would be so difficult as this…" But he rolled to his side, cupping her cheek and catching her eyes before she bridled at his teasing. She searched his face and he smiled. "I have promised you every pleasure within my power to give. I will not refuse you this, but you must make me a promise in return."

Her forehead furrowed, and he wished she did not look on him with so much suspicion. But it was surely better than the guilt and tears, and he could not say that he did not, in some ways, deserve a little of her mistrust. "What would you ask of me?"

"Honesty," he said. "Most especially in bed, but out of it as well. You must tell me at the first if you cannot tolerate my desires, and swear you will not let your pride hold your tongue. If you lie, little mouse, I will know, and I promise you that will be the end of this trial. Heir or not, and if need be, even the last night you spend in my bed altogether, for I will not see you harmed by my hand or for my pleasure."

Her eyes had widened as he spoke, and all to the better if he had inspired some small fear. After all, if he could not trust her even in bed, how could he trust her as his queen?

"And can I expect your honesty in return?"

"You have not lacked it, Princess." He brushed his thumb along her cheek, reveling in her softness. "But there is one more thing that I would ask of you."

She let out a sigh. "Of course there is. What more?"

Such impatience! Somehow he found it charming. And had he not asked her for honesty, just moments before? He grinned.

"If I am forbidden from taking any other lovers, so are you."

"For the duration of the trial."

"Until our son is born," he countered.

Her eyes narrowed. "And if this trial does not last beyond the next full moon?"

This time, he did laugh. "If you are so certain you will have no trouble matching me, I do not see why you should worry."

"Even so!"

"Even so, these are my terms. In the interests of getting an heir, if you desire satisfaction, I would have you come to me. For my part, I will not refuse you. At any moment of the day or night, you need only find me and I will grant you any pleasures you crave."

"*Any* moment?"

He traced the shape of her lips with his fingertip. "Any."

Her breath caught, and she licked her lips. "Oh."

He leaned down, pressing a kiss to her forehead, the tip of her nose, the corner of her mouth. "Then we are agreed?"

She hesitated, just for a moment, and then nodded.

Aphrodite, bless us.

And for the first time, he almost hoped that Hippodamia might be right.

***

Fingers brushed across his mouth, tracing the line of his lips, the bridge of his nose, the shape of his brow. He forced himself not to stiffen, nor even to open his eyes, but only lie still, his breathing steady as if in sleep, one arm around her waist to keep her near. Light filtered through his eyelids, blue and gentle, as if Apollo himself had barely risen.

She sighed, so soft and light he barely trusted his ears, and then her mouth found his, her body straining closer, pressing against the hardness below his waist until he groaned. Without thought, he shifted, rolling her beneath him. Her lips parted to his, her tongue inviting him deeper, even as her hands spread against his chest holding him away.

He growled and she laughed, turning her face from his to break the kiss and pushing him back. "I cannot leave Cyllarus and Hylonome to the mercy of your nobles."

"Can you not?" he demanded, dropping his mouth to her breast, careless of the linen which covered her body. If he had not time to remove it, he must make do. He had restrained himself last night, but what she had started this morning, he would finish. "Perhaps they, too, intend to take their pleasure before rising."

He flicked his tongue across the hardening point and her back arched, dark eyes darkening even further. "Pirithous..."

But it was moan more than denial, and he eased the short tunic up her hips. One of his, he realized absently, though he had not noticed how loosely it fit her the night before. He slid down her body, biting softly through the fabric as he went, marking the trail to that slick heat at the apex of her thighs. And then he tasted her skin, just below her navel, sweet as pomegranate, with the barest hint of salt. The perfect complement to the soft musk of her need.

"Please," she breathed, her fingers curling around his ears.

He spread her thighs and lowered his head, taking the bud of her desire into his mouth, teasing her with his tongue. She gasped, her thighs closing around his head, and he chuckled low, making her writhe even more.

Gods above, how he wanted to take her then. To lift himself up and slide deep inside her. He traced one finger around her entrance, teasing her with just the slightest pressure while his mouth worked. He had been careful of her before, not wanting to give her any discomfort with her first release. Nor did he wish to stretch her too far now.

He dipped one finger deeper as he tasted her. She moaned, lifting her hips, and he answered. Another finger joined the first, curling up to stroke the sensitive flesh, the heat of her center making him ache all the more.

She bucked, a throaty cry breaking from her lips and her fingers twisting into his hair. Her body clenched around his fingers, and she shuddered once, twice, a third time, with a second low moan. He stroked her again once she had relaxed, as she lay limp and panting. She shivered and laughed.

"Are all men so skilled with their mouths?"

He kissed his way back up the length of her body. "Not even half of them."

She stroked his hair, his neck, his back, until he had brought himself level with her eyes and had pulled the tunic over her head. All he wanted was to lie between her thighs, to have her body shudder around his while she found release a second time. He nudged her legs apart with his knee, wishing he had stripped off his kilt long ago, that he might sink inside her. The warmth of her center still teased him through the fabric, and she lifted her hips, wrapping her legs around his waist.

"Mia…" He groaned and dropped his forehead to her shoulder, his arms trembling. "I begin to fear you still wish to drive me mad."

She laughed again, clear and sweet and more joyful than he had ever hoped to hear. "I thought we had come to an agreement, my lord." She pushed against his chest, and he let her roll him to his back. "You cannot believe I would leave you wanting so soon?"

CHAPTER FIFTEEN

HIPPODAMIA

Her days passed quickly then, in eager anticipation of the nights, and Pirithous taught her more of pleasure with his mouth and hands than she had ever realized was possible. But it was not only the nights they spent together. Pirithous took her again out to the broad plain where the horses grazed, guarded by the young men. Two mares were with foal, returned lately from the Myrmidons, who had failed to keep them as prizes. The foals would be hers, and one of the mares, Pirithous promised, was Fire's get, a brilliant chestnut who bred as true as her dam.

"Colt or filly, it will be a fine foal."

They spoke little after that, for Pirithous had found excuse to part from Hylonome and Cyllarus, and he was determined to make good use of the time they had alone. Not that Hippodamia objected, for the rest of her days were spent preparing for the wedding feast, which could not come soon enough, and welcoming guests as they arrived for the celebration. Peleus was invited, of course, and King Nestor of Pylos, though the journey was long.

"Nestor will miss nothing, if he can help it," Antiope told her while they took their turns scrubbing tables one afternoon. Antiope would not ask servants to do anything she had not done first.

"When he is not invited, all of Achaea hears of the slight. But for all of that he is not so terrible for a man. At least he always brings a story. If he had been a younger son, he would have made at least as good a poet as he has a king. It is Peleus you must watch out for. With Dia's death, he is no longer bound in friendship to the Lapiths. That is part of why Pirithous was so determined to make peace—he could not risk the centaurs turning to Peleus instead. Theseus says Peleus has been hungry for the plains and the horses which graze upon them since he came into his kingship."

But it was the centaurs Hippodamia looked for. Her father, most of all, and Eurytion, that she might show him the horses Pirithous had given her, gold and silver bridles and all. He would have no reason to think she was unhappy then, not when he had seen for himself the generosity she had been shown—and the gentleness in Pirithous's eyes when he looked on her besides. He had made so clear his delight in her, she could not help but be encouraged. Indeed, he gave her far more pleasure than he took.

None would leave their wedding feast thinking Pirithous mean, either. Amphora upon amphora of wine had come from Athens, for Pirithous would serve only the best to his guests. He had traded, too, for honey mead, sweeter than anything Hippodamia had ever tasted, though it made her head spin and her feet unsteady. Two hands of oxen were marked for slaughter, and twice as many goats and sheep went up the mountain in sacrifice to Zeus, Hera, Aphrodite, and Poseidon.

"Come," Pirithous said, catching her by the arm the morning before the feast, his eyes bright with mischief. "I would have your help to choose the guest gifts, and you have spent enough time on your knees these last days."

Heat flooded her cheeks, for it was not only in scrubbing the floors that she had knelt. But he was already pulling her with him down a corridor, rarely used, and through two store rooms, filled with tables and stools, reams of rough-spun wool and broken looms. Cast-offs and discarded furnishings, too worn or too dowdy for use.

"This cannot be what you mean to offer?"

Pirithous grinned, stopping before a cracked stone altar as tall as her waist and at least twice as long. One-handed, he tipped it upon its end, revealing a door cut into the floor beneath.

"These upper rooms are what is left of Ixion's wealth, but for the horses, of course. What waits below is mine, and only a portion at that." He nodded toward an oil lamp upon a broken chest. "We'll want the light."

With some trick of his fingers he had it lit once she had brought it to him, and then he lifted the solid oak panel from the floor, revealing a stairwell of stone leading into darkness. Pirithous took her hand in his, leaving her no time for hesitation as he started down the stairs.

She followed, the lamplight illuminating nothing but more stone, roughly hewn and scarred by chisel and sledge. Then the bubble of darkness expanded, and the light no longer reached even the wall.

"Not much farther," Pirithous said, squeezing her hand.

Gravel of some kind crunched beneath their feet, the only sound but for their breathing, and then she saw the first spark of reflected flame. Pirithous let her go, cupping his hand around the lamp to shield it, and took three long steps forward, leaving her outside the light.

"Come here," he said. "Exactly here, and do not move."

"I can hardly see, Pirithous." In truth it made her uneasy, for all that she had slept her whole life in caves. This was different. The darkness crowded her, impossible to avoid. Even the stairway and the door behind them had been swallowed whole.

She saw the flash of his smile. "Just a moment longer and you will have no trouble with the dark."

He positioned her exactly as he wished, then left her. The lamplight turned his skin a glowing bronze, flashing here and there off something she could not see clearly as he moved away. She hugged her arms to her chest and shivered, covered in gooseflesh.

Pirithous stopped, crouched down behind a shadowed thing—a table perhaps, for it did not shine, or another altar made of stone—and the lamp's light jumped, then flared into a wall of golden flame, rippling out along a channel carved in the floor.

Hippodamia blinked away the glare, the light blinding her after so long in the dark.

"Look!" Pirithous called, bounding back to her, lamp forgotten. "And you will choose first what you wish to keep for your own. I promised you platters and cups and bowls, did I not?"

She looked, her eyes widening to take it all in, and still there was more. Mountains of golden tripods, cauldrons, platters, cups, piled higher than Pirithous was tall. The same again stood heaped in silver, and rich furnishings of olive, oak, cedar, ivory, and ebony, bejeweled with pearls and brilliant blue lapis, emerald, ruby, and quartz. Chests of bronze armor, swords, spear- and arrowheads rested in another pile, separate from the hoard.

Pirithous picked up a dagger, dull gray rather than gleaming bronze, though the handle shimmered, not quite gold or silver, but somehow both.

"It is forged from iron," he explained. "Stronger than bronze, and less brittle when worked and folded. I have never seen its like before, but if what their armorer said is true, we will see more of it, soon." He smiled shyly, sheathing the blade. "Forgive me. I meant to show you jewels, not knives."

"All of this is yours?" she asked, when he poured necklaces and bracelets into her hands until they spilled over, chiming against the stone at her feet.

"I have been raiding with Theseus season upon season, as far as our ships could take us. Beyond Troy to the far east of Colchis, and as far west as there is sea to sail upon." He picked up an arm cuff, gold wound in two spiraled discs wider across than her thumb, and then he dropped it again and chose another, solid silver snakes with emeralds for eyes. That one, he slid up her arm, his fingers caressing her skin. "We even went into the north one year, through the Thracians, one river after another, as deep inland as we could row. This is but a sampling of the prizes I brought back. We have caverns elsewhere, sealed with boulders even Heracles would have trouble shifting alone. And the fabrics are in the palace proper, of course. They would only rot down here."

He grinned when she stared at him, and tugged her toward the largest pile of gold. "Choose whatever you would like for yourself, and gifts rich enough to honor your father, as well. There is plenty—enough to make guest-friends of an army, if we could but feed them all. We will have a cup of gold or silver at every seat for our wedding feast."

"Are you certain?" she asked, her eyes drinking in the glitter of so many riches, piled as carelessly as the discarded furnishings in the storeroom above. "I can hardly imagine—it is so much, Pirithous. Too much!"

"Perhaps," he said. "But it will buy us peace for a time, I hope, and our children will never lack the proper gifts if they require the favor of hospitality from another." He tossed her a golden cup, embossed with horses running across a plain, manes and tails streaming behind them in the wind. "Ixion's house, our people, will never need to beg again."

***

The rest of that day was spent in the cavern, Pirithous encouraging her to choose gifts for her friends as well as her father. They emptied a yawning chest of a hodgepodge of silver goods and ingots and refilled it with cups and platters for the feast, guest gifts, and what jewels, once admired, Pirithous insisted she keep to wear when she was queen. He carried treasure up the stairs as easily as he might have lifted a skin of water to his lips, laughing when she frowned.

"Heracles held the whole world upon his shoulders, Princess, and though I do not quite have his strength, I am the son of his father, still."

"A true son of Zeus even in matters beyond pleasure," she teased him. "Though you have hardly given me opportunity to notice."

"And even less, come tomorrow." He set down the chest to close the door again, and covered it once more with the altar. "We need only wait for the sun to rise."

Her skin prickled at the promise in his voice, low and determined. "Before the feast."

His eyes met hers, silver-gray and intent. "The moment the sun breaks over the mountain, even if I must give up my own blood in dedication to Aphrodite to see her satisfied. We will go to our feast sated and content, your face flushed and your body warmed and well-loved, and no one will doubt that we have the blessing of the gods."

"And after the feast?" Her throat tightened with anticipation. To be joined at last, to be truly filled by his hard body, and feel his seed spill inside her—she smoothed the short tunic over her stomach, so he would not see the way her hands shook.

But Pirithous stepped toward her, tall and fine, his eyes liquid and warm. "After the feast, I will make you tremble with desire, pleasure, and need, until even the whisper of my breath against your skin sends you shuddering to your release."

It was a promise she meant to make him keep.

***

That night she spent alone, for Pirithous did not trust himself and Hippodamia could not blame him. The temptation of his body, and the moment so near when they might consummate the marriage so long planned would have undone her, even if he had disciplined himself completely.

But she did not sleep. Instead she stared out at the mountain and the road from the trees to the palace gate. The moon was nearly full, bright enough to darken the stars, and washing everything in silver. The light glinted off the golden bridles hanging from their pegs in the stables, always open for the horses to come and go as they wished. The halters they wore during the day were not full gold or silver, too heavy and too gaudy for such use, but all of the horses she had chosen were given gold and silver fittings between the leather straps over nose and brow, and engraved silver nameplates sewn to the leather as well.

So when the centaur came out of the woods to stand framed in the moonlight, all but liquid shadow even then, Hippodamia's eye was drawn to the movement, then caught by the stillness and tension of his figure. Not so much as a switch of his tail nor paw of his hoof against the earth, but bleak and heart-rending all the same.

Eurytion.

She did not think, only reached for the nearest tunic, rumpled but still scented with lavender and lightning, and slipped from her room into the corridors of the palace, down the stairs, and into the night.

She ran, her bare feet making no noise upon the stone inside or out, and Eurytion started at the sight of her, half-rearing in surprise. He charged forward to meet her and crushed her in his arms, lifting her up.

"Mia," he murmured, as if it had been years instead of days. "My fleet-footed fawn."

She laughed. "Let me down, Eurytion, or I'll have bruises before you're done."

He set her to her feet, but held her hands still, then her face, framed carefully. He stared at her so strangely. As if he had forgotten her features.

Hippodamia flushed, turning her face away. "It has not been so long that you should not recognize me."

"Too long, all the same, Fawn. Every night a torture, imagining what you must suffer. This marriage—it was wrong of Centaurus to take you from us, even for Dia, even for peace! Come away with me. This very night. This very moment. Let Centaurus make some other peace for our people. One that does not steal you from me, from even the hope of happiness."

She pressed her fingers to his lips, shaking her head. "You need not fear for me. Not for a moment. And tomorrow you will see, I promise you. Pirithous is more than kind, generous to the point of foolishness..."

Eurytion reared back, his black eyes narrowing as they raked over her body. "You wear his clothes." One hand caught at her hair, bringing it to his nose. "You smell of him, of musk and need. You gave yourself to him? Or did he take you—persuade you with his father's power that this was what you wished?"

"He is a good man and a better king!"

"And all those nights we spent together, dreaming of a future—dreaming of what you might do, if you were free—you forget them so quickly?"

"I was a child, Eurytion, with childish dreams. And you know as well as I what my future would have been. Death and blood was all that awaited me among the centaurs, but Pirithous can offer me a good life. Children of my own!"

He snorted, his lip curling. "He's bewitched you, just like all the others who surround him. But it hardly matters. The moment he leaves his palace, leaves you behind long enough for you to know your own mind, you'll come to me, call to me to take you from this place. You'll beg Centaurus to allow your return, and when he understands what your precious Pirithous has done, Dia's peace will shatter."

"Perhaps that is your dream, Eurytion, but it is not mine." Her heart twisted, though only half his words made sense. There was something in them, some breath of truth that curdled her joy. "It will never be mine."

She wrenched free of his hold and left him in the moonlight, wishing she had never come at all. Or better yet, that *he* hadn't.

Chapter Sixteen

Pirithous

He could not wait for dawn. All he had done half the night was lie restlessly, unable to sleep, unable to settle his mind into quiet. It was a night he would have spent exhausting the palace women, and lying alone in his bed while Hippodamia slept just beyond his door was maddening. Even if he could not find his release yet, her presence, her warmth, would be enough.

He rose, slipping silently through the bathing room. At the other end, her door stood open as if in welcome and he smiled. It seemed his little mouse had no wish to wait for dawn, either. His blood heated at the thought, his body hardening. Not long, now. The moon had already begun to set, its white rim kissing the ground. And he would lie beside her, ready for the first purpling of the sky…

But the room was empty.

He froze, searching the dim room for any reason for her absence. Her sandals sat discarded by the door to the hall, of course, for she hardly reached for them without reminder, and her short tunic lay puddled outside the bathing room. The rumpled bed told him only that she had been as sleepless as he, and the jewels he had given her were all accounted for, spread out upon the table near the hearth. Had she been stolen in the night, the thief would not have overlooked such wealth so near at hand.

He fingered the cuff she had chosen for Hylonome, staring blankly at the wall. Surely she would not run naked through the palace the night before their wedding feast? Naked upon the balcony he had no trouble believing, for he had caught her more than once leaning upon the railing in the dead of night, after waking for some other need.

"Mia?" he called softly, parting the curtains and stepping outside, smiling at his foolishness. It was only that there were so many guests suddenly crowding his halls that he could not help but think the worst first. Hippodamia would make a fine prize to the man who might steal her. Even bound by the laws of hospitality, he had no trouble believing some might be tempted, and Peleus had yet to arrive, after all.

Yet Hippodamia did not answer, nor turn to him with a smile. Instead he was greeted by the murmur of raised voices in the distance, and his gaze searched for the source of the sound. A centaur, blacker than the sky above, and a woman in a man's tunic stood upon the road.

He narrowed his eyes. Hippodamia, he had no doubt, though he could not see her face, and by the jerk of her movements and the pitch of her voice, she was not pleased.

Nor was he to find her so, for he recognized the centaur easily enough. Eurytion, it seemed, had decided to come. One last gamble to convince her not to wed, perhaps, and Pirithous could only pray the centaur's arguments fell upon deaf ears.

He gripped the railing, the stone crumbling in his hands. From such a distance, he could not hear the words exchanged, but he could feel Hippodamia's impatience. And something else, bitter on the back of his tongue, spoiling her contentment like the worm that has burrowed inside the apple, only revealed after the first bite.

She spun away from the centaur then, and Pirithous tensed. If Eurytion laid one hand of restraint upon her, peace or no peace, he would tear the offending limb from the centaur's body.

But Hippodamia continued on unmolested, her head held high. Pirithous stepped back before she saw him, and frowned. That she had gone to Eurytion at all made his eyes burn, the edges of his vision going white. She had sworn to him her affections remained her own, unpromised to any other, yet this foul beast had lured her from her very bed, when by all rights, she should have been thinking only of him and the pleasure he'd promised her as her husband.

It stung his pride, to be sure, but worse than that—whether she had turned from Eurytion tonight or not, his little mouse had lied. Something had passed between them to draw her out into the night, giving encouragement to the centaur's desires. And if she lied about that so convincingly, what else had she hidden from him? He knew for certain she had not lain with the beast, but had he not proven these last nights how much else they might have shared? And Hippodamia had been eager. Too eager for a maiden.

Pirithous retreated to his own room, for if he met her coming back to hers, they would both regret the result. His hands were fists, still gritty with stone dust, and while he wanted more than ever to claim her as his own, to leave her in no doubt as to where she belonged each night, to begin his marriage by taking her in anger was unthinkable.

She would have some explanation of course, and better if she came to him than if he forced her to confess, but the longer she waited, the longer she left him pacing in his room, the less he wished to hear it. It would only be another lie, another deception. And to think she had wept so prettily over even the thought of betraying him just days ago, then promised him her honesty!

He snorted. The sly mouse had known what she was doing from the start, tugging at his heart, playing upon his sympathies. From beginning to end, she had done nothing but manipulate him. Perhaps he had given Antiope too much credit in the matter. He could just imagine it now: Hippodamia and Eurytion, heads together in the night, deciding how best to bring him to his knees. Perhaps those times he'd found her looking out into the darkness, she had been waiting for some sign from the centaur, and he had been too great a fool to realize the truth.

The door creaked open and he whirled, his eyes blazing white. Hippodamia stood framed against the darkness of the room beyond, dressed in his own tunic. He could not quite stop himself from growling and her haunted face paled, her eyes going wide.

"Pirithous?"

How she managed to give her voice such a note of innocence, as if she were so unsure of herself, of him, he did not know, but he had no patience for it. "Should you not be in your bed, Princess?"

"I couldn't sleep…"

"Could you not?" He stepped toward her and she stepped back. "Poor little mouse, so distracted by the thought of her wedding day. Or was it something else on your mind? Someone else."

Her face reddened, her spine stiffening. "You cannot still think I would turn to Antiope?"

"Not Antiope," he agreed, almost snarling. "Though I suppose that is not beyond you, either. All that talk of how centaurs mate for life—how long would you have waited before you betrayed me?"

"What?"

"Eurytion, Hippodamia. And after you swore so solemnly you had no feelings for him but friendship. I should have known! The moment you asked that I allow him to stay with you—I should have known then that you lied."

"Pirithous—"

"Another lie, little mouse?"

"No!" She glared at him then, eyes alight with righteous fury. "Eurytion and I shared nothing more than a few kisses as children—it meant nothing!"

"And tonight? When you went to him in the dark, threw yourself into his arms? Did that mean nothing too?"

"I only wanted—"

"What, Princess? To reassure him that you had me wrapped around your smallest finger? That it would not be long now, before you might be reunited? Did you think you could convince me to let him stay? Is that what you wanted with all your talk of taking other men to your bed? Your centaur lover right beneath my nose?"

She slapped him. Hard enough to make his cheek sting and his head turn, and he clenched his jaw. He had almost forgotten the fire in her heart. The wildness. He should have known she hadn't been tamed. That her softening had all been part of the lie. Perhaps she had simply wished to use him for his seed before she left him for her people once more, his son in her belly to be raised by beasts and used against him, once grown.

"The only lover I ever wanted was you," she said, liquid pooling in her eyes. "Not Eurytion, not Antiope, not some palace slave. All I wanted was your loyalty in return for mine."

"Pretty words, Princess," he murmured. "A shame I cannot trust them."

Her chin lifted even as the tears spilled down her cheeks. "Then perhaps you should not take me as your wife."

Chapter Seventeen

Hippodamia

Eurytion had been right to worry, to fear for her. He had been right, and she had been such a fool. No matter what they shared, Pirithous's pride would always stand between them, worse than any mistress in his bed.

But Pirithous caught her by the arm before she turned away, his jaw working and his eyes cold. "I fear you have misjudged me again, my lady. There is no stopping now. The feast will go on, and when it is finished there will be no question as to where you belong. This peace will not be broken by me, and I will do everything in my power to ensure it is not destroyed by you or Eurytion, either."

She shook her head, jerking her arm free. He would never understand, and she had not the patience to explain. How could he believe she had no wish for this peace? After everything she had sacrificed—after everything they had shared!

"You're a fool, Pirithous."

"Then you will be a fool's wife." He nodded to the baths. "Call for your maid. Wash and dress. We go to the priest first, for his blessing, and I do not care if our guests are awake enough to follow. I would have this done with before your lover can interfere any further."

Lover! She spun on her heel, slamming the door behind her. Barring it, she was certain, would only enrage him, but she did so anyway. If he wished to be a brute, she would not deny him the opportunity to show the truth of his character.

In her own room, she splashed water on her face, scrubbing away the tears that stained her cheeks. She would not give Eurytion the satisfaction of knowing he was right, nor would she give Pirithous any proof for his claims. If he thought she would go running to Eurytion now, throw herself at any other, he would be sorely disappointed. She had known from the start that this marriage would be strange. That she had little hope of love, never mind joy. As long as he did not betray the peace it promised, she would suffer his accusations, even his anger, and have all she desired.

But she had given him no reason to mistrust her. None! And he had made up his mind before she stepped foot in his room. He had decided her beneath him from the beginning, from the moment he had laid eyes upon her in the megaron. That was why he had offered her the choice, not because he wanted her willing—for he certainly would not have her so now—but because he had *not* wanted her, had not trusted her or her motives.

Eurytion had been wrong about one thing, absolutely. Pirithous had not bewitched her. He would have had no cause to distrust her if he had, and she would not be so furious, besides. She had gone to him in honesty, for comfort in his arms, and instead he had turned on her like a maddened dog!

Not wishing to face her maid or any other, she did not bathe, only washed and dressed. Pirithous had chosen her gown from among his prizes in another storeroom, not so well hidden and just as neglected. Silk, he had called it, smooth and soft as water against her skin and dyed a pale yellow, the color of morning light. The girdle she had chosen for herself, purple leather with teardrops of gold that chimed against one another as she moved, with a sound as delicate as water trickling over stone.

She braided her hair loosely and waited for full dawn. Even Pirithous would not roust a priest from his bed, though she had no doubt he had been tempted by the thought. Perhaps by the time they reached the shrine he would see reason—surely he could not believe the things he had said. Not truly. And she had only wanted Eurytion to know she was happy…

But it seemed she had spoken too soon.

***

Pirithous did not speak to her at all as they walked the path up the mountain, Hylonome and Cyllarus following silently behind. Her father had arrived late the night before, and slept still, but he had already done his part by bringing her so far.

Theseus and Antiope waited for them at the shrine, bleary-eyed and rumpled, with a pure white horse tied to the altar. Whatever qualms Pirithous might have had over shaking the priest from his bed, they clearly did not extend to his cousin. She should have thought of it herself—sent her maid to Antiope, to wake her husband, and told them everything. Surely Pirithous would have listened to Theseus, if no one else.

"The priest says the omens are ill," Theseus warned, his voice too low for the centaurs to hear. "It would be better if you waited until tomorrow."

Pirithous shook his head. "It must be now."

Theseus's gaze slid to hers, questioning, but she only pressed her lips together. Now was not the time to speak against their union. Pirithous would only see it as further proof of her betrayal.

"Would you risk your kingdom simply to plow her?" Antiope demanded, her golden eyes flashing. "Have you not had enough of one another in other ways to sate your lust?"

Pirithous gave her a hard burning look. Antiope's mouth snapped shut and she turned her face away.

"Princess." Pirithous extended his hand, shifting his glower to her. Hippodamia gave him her hand without hesitation, but his fingers closed too tight around her own and his eyes glowed white. "Have you any last confessions to make? Perhaps you'd like to beg me to release you from your vow."

"I have told you already what I wished to say. All I have ever wanted is this peace between our people and your loyalty and affection. My feelings on the matter have not changed."

"You squeak a sweet song, little mouse."

"The truth need not be bitter on the tongue."

He grunted, drawing her forward more roughly than necessary. "Priest!"

At the altar, the priest stood before them, his face pale and grave. "I can promise only a fruitful union, my lord. Had I known what the auguries would reveal, I would have urged you to marry before now. Even yesterday, or perhaps tomorrow…"

"No," Pirithous said.

"But my lord—"

"No," he said again, his eyes flaring lightning white. "Whatever fate the gods bring us tomorrow, I will face it with Hippodamia as my bedded wife. To hesitate now will only bring excuse for war, besides."

The priest turned his anxious gaze to her. "My lady, I beg of you…"

"I have already given my promise to your king," she said. "I will not bring dishonor to myself or my people by breaking it."

Pirithous drew the knife from his belt and pressed it into her palm, wrapping his fingers around hers. "Much as I would prefer not to place a blade in your hand, this cut we must make together."

"Wait," Hylonome said, and the priest looked as though he might weep with relief. "What of Dia's peace? What do the auguries say of that?"

Beside her, Pirithous swore under his breath, and sparks of lightning crackled in the air, prickling her skin and turning it to gooseflesh. The priest swallowed thickly, meeting his king's eyes.

"The Lapiths will have peace, but only after they have paid for it in blood and sacrifice."

Hylonome's tail switched and she stepped back, the tension of her body expelled with a shudder of her hide. She bowed her head to Pirithous. "If the Lapiths must pay in blood, the centaurs will offer their share of the sacrifice. Centaurus would wish it."

Pirithous's hand tightened over Hippodamia's, the blade pressed to the horse's throat. The lightning faded from his eyes, from the air around them, and he inhaled deeply through his nose, looking down at her. Hippodamia held his gaze, willing him to see the truth, her truth.

It was only ever you.

The grim line of his mouth softened and something warmer flickered in his eyes. He nodded once, though whether it was acceptance of Hylonome's offer or in recognition of his own foolish pride, she did not know.

"If you wish it," he said softly, "we will wait until tomorrow."

Her whole body trembled with relief as she exhaled. "You have made me wait too long already."

"Now, priest," Pirithous said, and the barley the old man had withheld finally fell from his fingers, sprinkled before the victim with a fervent invocation to the gods.

They drew the blade across the horse's throat and the hot blood spilled over their hands. The horse sank slowly to his knees, unprotesting, and the priest let out a breath that was half-moan as he pressed a golden bowl to the animal's neck.

She did not hear the blessing he gave, and she did not care. They would have peace, for themselves and for their people. That was all that mattered.

CHAPTER EIGHTEEN

PIRITHOUS

The priest dismissed them, but when Hippodamia turned to follow the centaurs, Pirithous held her back. "I would have a moment alone with my wife."

Theseus frowned, searching his face. Pirithous gave him the slightest shake of his head. The madness had passed, and Hippodamia was his. Whatever Eurytion had hoped for, he would not have it. He could not have it. But even if they had waited until tomorrow, he was certain Hippodamia would have made the same choice. He had felt the conviction of her love, tasted and savored it like the finest wine before drinking deep.

Though he was not certain she realized even her own feelings, he could not help but be softened by them. He had no right to her affection, and he certainly did not deserve her love. He had offered her so little in exchange. Generosity, perhaps, when it suited him, but the rest? Mistrust, anger, insult. He had repaid her poorly.

"This way." He pulled her with him away from the main trail. "There is a pool not far from here where we might wash the blood from our hands…"

"No centaur would find fault in a little blood," she said, offering a hesitant smile. But even so unsure of herself, of him, she followed.

He wished he could take it all back. All his anger, all the things he had said. *Gods, forgive me.* How could he have been so blind? But he knew the answer. He'd known it from the moment he had nourished her fragile love with his own strength, unknowing, while she wept for the betrayal she had wanted so much to commit—hoping it might secure his affections, his loyalties. Hippodamia was so unlike the others, and for a breath, for a heartbeat he had feared…

She was the only woman he had ever known with the will to leave him. And it did not matter to her that he was king, or hero, or demigod. All that mattered was that he cared as much for her people as he did his own—that he cared as much for her as he did Dia's peace.

He led her through the trees, the path no more than the faintest of deer trails, the brush at times so thick he had to hold the branches back to allow Hippodamia to pass unscathed. She would bleed soon enough without the help of thorn and bramble, but he would treat her gently, carefully, for he had given her too much pain already this day.

And then they broke from the path into a clearing, edged by rose bushes which spilled in lush red and white blossoms over the bank of the pool. Petals fell like tears into the water with each stir of the wind through the branches, and a soft mist still clung to the grasses where the dappled sunlight could not reach.

"My mother used to bring me here when I was a boy. She said it was while she bathed here that Zeus came to her, and Aphrodite herself blessed them." As he hoped, now, that the goddess might bless their joining, if Hippodamia would forgive him. But he did not feel as though he had the right to ask it of her. Not yet.

One of her fingers coiled in the lace of her girdle, winding and unwinding the leather string. "It is no wonder the goddess favors this place, beautiful as it is."

"Even more so, with you here."

She looked up at him, then, searching, and he smiled, taking her hand to still the movement of her fingers. Her eyes closed, just for a moment, and she stepped into his arms, pressing her face into the curve of his neck. He smoothed her hair away from his chin and felt her shudder.

"I thought—I feared I had lost you. This. Everything."

"No," he said, pressing a kiss to her temple. "I am yours if you will have me."

"If!" She laughed, but it was weak, fluttering against his throat. "Oh, Pirithous! He said such awful things, and I only wanted you to tell me none of it mattered. He said you had bewitched me, and for a moment… but then you made me so furious, I knew it could never be true."

He smiled into her hair. "It would have done me little good to keep you so besotted, Mia. A queen must know her own mind, and I could not have trusted you to care for my people in my absence if the moment I left you, all you felt was loathing."

She drew back, staring up at him. "You cannot mean it was within your power?"

"I would have thought that the first warning Antiope gave you." But her face betrayed no understanding, troubled lines creasing her forehead instead. He smoothed them away with gentle fingers. He ought to have confessed it all to her that first night, but she had wanted so much to hate him already, and he had not wanted to give her another reason for mistrust. "I can feed the spark of some emotion already present, or share my own feelings with yours, but to impose my will upon another—it is a difficult and tiresome thing, and no honor to be had in the winning. To say nothing of what Antiope would have done to me if I had tried."

"She said you would never take me unwilling."

"Even now," he said, his voice hoarse, "if you wished me to release you, preferred instead to join the others at the feast…"

She pressed her fingers against his lips, held them there as she leaned in, her own lips parting, soft and inviting as they brushed against his throat, his jaw, his chin. He dragged her fingers away and claimed her mouth with his own, tasting her sweetness, her warmth. She shifted nearer, her body forming to his, all softness and curves, the silk teasing when he wanted her bare skin.

He tugged at the lacing of her girdle, the gold chiming where it was not crushed between them. The gown itself was a simple thing, made rich by its fabric and embroidery more than its cut. When the girdle fell away, he pulled the dress up over her head, and tossed it into the grass. The silk would wrinkle, but no one would be looking at her gown when he presented her flush-faced and glowing with pleasure.

Hippodamia unknotted his belt, the brush of her fingers so near his manhood he could only groan. She dropped to her knees and pressed kisses through the cloth, letting his tunic bunch over her forearms as they slid up his thighs. His hands shook, and it took all his restraint not to tear the fabric from his body, getting it over his head, for the moment it had risen above his waist, she had taken him into her mouth, swallowing him deeper than he had ever gone.

"Mia," he sighed, winding his fingers in her hair. "You need not…"

She drew back slowly, as if savoring his length, and he tightened, aching for more. But he did not want her mouth, not today. Today he would spread her thighs and let her guide him inside that slick, tender heat. He would repay her love and loyalty with pleasure beyond anything she had yet known.

"Come," he said, pulling her up. He needed to calm his desire, needed to go slowly, and it would not do to bring her to their wedding feast smeared with horse's blood besides, even if the centaurs would think nothing of it. To his people, it would signal only ill. "Bathe with me, little mouse, and the rest will follow."

Chapter Nineteen

Hippodamia

She was flushed already when Pirithous caught her by the waist, lifting her down into the water, but the cold she had braced for never came and she sighed at the warmth on her skin. Pirithous chuckled softly, sinking back into deeper water and drawing her with him.

"Did I not mention it was fed by a hot spring?" he teased, his hand sliding up her back, tickling the length of her spine.

She shivered and wrapped her arms around his neck, letting him support them both in the water. The hardness of his desire pressed into her stomach, and he tightened his arm around her waist, pulling her closer. His other hand abandoned her back, gripping her thigh instead, shifting her higher and guiding her legs around his hips, until he nestled himself against her center with a moan.

She echoed it, closing her eyes and tilting her hips just so… She bit her lip on a soft sound of pleasure as he teased her, holding back from the joining they both wanted. Heat blossomed through her, but not enough. She needed him closer, inside her. She needed to be filled.

"Even in the water, you're still so warm, so welcoming." His lips pressed against her shoulder, then followed the curve of her neck, and she tilted her head back. He grasped her bottom, moving her against him with that same delicious sensation, slipping his body against hers, but not inside. She whimpered, straining nearer, but he only laughed against her throat. "Soon, Princess, I promise you."

He caught her arm with his own bloodied hand, slipping it from behind his neck and drawing it beneath the water. The blood washed from her arm and hand with nothing more than his gentle touch, his hand gliding up her forearm, then down, his thumb massaging her palm, then each of her fingers.

She sighed, her head falling to his shoulder and her body melting against his, all liquid and warm. The things he could do with his hands, the way he touched her, firm and deft and confident. He always knew what she needed, and how to play her body until there was nothing else in the world but his hands, his mouth, and the growing need inside her, white and hot and so exquisite when it bloomed.

He lifted her up out of the water and set her upon the grassy bank, the cooler air making her skin prickle and the buds of her breasts harden. Pirithous tweaked one, and a flush of heat spread through her body against the sudden chill.

"Lie back, little mouse," he murmured, his other hand sliding up her thigh. When he stood, the water rose to the middle of his chest, and his eyes were dark as hurricanes. His thumb slipped between her folds, stroking between her legs. She shuddered hard, and when he urged her to part her thighs, lowering his head to take her with his mouth, she lifted her hips to meet him.

"Please," she moaned. "I need—"

One thick finger slipped inside her as his tongue flicked the place where his thumb had been, and she cried out, arching her back, her body flooding with warmth and need. He curled his finger, stroking something deeper, and she whimpered, feeling it build. She rocked her hips against his touch, against his mouth, needing more, begging for more. Her hands fisted in the grass, pulling tufts of it from the soft earth.

And then his mouth was gone, the absence of that warm, wet touch making her ache all the more. Another cry, half-moan, escaped her throat. So close! She had been so close.

But Pirithous hushed her, his body hovering over hers, and where his finger had been, the thick head of his desire pressed against her readied entrance. Her eyes flashed open, meeting his, and he pushed deeper, stretching her wider, filling her in a way his fingers never had. She clutched at his shoulders, his back, her nails scraping his skin as some small discomfort flared, then faded. He was so thick, and she needed him there, needed him.

He groaned and sank inside her completely, every muscle of his body tensed. "I've never…" He moved slowly, carefully drawing himself back, and she sighed. The feel of him, so deep, and she was whole.

"So tight," he murmured, and she wrapped her legs around his waist, pulling him deep again.

He fit her so perfectly, so completely, filled her to overflowing, and still she wanted more. "Please," she breathed.

He answered with another groan, one hand grasping her hip, holding her tight to his body. "I swore to myself I wouldn't hurt you, Mia, not like this. But I am not certain I have the strength to hold back."

She framed his face in her hands, curling her fingers around his ears. "It hurts more not to have you."

He growled and gathered her closer still, unwinding one of her legs from his waist. And then he rolled to his back and she straddled his body, gasping, the shift of her weight driving him all the deeper. His hands settled upon her hips, rocking her back and forth, guiding her until she found the rhythm and the heat spreading through her blood swelled into fire and lightning, prickling her skin, lighting her from the inside out.

Pirithous's hands glided over her ribs, his fingers pressing into her skin just hard enough. His mouth found the point of her breast, suckling, and the cresting wave of her pleasure broke at last, her body shuddering, clutching at his as she moaned her release.

But it was far from the finish, for Pirithous only laughed as she collapsed upon his chest, and rolled her to her back.

She had married a true son of Zeus, after all.

***

They bathed once more in the pool after, and helped one another dress. Pirithous combed his fingers gently through her hair, smoothing the tangles and picking leaves and rose petals from the strands. Her body was pleasantly sore in ways she had never imagined possible, but she had never felt so calm, so at peace, so whole.

"Will you forgive me?" he asked, his voice low and rough with emotion. "I will beg if I must."

She turned to look up at him, stroking his cheek. "As long as you are mine."

He turned his face into her hand and kissed her palm. "Then perhaps Aphrodite has blessed me, too."

Goddess, let it last. Give me the strength to match him in body and heart. Perhaps, in time, they might even find love, as Antiope had promised. She could only pray it would be so.

"Shall we join the others?" Pirithous asked. "I confess, I have no desire to share you, even the sight of you, but I fear your people will take offense if we do not feast with them."

"And yours will not?"

He flashed a wolfish grin. "The Lapiths know my appetites. They would find nothing amiss if I took my bride to bed."

She let her hand fall from his face, stepping back before he could tempt her further. "I would not mind the food or drink, and if we must eat to keep our strength, perhaps we ought to do our guests the courtesy of joining them for a time."

"A short time," he amended, and he caught her hand, his fingers tightening around hers.

Hippodamia laughed, her heart so light she feared she would float away but for his hold upon her. "A short time," she agreed.

Chapter Twenty

Pirithous

The wine had flowed freely in their absence, though the sun had barely reached its zenith, and Pirithous had ordered it well-watered out of deference to Hippodamia's guests. At her insistence, he had even set out pitchers of goat's milk for them, for whatever good it might do. At least the day had dawned clear, and long tables had been set within the courtyard for the centaurs, who had come in numbers far larger than he had wished.

Beside him, Hippodamia's delight shone in her eyes, and he hid his own irritation for her sake. But it was far harder than it should have been to release her hand when she tugged against his hold, intent on greeting her kin. Even more difficult to watch her run toward them without even the barest glance back. After the morning they'd had at the spring, she should have had eyes only for him, her entire being aching for more of his touch.

Instead, she flew into her father's arms, hugging him tightly, smiling and laughing as Hylonome and Cyllarus teased her for the delay. And it was not until Pirithous had joined them that she seemed to spare him any thought, stepping back from Centaurus and turning that smile upon her husband instead.

"King Pirithous has been more than kind to me," Hippodamia told her father. "And you are all to consider the cups at your places as his gifts to you."

"Our gifts," he corrected, forcing a smile to his lips.

Hippodamia slipped her arm through his, looking up at him with warmth and joy in her eyes. "For a lasting peace."

He let out a breath, and some of his own tension with it. Truly, he could not be angry when she looked on him with so much affection. He was fortunate she looked on him with any, no matter how much pleasure he had given her in recompense. But the thought only reminded him of Eurytion, and he could not help but lift his gaze from hers to search him out. Surely he would not have missed this. If only for one last opportunity to persuade Hippodamia of her mistake.

"Father, you must see the horses he's given me!" Hippodamia was saying. "Come, let me show you, and you can have no doubt of my husband's generosity. The horses upon the plain are magnificent, but they are nothing compared to the king's stables."

"She hardly exaggerates," Hylonome agreed. "I have never seen so many fine animals, some as beautiful even as the Mares of Magnesia."

"If King Pirithous will allow our absence, it would be my pleasure to see them," Centaurus said, smiling fondly at his daughter. The grimness of their last meeting had left his face, and Pirithous could hardly blame him for his relief after how things had begun. "But perhaps tomorrow might serve us just as well—"

"No." There. There was Eurytion, black eyes fixed on their small party, and Pirithous wanted a word with him. All the better if Hippodamia and Centaurus did not bear witness, for he was certain the centaur would not like what he had to say. He dragged his gaze back to Hippodamia and lifted her hand to his lips. "If my bride desires you to see her wedding gifts, I would not diminish her pleasure by refusing her the right. By all means, go. The feast has waited this long, and a trip to the stables will hardly keep you."

Her smile was all brilliance, and had he not just granted her permission to leave him, he would have thrown her over his shoulder instead and, centaurs or no centaurs, she would never see her wedding feast at all. When she looked at him that way, he could not bring himself to care for anything but the thought of when he might bed her next.

Hippodamia rose to her toes, pressing a kiss to his cheek. "I promise we won't linger."

And then she was gone, running off with Centaurus and Hylonome as he and Cyllarus watched. Pirithous waited until they had disappeared through the porch and out into the palace grounds before he turned away, searching for Eurytion once more. The centaurs were enjoying themselves, a sea of flanks and flicking tails, smelling of musty grass and damp caves. They roared back and forth across the tables, laughing loudly, and beside him Cyllarus grunted.

"If this is the welcome we might receive, you will find more centaurs making the journey to your palace, King Pirithous."

Pirithous half-shrugged. "An open hand is a small price to pay for peace."

And Eurytion had disappeared. He wanted to growl with frustration.

"Yet you do not seem pleased that so many have come to take advantage of your hospitality."

"It is not the many which draw my ire, Cyllarus," he said, baring his teeth. "Only the one. When this feasting is done, I promise you, Eurytion will not be welcomed beneath my roof again. I would not have him here even now if I did not think he would challenge his removal."

Cyllarus snorted. "What threat is Eurytion to you?"

"He threatens the peace, seeks to steal Hippodamia from me with his poisonous lies, and if not by those, I do not think he will hesitate to use force. If one of my men touched Hippodamia without her consent, whispered treason in her ears, I would have him killed. I have sworn to treat your people as my own, and I will.

With great pleasure, in Eurytion's case, should he decide to test me."

Cyllarus stared at him, nostrils flaring. "This is the peace you would offer us? Not a week has passed, and already you make threats against our people."

"I threaten Eurytion and Eurytion alone," Pirithous said coolly. "And can you truly say you would not do the same, were it your Hylonome he sought?"

The centaur looked away, but Pirithous did not miss the flick of his tail or the shudder of his hide, as if he wished to shed a swarm of flies. "Eurytion is protective of his charge, nothing more."

"You tell yourself the same lie Centaurus told me, but it does not make it truth. You are blinded, all of you, to the danger, and out of respect for my mother, this is my warning. To you. To Centaurus. To Eurytion himself. You will not get another."

He did not wait for Cyllarus to respond. This was his wedding feast, and he had more than the troubles brought by rowdy centaurs waiting to be addressed. Peleus's arrival, for one. If the Myrmidon king had not accepted his invitation, he would have had to send more men out to watch the river at the least—or, more likely, prepare for war.

Theseus met him inside, his expression grimmer than Pirithous liked, though he made an effort at a smile even as he drew him away from the tables and the guests. "Tell me you did not exhaust your bride even before she could be presented as queen?"

Pirithous shook his head. "She's with her father, showing off her horses."

"Better she were at your side," Theseus said.

"What difference does it make?" The words came out sharp, and he ground his teeth, hating the sound. It did not help that Theseus only said what he thought himself. In the woods he had been certain the gods had blessed him, but he had not been at his own banquet for even long enough to find a drink and already he wanted the whole thing ended. "The Lapiths have had a week to know her, and I have made it clear she was already queen in all but name. Whether she shows her father the horses before we eat or after, it hardly matters."

"Just as the omens did not matter?" Theseus asked, his voice low. "You did not hear the priest's warning in full, but we did. There will be blood spilled this day!"

Pirithous stiffened, wishing for the weight of a sword upon his hip. "Peleus?"

"He is here." Theseus nodded toward the dais. The Myrmidon king was seated beside Nestor, his sharp eyes seeming to count every cup of gold, and his jaw tight, as if he did not care for the tally.

Pirithous smiled. "And already regrets his coming, I see."

"You must have realized the trouble this would cause, Pirithous. You flaunt your wealth as if you fear nothing. If Zeus were not your father—"

"The gods have had their share, and those who have come today are bound by law. What risk is there in showing generosity to those who would declare themselves my friends? It is hospitality, Theseus, as the gods demand, and what is the point of it all otherwise? This marriage, the raiding we have done, season after season? I will have peace and prosperity for my people, that they need never fear again."

"And if the gods have other plans for you? For them?"

"I will appeal to my father, as you say. Shower Zeus and his priests in blood and riches until they are fat. Is that not what you've done? Turned to Poseidon and Athena for protection after giving offense to Artemis and Ares?"

"We offended them, perhaps, but no priest warned us of bloodshed at our wedding feast, and if one had, we would have waited!"

"Enough, Theseus." He grasped him by the shoulder. "Please, I beg of you. Peleus is here as my guest-friend. The centaurs have their peace and Hippodamia is clearly treated with honor and respect. The only blood that will be shed today is upon the altars to the gods, in sacrifice."

"You are a fool to ignore this," Theseus hissed. "And for what? Is planting your bride worth so much to you? More than the lives of your people?"

"There is nothing to be done!" He released him forcefully, and Theseus gave half a step. They had always been evenly matched, strength for strength, passion for passion. "Eurytion drew her from her bed, Theseus. What would you have had me do? Let her slip through my fingers? Let the peace Dia wanted turn to ash and blood?"

Theseus frowned all the harder. "Eurytion?"

"He would have her believe I've bewitched her," Pirithous spat. "If I hadn't taken her to wife, he'd have seen it as an insult. He'd be stirring up the lot of them, making plans to steal her away in the night. There would have been no hope of peace, then."

"But surely Hippodamia believed none of it?"

Pirithous rubbed his face, exhaustion creeping over him, as if he had been sustained until that moment only by passion and rage. "No, thank the gods. Though it did not stop me from making myself a fool. And now it is done, all of it. Whatever comes as a result—there is nothing any of us can do if the gods have other fates in mind, Theseus, but I could not risk losing…"

"Hippodamia," Theseus finished for him, and smiled wryly. "Though I think it had less to do with Dia's peace and more to do with the girl herself."

He only shrugged in response, unwilling to consider what he implied. "She is mine."

"I know the feeling well enough." Theseus sighed, his gaze shifting to the dais where Antiope sat, listening attentively to one of Nestor's tales. Peleus seemed less pleased with her company, but it was just as well. He was all the more likely to speak freely in her presence if he did not respect her as an equal, and Antiope could be relied upon to share what she might learn.

"Trust her," Theseus said, glancing back at him sidelong. It was not Antiope he spoke of, either. "It will be a long, hard road for both of you, if you don't."

Pirithous snorted. "I could hardly leave her to go raiding if I did not, and you know I would not give *that* up."

Theseus laughed, tipping his head toward the dais. "As long as you are sure to tell her which of your neighbors she should not trust in turn."

He pressed his lips together. Guest-friend or not, it would not stop Peleus from encouraging others to weaken him, however they might, that was true. And while the Myrmidon king had known Dia to be formidable, he was not likely to grant Hippodamia the same respect. "Perhaps it would be best if we did not raid for some time, yet. It would be unkind to leave our wives so soon."

"If Antiope has anything to say about the matter, she will not be left at all."

"May the gods save us all from Amazon brides." Pirithous clapped him on the shoulder. "And in the meantime, I must begin to speak with my guests. It would not do for Nestor to feel himself slighted, and I suppose I will have no choice but to exchange pleasantries with Peleus."

"Better those softer noises than the clash of swords in war," Theseus said. "And better you than me, all the same. The gods have shown him too many favors, it has made him far too proud."

Pirithous did not disagree. "You'll keep an eye upon Eurytion? And his kin?"

Theseus bowed. "Antiope and I, both. But perhaps you might send another horse up the mountain for Zeus, to be safe."

He did not like it, but he gave the order. Theseus might be overcautious and even grim at times, but it did not mean he was wrong. In fact, Pirithous could not remember the last time he had been mistaken in his caution, and the knowledge sat like stone in his stomach.

Because if Theseus was not wrong, another horse in sacrifice was unlikely to stop what was coming.

Whatever it might be.

CHAPTER TWENTY-ONE

HIPPODAMIA

Hippodamia put Podarkes through his paces, showing off, she admitted, if only to herself, but she wanted so much to reassure her father, to prove to him that this choice had been the right one, for more than just their people.

"He is a fine horse," her father said, when she brought the stallion to a halt beside him. He took Podarkes by the halter, holding him steady as she slipped from his back. Hylonome had left them not long before, intent upon returning to Cyllarus's side. "And as always, you ride well."

"He was Pirithous's favorite, I think, but he did not even lift an eyebrow when I claimed him for my own."

Centaurus laughed. "Was that the reason for your change of heart? That he gave up his prized stallion without a fight?"

She flushed, fussing with the fit of Podarkes's bridle, that she need not meet her father's eye. "It is more than just that. He is a good man, Father. Every one of his horses, he knows by name, and they nose about him, waiting for kindnesses. A bit of parsnip or a caress. He is good to his animals, as he is to his people."

Her father caught her by the chin, lifting her face. "And is he kind to you? Beyond these gifts and generosities—we all know what small meaning gifts can have, and I would not like to think he gives them only to make up for some other failing in his character."

"I cannot say he is perfect by any means." There was no use in being less than honest with Centaurus, after all. He always knew when she spoke half-truths. "But he is certainly kind to me. Kinder than I deserved, at first, until we came to an understanding. It is only his pride that gets in the way, now and then, but not so much that I cannot overlook it. And perhaps, one day, we might love one another, he and I. I was not certain of it at first, but now that I have known him, I think there is hope."

"Guard your heart, Daughter," Centaurus said, giving her chin a gentle pinch as he had done so often before. "Pirithous can give you children, wealth, riches beyond imagining, even peace for your people—but of love, the Lapiths know little, and I would not wish you to be disappointed."

"It is different, that is true, but Pirithous cares for me already, Father. He is mine as much as I am his. Is that not a place to begin?"

"And what if there is nothing more beyond it? If this is both the beginning and the end? Eurytion was not wrong when he said it was cruel of me to trade you this way, but I would see you content, at the least, satisfied with what you are given back. And I fear if you look for more, it will only bring you greater unhappiness."

"But I am not unhappy at all!" she said, and Podarkes tossed his head in response, sensing her frustration. "Whatever Eurytion believes, it's born of jealousy more than truth. Pirithous has given me more joy than I could ever have imagined, and I know this is not the end, Father. I have only to look at what Antiope and Theseus share to see what more awaits me."

Centaurus sighed. "A son of Zeus is not the same as a son of Poseidon, Mia."

"And I am no Amazon queen," she said bitterly, stepping back. Her father's words sounded far too much like Pirithous's own warnings, and they stuck in her heart like knives. "But can you not simply share in my joy? Pirithous is no centaur, but he is my husband, my mate! Do I not owe him at least the hope of love between us?"

"You twist my words, girl," he said, stamping a hoof. "You are new to this world, to these men. You cannot know their cruelty, and no matter what pleasures Pirithous might show you in his bed, he is still a man. Do not confuse his lust for love, or you will only be hurt all the more by his disloyalty. Give him his heir and be his queen, ensure our peace, but you owe him nothing more than that, and you are lucky if he returns even that much of your courtesy."

"Then I suppose I am very fortunate indeed," she said, turning back to Podarkes. The stallion's eyes rolled white, his nostrils flaring, but when she took a grip upon his mane and placed her hand upon his shoulder, he did not hesitate to help her to his back. "I must return Podarkes to his stall, but I see no reason why you must attend me. I'm certain our people already wonder what's become of you."

"Mia…"

She felt his touch upon her ankle, but Hippodamia tapped her heel to Podarkes's side and let the horse sidle away. "Enjoy your feasting, Father."

She left before he might see the tears threatening to spill from her eyes. What a fool she had been to think he might understand. Or perhaps it was worse than that. Perhaps he was right, and she did not know. Perhaps she was a fool to have any faith in Pirithous at all, even if he had not laughed at her dream of love. Not, she reminded herself bitterly, that he had ever suggested he believed in it, himself.

But she wanted so much to have a true marriage. For Pirithous to recognize her as his equal in all things, as his match and mate. She had the strength for it, she was certain, and it was too late now, besides. She had committed herself to him. To this marriage. To their future, together, bound by the gods.

Was it really so wrong to wish for love, too?

***

"Mia!" The creases of a frown cleared from Pirithous's brow the moment he caught sight of her inside the megaron. He did not seem to have taken his seat upon the dais yet, and came to her at once, excusing himself from the men he had been speaking to and taking both her hands in his. He must have been keeping one eye upon the entrance all the while to have spotted her so swiftly. "I was beginning to fear Podarkes had gotten the better of you."

"Even a Lapith stallion could not throw me if I did not wish to be thrown," she said, though she could not bring herself to smile. Her mood was more than soured, and she had taken her time stabling Podarkes, struggling to find some remnant of the joy she had carried with her from the spring.

Pirithous searched her face, the frown returning as a storm in his eyes. "Had I thought for a moment sending you to the stables would return you to me so grim, I would have insisted you remain at my side, little mouse."

She shook her head, smoothing the lines from his face and finding no little comfort in his concern. "It is nothing that you cannot make me forget easily enough," she promised, for she could not see how it would do any good to tell him of her father's concerns. No doubt it would only offend his pride, and what then? More than just her own mood soured, surely, and she would not let this feast be poisoned simply because she could not rule her own heart.

"If I could steal you away this very moment, I would," he said, catching her hand to press a kiss into her palm. She shivered at the gentle nip of his teeth against her skin, and he grinned slowly, much too pleased with her response. "But I fear now that we have come, it is not so easy to escape. My people are too eager to meet their queen."

"Queen." She swallowed her sudden panic. Pirithous may have called her princess, but it had been a courtesy, nothing more. Among the centaurs she was simply an adopted daughter of her father, who himself would never claim the title of king. Leader, yes.

Father of them all, as the son of Ixion, but nothing more. To be Pirithous's wife was one thing, even to run his household a task she felt equal to, but she had thought she would have more time before he named her queen. Time to learn what it was to be Lapith instead of Centaur.

Pirithous laughed as if he had heard her thoughts, but his eyes were warm, even gentle. "You need not fear, Mia. I will not throw you to the wolves, and Antiope will teach you what I cannot."

"Surely there is a more auspicious day, or some blessing needed from the gods?"

"Better to begin as we mean to go on, little mouse. And this way, we give your people no reason to claim insult later. I will see this peace sealed in every way possible before this feast is ended."

She felt like a mouse then, as she had that first night, when she had come upon him naked in his bath. But this was nothing she could run from. Centaurus had traded her for this peace, given her up to Pirithous that she might be a voice for her people as queen. That the Lapiths might show the same respect for the centaurs now as they had shown under Dia's rule, while she lived.

Hippodamia took a steadying breath, then nodded.

Pirithous cupped her cheek, his gray eyes alight with what seemed suddenly too near to pride. Her throat closed at the thought, her heart constricting. Because Centaurus must be wrong, if Pirithous could look at her like that.

And then he turned away, facing their guests and drawing her forward. He had only to lift his head and raise his hand and the hall quieted.

"Lapiths!" Those who had not seen his movements fell silent at the sound of his voice, obedient to their king. Pirithous grasped her hand, raising it high with his. "I give you your queen: Hippodamia, Tamer of Horses, Daughter of Centaurus, Princess of the Centaurs, and with the blessing of Zeus, my bride!"

There was a roar in response, but it was a moment before she realized it did not come from the guests inside the megaron. Her head turned even as her mind struggled, knowing what she would see and refusing it, all at once.

"Eurytion," she said, his name no more than a whisper, and then her guardian was upon them, a thick branch in his hands for a club, swinging it with all his strength. "Eurytion, no!"

Pirithous flung out his arm, pushing her back, but she ducked beneath it, twisting to place herself between them. Eurytion would not strike her, no matter how enraged, and Pirithous might be the son of Zeus, but centaurs were strong enough to daze even a demigod were he caught unaware. And if Pirithous fell, he would be helpless beneath Eurytion's hooves.

"Stop this!" she cried, throwing herself forward.

Pirithous caught a handful of her gown, and Eurytion's club arced down, as if he could not see her, could not stop himself from completing his swing. In that moment, her eyes wide with shock, she saw he was not alone. A dozen others charged with him, bellowing their hatred.

"Hippodamia!" Pirithous's arms wrapped around her, his body a living shield as the branch struck across his back, shattering against his flesh and bone. His eyes burned bright white, and wood smoke and lightning filled her nose. "Go to Antiope!"

Eurytion roared again. Pirithous pushed her away, sending her stumbling, and spun to face the centaur's charge.

"Go!" he shouted again, not even sparing her a glance. Eurytion had a stool in his grasp, and Pirithous caught him by the wrist, stopping the blow. But the centaur had more than just his fists, and Pirithous could do nothing to block the strike of his hooves when Eurytion reared. "Get to the stairs! To the roof if need be, but go!"

"This way, Hippodamia," Antiope said, grabbing her by the arm. "Hurry!"

"But Pirithous—"

"Has fought and won more battles than you could ever dream," she snapped. "Come, Mia. It is you he wants, and if we can but thwart him a time, he will calm!"

She tripped after the Amazon queen, casting one last look back. Pirithous had only his table knife, but Theseus was forcing his way through, sword in hand. The Horse Lord's son. But Eurytion was blind with rage. Had Poseidon himself risen up from the seas, he would not have stopped.

"He isn't after me," Hippodamia said, dragging Antiope to a stop. "It isn't me he wants, it's Pirithous!"

"Pirithous dead," Antiope agreed, urging her on again, and for all her own strength, Hippodamia found she could not match the Amazon. "And then you."

CHAPTER TWENTY-TWO

PIRITHOUS

It was the wine, Pirithous realized, the stink of it thick upon the centaur's breath when he did not dodge quickly enough. Eurytion had him by the throat, bellowing into his face. He grabbed the beast's arm, digging his thumb into the underside of the wrist until Eurytion's grip failed. Pirithous dropped, letting the fall become a roll. The more distance he put between himself and the centaur's hooves, the better off he would be. And he needed a sword, for he'd lost his knife almost immediately when it had stuck in Eurytion's side. If he'd struck anything vital, the centaur didn't show it, but the wine explained that too.

"She is *mine*!" Eurytion roared, and before Pirithous could find his feet again, another stool came flying at his head.

Pirithous lifted an arm to block it, then wrenched it from the centaur's grasp. "She was never yours, Eurytion." He stepped back, leading the centaur away from the passage Hippodamia had taken. "And this is no way to win her! Think of what she gave up for this peace, and you would have it shattered the very day it was born?"

"As if you meant to keep it!" The centaur reared, striking out with his hooves, and Pirithous barely had time to duck.

He'd already taken one hit that way, and his shoulder had not thanked him for it. He flexed his hand, testing the feeling there. If

Eurytion had not caught him so squarely upon the joint, sending spikes of hot pain down the length of his arm, perhaps he would not have lost his hold upon the knife.

But he did escape this time, and even risked a glance at the state of his hall. It wasn't only Eurytion fighting, but it was clear the aim of the others was different. Until that moment, he hadn't understood the screams of the women, but it was all he heard now. One of the palace women was sobbing in a corner, struggling to cover herself in the shreds of her gown. Blood stained the tiles beneath her, and her face was puffy with more than just tears. Another woman, the wife of one of his councilors, was being hauled back by the hair, the centaur's lust more than obvious.

"Pirithous!" Theseus's sword sliced cleanly through the woman's hair, freeing her from her attacker, and he sent a second blade skittering down the long table dividing them.

It stopped nearer to Eurytion than him, and Pirithous dove for the weapon, cursing as he did so. A crash followed him, pottery shards exploding in sharp knives where the sword had been. Pirithous rolled off the table, following the blade. He grabbed the sword, ignoring the stinging cuts across his forehead and arm, even the pottery sticking from his skin. Wine dripped from the table top, spilled from the shattered krater, but it was not as though he had never fought drenched just as completely in blood.

"This is your last warning, Eurytion. Turn back and call the others off, and perhaps this peace might yet be saved."

The centaur sneered. "Do you think I care for your peace? For anything you might offer?"

Pirithous bared his teeth. "If not for me, then for your princess. Think of Hippodamia!"

"It is for her sake I act now! For her freedom! Once you are dead, nothing stands between us."

"But for my shade, and the blood on your hands, no, nothing at all. And do you think she is so faithless as to overlook such ruin?" He spread his arm, indicating the megaron, the screaming—he must finish this. And quickly, for his people's sake. "Peace benefits us all."

"When you treat us like children? Insulting us with milk instead of honeyed wines? Peleus told us the truth. You and your people only laugh at us! But not after today. After today, they will think of us with terror in their hearts, and it will be *your* people who are hunted down like dogs!"

Peleus. Of course. Stoking the fire of Eurytion's anger, all the while pouring him drinks of unmixed wine, no doubt. Pirithous had wondered where he'd gone, and now he understood. And did Peleus fight against the centaurs, now? Make a show of his loyalty to the bonds of friendship? It was so well-twisted a plot, he might yet even fool the gods.

"If you do not leave now, I will kill you," Pirithous said calmly. Perhaps he could not touch Peleus, but he could do this much. And he would be lying if he said he did not want it. "Not even Hippodamia would blame me."

"Eurytion!" Centaurus's bellow caused the centaur to hesitate, and Pirithous narrowed his eyes against the glare, for the centaur king was framed by sunlight. "Enough of this! You bring shame upon us all, and worse!"

Eurytion's tail flicked, his lips curling as he turned to face Centaurus. "I? It was not I who sold my daughter! Our gift from the gods! She might have been our redemption, our hope, but instead you threw her at this cur's feet!"

"Our hope for what, boy?" Centaurus demanded. "What better hope than peace?"

"She could have given us children! Bred us back to man, more than beast!"

"You would have killed her in the trying," Centaurus snapped. "Wasted her life for nothing more than a fool's dream. The gods have made us what we are, fated us to this form, and who are you to subvert them? Just another whelp, unworthy of her love. Better she live with Pirithous than die for your pride!"

Eurytion reared, roaring, then charged, tearing the knife out of his own side as he did. Pirithous swore, vaulting back over the table to follow.

"No!" It was a woman's voice. Hippodamia's voice, from the gallery above, Antiope at her side, though the Amazon's attention was directed elsewhere, bow in hand, and arrows flying. Trust Antiope to protect the women, even over Theseus himself. But it meant she did not watch Hippodamia, who already scrambled over the rail.

Too slow.

They were both too slow.

CHAPTER TWENTY-THREE

HIPPODAMIA

The knife. Hippodamia hung from the balcony, her heart pounding in her ears, but even before she could think of falling, the knife was already slicing through skin and sinew and bone.

"No!" she cried again, her voice breaking on the word, and she reached one arm out, as if somehow she might stop it, might grab it all back. Antiope was shouting, grasping at her other arm, trying to haul her back up, but she couldn't. And Hippodamia couldn't do anything but watch her father's blood spray across the room.

Her vision blurred, hot tears searing her cheeks, and then Pirithous's arms wrapped around her, easing her down as he called for Theseus. For Antiope to shoot Eurytion down. The other centaurs were maddened with rage, even their lust drowned by Centaurus's blood, and more of them had spilled into the megaron now. She heard Cyllarus's voice and Hylonome's weeping, and Pirithous and Theseus stood together beneath Antiope and her bow.

She could not stop shaking. Could not stand upon her own two legs when Pirithous set her to her feet, and yet she found herself scrambling away, reaching for her father, his body slumping as she watched. "Father. Father, please!"

"Mia!" Pirithous caught at her arm, but she was wrenched from his grasp.

Eurytion had her. An arrow through his shoulder and another in his flank, but he leapt up, soaring over Centaurus's body even as she fought and clawed and screamed. "Father! No, let me go! Let me go!"

"Never fear, Fawn. You'll be free of them all."

She twisted in Eurytion's arms, all her sorrow twisting with her, turning her inside out with rage and madness. One hand closed upon the arrow shaft that pierced his shoulder. He hissed and met her eyes, his own wide with confusion. Eurytion, her protector. Her friend—no longer. Eurytion who had gutted her father before her eyes, killing every hope of peace.

Hippodamia tore the arrow free.

The shock of it made him stumble, his arm weakened enough that Hippodamia felt herself slipping. But not enough. Not enough, and she would not let him steal her, would not let him have his way. Not while her father's blood stained the painted floor, and the women wept, and the men cried out in shock and anger to have their wives and children borne away. Not when everything Centaurus had hoped for, worked toward, lay in ruins inside the megaron.

She aimed for his face. So near to him, she could hardly have missed had she not lost the advantage of surprise. The arrow point caught his brow, and when he turned his head, it sliced across the bridge of his nose, barely avoiding his eye.

Eurytion snarled, flinging her away. Blood poured down his face and he shook his head like a dog maddened by fleas, while Hippodamia struggled to arrest her fall, to right herself before he came for her again.

But he only staggered back, another arrow sprouting from his breast. Another, piercing his heart, and another his throat, his stomach and withers. Eurytion collapsed, ebony eyes still so wide, so lost. And there was Pirithous, fighting to reach her side. Antiope standing upon a sloping table top and letting her arrows fly.

"Mia!" Pirithous burst from the hall. How long had he been calling her name? She turned toward him, tripping over branches and stools, table legs and amphorae, their contents spilled upon the grass. Libations for the gods. When he caught her up, she let herself go limp, let the sobs break from her throat and her whole body shudder.

"My father," she gasped. "My father."

He cradled her against his chest, dropping to his knees and holding her tight. "Forgive me, Mia. I should have realized. Should have known. If I had only struck him down—"

"We have not time for your grief, Pirithous, nor your wife's," Antiope interrupted. How she had found her way to them, Hippodamia did not know. "The centaurs have stopped their rutting, but they have only begun to fight. Peleus rallied the men by cheering your name as Centaurus fell, and Cyllarus will not hear that it was Eurytion's doing. He will not hear anything but the cry for blood."

The words left a hollow, broken place in her heart. Centaurus fallen. Eurytion dead. How many others? How many others if Cyllarus would not listen?

She pushed Pirithous away, rose on shaking legs and forced herself to see. Men and women, beaten and still upon the ground. Centaurs, too, maimed and dead. And this, in the courtyard, was not the worst of it, she knew. But from the megaron, there came shouting yet, and battle cries. The centaurs were inside. Their guests were dying, and Centaurus was gone.

"He will hear me," she said, though her voice was so hoarse she could barely hear herself. "He will hear the daughter of Centaurus, and he will take what is left of our people and go."

"Mia, it is not safe," Pirithous began, his voice low and urgent. "I will not risk you!"

She met his eyes. "You called me queen, and now I must act as theirs. Surely you see that?"

His jaw worked, muscles twitching beneath the surface. "It will not end this. Even if they leave."

Her spirit twisted, but there was no use in denying it. "I know."

"And whose queen will you be then, Hippodamia?"

Tears pressed against her eyes, thickening her throat. To choose between her people and his should have been easy. But she did not know. She did not know what she must do but this.

"Pirithous, Theseus is still inside," Antiope said. "If they might listen, we must let her try."

He picked up his sword and stared at her hard, gray eyes flashing with emotions she could not name. She wished she could reassure him. Wished so much that she could promise to stay. "Pirithous—"

"Do not leave my side," he said, stopping her. His voice was raw. "Not today."

She swallowed all that she dared not say, and nodded.

Chapter Twenty-Four

Pirithous

With Antiope beside him, her bow traded for a small but no less deadly blade, they made their way through the brawl. Pirithous helped Hippodamia climb upon a table, the better to catch the attention of her people, before he took his place at her side.

"Centaurs!" Hippodamia called out, her voice ringing over the clash of swords and makeshift clubs. He had not realized she could bellow so, but he should not have been surprised. "Centaurs, hear me!"

It was the Lapiths who looked to her first, and Pirithous gestured them back with a flick of his sword. The megaron was in shambles, the hearth fire half-guttered, and even as his people retreated toward him, the centaurs followed, spittle flying with their roars.

Hippodamia cursed, and before he realized her intent, she leapt from the tabletop.

"Mia! Come back!"

But she ignored him, landing squarely upon the hindquarters of a roan-backed centaur, before launching herself again, from his backside to Cyllarus's own. The centaur reared, and Pirithous lurched, only to be caught by Antiope.

"Trust her!" the Amazon hissed. "She is no sheltered maiden! These are her people."

Before Pirithous could break free of Antiope's hold, Hippodamia had grasped the centaur's hair with one hand to balance herself, and caught his wrist with the other. What trick she used to snatch the table leg from his hand, he did not see, but a moment later, Cyllarus was back upon his hooves, bucking and spinning in place, trying to reach the woman upon his back.

"Listen to me, you fool!" Hippodamia shouted, and then lifted her head. "All of you! Listen! Centaurus would not have wanted this, and you will not win! If death is all you desire, run yourselves off the mountain's cliff, but stop this!"

"You protect him, after what he's done?" Hylonome called. "Has he truly bewitched you so completely that you would turn your back upon the most sacred of laws? Your father is dead!"

"And so is his murderer," Hippodamia snapped. She leapt from Cyllarus's back, allowing his own bucking to propel her, and landed lightly in the ashes of the hearth, cooling and clumped with the splash of blood and wine.

The centaurs hesitated then, at the sight of their princess so near the flames, and Pirithous leaned out to reach for her, hauling her back to the height and safety of the tabletop—and this time, he kept her hand in his.

"Centaurus's vengeance is taken, and mine as well!" Hippodamia called out. "Leave now and you will not be followed. Remain, and the Lapiths will have no choice but to fight, to defend themselves and their women! You cannot win a battle against the Horse Lord's son!"

Theseus pushed through the other guests surrounding their makeshift dais, blood smeared across his cheek and nose, and Antiope clasped him by the arm, pulling him up beside her. The centaurs shifted, Cyllarus and Hylonome exchanging a glance, and Pirithous would have sworn it was alarm he felt from them.

"Already you risk Poseidon's curse!" Hippodamia continued, her head held high and proud. If he had thought for a moment she lacked the strength to rule as queen, she proved her mettle now. Let Peleus note it well. "And what then? No other god will show us mercy or grant us aid. But if you leave now, there is still hope. Go to your caves and burn offerings to the Earth Shaker. Beg his forgiveness, his blessing!"

"And are we to leave you here?" Cyllarus called back. "Trust that no harm will come to you, after what your husband has done today?"

"What *I* have done?" Pirithous stiffened, his eyes burning with the insult. He had warned them! He had warned them of Eurytion this very day, and what had they done to stop him? Joined him in his slaughter, in his violence, and now they blamed him for that beast's madness? For all of this? "How dare you—"

Hippodamia squeezed his hand, stopping him with a glance. He could feel her determination, her resolve. "I will remain among the Lapiths as hostage, and I will speak with the king and his councilors on behalf of our people." She lifted her chin, staring down the centaurs who shuffled and grumbled amongst themselves. "Is that not half the reason Centaurus gave me to King Pirithous? That we might have a voice within these halls? I will not dishonor my father by abandoning my place so easily."

He had not realized how much it would mean to him to hear the words. She would stay. If not forever, at least for a time. But it was his people who shuffled and murmured to one another now, casting sidelong glances at their queen as if she were some witch. A curse of the gods meant to bring them ruin.

"We accept," Pirithous said firmly. And they were fools, all of them, if they thought for a minute she spoke anything but the truth. Oh, they dressed it up in words like alliance and peace, but the politics did not change. Hippodamia had been meant to be her father's voice, perhaps even his spy. Not that it should have concerned them. Centaurus had been honorable, though his people did not always live up to his example. "And We give Our solemn vow that Hippodamia will be treated with all honor and respect as Our queen."

Cyllarus snorted, hoof scraping against the plastered floor. "As you warned me, King Pirithous, now I warn you. Hippodamia may be human in form, but she is centaur in spirit. If she is harmed while in your keeping, you will pay in blood."

Pirithous bared his teeth. "Just remember who meant her harm this day, Cyllarus. For it was not me, nor any of mine. My men did not seek to defile your women!"

"Go," Hippodamia said, and though Hylonome gave them a long look, hesitation clear in the centaur's eyes, she turned to leave with the last of the others. Hippodamia watched them, her expression carefully blank, for all that Pirithous could feel too clearly the ache of grief and sorrow in her heart.

"It was the wine," he said quietly, hoping it might reassure her. "Eurytion and those who attacked with him were drunk on it."

"And all of them are dead, now. Incapable of making such a mistake a second time," Hippodamia replied, her gaze falling to the bodies littered throughout the megaron. "But I suppose that will not satisfy your people, will it?"

"Had it been your people who were attacked without provocation, would they be satisfied?" Pirithous struggled to keep his words gentle. There was so much bitterness in her voice, in her mind, and when she lifted her eyes to his, there was no warmth there to greet him.

"My people have lost more today than you will ever understand," she said.

"We both lost."

She shook her head. "Your people did not lose their king. They did not lose the favor of their gods. Some died, yes, and more were hurt. But your people will survive this day. Seeing what they have done, this savagery, I cannot say the same for mine."

She jumped down from the table then, all the pride of her bearing gone.

"Mia—"

"Let her go," Theseus said, his voice low. "There is nothing you can say that will bring her any comfort, and much you might that will only cause more pain. To say nothing of what your people will think, should you go running after your wife after everything they have suffered for her sake this day."

He tore his gaze from her slumped shoulders to the men and women who surrounded them. In that moment, he hated them all. "Peleus is gone."

Theseus grunted. "He and his men slipped away the moment he'd goaded the rest of the centaurs into battle with that nonsense about Centaurus's death. You may yet have two wars to wage."

"May the gods smite him." Pirithous tossed his sword away and vaulted down from the table. "For if they do not, I will. Sacred laws be damned."

"He drank from your cup, but he did not accept it for a gift," Antiope said. "And I cannot think the gods will find offense after what he has done today. The laws of hearth and hospitality are already broken by his betrayal in spirit, if not in deed."

"Would that he had not come at all," he growled. "No wonder he left his wife at home, if this was what he planned. I should have realized then that he meant trouble."

"Perhaps he only took advantage of the opportunity presented," Theseus said. "How could he have known of Eurytion's discontent beforehand?"

Pirithous nudged the corpse of a silver-white centaur and frowned. "How indeed."

For that question, he would find an answer.

***

Antiope tended to the women, for Pirithous did not think they would find any comfort from Hippodamia's aid, even if she might be persuaded to offer it. He and Theseus moved among the men, dead and alive.

For the dead, there was little to be done beyond offering gifts and sympathy to their sons and daughters, husbands and wives, removing the bodies with all proper ceremony and respect, and preparing a funeral pyre. With so many dead, and by such a violent end, they could not afford to take the time to entomb them all, nor risk the malevolence of their shades. Tomorrow would be another feast, more somber than today's, with games to honor the fallen. The prizes would come from his own treasury, but even so, he wished he might do more.

He wished he had listened to the priest. Put off this wedding for one more day. It could not have had a worse result. Eurytion would have taken insult and raged, but Centaurus would have ignored him. And when Pirithous married Hippodamia the following day, the centaur would have looked the fool for his unfounded fury.

Or perhaps Peleus would have goaded him, still. But how many others would he have been able to convince? Fewer innocents would have been lost, to be certain, and fewer women taken. It was their bodies which haunted him most of all, for he could not look on them without seeing Hippodamia's face, her lean form abused and broken. And this would not be the end of it. Those women who had survived the centaurs' lusts might yet be burdened with unwelcome fruit, and from what he had gathered, if the midwives' potions did not act as they should, the women faced death when it came time to birth.

But for the strength Zeus had given him, and the power of Antiope's bow, it might be Hippodamia's stomach budding in three months' time, her death he feared. If Hippodamia had not fought against her captor, had not done what she must to save herself…

"You can't mean to let them live on so near to us," one of his councilors, Plouteus, said, after Pirithous had clasped his hand and praised him for his courage. "You can't mean to give them peace again. Perhaps it's true they share Ixion's blood, my lord, but they're nothing more than beasts. Surely you see that now."

Pirithous murmured something reassuring, promised to post guards upon the palace walls, and distracted the man from the realization that his king had not answered him at all. Just as he had done with all the others who had asked the same questions, growing grimmer and grimmer each time.

"Even with a head start, we can find them. Hunt them down and let their shades fly to Hades. Won't rest easy until every last one's gone," another man said, closing his wife's eyes. "Queen's kin or not."

Pirithous grunted and moved on.

"I know what you're thinking," Nestor said when Pirithous finally reached him. No question, he was relieved to know the old king lived, though he would have a new scar or two to show for his adventure.

"And what am I thinking?" Pirithous asked, slumping down the wall to a seat on the filthy floor beside his guest. A true friend, Nestor, and truth be told, he could use some of his wisdom just now.

"You're thinking that perhaps your people will be satisfied if you only drive the centaurs from the mountain. Perhaps you might even make them Peleus's problem. Force them into his lands, and let the Myrmidons bloody their hands while you take your new wife to bed, conscience clear."

Pirithous snorted. If only Hippodamia were so easily deceived. "The first part, perhaps, but not the last. I would not send the centaurs to Peleus. Too great a risk that they might forge some alliance between them."

"Your people want blood, Pirithous. A chance to prove themselves, after this. To take back their honor and their courage, and know they need never fear this threat again."

"If there are no centaurs upon the mountain, there is no threat at all."

Nestor sighed. "If only the centaurs had not betrayed their trust. If this had all happened before the peace was struck, you might have convinced your people of that. But they can hardly take such an agreement on faith now, can they? After the centaurs have proven themselves false friends? The Lapiths will always wonder if they are there, hiding, waiting for the opportunity to strike again, to steal their women and murder them in their beds."

"And what comfort is that to my wife?" But he was uncomfortably aware that if not for Hippodamia, he would likely have agreed. Before he had met and married her, he would not have hesitated even for a moment to go to war, nor declared peace again until every last centaur was dead.

"Kings do not always have the luxury of pleasing their wives, Pirithous. Most especially when those wives are the result of failed accords. And after all, it is not as though you married for love."

No, he had not married for love. He closed his eyes and tipped his head back against the plaster wall behind him. But the way his heart twisted at the thought of telling her this, of seeing her face fall and her eyes fill with tears as he explained that the centaurs must die, he was not far from such a regard for her, all the same. Certainly he cared for her. Wanted her to be happy. And he had no wish to disappoint her love for him so soon, nor lose it altogether.

But after this, how could she love him at all?

If he had only waited another day to marry her.

If he had only listened to the priest.

If he had only forbidden Eurytion from the feast altogether, or slit his throat instead of trying to reason with him.

It was a good thing that Dia was dead, for she would never have forgiven him for the mess he had made of all this.

Nestor clapped him on the shoulder as he rose. "Be of good cheer, Pirithous. If you succeed in this war, men will sing of your name for ages to come. I'll teach them the song of it myself."

It was not much of a consolation.

In fact, he would have traded it all if he could only find a way to satisfy his people and still keep Hippodamia's love.

CHAPTER TWENTY-FIVE

HIPPODAMIA

After the maid had filled the tub with hot water, Hippodamia dismissed her. She bolted the door to her chamber behind the girl, and stripped the ruined gown from her body. Beautiful yellow silk. She could not even stand the sight of it, stained with Eurytion's blood. Tainted by the screams of the Lapith women, as her people had turned to brutes. Her people. The gods had truly forsaken them, to make them capable of this. Hippodamia threw the gown into the hearth fire, watching it burn until her eyes blurred from the flames and the scent of charred meat filled her nose.

Her bath was getting cold, and gooseflesh had risen on her arms as she stood naked before the fire. The blood hadn't limited itself to the fabric, and she shifted her gaze to her hands, staring at the rusted stains upon her skin, beneath her nails. She saw Eurytion's eyes, widening with shock and betrayal after she tore the arrow from his shoulder.

Hippodamia shook her head, blinking back tears, and took herself to the bathing room. There was no purpose in barring those doors, even if her own had been repaired, for Pirithous had already proven he would not be stopped from reaching her if he felt it needed. Whether he believed it needed or not this night, she was not certain. She was not certain even of her own feelings on the matter, yet.

The water was still warm when she slipped beneath it, but she made no move to wash the blood from her hands, only watched as it leached from her skin. Eurytion's blood. Eurytion's death. She wrapped her arms about her knees and pulled them to her chest. Easier to think of him than to think of her father, lost forever, and remember how wrongly she had spoken to him in the stables.

He had only wanted to warn her. To protect her from heartbreak. And why had she been so offended, so hurt? He had only spoken again the same words she had grown up hearing, the same warnings and the same concerns. But she had been so full of Pirithous's kindnesses, so determined to prove his affections. And who had she been trying to convince so desperately? Centaurus? Or herself?

She raked damp fingers through her hair, tearing it from its braid and wishing she could tear it from her scalp altogether. What a fool she was. So eager for her new husband, for all he had promised and all they might accomplish together, she had disregarded even her father's love. And now all her dreams were nothing more than ruined silk, burned to strange black ash, and blood.

Hippodamia shivered, a chill settling into her bones where the warmth of the water could never reach. She should have been in the megaron still. As queen, her place was at Pirithous's side. But what comfort could she give his people? She had none to offer her own. None for herself. And why should they trust her, besides? All their marriage had brought was death and pain, horror and war. She had no trouble imagining how his people responded now, their pleas to their king for vengeance and blood. And even in her own mind, she could not deny them some right to the call for war.

But it would not be enough. Could never be enough for this breach of trust, all because Eurytion had refused to abide by Centaurus's decision. Refused even to respect her own. Because the centaurs had turned to beasts before her eyes. And he thought

Pirithous undeserving? Pirithous, who had sworn never to take her unwilling?

To think she had descended the mountain so joyfully. Had it only been that morning when they had made love? It felt as if a full year had passed, so much had changed so quickly, and all the strength she had summoned to send the centaurs away had abandoned her now. If she had not stood in witness to their vileness—she wondered now, if the stories the Lapith women had told all these years, of being raped by centaurs and left in the woods, were true. Had she been so blind as that? Or was it only the betrayal of this day? The curse of the gods for Eurytion's treachery, when by all rights he ought to have been bound by the laws of hospitality and friendship.

The Lapiths would never trust her as their queen, no matter what came next. And she could not help but wonder…

What good would it do her, or anyone, if she stayed?

CHAPTER TWENTY-SIX

PIRITHOUS

Pirithous pushed open the door to his room long after moonrise, exhausted and heartsick. He had seen all his people settled, sent them all to their beds with full stomachs and bandaged pride. The guests, too, he had found rooms for, and set guards upon the palace walls, as he had promised his councilors. "Hippodamia?"

She was not in his room. He snorted at his own foolishness. After what had happened, he would be fortunate if she was willing to speak to him, never mind share his bed.

"Mia, please, we must—" Pirithous stopped himself at the sight which greeted him in the bathing room.

Hippodamia had her knees drawn up to her chest in the bath, her face hidden in her arms, resting atop them. She looked… fragile. Utterly broken. This was not the woman who had challenged him, declared him unsuitable for her affections, or herself his equal. It was as though her flame had been smothered, and seeing her that way made his heart ache in sympathy and grief.

"Ah, little mouse," he said gently, crossing the room to her. She did not so much as twitch when he knelt beside her, though when he lifted a hand to her hair, stroking it from her face, she shuddered. "Today, you showed the bravery of a lion. Proved yourself a fitting bride for any hero."

Not a shudder, he realized, but a sob. All but silent. And still, she did not lift her head. Shock, perhaps. He'd seen it before, while raiding. Seen it in the boys, after they fought as men for the first time. Hippodamia was no sheltered maiden, Antiope had spoken true on that score, but she had seen her father struck down before her eyes, and had a hand in the death of the centaur who had been her guardian and childhood friend. She had seen her people lose their minds to lust and act with unspeakable violence toward the Lapiths. And all at her wedding feast, a banquet which should have been a joyous occasion. Better they had stayed at the spring. Or given in to desire, and gone straight to their marriage bed.

"I wish I were worthy of the honor," he said, more to himself than her. He pressed a kiss against the side of her head. And then he gathered her up, lifting her from the water, long since grown cold. Her skin was chilled and prickled with gooseflesh, her body stiff in his arms. "Let's get you warmed and fed."

She curled in upon herself all the tighter when he laid her upon his bed, rolling away from him with nothing more than the smallest sniff against the tears that dampened her cheeks and caused her hair to stick against her face. Pirithous sighed, sitting down beside her. How he wished he could reassure her, offer her some comfort. But the words would only be hollow, and he would not lie to her. Could not bring himself to betray her trust in that small way, even if he must turn his back upon her people.

"I know you do not wish to speak of it, or even to know it," he said, smoothing her hair back. "But I would have you hear it from me, Hippodamia, and know I take no pleasure in the telling."

She went still, and even her breathing seemed to stop.

"My people will accept nothing less than blood," he forced himself to say, the words bitter upon his tongue. "If I wish to remain king, I must give it to them."

Hippodamia rolled to her back, the first response she had yet made to his presence, but the way she looked at him, the anguish in her eyes… "Is your kingship worth so much to you? Your pride? Is it truly worth the lives of so many in exchange?"

He shook his head, unable to meet her eyes. "What do you think will happen, Mia, if I forbid this war? If I refuse them the right to take their vengeance?"

"You will save my people!"

"No!" The word came far more harshly than he meant it to, and he clenched his jaw, inhaling sharply through his nose and forcing himself to calm.

He had been over it so many times in his head, spoken at length with Theseus and Antiope, even with Nestor, though the old king had been anything but helpful. There was no other way. Their hope for peace was shattered, and if he meant to salvage anything at all, only one path lay open to him, and it was not one she would wish him to take.

"If I do as you wish, as *I* wish, I will be exiled," he said slowly, careful now to weigh his words. She must understand this, if nothing else. "If we are fortunate, perhaps they will allow you to come with me, and if it were only that, Hippodamia, I would go. I would flee with you to Athens and live on, dishonored but at peace, I swear it."

Her eyes narrowed, as if she distrusted even that. He took her hand, held her gaze, and all but willed her to believe. It was not only her father's wish for peace, after all. It had been Dia's, too. And the centaurs—perhaps they were not his kin by blood, for he was far more Zeus's son than Ixion's, but they were his responsibility, all the same. Ixion's legacy, like everything else he had been given.

"It is far more likely that they will make an example of you," he went on, though even the thought of it made him sick, souring his stomach with fear and rage. "Kill you first, as a message to your kin. And while they make war, Peleus will ready his own men. He will wait until the worst of it is over, until the Lapiths have driven the centaurs from the mountain, and the centaurs have weakened us in turn. And then he will strike. He will take our land and our horses and all our wealth, and he will turn our women and children into slaves after he slaughters our men. There will be nothing left of the Lapiths or the centaurs, either. Everything will be lost. Both our peoples, wiped from these lands."

"You cannot be certain," she said, her eyes wide, her voice so small. It was a child's denial. "You cannot be certain that is the way of it. The priest said there would be peace!"

"Paid for in blood."

"But they will have it, either way. Whether you remain as king or not, they will have their blood."

"And if I am no longer king, there is certain to be more of it spilled. Zeus will have no reason to watch over my people. The gods will forsake them, just as you fear Poseidon will forsake yours. But if I stay, Mia—if *we* stay—perhaps we can soften the blow."

She made a strangled sound, pulling her hand free from his. But at least she was sitting up now, and responsive. "You would have me stand at your side while you declare war upon my people? You would ask that of me?"

"Not war," he said quickly, watching her all the more closely now. He was not certain how she would respond, but he could not lose her. Could not stand the thought that she might join the centaurs instead, to stand against him, that it might be her head brought to him before they were through. "My people will not trust yours in word or deed, but I do. If they will leave the mountain peaceably, I will delay a hunt for as long as I am able, to give them time to go."

"And your people would be satisfied by this?" she demanded.

"They will be satisfied when I promise them a bounty for every centaur's head they bring to my hall. They will believe I wish to see them hunted to extinction, that I have joined with them in their anger. But when they begin their hunt, your people will be gone."

"Gone from the mountain, but still endangered," she accused. "If the Lapiths will not be satisfied by anything less than blood, and you promise them a prize besides, they will hunt them well beyond the mountain's slopes. And it will not only be your people who stalk them. My people will never have peace, never know safety again."

He could not argue that truth and would not insult her by trying. She was not wrong, but it was the only solution he could see. "I can limit the bounty, declare that only my people will receive a prize. And perhaps in time, they will weary of the hunt. But is this not better than outright war? At least they will have some hope of escape, of survival!"

"And why should they agree to this, Pirithous? Why should they leave their mountain at all? You do not consider their refusal, and they are not likely to be welcomed elsewhere. Not after your guests leave, and word of all this spreads."

"Because if they remain, Princess, they will die." It was cruel of him, perhaps, but what good would coddling do either of them? "Do you not see? Even this much risks more than I wish, but I will do it. For you. For those of your people who are innocent of this crime."

She lifted her chin, tears shining in her eyes. "And if I choose instead to return to my people? To stand with the guilty?"

He pressed his lips together, determined not to let her see how deeply those words cut. After only seven days, they shouldn't have. He ought to have been bored with her, by all rights. Happy that she might give him excuse to take another woman to his bed. But his heart twisted, and his hands balled into fists. "Do not make that choice."

"What good does it do me to stay, Pirithous?" The tears spilled out, and her voice caught. "What good does it do you? Your people will never trust me now, never accept a child of my body as king. I will always be looked on as the cause of all this pain."

He could feel her despair, and it made him ache all the more. "My people will know that the blame for this falls upon Peleus, Eurytion, and myself alone," he said firmly. It was no more than the truth. "They will not fault you for any of it. I will see to it, and Theseus and Antiope will grant their support to the cause. No one argues with Theseus's judgment, even if they might question mine."

She stared at him, her eyes wide as moons, all disbelief and confusion. "I don't understand."

Pirithous reached out, cupping her face in his hand and brushing the tears from her cheek with the stroke of his thumb. That she could believe even for a moment he would not do everything in his power…

"You are my wife, Hippodamia. It is both my duty and my honor to protect you, to safeguard you in your father's place. Even if I did not care for you, I would not dishonor Centaurus's memory by allowing my people to mistreat you in any way. You are their queen, both Dia's choice and mine."

CHAPTER TWENTY-SEVEN

HIPPODAMIA

She let out a shuddering breath, catching his hand and holding it tightly against her cheek. Holding him tightly. *Even if I did not care for you.*

"You cannot have doubted me?" He spoke so gently she thought she must have imagined it. Pirithous could never be so insecure, so worried of what another might think of him. "I know I have been a fool, Hippodamia, but you must realize I have no desire to give you up. Indeed, it has been my fear that has driven me."

"A son of Zeus, afraid?" she asked, baffled that she might have caused him any such emotion. He was so sure of himself, always. So confident. "What could you possibly have to fear?"

"Surely I do not fool you so completely?" His smile was strange, as if he laughed at himself. "I feared you would leave me, Mia. For the first time in my life, I feared a woman had seen what I offered and found me wanting all the same. Not worth even the peace I might bring you, and now—" He turned his face away, his hand slipping from beneath hers as he did so. As if he could not look at her, his shame was so great. "Now I cannot even give you that."

"Pirithous—"

He held up his hand, stopping her, and when he met her eyes again, she could see his resolve. "You asked what good you might do me by remaining, and I do not know the answer. But I can tell you what good I might do you, if you stay. Perhaps I cannot promise the peace our parents desired, but no harm will ever come to you while you live as my wife. I will give you children. As many as you wish. And I will take no other woman to my bed without your full blessing. I will shower you in gold and silver and jewels. I will even give up my raiding, but for reasons of dire need, to remain at your side. And I will beg of you, Mia, if I must. Beg you to stay, to be my queen. I did not know it at first, could not see why Dia chose you, but I understand it now. There is no other woman I could trust, no woman better suited to the duty. If it is not you, the Lapiths will have no queen at all."

He said it all so fiercely, as solemnly as any vow, and it was clear he meant it. All of it. But he could mean every word, and it would not matter if his people did not approve. Kings were not kings simply because they were born princes. Centaurus had taught her that, and Pirithous himself had now confirmed it.

"Will your people accept me?" she asked, though she hated that she must. "Truly, Pirithous. No matter what it is that you desire, do you truly believe they will trust me as you do?"

"In time." His eyes flashed lightning white, his jaw going tight. "I will make it so, I promise you. And in this one thing, I will not be denied. If they wish for a queen, it must be you. If we had not married already, perhaps it would be different. But we have, and with Zeus's blessing. The priest will say as much."

She was not certain the worth of such a blessing when it had only brought them bloodshed and war, but she did not dare speak such blasphemy aloud.

"Do not give up on me so quickly, Princess. Give me time to make this right."

She shook her head, hating to see him so desperate as this. He was a son of Zeus and a king, and in the end, he must act in the interest of his people. That was his duty, more than even what he owed his wife. And that he blamed himself for Eurytion's foolishness… "It is no more your fault than it is mine, Pirithous. I stood beside you at the shrine. I went to Eurytion in the night, and perhaps if I hadn't, perhaps if I had remained in my room, we might never have argued."

He smiled sadly, stroking her cheek. "I think he would have found excuse enough, regardless. He was determined, Mia. From the first, I knew he would be trouble to us. To Centaurus, too."

From the first. "That was why you shamed me," she realized, catching his hand by the wrist and stopping his caress. "That first day, at the shrine. When you made me speak of my affections. It was not only for your pride, then, was it?"

His lips pressed thin, his expression guarded. "I knew he coveted you. And I hoped that if you denounced his affections, he might resign himself to our match. It was not, perhaps, the kindest way, but I felt it needful."

"I hated you for it!"

His eyes crinkled at the corners. "Happily, it did not last."

"But you couldn't have known I would forgive you. And what would you have done if I hadn't? Taken me to wife and endured?"

"What is a shrewish wife in exchange for peace?" he teased, lips curving. It was not quite a smile, but it was no less smug. "You are not the first woman to scorn me, little mouse, though I hope very much you will be the last whose affections I must win for my people's sake."

"Just theirs?" He was insufferable, truly, but his teasing reassured her all the same.

"For mine, too," he admitted, pressing a kiss against her knuckles. "But I did not realize it then." Pirithous met her gaze and held it, his gray eyes beseeching. "Tell me you will stay, Mia. That I need not fear it will be your head brought to me in exchange for a prize. Tell me you will stand at my side as queen."

She wished she could. In that moment, his eyes upon her, she wished so much that none of this had happened. That Eurytion had never come, and the only displeasure of their wedding feast was the waiting until they might slip away to their marriage bed.

She wished she could, but she did not see how. For all that he might promise her, and all that he might give, she was not certain she could live with herself if she accepted. And to live her life among a people who hated her own, hunted them down? Even for love?

But Pirithous had been very careful not to promise her that, and the realization twisted her heart just as much as the rest.

"I'm sorry," she said softly, dropping her gaze.

His fingers tightened around hers. "Then we must at least enjoy the time we have left."

It wasn't the response she had expected, and the way he said it sent a shiver down her spine. Nothing about his words spoke of surrender, of resignation or sorrow. He was all self-assurance now. Confidence and determination.

He had not given her up.

But if not because of love, then why?

***

It was a subtle campaign, Hippodamia decided. He made no demands upon her that night, only held her in his arms, stroking her hair and soothing her grief. His kisses were soft, all affection and kindness. Like the first they had shared, when Centaurus had put her hand in his before the palace gates.

But of course, that reminded her that her father was gone, and when the tears welled up, then spilled, Pirithous hushed her gently, brushing them away with a tenderness that surprised her.

"Tell me," he murmured, nuzzling her ear. "Let me help."

And so she spoke, haltingly, of her argument with Centaurus. Of the way she had dismissed his wisdom, though she did not say precisely what it was he had warned. What she had done was awful enough without insulting Pirithous, as well. And what good would it do to reveal her loyalty, so foolishly misplaced? It would only give him hope for what she was no longer certain they could ever have.

"What rites would you have performed?" Pirithous asked, when she had finished. "I will see them done, for Centaurus deserves the honors, one king to another, and I would not have you feel that you have not done your duty."

"I would see his body cleansed and anointed myself, but it must be returned to my people, Pirithous. He must be given up to them, that he might return, too, to the mountain itself."

He pressed his lips together, his gaze growing distant. "Perhaps Theseus and Antiope might do us that kindness. And deliver my bargain to Cyllarus, besides. Your people are much less likely to strike at Poseidon's son on such an errand, and mine will recognize the wisdom of it far more readily if the suggestion comes from Theseus's lips."

She knew it was true, but she hated the thought. Hated that she could not see her father's body given back to the Horse Lord. "Is there no way I might accompany them?"

"If you do, and the centaurs disappear from the mountain, my people will believe you betrayed them by giving warning."

"And will they not think the same of Theseus?"

"After he and Antiope fought so fiercely for the Lapiths?" He shook his head. "Even if they had given only a token wave of their swords, there is not a man in Achaea who would dare speak such slander against the king of Athens. Not when he is known so well for his judgment and wisdom. If Theseus sees fit to warn them, and perhaps some might whisper it is so, they will think it is proof of his greatness, not a reason for mistrust."

She bit her lip on her reply, rolling away from him in the bed. What good would it do to object? To remind him that she had fought against the centaurs too, had helped to kill Eurytion as he had carried her away? What difference did it make at all if his people would not trust her, even after she had defended them and sent the centaurs back up the mountain? She was not even certain she would stay.

But it stung, all the same.

"You cannot be angry that they love Theseus?" he said, shifting to lean over her. His hand found her waist, his thumb caressing. "He is the hero of Attica! Of course they would trust him, after all he's done."

"Of course," she said, staring at the plaster wall, painted with horses racing along a plain. "But they will not trust me, though I have fought at your side. Just as you did not trust me the night before we were wed. Always, they will look for my failures, my mistakes, and hold them against me, see them as proof that I am disloyal and unworthy of their king."

He pressed a kiss to the point of her shoulder. "Only time will change that. Once they come to know you, it will be different. You need only stay. Show them where your loyalties lie. Stand at my side long enough, and they will stop seeing you as the daughter of the centaurs, and begin to see you as a woman, instead. As their queen."

"Stay, and smile proudly when they roll the heads of my kin across the painted floor? Lie to them with every breath to prove I am worthy of their trust?"

Pirithous sighed, lying back on the bed. "I would not ask that of you."

"Perhaps you wouldn't, but your people will. And if I turn away from the sight, they will think I am weak, see it as betrayal."

"We are married, Mia. You are bound to me. To them. They will see that you do your duty, that you are loyal to that binding and faithful to the gods. You judge them too harshly."

"If they believe that in returning my father's body to his people I will betray them, even after I have fought to protect them, how am I wrong?"

He made a low noise of frustration at her back. "Even if Eurytion had not struck at us today, my people would not have loved you overnight. Would you have been so offended by their mistrust then? Demanded they give you what you had not yet earned with your deeds? They have known you for only a sevenday,

Mia! And at that, little of it was spent in their company. They will not trust you simply because you were made their queen."

Her face flushed, and she sat up, throwing the linens off. "Do you think it was nothing to me to strike at Eurytion? Is that not deed enough, that I turned against my own when they acted unjustly?"

"You were attacked," he said. "Of course you would defend yourself! But you expect them to understand what they cannot know. To them, Eurytion is just another centaur. They do not know he protected you from childhood, serving as your guard and guardian, nor can they realize how you trusted him, even cared for him. To see him murder your father..." He caught her by the hand, tugging her back down. "Mia, they do not know what they witnessed. And how will they know, fully, what you have suffered, the loyalty you showed, if you do not stay to explain it to them?"

Always it returned to this, and even as she let him settle her at his side, allowed her body to soften against his, her thoughts raced. By law, she belonged to Pirithous now. She was his to protect, to lock away, if he desired it. But their marriage had also been a covenant of peace, one she was bound to honor. Remaining at his side while his people hunted hers could not be the right choice. Certainly it would not bring peace.

By all rights, she should have left with Cyllarus and Hylonome. Should have led her people back to the mountains, never to return. The priests would have been persuaded to void their marriage. After the spilling of so much blood, they ought to have been wringing their hands, begging Pirithous to give her up. A quick death. A sacrifice to appease the gods. No doubt it was only Pirithous's will that prevented it.

"Will explaining change anything?" she asked. "Will it stop them from hunting my kin? Sate their lust for blood and vengeance?"

He was silent for a moment, long enough to prove his uncertainty. "Surely you owe it to your people to try? Leaving us—

that is a simple thing. But there will be no coming back, if you do. I would not have you regret it, as I know I will."

"Because you believe I am the only worthy queen for your people," she said, the words bitter on her tongue.

"Is that not reason enough?"

For him, perhaps it was, but it only made her heart ache that much more for the things he did not say. Did not feel.

What if her father had been right?

If she stayed, and he never loved her, and her people still died, would she not regret that more?

"Sleep, Mia," Pirithous said, tucking her head beneath his chin. "Perhaps in the morning light, our path forward will be that much clearer."

CHAPTER TWENTY-EIGHT

PIRITHOUS

He didn't take his own advice, but lay awake in the bed long after he had pushed Hippodamia's frustrations toward exhaustion and sleep. She needed rest, and he did not feel the slightest bit guilty using his power to encourage it. Not when she clearly turned the same arguments and worries over and over again in her thoughts.

It wasn't that her fears were without merit. He understood them well enough, even worried at them himself. But nothing could be solved by talk, only action, and for that they both must wait until morning.

He cursed Eurytion silently for bringing all this to the fore. And what would he do if the centaurs did not accept his offer? What would he do if instead, the Lapiths hunted Mia's people to their doom?

Pirithous snorted at himself and forced the thoughts away. He was no better than his wife, agonizing over things he could not control.

Except… perhaps he could, in some small way. Perhaps Theseus would, on his behalf. In the megaron, the others had looked to Cyllarus, allowed him to speak on their behalf. If any small part of Cyllarus wanted peace, wanted to protect his people, surely Theseus could inflame those feelings, encourage them to blossom into action and acceptance. Pirithous did not dare to risk influencing his own people in such a way, but if Theseus could only drive the centaurs from the mountain, surely it would do more good than harm in the end.

He lost nothing by asking. Antiope would not approve, of course, but neither would she wish Hippodamia to suffer needlessly.

No one who knew Hippodamia could ever wish her ill. Even Eurytion had acted, in some small part, out of what he believed to be her interests. To save her from a loveless marriage to a pirate king who would only dishonor her.

And perhaps Eurytion was not so wrong after all, though Pirithous hated to admit it, even to himself. Hippodamia deserved better. She deserved the peace she had traded herself for, at the very least. The respect of the people she ruled, as well. By all rights, he ought to have been able to give her that much. The Lapiths should have loved her—would have had no reason not to, if not for the fool centaur.

If only Centaurus had lived.

If only Eurytion had never come.

If only he could trick his own mind as easily as he had Hippodamia's, and put himself to sleep to break the pattern of his thoughts.

Pirithous closed his eyes and inhaled deeply, catching the scent of rose petals from Hippodamia's hair. How she still smelled of the spring he did not know, but his body stirred in answer. He wanted her, to be sure, every soft movement of her body against his reminding him of the sweetness of what they had shared. But for once, perhaps even for the first time, it was not desire which overwhelmed his senses. His need for her did not build into an ache, impossible to ignore, but rather, with each caress of her breath against his skin, each unconscious shift of her body, searching for his, it seemed to quiet.

He could not lose her. Even if the peace between them, so newly won, had been shattered, he would not give her up. And more, he would have it back. Would have *her* back, and no more of this talk of leaving. She was his wife, their union witnessed by Aphrodite herself, and he would not surrender her so easily. The time for fear was done, and she had bound herself to him willingly. Every law, sacred or otherwise, supported his right to her now.

Tomorrow, he promised himself. The new day would dawn, and he would make his wishes known. Hippodamia was his, and she would remain so, no matter what became of her people.

It was the only way *he* would have any peace.

***

A knock on the door brought him awake, though Hippodamia slept on, curled against his side. He slid his arm out from beneath her head, glad for all his practice if it meant she would not be disturbed, and rose.

"My lord?" his steward called, his voice low.

"A moment," Pirithous said, glancing back at Hippodamia, her brown legs tangled in the bedding. Leaving her made him ache, and he wanted nothing more than to wake her with slow kisses, tease her to whimpering completion before she opened her eyes.

But she was not likely to welcome his desire, and he did not trust himself if she refused him. So instead, he belted a kilt to his waist and stepped out into the hall.

"My lord, I thought you should know there is agitation over the bodies."

"What bodies?"

"The centaurs, my lord. The men want to desecrate their remains."

Pirithous swore. Of course they would, maddened by heartbreak and grief. And he had not even thought to guard them. If Centaurus's body was polluted—

"I will see that the bodies come to no harm. Go to King Theseus. Drag him from the arms of his queen if you must, but rouse him and tell him what you have told me, and that I require his judgment in this matter."

"Yes, my lord," the steward said, bowing quickly.

Pirithous did not watch him go, slipping back inside his room with the silence of a shadow. He dared not wake Hippodamia now, but he needed his sword and his crown, if nothing else. Reminders of his authority, both. And he must hurry. Judging by the light, it was well past dawn. He had slept much later than he had meant to, giving his people far too long to dwell on their losses without direction. Theseus would have absented himself out of respect, to allow Pirithous's voice to rule without interference and give the Lapiths time to grieve in privacy.

He pulled his sword from the brackets on the wall, and collected his golden circlet from the table beside the bed. Hippodamia stirred, rolling toward the place where he had been. He paused only long enough to press a kiss to her forehead and persuade her mind into deeper sleep once more. Better if this were settled before she woke, and that the ruling came without her voice.

He left her, slipping the sword onto his belt after the door had shut behind him. A king did not run through the halls, but he moved with swift purpose all the same. They had cleared the bodies from the megaron and the courtyard, piling them within the inner yard on the far side from the stables and roping the area off to keep the horses away.

His men were already there.

"King Pirithous!" Plouteus greeted him with a smile, rope looped over his shoulder. "We thought to string them up to teach the boys where to strike. We will not be caught unawares again."

"Indeed, we will not." It was Eurytion, his black hide matted and smeared with blood and gore. There were ropes already wrapped around his hooves. Pirithous drew his sword, slicing the bonds from the flesh. "But nor will we offend the gods with barbarism."

"They are nothing more than beasts!" Plouteus spluttered. "What offense can it give?"

"The centaurs belong to Poseidon." He met his noble's eye, holding his gaze until the man looked away. "I will not bring the fury of the Earth Shaker down upon my people. Not this day, and not for these reasons."

"And how are we to learn to protect ourselves?" one of the other men called out, Kotullon. His father had been one of the men lost in the fighting, and Pirithous could not blame him for his anger, but even so.

Even so.

"This centaur's name was Eurytion," Pirithous said, his voice cool. "He was Queen Hippodamia's guardian during her youth, charged with her protection. When he fought yesterday, it was for her protection still, misguided though he might have been. She helped to slay him with her own hand, though until that moment she had counted him the dearest of friends. These centaurs are Our kin twice over. Once through Queen Hippodamia, and once through Ixion and me, your kings. Will you deny it?"

Kotullon's hands balled into fists. "He led the charge against us, goaded the others on!"

"*Peleus* goaded them," Pirithous corrected him sharply. "But even if a brother betrays you, his murder does not come without sin, without penalty and price. Will you bring the anger of the gods upon the head of your wife, your child, your widowed mother? Have they not suffered enough already? Lost enough?"

"You only stop us because of *her*," Kotullon mumbled.

"Say it again, Kotullon." Pirithous ground his teeth, lifting his sword. "Look me in the eye and say it once more."

"My lord, he does not know what he says," Plouteus said, catching the boy by the shoulder before he could respond. Kotullon's jaw was working, his face flushed, but he kept his eyes downcast. A sulking child.

And that was all it was, Pirithous thought. A boy's sulk. But it did not change how he must respond. "Then he should not speak at all. And let it be known now, I will suffer no slight to the queen. What happened at the banquet does not change that we are married. She is mine, and all matters of her honor touch my own. Queen Hippodamia is owed our respect and our kindness, and I will tolerate nothing less from my people. Am I understood?"

"Yes, my lord. Of course!" Plouteus bowed. "We meant no disrespect to the queen. It is only—the things she said, the promises she made to the centaurs—surely she spoke out of turn? Without your blessing?"

"Queen Hippodamia acted in the interests of us all," Pirithous growled. "Or would you have preferred to keep fighting? For your own blood to stain the floor of the megaron?"

"She promised them we would not follow, that they might leave in peace," Plouteus pressed.

"And so they did. Who of us, at that moment, wished to pursue them?" He kept his response carefully neutral. "We needed time to see to our dead, and Queen Hippodamia gave us that, and more."

"There," Plouteus said, squeezing Kotullon's shoulder. "You see, Kotullon? It is as I said. King Pirithous is with us, and Queen Hippodamia is his tool, that is all."

Pirithous bared his teeth, his hand tightening around the hilt of his sword. "Was Dia the tool of Ixion?"

"My lord—" Plouteus took a step back, his eyes going wide.

"Was she?" Pirithous demanded. He felt the lightning in his veins, the spark of it dancing along the edge of his sword. "Would you have dared speak of her so dismissively? She who sheltered you, protected you from Ixion and his madness? Guided you and led you to prosperity after his death?"

"N-no, my lord. Of c-course not."

"And the woman Dia chose to lead you upon her death, do you think she would choose one only to be my tool? To be used by me and cast aside so easily?"

"B-but the peace—" Plouteus stumbled over Eurytion's legs, pulling Kotullon with him nearly to the ground as he fought to right himself.

"Perhaps you think I am bewitched by my bride," Pirithous said evenly. "But do you think Dia would be so easily taken in? That she would marry her only son to a witch, no matter what the centaurs offered in exchange?"

"No," Theseus said from behind him. He clasped Pirithous's shoulder, and relief flooded him as it never had before, a wave of calm washing over him on its heels. Theseus's calm. His power. "Sheathe your sword, my friend. We are all unsettled by what has come to pass, but I would not give Eurytion's shade the satisfaction of knowing he turns us against one another."

Pirithous snorted, eyeing the centaur's corpse with distaste as he put his sword away. He thought it far more likely that Peleus had hoped for such an outcome more than Eurytion. "I cannot say I am not glad of your wisdom, Theseus. And your friendship, now. Antiope still sleeps?"

"She offers your queen what comfort she may," Theseus said, nodding to the men who stood idle. "I cannot begin to imagine the depths of her grief. To lose her father, find herself betrayed by her protector, and see the peace she worked so hard to build lost with the deaths of her new people as well as the old—you were wise to send her to her bed, Pirithous. Now what is all this? Surely your men would not insult their queen's honor by defiling the bodies of her kin?"

"No, King Theseus," Plouteus said, his face flushing. "Of course not."

"It is only right and proper to allow them the opportunity to collect their dead," Theseus said, frowning. "But I cannot blame your people for not wishing the centaurs to return, nor would I permit them within my walls, if I were king. Would you allow me to be of service to both your peoples? Let me arrange for the disposal of their bodies. Antiope and I can see them taken up the mountain, where the centaurs might claim them peaceably."

"You would have my thanks," Pirithous agreed. "Speak with Hippodamia upon the matter. She can tell you where best to leave them. And if you would be so kind as to deliver them a message from me, as well?"

"All the better to have the protection of Hermes on this errand, though I must admit I do not think the centaurs are likely to strike at us."

"Certainly you will be much safer than any of my people, but we cannot afford Poseidon's ire, and I will not refuse Centaurus the honors he is due, one king to another, no matter what his people have done. He surely sanctioned none of it, after working so long for peace."

"Anyone who believes otherwise is a fool," Theseus said, his gaze flicking to the men surrounding them. "Plouteus, perhaps you will show me where I might find a cart for the task I have been set?"

Plouteus bowed deeply. "Certainly, King Theseus. It would be my honor to serve you."

"And Kotullon, if you would speak to the horsemaster? Machaon is his name, is it not? I will need a steady team for the work."

The younger man glanced first at Pirithous, as was proper, since the horses belonged to him, but when he gave his nod, Kotullon bowed as well, and left.

"Those of you who wish to help King Theseus load the cart, stay, but he will not wish to have others underfoot," Pirithous said, after Plouteus had guided Theseus away. "We could use more wood for our pyres, if you wish to be of use. The funeral games begin at dusk, and I mean for the fires to burn like beacons in the night."

Then he left them, too. Guarding the remains would only convince them he had sided with their enemy and undo all Theseus had accomplished with his easy manner. What he would have done without his support…

Likely Kotullon would have lost his head, and Plouteus would have spread the word of the king's madness. By evening, his people would have believed him Ixion come again, and he would have been fortunate to keep his throne. Pirithous shook his head, cursing his own foolishness. It was one thing to act rashly while Dia ruled, another altogether to lose his temper now. They would think it Hippodamia's influence, and all the more so when he took offense so easily on her behalf.

"Perhaps I was wrong, King Pirithous," Nestor said, when he reached the courtyard on his way back to his rooms. "The way you defend your queen, I begin to think you may have married for love, after all."

The polite smile he had meant to give in greeting froze upon his face, and Pirithous found himself rooted to the earth. "How could I have, when Dia arranged all? I had not even met my bride until my mother's funeral banquet, but seven days ago."

"A sevenday during which, it seems, you spent little time apart."

He shrugged, forcing a lightness into his words which he did not feel. "She swore she could never care for me, and I found the challenge of winning her a pleasant distraction."

Nestor laughed, clapping him on the back. "Tell yourself that, lad, if you must. But it will not change the difficulties which face you now, and I do not think even your loyal King Theseus will have the power to save you in the eyes of your new wife."

Chapter Twenty-Nine

Hippodamia

A *pleasant distraction.* Hippodamia slipped back into the shadows of the stairwell and shut her eyes against the sting of tears. Her nails bit into her palms, her whole body flushing with humiliation. That was all she was to him, all she had ever been, and she was a fool to have believed anything else, even for a moment. Centaurus had been right. So right.

Pirithous excused himself from Nestor with a derisive laugh, mumbling something about bread and cold meats and keeping his bride's strength up, and her stomach twisted, bile rising in the back of her throat. Gods above, but she had known. She had known from the start this was what she had agreed to, so why did it make her want to heave up her empty stomach now?

"Mia?" Antiope said, catching up to her. She'd gone back to her own room for something; Hippodamia didn't remember why. No longer cared at all. "Are you ill?"

"I was just a challenge. A distraction."

Antiope pressed a hand to her forehead. "Perhaps you should rest, yet. Pirithous is sure to return before long."

She shook her head. He'd told her himself, when she'd declared herself incapable of loving him. She'd realized then that he'd taken it as a challenge. But she'd thought—and why should she have thought it at all? They'd only had seven days. Just as Pirithous had said. How could she expect him to love her in just seven days, regardless? It was a dream. From that first kiss on the plain with the horses, to the time they had spent at the spring. A dream turned to nightmare upon waking.

"I don't want to see him," she heard herself say, her voice strange. "I can't."

"Mia, you cannot blame him. If war comes, he has no choice but to win. It is his duty, and his people asked for none of this."

She swallowed, opening her eyes at last. Antiope's gaze was warm with concern and sympathy, but it did nothing to ease her feelings. "We never should have married. I thought I had resigned myself, but not to this. Not to any of this."

Antiope sighed, cupping her cheek. "You should not blame yourself, Hippodamia. Or your marriage. Pirithous did what he believed was right, and so did you. If you had delayed, it would have insulted more than Eurytion."

"I'm nothing to him, Antiope. I bring nothing without this peace, and how quickly I gave in to him, how easily I gave myself up!" She jerked free, running up the stairs, back to her room. Away from Pirithous, who had gone to the kitchens, and Antiope, who had married for a love beyond anything Hippodamia would ever know. Because she was just a game to Pirithous. A pleasant diversion. And what use would he have for her now?

There was no greater distraction than war, and Eurytion had given him that. Or did he mean to use her as his noble excuse? To claim that whatever came was only in defense of her honor, all the while knowing she would give up even that for the safety of her people. Hadn't she already? At the shrine, when he shamed her. And for nothing. For nothing at all, for Eurytion had still come for her, still tried to take her from him. To free her from him.

Perhaps she should have let him. There was no hope of peace, and Centaurus…

She barred her bedroom door behind her, slumping back against it. Antiope called to her, voice low and urgent, but she said nothing, did nothing. She had remained to honor her father's memory, his desire for peace, but if there was no hope of peace, what purpose did it serve to stay? What purpose could she serve if she was nothing more than a challenge to Pirithous? He would hardly respect her opinions, listen to her counsel! Centaurus had been blinded by his dream, and she, even more so.

Pirithous had blinded her, but now she could see.

***

She gathered her belongings, what few she had, wrapping them in the bundle of her tunic. All the gold and silver, all Pirithous's gifts, she left behind. Their weight would only slow her, and she had no need of baubles on the mountain.

"Hippodamia, please," Antiope said. "Am I not your friend? Will you not let me help you?"

She hesitated, hugging the bundle to her stomach. Antiope. She would miss Antiope. And if she owed anyone an explanation, it was the Amazon queen. The wife of the Horse Lord's son. Perhaps Antiope would even help her, though Theseus surely wouldn't. He was too loyal to Pirithous.

She crossed to the door, bundle still in her arms, and unbarred it. Antiope pushed it open at once, shutting it firmly behind her again before staring hard into her eyes.

"I'm leaving," Hippodamia said, not waiting for her to speak. "I will not remain here as queen to a people who mistrust me, or as wife to a man who has deceived me from the first moment."

"It is not easy, I know," Antiope said gently, holding out her hands in friendship. "Perhaps I do not know what it is to be deceived into love, but I know the struggle of being queen to a people who distrust everything that I am."

Hippodamia hugged herself harder, giving Antiope the same distance she would a poisonous snake. "And perhaps if I had Pirithous's love and admiration as you have Theseus's, it would be different."

"You are so certain he cares nothing for you." She let her hands fall, and her eyes darkened with sorrow. "Do you think so little of yourself, Hippodamia, that you do not see how worthy you are? This is the trouble with the world of men, the way they teach women to doubt, to see themselves as such small creatures. But you burn so brightly, and you are so wrong to think you bring nothing to this marriage beyond the peace between your peoples. Were Dia living still, she would laugh at such a thought!"

"But Dia is dead, just as my father is," she said, the words sharp on her tongue. "Let their shades laugh or weep, it hardly matters now."

Antiope drew back, shock written clearly in the lifting of her brows. "You let your grief speak for you."

"Better than letting foolish dreams blind me to the truth." Hippodamia's hands fisted in the fabric of her bundle. "I thought to ask you for your aid, but I see now I was wrong to believe you might help me."

"Help you to leave?" Antiope barked a laugh. "Why would I, when it will serve nothing but your death? When it would mean another woman, a weaker woman, made queen in your place? No! I am Amazon still, Hippodamia. I would not see Dia's legacy destroyed so easily as that."

She had been so wrong. So wrong in so many ways.

"We were never friends," she said, surprised at how deeply it cut. "You only wanted a strong queen. A woman who might rule in partnership with a man, as his equal, perhaps even his better."

"No, Mia." Antiope's lips thinned, and she reached out, but Hippodamia stepped back. "Yes, I hoped you might lead, that in Thessaly at least, women might keep what little power they had won. But that is not all. How could it be all?"

Wasn't it? How could she trust any of it? Any of them. There was a reason centaurs did not mingle with men. A reason they kept to themselves and their mares. Humans were snakes. Liars and thieves and manipulators, no matter their sex. "If that is what you wished, your dream is dead too. Better another woman take my place, one born of these people. I'm certain you can teach her the strength she requires."

"If you leave, they'll only hunt you! Can you not see how much pain that would cause us all? Would you drive Pirithous into madness, like Ixion? You think he does not care for you, but you are wrong. We all do! And I promise you, if you leave him, you will cost him his crown. Exiled, he will be worse than powerless. There will be no one to stop the Lapiths from slaughtering your kin, then."

"Mia?"

Pirithous. She could hear him now, the scuff of his sandal upon the tiles. When he wished to, he could move as soundlessly as a leopard, and she could only thank the gods he gave her as much warning as this.

She made for the door, but Antiope reached it first, holding it fast. Hippodamia shoved at her, grasped the handle and heaved.

"I will not let you do this, Mia."

Antiope might as well have been stone, and no matter how much of her life she had spent in exercise, Hippodamia would never have the strength of a daughter of Ares. Never have strength enough at all, and that, too, was another reason to go.

Antiope did not move even a finger's width, and her voice was low and hoarse. "Out of love for you, I cannot."

"Theseus has agreed to take the dead to your people. He waits only for you to anoint your father's—" Pirithous stopped, and Hippodamia did not need to turn to know he had pushed open the door from the baths and seen them. Seen her, clutching her bundle, tearing at the door.

Tears rose, flooding her sight until everything blurred. "Please," she begged, though she did not know to whom, or for what. "Please."

And then Pirithous had her, his hand closing upon her shoulder, spreading warmth down her arm. She tore herself from his grasp and ran, grateful for her tears now, glad that she could not see his face. If she could only make it through the bathing room, she could bar his door on the other side. She need only reach the stables, reach Podarkes, and he would never catch her.

"Hippodamia, stop!" He was faster. She had forgotten how fast, for she had not even reached the tubs before he caught her again, fingers tight around her arm, just above the elbow, jerking her back. "Gods above, girl! Have you gone mad?"

"Let go!" She struggled against his hold, but he only lifted her off her feet.

"What's happened?" he demanded, though his head had turned back to her room, to Antiope. As if she were not there, in his arms, fighting against his hold. "If that fool steward opened his mouth—"

"And tell me what?" she cried. "That I was nothing more than a *pleasant distraction* for his king? A challenge to his pride he wished to conquer?" She freed one hand and slapped him.

"Ow!" He nearly dropped her, and even through her tears she could see astonishment in his wide eyes. But he only took a firmer grip upon her wrists, even if her feet touched the floor, and dragged her back into her room. "Who whispered such bile in your ear, wildling, that you would take it so to heart? You know what you are!"

"I know the sweetness of your tongue, the lies you weave so carefully while you ply me with pleasure. Nothing more!"

He shook his head, his gaze shifting to Antiope, still standing at the door. "I cannot believe this of you, but who else's words would carry such weight?"

"I do not know," Antiope said. "I left her to find my sandals, and when I met her again at the stairs, she was frozen with it. She would only say that she was just a challenge, a distraction."

"When?"

"Not long ago. I thought I heard Nestor in the courtyard, but why would he say such a thing?"

Pirithous swore, the viciousness of his curses startling her back. And this time, he released her. So suddenly she half-fell upon the bed, but she did not waste time before finding her feet again.

"*Your* words, Pirithous. Your words, like knives through my heart. I should have listened to Eurytion. To my father! But I wanted so much to believe better. To dream." She grabbed up her bundle, dropped in her struggle against him. Pirithous watched her, eyes narrowed. "I'll spare you the trouble of ridding me from your bed by leaving it now. Cyllarus will need my help, and as you said, I was their princess. Now I will be their queen."

Chapter Thirty

Pirithous

If she thought for a moment—but she did, that was obvious. She thought he would simply agree to let her go.

"No."

She stiffened, lifting her chin. The tears were dry, now, and her eyes flashed. "I'm certain the priests will release you from this ill-fated marriage. It will be nothing to turn the bloodshed of yesterday into a message from the gods."

Pirithous shook his head. "Antiope, I would speak with my wife alone."

For once, the Amazon queen did not argue, though the look she gave Hippodamia, filled with grief and longing, did not escape his notice. Something more had happened between them, but he had not the time to spare for it. Not while she stood before him, demanding the right to return to her people. He waited only for the door to close behind Antiope, though no doubt she stood yet at the other side, listening. All the better if she heard, and gave Theseus the news, so he would not have to repeat himself later.

"I have no interest in being released from the bonds of this marriage, Hippodamia." She drew a breath, but he lifted his hand, silencing her with a hard look. And if his eyes burned with his father's lightning, all to the good. "Centaurus placed your hand in mine, and there it will remain."

"For your pride," she accused, her lip curling.

"By my desire!" His hands balled into fists, and it took all his will not to grab her and shake her until she understood. "You are *mine* by sacred law and right. My wife and my queen. With Aphrodite's blessing, besides!"

"Aphrodite!" She whirled, then spun back again, hurling the small bundle at his head. "How dare you use her name!"

He caught it easily, tossing it aside, even as he longed to reach for her. "You were willing, Hippodamia. Do not deny it, now! You wanted me as much as I wanted you."

"And if I have no desire for you now? If I refuse you, what then? Will you still insist upon keeping me? Lock me in my room as a prize, until I wither away? If it is only your desire which drives you, what use am I then?"

"You twist my words," he growled. "Are you so determined to find misery here? Have I not treated you with all honor and respect? Given you pleasure beyond any you might have hoped for in some centaur's arms?"

"My people have need of me, pleasure or not. Would you have me turn from them? Would you turn from yours?"

"It does not matter," he said. That she asked him that, after all he had promised her the night before—how could she not see that he had turned his back upon his own people for her, already? How could she believe he did not do everything in his power to save hers? For her sake! For her love! "The choice is not yours to make, not any longer."

"I am not Lapith, that by marriage you might own me, Pirithous."

"Do you defy even the laws of the gods, then? Are your people so savage as that?"

She flew at him, hands balled into fists, a strangled cry slipping from her lips. He let her strike him, let her pound her fists against his chest with a force so surprising he stepped back, bracing himself against her fury.

"I hate you!"

Those words—they lodged themselves in his heart, bruising far more than her fists. He swallowed against the tightness in his throat, the pain of knowing she no longer wanted what he might give. But all the same. He would have her know. He would have her hear the words, even if she did not believe them. He scarcely could himself.

"And I love you too much to let you die."

***

Antiope waited outside the door, just as he had thought, her face grave. "She will not sit quietly in her rooms."

"No," he agreed, closing the door firmly behind him. Hippodamia had exhausted herself between pummeling him, weeping, and fighting, and in truth, he was worn thin, too. Pleasure may not have tired him, but this did, this love for her she would not accept. Far more than he wished to admit. "Are you with me, Antiope?"

"Like you, I would not see her throw her life away for a cause that is lost already. Nor see your people lose a worthy queen."

"Will you guard her?" He did not know who else to ask. Who else he could trust. And perhaps Antiope might reason with her in ways he could not. "If I let her go, my people will believe they were betrayed, beginning to end. They will think Centaurus fooled Dia, and that Hippodamia deceived me. It will be war then, open and bloody."

"If you let her go, she will die. After Eurytion, her people will not trust her any more than yours."

He let out a breath, but it did nothing to ease the tightness around his heart. He had not even considered how her people might respond. "Perhaps if you tell her so, she will believe it. She trusts nothing I say, now."

"It must be grief."

"I can only pray." But he was not sure he believed it. Without trust, their marriage served nothing. It had been so from the start, and Eurytion's attack had not helped matters.

"I will watch her, Pirithous." Antiope touched his arm, and when he met her eyes, they held no sharpness. Only sympathy. "And you can be sure I will do everything in my power to keep her safe."

He nodded. "When she wakes, she must see to Centaurus's body. Send for me, and perhaps between the two of us we will keep her from escape."

Her lips curved. "She is fleet and strong. If you were anything less than a son of Zeus, she would have slipped from your reach already."

"If I were anything less than a son of Zeus, she would have been right to go." And then he left her. There was much yet to do, and if he did not address his people soon, and clearly, they would go to war without him.

As it was, he was not certain he could stop them.

He was even less certain he wished to.

***

"We await the queen's direction," Theseus said, meeting him in the megaron. "And I've set one of the younger boys to watch the carts. Should any of your people grow restless, we will know of it."

Pirithous had already sent runners to find and gather his nobles, and now he took his seat upon the dais to wait for their arrival. Theseus stood beside him, a forgotten coil of rope in his hands, which he twitched absently against his thigh.

"Antiope is still above?" he asked.

Pirithous grimaced. "Hippodamia is… unwell. Your wife was kind enough to sit with her, that she would not wake alone."

Theseus's eyes narrowed. "She has great affection for your bride."

"Indeed." Pirithous stared into the hearth fire, watching the jump and flicker of the flames. "I only hope Antiope's friendship might grant her some peace. But I fear Hippodamia was right—we have lost much."

"Too much?" Theseus asked.

"Perhaps."

Theseus limited himself to a grunt in response, no doubt because Plouteus had arrived, with a handful of the others. They presented themselves to Pirithous, bowing with all appearance of respect, and Pirithous nodded stiffly back, wishing Dia still lived. That he had been king in more than just name for longer than seven days. He ought not to have left the ruling of his people to his mother for so long, or at the least, he ought to have stood at her side with greater frequency, to understand his duties more fully before she had gone.

But if he had stood beside her, it would have been his judgment the people looked for, and how could he have given it when he knew so little, and cared even less? He was not Theseus, renowned for his wisdom. Nor had he inherited Dia's serenity and perception. He knew how to fight, how to raid and rustle and thieve. But to command more than a small band, made up of men he knew as brothers? And as more than brothers when there had been need.

Perhaps it would have been different if Eurytion had not led the centaurs in such a brutal attack, but as things were now, he did not trust his mother's councilors. Not with his wife, or the shape of his kingship. They saw only a threat, an affront to Dia's legacy and an excuse to throw away a peace they had never truly desired. But he saw Hippodamia's tears, her grief, her bowed shoulders and her stillness in the tub, lost in the sorrow of knowing her sacrifice had ended in failure and loss. He saw the blood of his people spilled upon the floor, too much already, too many widowed and orphaned, too many broken with grief. And how many more before those who lived were satisfied?

He rubbed his forehead, slumping back in his chair. He needed time. Time to determine for himself the right action, and time for

Hippodamia to come to terms with her grief. Time for all the Lapiths to grieve. For if they went to war now, reckless and angry and broken, he would lose too many men. No doubt Peleus hoped for such an outcome, and Pirithous had no desire to satisfy him.

"My king, we have assembled as you asked," Plouteus said, drawing him from his thoughts.

Pirithous gave a short nod. He did not dare glance at Theseus. Here, in this megaron, he was king alone. And he must speak his own mind boldly, even without support.

After another moment, he rose.

"We have lost much," Pirithous began, his gaze touching on each of the men before him. Not only his mother's councilors, he realized, seeing faces he had not expected among them. Melanthos, one of his best raiders, and Atukhos, who never returned from their time at sea without some injury or another, but somehow always lived to fight again. They touched their fists to their foreheads in respect, gold rings and bracelets and armbands flashing in the firelight. Somehow he had not considered that his men had grown rich enough to be counted as nobles among the Lapiths, but it heartened him now. Lightened him to know he might have their support, even their counsel.

"We have lost much," he said again, nodding to Kotullon, and the others who had lost fathers or brothers, daughters or sons or wives. "And I would give all those who were lost the honors they deserve in death. For the men who died as warriors, we will have games. Seven days of games, with prizes from my own treasury. For the women and children, we will feast at banquet for those same days, with food and wine from the palace's stores. None will be turned away from our table."

"What of the centaurs?" one of the men called out. Not Kotullon, at least. Perhaps he had silenced at least that much dissent. "Games and banquets are all well and good, but you cannot mean to let this insult stand!"

Pirithous held up his hand, quieting the murmur of agreement. "It does us no good to enter battle without our wits. The anger in our hearts will make us careless and weak in ways we cannot afford. If our only enemy were the centaurs, perhaps the risk would be less, but we must not forget that Peleus and his Myrmidons wait just beyond our borders. Nothing would please them more than for the Lapiths to go unprepared to war against the centaurs, that once weakened, we might be conquered by the Myrmidon army all the more easily in our turn."

There was more than murmuring this time. A cacophony of voices, half in agreement and half made furious by his suggestion. Had they worn their swords, Pirithous had no doubt that hands would have settled upon hilts, with blood drawn before they calmed. He let them fight amongst themselves, sharpening their arguments and their tongues upon one another. When they spoke again with one voice, or two, he would answer readily enough.

"What would you have us do, my lord?" Melanthos asked, shouting to be heard above the others. "If we do nothing, all of Thessaly will believe us cowards. More than just the Myrmidons will come raiding, thinking us ripe and ready for plucking."

"We must act!" Pirithous agreed, meeting his friend's eye. "And I give you my oath that we will. But not this day, nor the next seven. As has ever been my way, I will not allow men blinded by grief to throw themselves headlong into battle. When the Lapiths ride out against our enemies, we will do so with clear minds, and be all the more dangerous for it."

Melanthos grinned, recognizing the phrasing from years at his side, raiding upon foreign shores. "And all the richer?"

"Those among the Lapiths who abide by the rule of their king will certainly find themselves rewarded."

"Then for these seven days, my sword will remain within its sheath," Melanthos said, bowing low. "And I would encourage these others to swear the same. Never once in five years has King Pirithous led his men astray, nor taken us into a battle we could not win. I do not believe he leads us poorly now."

"Nor do I," Theseus said, raising his voice above the din, and Pirithous was glad of his support. "Whether it is what you wish to hear or not, for a son of Zeus, King Pirithous speaks with the wisdom of Athena."

"Go home to your families," Pirithous said. "Make love to your wives and give comfort to your daughters. Train with your sons, if you wish, and compete in the games to honor those we have lost. Clear your heads of bloodlust and vengeance, and when the pyres no longer burn, come to me again."

And he would pray, in the meantime, that what he offered them would be enough.

CHAPTER THIRTY-ONE

HIPPODAMIA

She did not like to be watched, Hippodamia decided, struggling to hide her grief and pain behind a mask of indifference as she knelt beside her father's ruined body. She had washed it carefully of blood and filth, a task made all the more difficult by the fur which had matted and clumped. He looked so much smaller in death. More than anything, she wished to weep, but surrounded by Pirithous and his men, she could not. Would not give them the satisfaction of seeing her so broken. Bad enough Pirithous already kept her as a true hostage, guarded by Antiope and held against her will. And if his people realized how reluctant a queen she had become, what would they think of their king?

"Dare I trust you with the knife?" Pirithous asked, his voice so low she doubted even Antiope had heard. She was the nearest to them, for all the others looked upon Hippodamia warily, uncertain of her purpose.

She snatched it from his hand, glaring, and his lips twitched as if he wanted to smile. Her fingers tightened around the hilt. "Perhaps you shouldn't."

"Theseus feared, before we met, that you might slit my throat while I slept, but I must admit, it was never a concern of mine. Even less that you might attempt to do me any harm now, with so many watching." He tilted his head at the lamb he had brought, solid black and as calm and quiet as anyone could hope. "Particularly if you wish your father's body to remain unspoiled long enough to complete your rituals."

She narrowed her eyes. "A threat of that kind is beneath even you, Pirithous."

"It was no threat. But I am certain you realize my people are not so sympathetic to your grief as I am." And then he did smile, as he scattered the barley for her sacrifice. "And I should think you know the only thing I desire beneath me is you, little mouse."

She flushed, busying herself by wiping the blade clean with the hem of her tunic, that he might not see how his words affected her. And he dared speak so while she prepared her father's body! She would have slapped him, had they been alone.

"You can hide your face, Hippodamia, but not your heart. Your desire is as familiar to me as my own. Just as your love has become."

Love! She pinned the lamb against her side and cut its throat in one smooth stroke. How dare he claim she loved him. "And my anger?" she demanded. "You should know it better than the rest by now."

She ought to have been praying, but it was all she could do to direct the flow of blood into the golden offering bowl. Her hands shook, and her stomach twisted into knots at the thought of what she must do next.

"It is an old friend by now, and I confess, I do love the color it brings to your cheeks, the brightness to your eyes and the fire to your heart. Your anger gives you strength, Princess."

Strength. She looked up from the bowl to find his gaze intent upon her, but not with lust, or even desire. He studied her with compassion, and the realization made her flush again. He was provoking her, true, but for more reason than his own amusement. He was trying to distract her. To lend her the strength she would not accept, otherwise.

"Tell me what else I might do to help you," he said softly. "Let me show my people the honor Centaurus deserves, one king to another."

If he thought she would forgive him simply because he showed her kindness now—

"It is not my intent to offend you, Mia. But if you wish for any kind of peace, it must begin with us, here and now."

She let out a breath, her throat thick with grief. "What hope is there for peace?"

He crouched beside her, taking the golden bowl from her shaking hand. "None if you will not trust me. But together? I have bought us seven days in which to find a way. If nothing else, we might soften the blow. Turn a river of blood into the trickle of a stream."

"By allowing my people to be hunted like dogs again, as we lived before under Ixion's rule? Centaurus would never agree to such a scheme."

"Centaurus would see that I work to save his daughter as well as his people. But not even the gods hold absolute power. And son of Zeus or not, I am newly king. Had I proven myself already, perhaps things would be different. Perhaps things might yet be made different in time, if you remain at my side."

"You have made it clear I have no choice in the matter." That was the only difference between the previous night and this new day, and she hated him for it—how could he have thought for a moment that she would not? But she nodded to the lamb, its small body drained of life, and took up the bowl again. If Pirithous wished to show her father honor, she would let him. For Centaurus. "Make of the rest an offering to Poseidon Horse-Lord. We will burn the fat and bones with herbs over my father's body after I anoint him."

He did as she asked, working silently at her side, and she used the blood to stain Centaurus's body with the Horse Lord's mark, as Chiron had taught her when she was small. His forehead, his cheeks, his chin, his throat, and the place over his heart.

"Have you no need for oils or shroud?" Pirithous asked, when she stepped back to study her work.

She pressed her lips together. "We do not burn our dead, nor seek to preserve their bodies in this world. The centaurs will entomb him within the mountain's heart, his body whole."

"And the rest of the blood?"

Hippodamia swallowed, staring at the bowl in her hands, and the blood inside. "It is for me. To draw his wounds upon my body, and mark my grief upon my face."

He fell silent, just as she had feared he would. He would forbid her from it, she supposed. Because of his people. Because when she smeared the blood on her face and her body, they would see she grieved for her father above all, and that her heart still belonged to her people.

Pirithous gave a grunt and turned away, his shadow shifting enough to make the blood shine in the sudden light. "Enough," he said, raising his voice to the others. "We have let you watch this far at your queen's insistence, that you would not suspect her of sorcery, but allow her now to pray in private."

She looked up, startled, and Pirithous gave her a grim nod. "Whatever you must do, We would share in it, for Centaurus was Our kin, too, as Ixion's son, and a loyal friend to the Lapiths all his life."

He said it for the men who still lingered, she knew, but he could have said nothing at all, or simply hurried them on their way. "Why are you doing this?"

"You are my wife and my queen, Mia. We are as bound in grief as we are in joy."

She shook her head, fighting back the tears that pricked behind her eyes. "I am only another prize."

"Because I sought to win you?"

"Because, by your own admission, I am something to be owned. And then you call me wife and queen, claim I have your love, and make a show of presenting me as your equal—" Her voice broke. "Do you not see that it cannot be both? I am either your equal and free, worthy of your respect and your love, or I am little more than a slave, and worthy of nothing!"

He stepped forward, cupping her cheek. "Mia—"

"Whether I stay or not, the choice must be mine, Pirithous. Not my father's or your mother's, or even yours alone, but mine. Ours!"

He shook his head, letting his hand fall away. "Every other choice, I swear to you before your father's shade, we will make together. But not this one. You are my wife and my queen, and I will not lose you."

She closed her eyes, her hands gripping the bowl so tightly she feared it would warp between them. She would not cry. Would not weep. Would not let him see her pain. She had been a fool to ask it of him. A fool to believe he might be capable of more. No matter what he said, in his heart he was no better than a pirate, seeing something he desired and taking it for his own.

"Mia, please understand. It is for your sake more than mine."

"Go," she said, turning her face away, for the tears pressed against her eyelids, threatening to spill. "Just go."

***

She streaked her face with blood, though her cheeks were damp already. And when she struggled to paint the wounds upon her own skin, to even remove her tunic, Antiope offered steady hands and silent sympathy. The cut of the knife, from her shoulder through her breasts, Antiope drew faithfully, and then the second from her ribs and across her belly, ripping through the muscle and into the gut. Her father had bled to death quickly enough, the blood of the lamb nothing to what had spilled in the megaron. And in his last moments—when she might have said goodbye, might have heard his final words, or begged his forgiveness for her foolishness not long before—she had been torn from his side.

That was the wound that cut deepest. That Eurytion would be so cruel as to deny her that small comfort after striking Centaurus down. That she would have to go on without her father's wisdom, her father's love.

"If only I had not gone to him that night," she said, dropping to her knees beside her father's body in the grass. "If only I had listened to you at the stables. Trusted you. If only I had not been so blind. I would give anything now to take back my anger, to make the last words I spoke to you words of love."

Antiope touched her shoulder. "No one blames you for what happened, Hippodamia, least of all Centaurus. And I am certain he knows your heart."

"I was so angry…" She pressed the heels of her hands against her eyes to stop the tears from smearing the blood on her face. "I behaved like a child."

"Then behave as a woman grown, now," Antiope said gently. "Until the flesh is gone from his bones, his shade remains. Let him see you have taken his words to heart."

Hippodamia laughed, her heart twisting. "His words. How could I deny them now? He told me to guard my heart. To restrain my hope and resign myself to the truth of my marriage. That Pirithous was just a man, and no matter how much pleasure he gave me, I should not confuse it with love. How much less it would hurt now, if I had only believed him!"

"And yet, he does love you."

"The love of a man, with all its failings. He confuses it with affection, with desire, and love or not, I am still owned. Not an equal, or a partner, but a thing to be locked away with all the rest of his gold."

"Your people and mine have much in common, Mia. The kind of love you desire does not come so easily for men as it does for us, but it is not all so hopeless as that. Pirithous, for all his faults, *does* wish for a partner. He needs a strong queen, an equal, even if he did not know it at first. Give him time to grow accustomed to the thought, and before long you will have all that you want from him in love, I promise you."

"As you have with Theseus?" She looked up at the Amazon. "Do you truly believe him capable of that?"

Antiope's lips twitched. "Even Theseus needed a guiding hand at first. And Pirithous had little love for me in the beginning, but we have grown used to one another. Is that not proof that he is capable of change, at the least?"

"Perhaps." And perhaps as long as there was some small hope for peace, she served her people better as Pirithous's wife. The longer she stayed among the Lapiths, the more she would know of their intent, certainly, and even if she could do nothing else, with that knowledge, if war came, she might find some means of helping the centaurs avoid destruction.

"For whatever it is worth, I do not think he sees you as a prize at all," Antiope said, after a moment. "I think, rather, that he fears what he will become if you are lost, and all the more if he does not do all in his power to protect you."

"Why should you think so?"

Antiope smiled. "I have never seen him look at a woman the way he looks at you. The others he only regarded with lust, but when he looks at you, it is with warmth and affection, even respect."

"Pirithous thinks I am weak. That is why he stifles his desire." Hippodamia fed what was left of the blood into the flame in offering to Poseidon. There was nothing left she might do for her father beyond that. Nothing she could ever do for him again.

"What?"

She did not look up, though Antiope sounded honestly startled. "That is why, in the beginning, he would not promise to give up the others. He believes I have not the strength to satisfy his desires without exhausting myself in the trying. That he will do me some harm if he gives himself up to his lust. That is all that you see, Antiope. Restraint. Because I am not a daughter of Ares, or Zeus, or Poseidon, or any other god. Just a foundling child, left to die. Because I am weak."

Antiope snorted. "If he did not care for you deeply, he would not worry himself over such nonsense. He would take you to his bed and keep you there until he grew bored. And I promise you, Mia, if he did not love you, he would lose interest in your company long before he exhausted you in his bed."

She stared into the smoke and flame, willing her heart to calm, her thoughts to steady.

But what if… what if Antiope were right?

Chapter Thirty-Two

Pirithous

Pirithous lit the first pyres that night as the sun sank behind the mountain and disappeared. Hippodamia joined him without argument, and though she did not reach out to him for support, he was pleased that she did not hide herself away. In the firelight, it was harder to see the blood painted upon her face, but he could feel her grief, all the same. How much he wished she might accept some comfort at his hand, even distraction. But perhaps that was what all of this was—her anger, her resentment, her stubbornness. As long as she fought against him, she need not think of the greater pain and loss.

"We must speak," Theseus said, coming to stand at his side. They had returned just before dusk, and Pirithous had not had the time to meet with them as yet, busy as he had been seeing to his people and giving his sympathies to the families who grieved. "Before the feasting begins."

Yes. He supposed they must. "Cyllarus?"

Theseus's expression was grim. "Best bring your wife as well. She will want to hear it."

"Mia." Pirithous touched her wrist, and she flinched, crossing her arms, no doubt to keep him from taking her hand. He pressed his lips together, unwilling to let her see the hurt it gave him. "Let us give them some privacy for their grief."

Her eyes narrowed, but whatever she saw in Theseus's face seemed to stop her objections. She swallowed, her arms tightening about her own middle. "Of course."

Antiope waited for them beyond the pyre's light, and Pirithous led the way forward. His rooms looked out over the palace gates and Hippodamia's balcony offered a view of the stables, but he dared not miss the return of his people from the pyre. Hippodamia's absence from the banquet might not trouble his people overmuch, but his would certainly be noticed, and his control over the Lapiths was tenuous enough already without adding more insult to their injuries.

"Here." He opened a door to a bare room, furnished only with straw pallets upon the floor. The room he had given to Hylonome and Cyllarus. He crossed to the windows, cracking one of the shutters that he might keep watch. The pyre licked at the sky outside the walls, burning brightly still. By all rights, the feasting ought to have been done in its light, but with the centaurs lurking, the risk was too great.

"You spoke to my people," Hippodamia said, after Antiope had shut the door behind them. Pirithous spared her a glance, but the room was dark without the light from the hall. Not that he needed to see her to know the tight knot of worry in her heart.

"For all your riches, you seem poor in lamps," Antiope grumbled. "Go to your wife, Pirithous. I will keep watch."

He grunted, moving nearer to Hippodamia. And this time, when he touched her, setting his hand upon the small of her back, she did not flinch from him.

"What news?" Hippodamia pressed. "Please, I would know that my father's body was safely delivered, at the least."

"Cyllarus accepted the bodies," Theseus said. "Centaurus will be laid to rest with his kin, and the centaurs are grateful to you, Hippodamia, for seeing him safely returned."

"To Hippodamia alone?" Pirithous asked, though he knew the answer. Theseus would not have phrased it so if his meaning had been different.

"Cyllarus believes you killed Centaurus, Pirithous. And it appears those centaurs who witnessed the truth of that moment did not live to tell the tale. I tried to reassure him, but even from a son of Poseidon, he would not hear it."

"You fought for Pirithous," Hippodamia said, her voice small. "Your loyalties are to him."

"My loyalties have little to do with it."

But Hippodamia shook her head, a quick movement of a lighter shadow in the dark. "My people have always been passionate. Cyllarus is ruled by his grief more than his reason, and I cannot blame him for it. Nor should the Lapiths, if they lust so for war against the centaurs."

"Centaurus had more sense than that," Pirithous said. "He must have had, to bargain with your hand."

"My father was a different breed. With his death goes his wisdom. But if it is Cyllarus who speaks for my people now, it is worse. He is in rut still, from his own mating with Hylonome. Another month, and perhaps he would be more willing to listen, but his blood runs too hot for that now."

"There is more," Theseus said. "He took insult from your offer of escape. Cyllarus claims the mountain for his people, and will not be moved from it. Not when, to his mind, it was the Lapiths who broke this peace and all hope of reconciliation with Centaurus's death."

His stomach sank. Hippodamia had warned him, but he had hoped the centaurs might see reason enough to save their hides. And now he had no choice. In seven days his people would come to him, ready for battle, and he would do—what? He could hardly offer prizes for their heads now, or his people would see the whole herd slaughtered before the month was out.

"I should have been the one to go," Hippodamia said, half-moaning. "Even if he had not believed me himself, the others would have. Hylonome would have listened!"

"Hylonome seemed as convinced as her mate," Theseus said. "And truly, I think Cyllarus would have seized you, had you come. He is uneasy about leaving you among the Lapiths, and demanded your return, lest some harm befall you."

Pirithous snorted. "The only harm to befall Hippodamia has come at the hands of her own people, not mine."

Hippodamia made a strangled noise, shifting away from his touch. "He means to attack. As hostage, my life is forfeit if he leads the centaurs against the Lapiths. That is why he fears for me."

Pirithous opened his mouth to object, then shut it again, meeting Theseus's gaze in the dark. Surely they were not so foolish as that! And yet…

"Mia, are you certain?" He caught her by the arm, forcing her to face him, though he was not certain how much of his expression she could see. He had no trouble making out her features now, his eyes adjusted to the dim light. Her eyes shone much too bright. He stroked her cheek, his thumb meeting dried blood and the dampness of fresh tears. What he would have given to kiss them away. "Perhaps it is only his mistrust of me."

She shook her head again, dropping her gaze. "I thought if I offered myself as hostage it would be enough to stop them from such foolishness, that they would not risk my life, and I might yet save theirs. But I was wrong. I was wrong, and better if I had left with them to speak with my father's voice—I might have filled the place Cyllarus has taken and stopped this, but now it's too late."

At the window, Antiope stirred. "Your people come, Pirithous."

He took her face in his hands, willing her not to look away. "None of this is your doing, Mia. And even if you had gone with them, it is likely they would only have attacked all the sooner."

"Pirithous," Antiope warned.

"Mia?" She had to believe him. And while he would not use his power to manipulate her, he did use it then, to show her his love, to offer her what comfort and sympathy he could. He dropped his forehead to hers and kept his voice low. "I would not ask it of you, but if what you fear is true, it is more important than ever that you stand at my side."

"Of course." She swallowed hard, her eyes closing, and what thoughts spun through her head, only the gods knew. "Forgive me. I—I am ready."

He let out a breath and took her hand, holding it firmly. "You are not alone, little mouse. Remember it, I beg of you."

***

He dosed her cup heavily with wine during the feast, until she all but dozed against his shoulder, far more relaxed than she had been in days. At the first opportunity without giving offense, he excused them, lifting her in his arms and carrying her from the megaron. Up the stairs and down the hall, he shouldered open his door and continued through to the bathing room.

The blood on her face had smudged with her tears, the once-distinct stripes blurred into smears upon her cheeks, but she stirred when he set her down upon the lip of the tub.

"No," she mumbled, swaying. "Can't wash it away."

He raised his eyebrows. "By rite or by stubbornness, little mouse?"

She slumped slightly, rubbing her face. "They'll forget."

"Who?" He lifted the cauldron of water from the fire and poured it into the tub, watching her carefully, lest she tip.

"Lapiths. Think they're the only ones… But my father. My father, and without the blood, they won't remember."

He set the cauldron aside and crouched beside her, cupping her cheek and looking up into her eyes. "I won't let them forget, Hippodamia. Centaurus died for their sakes as much as yours. Died for me, too. He'll have a feast day, I promise you, and all the Lapiths will honor his sacrifice."

Her eyes brimmed with tears, and she pressed her fingers to his lips. "Can't make them love us."

"But I will try, all the same," he vowed. "You and your father, if no one else."

He dropped his hand, giving her chin a gentle pinch before letting it fall. And then he stood, unknotting his belt, and pulled his tunic over his head. Her eyes went wide, and she tightened her grip upon the edge of the tub until her knuckles whitened.

"Your shoulder."

He shrugged, though it pleased him that she noticed, for the night before she had said nothing at all. "It is nothing."

"A hoof mark." She rose unsteadily from her perch and touched it, her fingers feather-light against his skin. She seemed more alert now, if still just as sopped. "Your back?"

"Sore to the touch, but nothing worse." He caught her hand, bringing it to his lips and pressing a kiss to her palm. "Zeus may not have given me Herakles's strength, but I am not without power of my own. I am well, little mouse, have no fear."

"If the centaurs come…"

"Then I will fight to defend my lands, my people, and my wife. And even if they came tomorrow, it would not slow me enough to matter."

"Pirithous. My Pirithous." His name was barely more than a breath from her lips, and she traced the bruise again, then the small scabbed scrapes and marks on his arms, the scars upon his chest. His blood heated with each caress, but he dared not press her. Would not take her when she was so far from herself, willing or not. "Promise me you'll live. I can't—without you, I can't."

"Can't what, mouse?" he asked gently, for the way the words broke twisted his heart and cooled his ardor. So much grief and despair, so much pain. If only he could take it all away, lift the burden of so much sorrow from her shoulders and scatter it among the stars.

"Live." Such a small word to carry such bleak fear. "My father, Eurytion, then you. I don't know. Where to begin. What to do.

This. All this. So much is ruined, nothing as it was meant, and everything spills more blood."

"Shh." He stroked her hair, letting his fingers tangle in its softness. She leaned into his touch, and he wanted to pull her into his arms, hold her so tightly that none of this pain could reach her again. "The gods test us, that is all. But we will conquer this, Mia. And I will come back to you, blood unspilled, body unbroken. There is nothing to fear. And even if not, even if by some cruel trick, I am struck down, you are not alone, even then. Antiope and Theseus will protect you, shelter you. You'll have a place in Athens, if it comes to that."

She pressed her hand flat against his chest, over his heart. "Promise me."

He kissed her forehead. "I promise you, I will live."

***

She let him bathe her, then, and he scrubbed the blood from her skin, though he could do nothing for the bruises those same marks had left upon her heart. Half-drowned in wine, she tried to wash him in return, pulling him into the tub with her, despite his objections. Gods above, how he wanted her. The soft touches of her fingers upon his scars lit a fire in his blood, the way her forehead furrowed in concern over the small cuts and scrapes. He'd been fortunate to escape with nothing worse, but he dared not speak of it. Eurytion had not been weak, and when it came time to face Cyllarus, by far the larger beast, he could not be certain of the outcome, no matter what promises he'd made.

And he would face Cyllarus, he had no doubt of that. If the centaurs believed him Centaurus's murderer, they would all come in search of him, above all. And had it been his king dead at another's hand, he would have done the same. Provided that king had not been Ixion.

When Hippodamia's hands fell lower, seeking his desire, he caught them up, caught her up, and carried her from the bathing room before he forgot himself. Before he forgot how much wine he had given her, and how furiously she had refused even his love, just that morning. He did not forget the things she had said. Did not forget she had no wish to remain his queen.

"To bed," he said gently, wrapping her in a towel once they reached his room. "We both need our rest."

"A son of Zeus has little need for rest when there is pleasure to be had," she said, reaching for him again. "Is that not true?"

He smiled, but shook his head as he captured her hands in his. "You've had too much wine, Mia, and I am not so great a fool as to think it is not the drink that speaks now. Even a son of Zeus has more sense than that."

She lifted her chin, drawing breath to fight him, but he stopped her with a kiss. A soft brush of his lips upon hers, and a hand in her wet hair. She closed her eyes, leaning into his touch, but he did not give her more; could not, not without risking everything he desired.

"If it means tomorrow you might love me clear-headed, I will wait," he said against her ear. "But I promise you, Mia, when the time comes that you want me, truly, of your own accord, you will not rise from my bed for days."

He drew back, and her eyes met his, wide and wild and far too bright, and if he had not filled her cup with his own hand, knowing full well how poorly she handled her wine, he might have believed her sober. Sober enough, in any case, he feared. Certainly awake enough to slip away in the night, if he did not keep her near. He stroked her cheek, searching her face.

"Sleep beside me this night, so I know you are safe, I beg of you."

She swallowed hard, then nodded, and for that moment he could breathe freely.

For that night.

But when Cyllarus came, what then?

Chapter Thirty-Three

Hippodamia

Her head felt ripened to bursting, and her mouth seemed as though it had filled with wool. Hippodamia groaned, squinting at the too-bright sun and rolling away from the window—into Pirithous.

He chuckled softly. "You are no child of Zeus, that's certain."

She narrowed her eyes, glaring up at him. How he could be so widely awake and so good-humored she did not know. Nor was she quite sure what she'd done the night before to make herself so miserable upon waking. The last was perhaps the more disconcerting puzzle of the two.

"What happened?"

"Just too much wine, that's all." He offered her a cup, helping her to sit up beside him. "Drink that, and you'll feel better after you've eaten."

She frowned at the contents, clearly not water alone. "What is it?"

"A potion for the headache. I'm told overindulgence is often followed by one, though I can't say I've ever experienced it for myself, thank Zeus. Antiope thought to have it sent up for you."

"How thoughtful." She wrinkled her nose against the smell. "Are you certain cold water would not serve just as well?"

"Not in the least," Pirithous said. "But I rather think Antiope would not lead you astray."

Hippodamia snorted, eyeing Pirithous sidelong, for someone had filled her cup the night before, and if she had mixed her own wine, it would have been much too weak to leave her feeling so ill. "Unlike my husband?"

"Your husband thought it would be best if you forgot yourself and your troubles for a time, and saw you safely to your bed, unmolested."

She took a sip of the potion, forcing herself to swallow, though it was far too bitter for her liking. Better to hide in her cup than to let him see the flush in her cheeks. Perhaps she did not quite remember everything that had passed between them, but the roughness of his voice as he promised to keep her in his bed for days was not so easily forgotten.

"If I overstepped, I beg your forgiveness," he said after a moment. "I only thought to give you some small moment of peace before the storm swallowed us whole."

The storm. She let the cup drop from her lips and stared at her reflection in the liquid. Her people. "Pirithous, I must try. To stop this, somehow. To stop them."

He sighed. "If I let you go to them, they will not give you back. There will be no stopping a war either way, then, for your people will have no reason not to attack, and mine will have even more reason to want their blood spilled. I know it is difficult to stand by, to do nothing, but there are times when taking no action is the best course, the only course that will not make matters worse."

"And how often have you done nothing when it meant your friends, your family might die?"

His jaw tightened but he did not flinch from the question, only met her gaze. "You forget I am Dia's son, born while Ixion reigned in all his madness. Did you never wonder why I kept away? I spent my days with the horses, and when that was not distraction enough from the trouble Ixion made, I left to raid."

"And if I did the same, your people would say I betrayed them. They would say I left to allow Cyllarus the freedom to attack."

"Which is why I would have you stay," Pirithous said, taking the cup from her hands. "To prove your honor."

She snorted. What had honor brought her father? Her people? Or the Lapiths, for that matter? Nothing but blood and death and heartbreak, and now this. And yet, her father had believed so strongly in this peace, in her marriage to Pirithous and the alliance of their peoples. He had died for it, and after all that he had done for her, the way she had spoken to him...

She would not give up on his dreams. Perhaps she could do nothing else, but she could do this. She could honor his memory, and if it meant giving up her life for the same cause, so be it.

But to give in to Pirithous so easily—he had caged her so completely, and dared to call it love. She was still not certain she believed him, but she knew her own heart. She wanted to trust in his love, however confused he might be. Maybe all the more because she had lost so much else. What did she have left, if not Pirithous?

"You must allow me to meet them when they come," she said. "If you will not let me go to them, if you refuse to grant me the freedom to act as I believe I must, to leave if it would benefit our people, you must at least give me this."

"Mia…"

"No, Pirithous." She lifted her chin, staring into his eyes, willing him to see her resolve. "You will not make excuses. You will not sit here and tell me that my life is too precious, when you would spend your own taking the same risks. If I remain here at your side, as your wife, as the peacemaker my father hoped I might be, you must allow me to act as such! Or what is the purpose of any of it?"

His gaze slid away from hers, his lips pressed thin. "And after? When your kin are vanquished, what then?"

"I will know I have done all I could," she said, ducking her head to catch his eyes again. "Do you not see, Pirithous, that to refuse me this would twist our marriage into nothing but resentment and bitterness? I would always wonder what might have been, if you had only let me attempt to reason with them. I would hate you for locking me away. For keeping me safe at the expense of my people, even of yours."

He closed his eyes and let out a breath. "Will you at least allow me to stand at your side?"

Her heart wrenched. Because she didn't dare. Knowing her people, even the sight of him would enrage them beyond reason, and it would all be for nothing.

His eyes opened when she did not answer, his hands tightening around the cup he held. "Mia, I beg of you, grant me that much in compromise if you will risk your life this way."

She shook her head, her throat thick. "Perhaps Theseus or Antiope. But not you, Pirithous. It cannot be you."

***

He did not take it well, of course. She had not expected him to. Had not truly expected him to agree to her terms at all. But he had, though it had seemed to pain him deeply, and Pirithous had left her almost at once, mumbling something about speaking to the men upon the walls.

And for the first time since he had found her in the bath after their wedding banquet, she was truly alone. Without a guard or a companion, or Antiope lurking just outside her door.

Hippodamia closed her eyes, falling back into the bedding, and lay still in the empty room. Empty, but for her grief and the shades of the dead whispering too near. There was little she could do to help them, but for the living, at least, she might act. And perhaps, if Poseidon blessed her, if the gods saw fit to spare both their peoples, she could prevent a war.

If she could only find the right words.

But that had been Centaurus's gift, not hers. He had spoken with such authority, such wisdom, and who was she? Not even a true centaur. Nothing more than a foundling child, of no consequence at all but for the fact that Centaurus had chosen to raise her as his own, and with her marriage to Pirithous and her father's death, she was even less of a centaur now, the bonds between herself and her people strained to breaking by Eurytion's jealousy and rage. She did not have Centaurus's blood, only the memory of his affections. Nor did she truly have power or strength enough to win leadership that way—not fighting against another centaur.

She had her skill with a horse, a deep knowledge of her people, and her father's name. It would make for a golden tripod, more decorative than practical in any way. Good for nothing more than the bluster of a prize.

She would simply have to hope that Podarkes could outrun the centaurs when she failed.

***

There was nothing to do but wait, then. The Lapiths held their games to honor the dead and Hippodamia stood upon the wall, wrapped in one of Pirithous's wool cloaks against the wind and keeping watch with the guards. She hadn't been certain she would be welcome at the games, though none had questioned her presence at the pyres the night before.

"Lady?"

She tore her gaze from the mountain as Theseus joined her. Kind as his wife had been, Hippodamia had not spoken much to the King of Athens, and what time they had spent together had always been in the company of Pirithous or Antiope.

"Pirithous said you had need of me," Theseus said.

She pulled the cloak tighter around her shoulders, and could not quite bring herself to meet his eyes. "I am not sure why."

"Are you not?" he asked. "I had thought whatever rift had opened between you bridged at last, or surely Pirithous would not leave you upon the wall without a guard."

"I have given him my word I will remain. Offered in compromise, though he did not care overmuch for my terms."

"Ah," Theseus said, and she could feel his eyes upon her. "Something to do with your people?"

Her heart twisted, realizing at last what Pirithous had meant by sending him. "I told him he must let me meet them when they come. To reason with them, if it is possible. He asked to stand beside me, but I feared it would only inflame Cyllarus's fury to allow it. I told him it would be better if it were you or Antiope."

Theseus was silent for a moment, and when she glanced at him sidelong, he seemed to be staring at the mountain, just as she had. "I do not think they will listen."

"You are known for your justice, King Theseus, for your wisdom and judgment. Surely you understand why I must try, no matter how little hope of success there might be."

"Yes," he agreed. "And I understand, too, how difficult it will be for Pirithous to watch you ride out from the safety of his walls, utterly impotent while you risk yourself for his people."

"Is that not the queen's right? Her duty, even?"

"In the absence of the king, perhaps."

"And I stand in the absence of my king, my father, Centaurus."

Theseus grunted. "It would save Pirithous some face if presented in such a way, even if it will do nothing to ease his fears, but I am not certain it will do you any service in the eyes of his people."

"His people will see the proof of my loyalties with their own eyes if I am forced to flee from mine. What can they possibly say then? What resentment can they possibly hold?"

He laughed, short and sharp. "Those who suffer, twisted by pain and grief—they will find a way to place the blame upon your shoulders if they desire it, I promise you. But the rest… It will certainly prove your bravery, Lady, if nothing else. And if you desire it, if you believe it will do any good at all, I will stand at your side. For Pirithous's sake, as well as yours. Better if it is me than Antiope, though I know she would not refuse you."

She met his eyes, then, at last, straightening beneath his gaze. "Better because you have just as little desire to watch her ride out from the safety of these walls as Pirithous does me?"

Theseus smiled, and she felt its warmth as a glint of sunlight on water. "As little as you wish to see Pirithous ride to battle, when that time comes."

"Yes, but Pirithous would never let my fears stop him from acting. Just as I will not let his fears rule me, in this. We have the same right, King Theseus, as you do. To risk our lives for those we love. To act in their interests. To protect our people and our families."

"Who exactly do you wish to convince, Hippodamia?" His eyes were laughing now. "Or do you forget I married an Amazon?"

Her face heated. "An Amazon you would prefer to keep hidden behind strong walls."

"And would you not wish to protect Pirithous, if you could? To shelter him from the rage of the centaurs when they come boiling down the mountain? Is that not what you seek to do with this compromise of yours?"

She let out a breath. To protect Pirithous, yes, though she had not realized until that moment how desperately she wanted to keep him safe. "I wish I had never come to him at all, if war is all it's wrought. I would not have him suffer because I failed in my one duty. I would not have any of the Lapiths suffer for it."

"Do not take so much upon yourself, Lady. It was not your failure which brought about this unpleasantness. You did everything that you ought, and Pirithous did not make it easy, I know."

"Not at first," she said, frowning at the mountain. It felt so long ago now, that day. When Centaurus had placed her hand in Pirithous's she had not imagined it possible to care for him this much. Nor had she imagined the conflict that would follow. It had all blindsided her. Eurytion's folly. Pirithous's generosity. "But that was before I knew he was kind."

"Sometimes I think he hides his best qualities too well," Theseus said. "As if he fears Ixion still looks over his shoulder, waiting to twist every good thing into madness."

She shook her head. "He hardly speaks of Ixion to me."

"He does not speak of Ixion at all," Theseus said, "but that does not mean he is not haunted by him. Everything Ixion destroyed, Pirithous has rebuilt. Everyone Ixion wronged, he has repaid. The centaurs were the last of it. To bring about a peace between your peoples was not only Dia's hope, though I doubt Pirithous would ever admit to the reason why."

She swallowed. She had been young enough to escape the worst of Ixion's rule, but his blood ran through every centaur's veins. "You do not think this is Ixion's madness, still?"

Theseus said nothing, but she did not think he ignored her question, only turned it over in his mind and did not care for the truth which presented itself.

"Centaurus was not mad," she said into the quiet that stretched between them, for she did not need his answer. Not truly. She had only to remember what had become of her wedding feast, the wildness which had overtaken her people, turning them into beasts. "But perhaps the rest of us are."

"Not you, Lady," Theseus said gently. "In this one instance let it be a comfort to know you do not share their blood."

She wished it was. But it only left her feeling emptier than she had begun.

Chapter Thirty-Four

Pirithous

The last of their guests, save for Theseus and Antiope, had gone by the following morning. Pirithous was glad of it. Even Antiope he would have sent away, if there had been any chance she might go. As it was, all he dared do was place more men upon the wall, and hope what Hippodamia feared would not come to pass.

"Antiope and I went riding this morning," Theseus said, joining him on the wall.

Pirithous had not precisely been pacing it, but he had certainly been prowling with the excuse of seeing to his men. Hippodamia was with Antiope in the kitchens, overseeing the preparations for the evening feast, and it seemed if he could not be in bed with his wife, he could have no peace unless he was moving. Or perhaps he simply had no peace at all.

"It is not only the centaurs who watch your walls, counting the men you set upon them," Theseus went on, unbothered by his silence.

"Peleus," Pirithous agreed. "He waits to see what will be left of us after the centaurs come, I'm certain. Or else he waits until we ride out against them, hoping to take the palace and the horses while my back is turned. He stands to gain much from this war he's started."

"I have men in Athens who would be willing to fight," Theseus said. "Or at least remain behind the walls to guard your back, and ensure Peleus will not have the opportunity he seeks."

He shook his head. "It is too late for that now. And even if it weren't—this is my fight, Theseus. These are my people. We will succeed or fail together. Against Peleus and the centaurs both, if it comes to that."

"But you need not succeed or fail alone," Theseus said.

"Which is why I have not sent you home, my friend." He smiled, clapping Theseus's shoulder. "Though if you wished to go, to keep Antiope safe—"

Theseus snorted. "She would not leave now even if I begged, and I would not abandon Hippodamia, for your sake or hers, besides. Antiope would never forgive me if I let your wife ride out to meet the centaurs alone. Though I must confess to you, Pirithous, I do not know what help I will be. The centaurs do not trust me, and I do not believe there is anything Hippodamia might say that will sway them from this course. Cyllarus is angry. The others want vengeance, thinking it will ease their sorrow. Whatever peace you hoped to forge is lost."

"I hope only for my wife's peace, now," Pirithous said. "And she will have none if she does not do this. Keep her safe if you can, bring her back to me behind the walls. Beyond that, I hope for nothing."

Theseus nodded. "She will have my sword to shield her, and Antiope's bow, from the walls. We will bring her back to you whole in body, if not in spirit. Failing her people, Pirithous—it will not be without cost. She may not have peace, even then."

"Her failure is mine, too, Theseus," he said quietly, the truth of the words heavy in his heart. "Our marriage was meant to unite our peoples, that one day our son might rule centaurs and Lapiths as one. I should have known Peleus would interfere. I should have delayed our wedding when the priest warned me of the omens. But

I was too angry, too stubborn, too jealous to see truth or reason. I wanted her to be mine."

"Because you loved her," Theseus said.

"Because I did not trust her," Pirithous said. "Because I was blinded by desire, no better than Cyllarus, with his mind fogged by rut. Now I am hers, lost in her, and she is less mine than ever."

"You cannot own an Amazon, Pirithous," Theseus said slowly. "I begin to think the same is true of the centaurs as well. But Hippodamia has promised to stay. She has chosen you. I think you are wrong to think she is not as much yours as you are hers."

"Until the centaurs come, and she rides out to meet them, I do not think I will ever know for certain."

Theseus grunted. "You still don't trust her."

"I trust that she will do what she thinks is best, and if it will avert a war, I do not doubt for a moment that she will return to the centaurs, to her people." Pirithous pressed his lips together. "And I cannot blame her for it. I cannot say, were I standing in her place, that I would do any different."

And perhaps that was what frightened him the most. For they were much alike, when it came to honor and sacrifice and duty. Too much alike, when it meant she might leave him, and after all they had shared, he might be forced to let her go.

***

Pirithous made the games more competitive. More sword work and spear throwing, more bow hunting, with man- and centaur-shaped targets. He dared not whisper of an attack, or incite his own people into rage, but he could train them, still. He *would* train them, still.

He and Theseus took turns walking among the men and boys, correcting their draw on the bow, their grip upon the sword, their form as they threw, and the funeral rites became something more. He could only pray what little preparation he could offer would be enough. That perhaps it would save one of the boys, too young to know better how to fight.

And then he sent Antiope to gather the unwed girls and young wives yet without children, allowed her to organize them for their own games, with their own prizes. He gave them bows and arrows and sticks for swords, and he watched them as they learned to use them. It would not be much, and when it came time, they would learn quickly that playing at war was not the same as killing, but at least they would have some small hope of defense.

"It will not work," Hippodamia said, appearing at his shoulder on the second day, while he watched the girls, smiling and laughing and following Antiope's every move. He ought to have realized his wife would hear of it, with Antiope in charge. "You teach them to fight against men, not centaurs. Men attack with a sword or spear or fists, but centaurs have all those things and their hooves besides."

He glanced at her sidelong, but her face was impassive, and all he could sense of her was resignation and pain. "I pray it is only men they must defend against. If the centaurs reach this far, we will have lost one war and invited another."

"If the centaurs reach this far, and these women do not know how to defend themselves, they will be worse than dead. It will not be clean, Pirithous, or painless. They will be raped and planted, and if their wombs quicken, they will not survive the result." She pressed her lips together. "Put Antiope atop a horse, the steadiest you have, and I will show them where to strike."

His heart constricted even at the thought. She should not have to teach his people how to kill her own. Already she did too much for them, gave too much of herself. "I will not ask it of you."

She met his eyes, her own dark with grief. "You haven't, but it is only right, Pirithous. Whatever has happened, whatever will happen, the women and children of the Lapiths are innocent." A smile ghosted across her lips, more sorrowful than anything else. "If it were the men, perhaps I might feel otherwise."

"If it were the men, I would forbid it," he promised her. "No matter how angry it made you, I would not let you take the stain of more blood upon your hands."

Her hand found his, shy at first, and then holding tightly. So tightly. "You cannot protect me from this, Pirithous. Just as I cannot protect you."

He brought her hand to his lips, pressing a kiss to her knuckles. "But you are determined to try, all the same."

"No more and no less than you would do, in my place."

"I am no hero," he said. "And I am not so selfless, no matter what you might think."

She shook her head. "You do not give yourself enough credit. Everything you have done has been for your people, even for mine, at no small cost to yourself. If that is not selflessness, what is?"

"Is it so selfless, when much of what I have done these last days has been for you? To keep you here, at my side?"

"Perhaps that is what you tell yourself, but I do not believe it is wholly true. It is not only for me. Not only for yourself and your interests that you've acted. War with the centaurs will do more harm than good, for both our peoples. You know that as well as I."

"It is convenience, that is all," he said. "For I think of little else but you. It keeps me awake at night, even when you are in my arms, sleeping soundly. You've promised me you will stay, but I fear the moment my eyes close, you will slip between my fingers and disappear into the night. I worry you will go to them, all the same, leaving me behind. Because you know the cost of war. Because you think it will spare me some greater pain. But I promise you, Hippodamia, it will only amplify my grief, my sorrow. It will only make every suffering that much more difficult to bear if you are not with me. If you are lost to me, and there is war, still."

"Do you think I would throw away our marriage so easily?" she asked, her eyes going liquid. "That I would destroy what we have built for so little?"

"I think you will do what you must, mouse. That your loyalty to your people is greater, perhaps, than your love for me." He sighed, brushing a tear from her cheek. He had not meant to make her cry, but surely she must realize how difficult this was for him, as well. "Perhaps it should be. Perhaps it is only right that it is so, when they have raised you from infancy, and I have guarded you for little more than a sevenday. Why should you remain with me, with my people, at all, but for duty? But for the desire to honor your father's dream? Your father's hope for peace? And if peace can only be found by leaving…"

She closed her eyes, turning her face away, and another tear slipped from beneath her lashes. But she did not deny it. She did not argue his reasoning, did not fight against his words. Her silence hurt his heart all the more.

"I will have the horse brought," he said, loosening his hold upon her hand. "And then I'll return to the men."

"Please." Her fingers tightened around his, her gaze skittering away. His little mouse, once again. "Please stay."

"Mia—"

"You promised me you would live, Pirithous. That you will return whole and unbloodied, unbroken. Wherever I am, I would have it so. Let me do this small thing. For you. Just for you."

He searched her face, smoothed the frantic, worried lines from her brow. He hadn't expected her to remember his vow, drunk as she'd been. And he was not certain, even with her help, that he could keep it. He was not so sure he wanted to, if she meant to leave him. And if the centaurs fought through them, reached the palace—it would not be long before Peleus followed and took everything that was left. He would be a king without a people before this was over. But if she stayed…

He had to believe she would not leave him.

"Are you certain?"

She nodded, her mouth a firm line.

"Then I will stay and watch, and learn. For you. Just for you."

Chapter Thirty-Five

Hippodamia

The centaur's heart is here," Hippodamia said, touching the breast of the horse. Pirithous's Fire, steadied by age and experience, she supposed. She did not so much as blink when Hippodamia placed the tip of the wooden sword to her hide, showing the best angle for a strike. "Encased by the ribs. Difficult to pierce, but not impossible. Particularly when he rears."

She could not look at Pirithous. Would not look at him, though she knew he watched, as she'd asked. That she might show him how to live, she told herself. It was not the same as showing him how to kill.

"But if you fear you do not have the strength or the aim, keep to his flanks," she said, stepping back behind Fire's withers. "A centaur's torso does not twist so easily as a man's, too thick with muscle to support the sharp bend of the back. But you must be careful, still, of the hind legs and the hooves. A kick will kill you as surely as a sword or the blow of a club. Perhaps even more easily."

The girls watched her with wide eyes, following her around the horse. She could not bring herself to smile, or even to meet their eager gazes. The women stood farther back, wary and whispering. She did not know what else she could do to convince them of her loyalty, her determination to keep them safe. Was teaching them how to defend themselves not proof enough that she bore them no malice?

"And if a centaur should catch hold of you," she went on, stroking Fire's neck as she ducked under her head, "his forehooves are just as dangerous as the rear, sharp enough to cut a snake in half. He will trample you, if you fall beneath him. He will strike with them, if you are near enough and he has no other weapon to hand."

"Then we will practice attacks from the side," Antiope said, sitting atop Fire. "Since that is safest and most deadly. A blade through the intestines will bleed out, if it does not poison them as well."

"Here," Hippodamia agreed, patting Fire's barrel. "A sword could be buried deep, and the centaur would likely be maddened by the pain. Perhaps enough to distract him from whatever lust burns in his veins."

Antiope swung down from Fire's back, passing Hippodamia the reins. "Lyco, you begin. Aim for his flanks."

The woman lifted her bow, fitting an arrow and drawing it back. Pirithous had brought a straw-stuffed target from the men's games for their use, and Antiope had been more than pleased to have Hippodamia's guidance and help in teaching the girls where to aim.

She pressed her face into the horse's neck, unable to watch the arrow sink into the straw, knowing that they imagined her people in the target's place. Centaurus's people, whom she had promised to protect. *Poseidon Horse-Lord, forgive me. Forgive my people. Forgive us all. Save us from this war.*

But she knew in her heart the gods had forsaken the centaurs. If Poseidon had still blessed them, Centaurus never could have died. Cyllarus would not be intent upon war. Eurytion had ruined everything—Eurytion and Peleus, together, if Pirithous was not wrong.

"Well done, Lyco," Antiope said, after the arrow struck with a meaty thump. "Now you, Eritha. The rest of you will have to rely upon your blades, for you have no hope of hitting anything with an arrow, and it will take more than seven days of games to teach you any skill with a spear."

"But you will teach us, Lady, will you not?" Lyco asked. "After the games have ended?"

"Antiope must return to Athens with King Theseus," Pirithous said, though when he had moved to join them rather than only stand upon the edge of the field, Hippodamia was not certain. She turned her head, peeking through Fire's mane to find him beside her, his hand upon Fire's flank. "But I have heard that our queen has some skill with a bow. Perhaps she will teach you, instead."

She straightened, giving Pirithous a narrowed glance. "I know how to hunt with a bow, of course, but little more."

"That is more than most of these women know," Antiope said, scowling at Pirithous. "And if they are willing, they should be taught. Hunting a man is not so different from hunting a deer or a rabbit, after all."

"I—" But what was the point in refusing? Either the centaurs would come and the women would be left to their own defense, or Pirithous and his men would win, and they might still face Peleus. And if she remained… If she remained, there was no reason why she should not teach them all that she knew, that in the next war, whenever it came, they might protect themselves.

Hippodamia swallowed, giving Lyco a nod. "I will teach you everything I know. And when next the Lapiths see battle against their walls, you will guard your men and yourselves from their height, with bow and arrow."

Antiope clasped her arm, as the warriors greeted one another, and smiled fiercely. "I will hold you to that promise, Queen Hippodamia."

She met the Amazon's eyes. This promise was what Antiope had wanted from the start, why she had befriended her. To see the Lapith women made equal to their men, granted the power to protect themselves and their children. To see that Dia's legacy was not lost. But even knowing, it still stung. "One way or another, they will learn."

"Let it be the more peaceful way, if there is a choice," Antiope said, her gaze shifting to Pirithous, over her shoulder. "You will see this is done? Your word as a king. Sworn upon the Styx."

"If it is my queen's will, it is mine as well," Pirithous said. "By the Styx, I will give them bows and arrows, and let Hippodamia teach them to hunt and shoot."

Antiope's mouth thinned, her gaze falcon-hard, and Hippodamia was not so foolish that she did not know why. Pirithous did not make promises carelessly, always aware of his own interests, his own desires, and turning the needs and wishes of others to his own cause. It was his gift, to make others believe they shared in his vision. To force others to share in it, with careful promises.

He would give Antiope what she wanted, Hippodamia knew, but only if she and Antiope served him in return.

Only if she stayed to teach them herself.

Only if she remained his queen.

Hippodamia's fingers curled tightly into Fire's mane, and she was glad for the horse, for her steadiness and her warmth. Horses made truer friends than men and Amazons, no matter how insistently she prayed otherwise.

Thank the gods it was Theseus who would ride out at her side to meet the centaurs, and not his wife.

***

"Tell me, Mia," Antiope said later, as they walked Fire back to the stables together. "Do you mean to leave him?"

The girls and women had been sent back to their homes to prepare for the feasting, and Pirithous had left some time earlier to watch the men and grant them their prizes. If Hippodamia had been given her way, she'd have walked alone.

"I do not mean to do anything but speak to my people," she said, keeping the old mare between them. "But if there is some way I might secure a peace between us, of course I will see it done. And surely the lives saved are more valuable than a girl's skill with a bow, even to you."

Antiope caught Fire's bridle, pulling them both to a stop. "You still mistrust me."

Hippodamia did not look at her, staring ahead at the barn instead. "If your people came to Athens, intent upon war, and the only way to bring peace was to leave Theseus, would you not go? To save the lives of Amazons and Athenians alike?"

"It is not a fair question, Mia," Antiope said. "Theseus and I married for love, knowing the risks. Knowing we courted war. We weighed those risks together."

"And I married for peace," she said. "I married to keep our peoples both safe. Not for love at all, though perhaps—perhaps I am fortunate enough to find some small taste of it, however flawed. But that does not change my purpose. I cannot let it."

"You can," Antiope insisted. "And perhaps you should. If Centaurus loved you as a daughter, truly, he must have wanted more than to use you. He must have wanted you to have some opportunity of happiness, no matter how small. Do you honestly believe you could have any kind of life among the centaurs now? Any kind of love? Or children?"

She flinched, tugging Fire forward again. There was nothing Antiope would not say to convince her to remain, Hippodamia reminded herself. For Theseus's sake. For Pirithous's. For the girls and women of the Lapiths. For herself. The friendship they had forged had only ever been secondary to all the rest. That much had been made clear long before now.

"Mia, you cannot tell me it is not true," Antiope said, skipping to catch up again. "You cannot tell me your father would have wanted you to die alone in misery!"

"You know nothing of what my father wanted. Nothing of my father at all."

"I know love," Antiope said. "I know that when Centaurus put your hand in Pirithous's, he gave you up with pride and pleasure to something better. And now you would throw it all away. His last gift to you."

She shook her head, her throat thick with tears and grief. "He never believed Pirithous could love me. Perhaps if he had, if his last words to me had not been a warning, I would be persuaded now. But I am not a fool, Antiope. And I will not forget my duty so easily just because it does not match the desire of my heart. Or yours, for that matter."

"This isn't about me, Mia," Antiope said. "It has never been about me, no matter what you tell yourself. I only care for you and your happiness. For Pirithous's, too. You were meant for one another, and you will find nothing but misery apart. Do you think I left my people so easily? Betrayed my vows to the gods upon a whim? When we find our match, we owe it to ourselves, even to the gods, to join with them and become whole. Is that not what your people believe as well? You said yourself that centaurs mate for life, and I cannot imagine that Hylonome would ever abandon Cyllarus."

"Perhaps not," she agreed. "But she would sacrifice herself for him. She would throw herself between his body and an arrow aimed at his heart. She would die for him, as he would for her."

"Is that what you think you're doing?" Antiope asked. "Giving up your life for Pirithous's?"

"He would do the same for me. He *will* do the same for me, if the centaurs come. He will march out with his sword drawn, to protect me. To protect all of us. And I have no right to do any less."

Antiope fell silent, keeping pace on the other side of Fire, and Hippodamia tried not to think of what Cyllarus would do if Hylonome died. What any centaur as well-matched would do, if they lost their mate. But whether Pirithous loved her or not, she could not imagine he would drive a blade into his own heart, nor did she think he would be so easily convinced that his life was not worth living in her absence.

Men were not so devoted to their wives. Not even Theseus, no matter what Antiope told herself.

And not Pirithous.

Pirithous knew only how to live.

***

She spent the evening in the stable, grooming Podarkes carefully as an excuse to avoid the funeral pyres. Too often the men and women, even the children, looked on her with accusation and anger in their eyes, reminded by the flames of what they had lost when Pirithous had taken her as his bride. After spending all day teaching them to fight, she could not bear to see it. It was as if the Lapiths could not believe she meant them well—as if, as Theseus had said, they were determined to blame her, no matter what she did to prove herself. No doubt they would find just as much offense in her presence at the pyres as they did in her absence, regardless.

Podarkes nuzzled her, his soft nose tickling the curve of her neck, and she closed her eyes, hiding her face against his cheek. "If only your people were as kind-hearted as you," she murmured.

The horse whickered, then drew suddenly away, tossing his head and sidling back. She turned to see what had startled him, and found Pirithous leaning against the post of the stall. "Do you think all of us are so lacking, or just the grieving widows standing too near the flames?"

She flushed. "I do not mean to begrudge them their grief. Only the way they look upon me, as if their husbands had died at my hands. Eurytion killed my father, too, and not only his body, but his hopes and dreams as well. His and mine. He destroyed everything I had worked toward, trampling our peace under his careless hooves. I share in their grief, their sorrows, their pain, but they cannot see it. Will not see *me*."

"They only need time, mouse. We all need time."

"And time is the one thing we do not have," she said, running a last handful of straw down Podarkes's back. "I'm sorry, Pirithous.

I'm sorry I went to meet Eurytion that night. I'm sorry I did not refuse to marry you when the omens were so ill. I am sorry that instead of peace, I gave your people war."

"Mia—" He breathed her name into her hair, so close behind her she could feel the heat of his body against her back. "My little mouse, there is blame enough for all of us to choke upon a share if we wish, but I do not believe for a moment that any of it is yours. I do not believe for a moment that this was not all my folly, from the start. And if I have lost you because of it…"

His voice broke, and he dropped his forehead to her shoulder, one hand fisted in her tunic, at the waist. "Gods above, Mia, I will never forgive myself. I will never forgive myself for ruining this."

Her mouth was dry, her throat tight with words she could not say, promises she could not keep. She wanted to tell him he would not lose her. That she would stay in his arms forever, no matter what came. But she would not lie, could not bring herself to betray his trust so utterly as that. So she only turned, letting him draw her against his body, and found his lips with hers. Found the tears upon his cheeks with her fingertips and brushed them away, wishing she could brush it all away so easily. With just a kiss and a touch and the softness of her breasts pressed against hard muscle.

He kissed her back, his hand knotting in her hair, drawing her out of the stall, away from Podarkes. They tumbled into the hay a moment later, Pirithous cushioning her fall before rolling her to her back. His mouth had left hers, following the line of her jaw, down her throat, across her collarbone, leaving fire behind. Her back arched, her hands upon his shoulders, and the heat of his breath through her tunic, over her breasts, made her ache all over. He bit her through the linen, suckled her hardening nipples as they tightened in response.

It had been only days since they had made love, but it felt like those moments at the spring were years ago, her body was so hungry, so desperate for his. She wanted him. Wanted him safe and whole and home, his heart beating hard and fast against her own.

But his hands did not drift below her hem, did not search for the skin of her thighs beneath. His fingers did not pluck at the knot of her belt, did not curl into the cleft between her legs. And then his mouth had gone, too, his face turned away.

"I can't," he said. "Not if this is goodbye. Not if this is the last time I'll ever love you, ever know you. Tell me it isn't. Tell me you'll stay."

She drew his head up, searching his face. "Would you have me lie?"

He groaned, burying his face in the curve of her neck. "Tell me—tell me at least that you love me. Tell me that is not a lie."

She closed her eyes, twined her fingers through his hair. It would never be a lie. It would never be a lie, but if she said it, she would shatter. "Pirithous..."

"Please, Mia. If I must let you go, at least let me have your words. Let me know your heart."

"Oh, Pirithous." She brought his forehead down to hers, their noses brushing. "Pirithous, of course. Of course I love you." She swallowed the rasp of her voice, opening her eyes to stare into his, like moonlight shimmering through clouds. His expression blurred with her tears, but she took his face in her hands, held him steady, held him close. "If I go—it will not change that. I will always love you. I will always want to be with you. To be yours, again."

"Mia." He stroked her hair. "My little mouse, don't go. You don't have to go. We will fight. My people. The Lapiths. They want to fight. Just stay with me. Be mine, be mine and I will be yours."

The tears spilled, a sob heavy in her chest. "I wish I could promise you more."

He let out a ragged breath and kissed her. Kissed away her tears. Kissed away everything but him.

Chapter Thirty-Six

Pirithous

He made love to her in the hay, his horse-tamer, his little mouse. Not so shy anymore. Not afraid of anything at all, but perhaps for love. The love her centaurs would steal from her, if he did not stop them. If he did not stop her.

He had to stop her, and this was how he would begin. "I love you," he murmured against her throat, against her lips, whispered in the hollow between her breasts. "I love you, Mia. My love."

She arched against him, her fingers twisted in his hair, in his tunic. He pressed his thigh between her legs, giving her the pressure she needed without the satisfaction. She could beg, and plead, just as he wished to. She could pray to the gods for release, but he would not grant it. Not until she was his. Not until she had promised herself to him.

To him alone.

He unknotted her belt and drew her tunic over her head. The hay made a coarse bed, but she was strong, raised to race through the woods on horseback with branches tearing at her arms and legs. She stretched out upon the hay pile like a cat, the expanse of her bared brown skin a banquet of pleasures laid out for his tasting. He bowed his head, offering her the honors she deserved, praying at the altar of her beauty with hands and mouth and tongue.

Her hips rose with a whimper, her legs spreading of their own accord, but he would not dip between her thighs. Would not touch her below the waist with more than just his leg wedged between hers. She rubbed against him, rocked, squeezed. When he suckled her breasts, she writhed.

"Pirithous, please!" It was nearly a sob, a cry of need.

He lifted his head, letting her see his smile. "Stay with me."

She shook her head, grasping at his sides, his arms, fumbling with his belt, his tunic, searching for his skin. She was strong, but he was stronger. He rolled to his back, pulling her with him. She straddled his hips, the linen trapped between them, and she whimpered again, frustration and desire. The warmth of her center, the sight of her naked, but for a touch of light and shadow, and the pieces of hay in her dark hair. He wanted her. He wanted her to be his.

"Please," she breathed again, both her hands upon his chest. She had settled atop him so perfectly, had it not been for his tunic, he would already be inside her.

He lifted his hips, letting her feel his length. Teasing her. "Promise me."

She kissed him instead, the flare of her desire, her love, her desperation white-hot and needy, filling him up and adding fire to his own need. His hands settled upon her hips, but she rose up on her knees, laughter rippling through her kiss.

She had always been quick. Beautiful and brilliant. A perfect queen. His match in every way. And now she proved it, teasing him as he had teased her. Nipping at his earlobe, at his throat, dropping kisses across his collarbone, until she met linen instead of skin. One hand slipped between their bodies, her fingers wrapping around his desire.

"No more clever words," she said. "No more sly promises."

He groaned as her hand moved, warm through the linen, caressing, taunting, making him throb. She had learned so much, come so far to touch him so boldly, and he never wanted her to stop.

"Just love me, Pirithous," she murmured, her lips against his. "Let me go with your love."

He gathered her in, shifting forward, and helped her pull the tunic up over his head. Helped her fit her body to his, and gloried in the soft, breathy gasp she gave as he sank deep inside her warmth, filling her at last. They sat that way, breathing hard, as if joining alone was all they needed. And he knew, in that moment, as their hearts beat together, their foreheads meeting, and her nose against his, he never wanted anything else but this. Never wanted to move, if it meant she was forever his.

"I love you," he said again, without artifice this time. A selfless promise, instead of a bond. "I will love you, no matter what comes."

"Pirithous." She shuddered, her body clenching around his, and slowly, so slowly, as if she could not stand, either, for it to end a moment before it must. One hand upon her hip, he guided her, slow and easy, and he kissed her just as tenderly. Her body molded to his, and he held her so tightly, so carefully, keeping her now as he could not keep her later.

If this was to be goodbye, he would make it last. They would make it last, together.

As much of forever as they could have.

***

He left her sleeping, covered by the rough-spun wool of a horse blanket. Much as he would have preferred to stay with her, skin to skin, to linger in the warming bonfire of her love, he could not miss the banquet. Not without hurting his people. And they already suffered enough without such a slight from their king.

So he went and sat at the table in the megaron, with Theseus at his right hand, and he ignored Antiope's knowing glance when his wife did not join him. Hippodamia needed her rest, needed all her strength if she meant to stand against her people. And he knew well enough by now that he had not stopped her—could not stop her. Love only fed the flame of her need to act, it seemed. Not that he ought to have been surprised. He wanted to protect her all the more fiercely with every joining, every kiss, every touch, every glance and word exchanged. He wanted to protect her *because* of love.

"Your people grow restless, Pirithous," Theseus said. "And for that matter, so do I. How can you stand the waiting?"

"Would you ride out from the shelter of the Rock if you knew an army was on its way to break against your walls?" Pirithous asked, his lips twitching at his friend's impatience. "I thought you were supposed to be the more restrained of the two of us."

"Which accounts for my astonishment that you have sat by this long," Theseus said. "And while your walls are strong stone, this palace is hardly as solid as the Rock of Athens. Surely you should at least be gathering supplies in case of siege."

"Centaurs do not lay siege," Pirithous replied, unable to keep his good humor, or even the appearance of it. "I do not need Hippodamia to tell me that. Nor should you."

"It is not only the centaurs you have to concern yourself with," Theseus said, his voice low. "They will come like a tidal wave, and break, to be sure. At what cost, we cannot know. It will be violent and fierce, but it will not last. Peleus, though—his Myrmidons will not be so easily undone. They are disciplined, Pirithous. Hardened and determined men, and excellent fighters, all of them."

Pirithous pressed his lips thin. The truth was, he did not wish to think overmuch of Peleus. Not when he had the centaurs to concern himself with first. If he could only keep his men behind the walls, keep the gates barred and barricaded, they might repulse them with little in the way of casualty. But he had only to look around the megaron, watching his men feast with hollow eyes and grimaces instead of smiles, to know their blood still ran too hot for reason. The centaurs would come down the mountain, and his people would charge out to meet them.

"Centaurs!" Melanthos burst in through the doors, gasping for breath. Pirithous had set him upon the wall, along with a number of his other men—those he knew would remain loyal, no matter what came. "The centaurs are coming, my lord! Down the mountain, with arrows aflame and already flying."

Pirithous cursed. And Hippodamia lay naked and asleep in the stables, unprepared. He had not expected them at night, but he should have. He should have known they would not war like men. "Send word below. Bring the women and children inside the walls, with any livestock and supplies they can carry. But quickly!"

"I sent men already to warn them," Melanthos said. "But if the fire catches—"

"Yes, I know." The horses would panic if fire broke inside the walls. To say nothing of what it would do to their crops, outside. Pirithous rose, lifting his voice above the roar of the men all leaping from their seats. "Get your women and children to safety first! No man is to meet the centaurs until all have been brought inside the walls. We will fight together!"

"Hippodamia?" Theseus asked. Antiope was already gone, no doubt eager to retrieve her bow and find a place upon the wall before the men began to crowd it.

"The stables," Pirithous said. "Asleep!"

"Not for long," Theseus said. "Will you come?"

"I'll need a horse, regardless," he agreed. "Or they will not hear a word I say. Melanthos! Get back to the wall and send Atukhos and a dozen of the young men to the horse pastures. If the centaurs charge us, it will not be long before Peleus seeks to take advantage of our distraction, and I will not lose our horses so easily."

Melanthos shoved his way through the others to escape the megaron, and Pirithous followed with Theseus at his back. He must get to the stables. He must reach Hippodamia before she woke and heard the word of it herself. She would be too eager to ride out, too desperate to wait for Theseus to join her.

Once they were out in the yard, free of the press of people, he broke into a run. He did not need to look to know Theseus kept pace. Straight through the palace courtyard and around to the stables. Machaon would be there shortly, no doubt, once word reached him, but Pirithous worried less for the horses and more for his wife. If she had heard, and gone already—

"Theseus!" Antiope waited for them, a sword belt in her hands and her bow and quiver upon her back. "Your sword. And your promise that you will take care. I can only do so much to protect you from the wall."

"Mia?" Pirithous demanded.

"Inside, yet."

He left Theseus with Antiope to their goodbyes, and pushed through the stable door. Deeply shadowed, the lamps unlit and the moon hidden behind the clouds, he clipped his elbow against a stall before he slowed. "Mouse?"

"Pirithous!" She caught him by the hand as he neared Podarkes's stall, and threw herself into his arms. "You're here. And I must go. I must go, before it is too late."

She had dressed, the soft linen of her tunic smelling of horse and hay as he crushed her against his chest. "I know."

"I'm sorry," she said. "I'm so sorry."

"No," he said, framing her face in his hands. "As long as you live, that is all that matters. Go and do what you must, but promise me you will protect yourself, too. Let Theseus guard you, and do not risk your life more than necessary."

She gulped back a sob, nodding once, and he let her go, reaching for Podarkes, already bridled. If he did not busy himself, he would throw her over his shoulder and haul her back into the palace. He threw a blanket over the horse's back and drew him from the stall. Dimly, he knew Theseus was seeing to his own horse, Antiope helping him, but he could only hear Hippodamia. Her hitched breaths, her soft touches. He found the glint of her eyes in the darkness and drank in every shadow of her form.

She caught his hand again, and slung an arm around his neck, pulling his head down for a frantic, desperate kiss. He savored the taste of her mouth, even the dampness of her tears beneath his fingertips, before she tore her lips from his, and he lifted her up onto the horse's back.

"Go!" he said. "Before I change my mind."

She hesitated only a heartbeat, then swung her leg over Podarkes's withers and kicked him into a gallop, Theseus right behind.

They had no more time.

Chapter Thirty-Seven

Hippodamia

They rode against the rush of people streaming toward the main gate of the palace, but there were men enough upon the wall, and at the sight of them charging toward it, the back gate lurched open. Hippodamia had wondered at the village's placement upon the riverbank, but she was glad now to know they would have that much more shelter, that much more protection. The centaurs would have to circle the palace to reach it, coming within range of the archers on the wall, and it gave her time before they clashed against the Lapiths, besides. Before the lust for blood overcame any hope of reason.

She could see them, now that they were beyond the wall, with their flaming arrows fitted to their bows. The first round of arrows guttered in the open field and the grasses before the wall, and the centaurs still stuck to the tree line, darker shadows against the black of the wood where they did not carry flame.

"Hippodamia, Tamer of Horses, Daughter of Centaurus would speak with Cyllarus and Hylonome!" Hippodamia called, reining Podarkes in before she entered the range of their bows. And how far might Antiope's arrows fly? Farther, she thought, than the bows of the centaurs could reach.

"And who rides with you?" a harsh voice shouted back.

"Theseus, Son of Poseidon Horse-Lord!" he answered for himself.

Hoofbeats sounded against earth, hard and fast, and Hippodamia held Podarkes steady, her chin high and her back straight. She would not let them frighten her. Would not let them think her weak. Not now.

The galloping shadows resolved into two forms, and Cyllarus and Hylonome slowed their charge, stopping only near enough for her to recognize them, with wary glances at the wall at her back.

Cyllarus reared, too restless to keep still even when he dropped again to four hooves. "Theseus has delivered you, as we asked."

"Theseus stands at my side as guard and witness. I am here only to ask for peace. To beg you for it, if I must."

Cyllarus sneered. "Peace! With the man who killed your own father?"

"Eurytion killed Centaurus," she said, letting Podarkes toss his head, that Cyllarus might see the sign of her anger in the shift of his weight, the flick of his tail. "Eurytion murdered him, to steal me, to break the peace my father forged. And you have taken up his purpose, like foals too young to know the difference between passion and truth."

"Do you think it matters?" Cyllarus demanded. "Do you think truth will stop them from hunting us down? Whether Eurytion or your husband killed Centaurus, it changes nothing. Your precious Lapiths will not rest until our blood has watered the mountain! Your king has admitted as much, himself."

"The centaurs began this war," Hippodamia said. "The centaurs broke the peace. You have a duty to make it right, not worse! If you had offered terms, Pirithous would have listened. He would have done everything in his power to keep peace between our peoples."

"He has no power," Hylonome spat. "If he did, he would not have told us to run. To flee before his people came for our blood."

"The centaurs wronged them," she said. "Wronged *me* because King Peleus whispered lies in Eurytion's ears, knowing what he would start. Do you not see this is what they want? An excuse for war and butchery! Peleus makes fools of you, using you for his own ends, his own reasons. If you had gone, shown that you meant no further threat to the Lapiths, Pirithous and I might have persuaded them, in time, to give up their anger, their thirst for vengeance. But not now. Not ever again, if you continue on this path. You sentence our people to death, if you charge!"

"But the Lapiths will die with us," Cyllarus said, baring his teeth. "And when we are finished, King Peleus will kill the rest. We will have peace after that, the fool men in their palaces too weakened to bother with hunting us. Peace on our terms!"

"It is no use, Lady," Theseus said, his voice low. "He is committed. And by the sound of it, Peleus has struck his own bargain with your people, now. One in which you have no place."

She shook her head, and beneath her, Podarkes stamped the earth. "You are blinded by lust and rut, Cyllarus, if you think Peleus will treat you with anything but contempt. The Lapiths are our brothers, our blood, through Ixion."

"And Ixion is dead," he snarled. "Pirithous is no son of his, no kin of ours at all. You plead with me for your own sake, that you might return to your husband's bed without guilt. To save *his* life, more than ours. And now that I know it, now that we all have seen where your loyalties truly lie, we need not worry ourselves over your sacrifice. Go back to your palace, go cower behind your walls, and when your husband dies, you will see the truth in how quickly the Lapiths turn you out."

"Come, Mia," Theseus said, catching hold of Podarkes's bridle. "You need not listen to this. You have done your duty to your father's dream."

But she had one last thing to say, and she raised her voice, lifting it to be heard even by those who waited in the trees.

"At the shrine, you promised that if the Lapiths must pay in blood for peace, the centaurs would offer their share of it in sacrifice. You knew the omens, and you agreed to the price. If you do this, if you fight this battle against the Lapiths, you are oathbreakers and betrayers! You are *beasts*."

Cyllarus growled, drawing a sword from a scabbard across his back. Theseus jerked Podarkes's bridle, cursing, but Hippodamia dropped from the horse's back to stand before the centaur she had once counted as a friend. She lifted her chin and spread her arms wide as the point of the blade pressed against her throat. A blade he should not have had at all, for centaurs did not carry swords. None but Chiron knew how to forge metals from the earth, and men were rarely willing to trade good bronze up the mountain.

"Go ahead," she said. "You are so determined to destroy everything Centaurus built, everything he worked toward, why should you not begin with me?"

"Cyllarus, stop this," Hylonome hissed. "You cannot strike her down this way. Not here, not now. Sheath your blade and leave her to the Lapiths. That is punishment enough for her betrayal."

The tip of the blade pressed harder against her throat, pricking her skin, and she felt the cold chill of her blood welling beneath its edge.

Then Cyllarus reared, twisting away from the arrow that had appeared in the ground at his hooves. Hylonome cried out, and that time, Hippodamia heard the *thwip* of the arrow as it flew through the air, sinking into the dirt.

"Come, Lady!" Theseus urged, whirling upon his horse and offering his arm to her. "Quickly!"

Hippodamia grasped it, swinging up behind him onto his mare. Podarkes followed close at her tail as Theseus kicked her into a gallop, back toward the wall and the gate. She could hear the thunder of hooves behind her, and knew the centaurs charged down the mountain, chasing after them. But if nothing else, she had given Pirithous and his people more time. Time to find safety. Time to gather behind the walls. Podarkes squealed and charged ahead, leaving them choking on dust, and Theseus pushed the mare faster.

The gate opened just wide enough to allow them through, and arrows thudded hard against the wood at her back as it closed again. Pirithous had Podarkes by the bridle, and torches were lit inside the walls, blindingly bright after the darkness on the mountain.

"Easy," he said, but he handed her horse off to Machaon the moment their eyes met, and he half pulled her from the mare's back, searching her face, her body for any sign of injury or harm. He touched her throat, his fingers gentle. "He cut you."

She buried her face in the curve of his neck in answer, her mouth too dry with dust to speak and her thoughts too scattered. He wrapped her in his arms, and if he felt her trembling, he made no mention of it, only tucked her head beneath his chin.

"Brave mouse," he murmured. "All the women and children are safe because of you. Inside the palace, now, where I would send you, if I thought for a moment you would go."

She might have laughed if her chest were not so tight with sorrow. "He would not listen. He says I have betrayed them. And Peleus. They've come to terms with Peleus."

"That sword was Phthian bronze," Theseus said, though she had not realized he stood with them still. "No doubt he means for the centaurs to weaken you, to waste their lives in order to tire your men. I expect Peleus will be here by morning, hoping to catch you exhausted by a night of battle."

"Then we will have to save our strength," he said grimly. "I will go and speak to the men, ask for half of them to remain behind, in reserve. Even to rest, if they are able, assuming the centaurs do not break down our gates."

"My lord!" a man called, half-frantic.

Pirithous grunted, releasing her from his arms too soon to take her by the hand instead, squeezing tightly. "Antiope is on the wall with a bow and quiver for you. Go to her, and do not take any further risks, I beg of you. Unless there is anything else I should know?"

She shook her head. "Nothing that Theseus cannot tell you. But you must live, Pirithous. It is you they want dead more than anyone, to punish me. To punish us both."

He grinned, bringing her fingers to his lips. "I would not give them the satisfaction, I promise you. And this time I will know how best to defend myself."

It was a relief to know he spoke truly. That she had shown him the way herself. And from the wall, she would be better able to watch him, even to guard him, if she must, though her aim was not so well-honed as Antiope's, and she had never thought to hunt her own people with the bow.

"I will find you when this is over," Pirithous promised. "But if Peleus comes before we finish, do not stay atop the wall. Go to the palace. To the storeroom. You remember? Antiope will know how to shift the stone. Bring as many of the women and children with you as will follow. You will be safest there."

"And you?"

He closed his hand upon the pommel of his sword. "I am a son of Zeus. Unless Peleus brings Heracles to fight for him, he will not win. At worst, I will simply be a few horses poorer come nightfall."

She prayed to the gods he was not wrong, and went as he asked, to join Antiope upon the wall.

***

There were arrows still to fear, even upon the walls, and she and Antiope took shelter half-bent behind the stone, their own arrows nocked and ready to fly as needed.

"You are a fool!" Antiope said, her eyes liquid in the moonlight. Upon the wall, they depended on shadow for safety, and Antiope had nearly knocked one of the men senseless with his own brand when she saw him trying to light a torch. But now her fury was directed only at Hippodamia, and she could not deny that she deserved it. "Pirithous did not see what happened, his eyes spoiled by the fire, but I did, and if you ever do anything of the kind again, it will be *my* sword at your throat, I promise you."

"He would not have killed me," she said, though she was not so sure she believed it, now. Her fingers itched to touch the soft scab at her throat, but she forced herself to fidget with her bow instead. A better excuse not to meet Antiope's eyes.

"You make a poor liar," Antiope snapped. "And as long as you are on the wall with me, you will do as I say. I will not have Pirithous holding your injury over my head for the rest of my days, and I do not intend to let you put yourself in danger again."

She glanced over the top of the wall, catching glimpses of fire and centaurs racing past, some with clubs, others with swords. Pirithous had kept the men inside the walls, so far, but she knew it would not last. Already, smoke rose in thick black plumes, blocking the stars. The houses were burning, along with the goat sheds and the fields. And the men wanted blood, just as the centaurs did. Putting out fires inside the walls would not sate them for long.

"What will we eat when this is over?" she heard herself say, her gaze caught upon the burning grain. "The wheat is utterly lost."

"Pirithous has stores, and plenty to trade for more, if what he has set aside is not enough. But Theseus is sure to offer foodstuffs, and unlikely to accept anything in payment for the kindness."

"Hylonome and Cyllarus want Pirithous dead, in the hopes that the Lapiths will turn upon me after he is gone. That I might suffer for my betrayal. For speaking as my father would have, with reason instead of rage."

Antiope grasped her wrist. "If the Lapiths send you from their midst, you will always have a place at my side, in Athens. And as Pirithous's bride, Theseus would give you his protection even if I did not insist upon it. You have nothing to fear, Hippodamia."

But it was not fear of losing her place among the Lapiths that chewed at her insides. It was not fear of how they might treat her. It was fear for Pirithous. Pirithous, who was all she had left.

CHAPTER THIRTY-EIGHT

PIRITHOUS

Pirithous did not like dividing his men. A few dozen at each of the gates, ready with swords and dressed in leather armor; his best archers upon the walls, half-blind in the dark; and the other half of them held reluctantly back, though Pirithous did not think they would remain so for long. Had he men and space to spare beyond that, he would have sent them for his horses, but even with the delay Hippodamia had provided they could not have returned them to the shelter of the palace in time.

He could only hope that Atukhos would scatter the herds, that Peleus would not find them so easily raided in any great number. A few mares here or there did not matter, but the wealth of the Lapiths depended upon the herds, and with the crops burned, they would need to trade the horses for food, or risk starvation come winter.

"My lord, we cannot wait here, putting out fires inside the walls and letting them destroy our fields and our homes," Melanthos said. "The men do not have your patience, and I must admit that mine wears thinner by the moment, as well."

"Short of breaking down the gates, the centaurs cannot breach our walls. We are safe, Melanthos. And what is the rest? Nothing we cannot rebuild, or plant again. Nothing we cannot recover, given time."

"Perhaps if they had not already killed our brothers, our fathers, raped our wives and daughters, it would be easier to cower behind these walls, to let them have their way this night. But not after what we have already suffered at their hands. This is insult added to grave injury, to grief. We who have fought with you will do whatever you ask, but you cannot ask this of the others. These men will not be satisfied by anything less than blood."

"And as their king, I should let them throw themselves upon centaur swords?" Pirithous demanded.

Melanthos looked away, staring at the gate, where the constant thud of arrows and clubs could be heard over the voices of his men. "You are my king, Pirithous, and I am proud to name you so, but these others—they do not know you as I do. To them, this is weakness, not strength. To them, this is proof you have betrayed us to the centaurs by your marriage to Hippodamia. If you wish to keep your throne, you must let them fight. You must lead them in battle—now, tonight."

He knew it. Had known it from the start. But he liked hearing it even less than he cared for dividing his men. And even worse, it meant opening the gates, and if even one man's courage failed then, the centaurs would have opportunity to invade the palace itself. And he could not afford that fight. Not now. Not with Peleus and his Myrmidons waiting for the sun to rise.

"I want our men at the gate when it opens. The blooded raiders, ready to cut down any centaur who forces his way through. Gather them, and we will fight."

Melanthos nodded, his lips curving in anticipation, and left him. Pirithous glanced up at the wall, at Antiope and Hippodamia huddled against the stone, taking turns shooting into the dark beyond, harrying the centaurs for whatever good it would do. He wished he could stay at her side. Wished he could sweep her away from all of this, that she need never watch her people die.

"Which gate will you open?" Theseus asked, rejoining him not long after. Pirithous had sent him off to the village gate to check on the men there, but Melanthos would surely have spoken with him. Not that he intended to allow Theseus into the fray. If Pirithous failed, he needed someone he could trust inside the walls to keep his people safe. To keep Hippodamia safe.

Pirithous grimaced. "I suppose that depends a great deal upon how much smoke cloaks the village. The centaurs have better vision in the dark, and I would rather not watch my men choke to death before they see battle."

"It would provide them more cover than the mountainside. The centaurs seem less intent upon breaking through at the main gate, besides. Too busy destroying the buildings beyond the walls to bother with what they cannot yet reach."

"Then they make the choice for me." And he could only hope it was not some cunning on their part, to drive him out with the river ahead and the walls behind. If Cyllarus had planned this—or even hoped for it—he would be leading his men into a trap. "What is there to be seen from the walls?"

Theseus shook his head. "Smoke more than anything else. Movements and shadows. We must keep the men close to the ground and pressed against the walls until they escape its cloak."

"Not we," Pirithous said, clapping his friend on the shoulder. "I need you here. To lend the men upon the walls your wisdom, and guard the mountain gate against invasion. Hippodamia, as well."

"Your wife seems well able to care for herself." Theseus's gaze shifted over his shoulder, and Pirithous knew he watched the women. "She will not be in any real danger unless this ends badly, but I suspect Antiope would serve her well enough as a protector, even so."

"If I do not survive the battle, I would know you live to shelter her in Athens. She has no one else, nothing else but us, now."

Theseus grunted. "It is a good thing we did not marry before now, or neither one of us would have any reputation at all, the way we are so desperate to live for our wives. Go then, and may Zeus and Athena see you safe. I will guard both our women and your palace, though I hope you do not expect me to stay behind when Peleus comes."

Pirithous grinned. "You may be among the first to fight against the Myrmidons, I promise you. At least they will fight like men rather than beasts."

"Go!" Theseus said again, his smile wry. "Before I change my mind."

***

He did not know how many centaurs waited beyond the walls, and though many of his people were desperate to spill their blood, there were only a few dozen he could trust to keep their heads in battle. Less than half of the men who would follow him through the gates.

"We are ready," Melanthos said, touching his fist to his forehead. "The gate opens at your word."

"Be wary," Pirithous told him. "If this is a trap meant to lure us, I would not have the bulk of our men caught unawares."

"Centaurs haven't the cunning for ruses, my lord," Melanthos said.

Pirithous bit his tongue on an argument, and gripped his shoulder briefly in answer, instead. Melanthos might not agree, but he would do as Pirithous asked. He always did.

From the main gate, he could not see Hippodamia. Did not know if she realized he had gone to lead his men. She would know it soon enough, he supposed, and he could only hope she would not watch too closely.

"Cyllarus and the centaurs have come for our blood," he called out, raising his voice to be heard even upon the walls. "They accuse us of false crimes, of false friendship, while they break our most sacred bonds of hospitality and alliance. They have murdered our men, raped our women. They offend the gods and betray your queen! Tonight, we fight for those they have taken from us. And we must win!"

The men roared, swords thumping against the wood and leather of their round shields. Leather armor and hide shields would do little to protect against the swing of a club or the kick of powerful hindquarters, but they would prevent an arrow from sinking too deep into a man's chest, perhaps even stop it from drawing blood altogether, if the gods were with them. Melanthos and most of the rest of his raiders wore bronze chest plates, greaves, and bracers, though Pirithous was not sure how much good that would do them against the centaurs, either.

He jerked his chin at the gate, and the heavy wooden bar was removed, the wide doors groaning slowly open.

"Stay low and close to the walls!" Pirithous commanded. "And keep together."

Otherwise they would be run down, one at a time. But it would do him no good to say as much. The men who would obey would live, and those too rattled to listen would break from the line no matter what warning he gave.

He did not wait for the gate to open fully, but slipped through with Melanthos the moment he could fit, crouching low. He'd abandoned his bronze helm, and chosen a wooden shield wrapped in hide rather than metal. The bronze would only reflect the fire light, and he preferred the cover of shadow. Sometimes, in the night, he could convince a tired guard to ignore the evidence of his own eyes, but against the centaurs, he was unsure of his power. Lust and rage were not easily squelched, and while he could easily fan the flames of those emotions, it would only give the centaurs greater strength in the moments when he would no doubt wish them exhausted instead.

He kept his blade behind his shield, the better to keep the bronze from glinting, and when no centaur came charging out of the haze of smoke, he thumped his hilt against the wood, signaling the others even as he continued on. He would not take them into the village to choke, where they would not see the centaurs coming, but if they followed the wall, perhaps they would catch their enemies by surprise, and more importantly, spear them in their flanks as they charged by.

Perhaps he should have told his men where to aim. Perhaps it had been his duty to share what he had learned. But he could not bring himself to betray Hippodamia so completely as that. The centaurs had wronged them, no question, but it was Cyllarus who had brought them down the mountain this night, Cyllarus who had refused all reason in the wake of Centaurus's death. It was Cyllarus who needed killing, and then—but he knew better than to believe the centaurs would turn back. If anything, Cyllarus's death would only deepen their rage. They were true sons of Ixion, after all. Steeped in his madness. Driven by it, now. He had been a fool to think they would respond otherwise, after Centaurus had died.

But he had wanted to believe, for Hippodamia's sake, that all this slaughter might be avoided.

He did not need to look to know the men had followed, slipping as silently through the gate as he and Melanthos had, a moment earlier. He could feel their anticipation, their excitement, their anger and their fear, so loud and distinct he could have counted each of them by it. Melanthos was cool, relaxed and ready. Plouteus was determined and angry. Kotullon was impatient and so terrified Pirithous expected the centaurs would smell the sourness of his sweat even through the smoke. The rest of his raiders were scattered throughout the column, the better to lend confidence to the unblooded men and hold the line if the centaurs charged. Spots of calm in the storm of emotion that raged at his back.

He wished he had not sent Atukhos up the mountain. Melanthos was steady, but Atukhos never went into battle without a joke upon his lips, and Pirithous could have used his humor now.

The *thunk* of the gate being closed and barred sounded only dimly in his ears as he crept around the corner of the wall. He'd seen flashes of movement as he went, but nothing near enough to strike at. The centaurs must have moved down the bank, to the river's edge. Pirithous prayed they did not burn his ships.

All the gold and prizes he had hoarded, thinking he need never raid again, that his riches would ensure his people would never be made poor again after Ixion had bled every scrap of wealth from their bones, until they had been forced to sell their own children to the palace for his favor, and now this. He would be fortunate indeed if he did not have to trade even his horses for the supplies they would need to rebuild.

Pirithous raised his sword, catching the moonlight on the blade to signal the men to halt as he peered cautiously along the next expanse of wall. This was not any different than a night raid, he supposed, though he had never thought to use those skills to defend his own lands.

The wall curved outward, offering him little in the way of sight lines, but the crops were burning, bright as a bonfire. Without the shadows, they would be exposed. He made his blade flash again, then thumped the hilt against the stone. *Move quickly.* The village men would not understand the nuance, but his raiders would. A glance over his shoulder gave him nods in return, his men poised to run low and fast.

He lifted his sword—no reason to keep it behind his shield in the blazing light of the fields—and darted around the corner. The smoke was not so thick here, no longer trapped by the walls, and drifting toward the river. He filled his lungs, grateful for the clearer air, and prayed to Zeus for protection as he charged around the bend of the long curving wall.

They caught the first centaur by surprise, and Pirithous stabbed him straight through the heart before he had time to call out. Melanthos overtook him while he withdrew his blade, launching his spear in a clean arc. The tip punched through the next centaur's torso. A worthless throw, though he did not know it, by his whoop of pleasure. Behind him, the other men gave war cries, charging forward against their foes.

"Keep together!" Pirithous roared, for the centaurs had seen them now, and begun to turn, galloping full tilt and calling back to the others. The beast who had taken the spear through the shoulder had torn it free, rearing up and waving it at the sky. "Aim for the barrels, not the torsos. Watch those hooves!"

Melanthos cast him a sharp look for such a quick response, but Pirithous ignored the accusation in his eyes. He had needed Melanthos's bad throw for an excuse, needed to see with his own eyes what Hippodamia had told him before he commanded his men. And the centaurs were upon them as soon as the words had left his lips. So fast. Too fast. Pirithous ducked and swung, feinted and jabbed. They had not recognized him yet, but he could see Cyllarus. Standing on higher ground, watching both the mountain gate and their advance. The coward did not even risk his own hide.

The other centaurs did not matter. Just a shield of flesh, a bulwark of hooves and tails and wordless roaring. His eyes burned, his father's lightning in his veins, and he cut them down. Cut his way through. Cyllarus would not leave alive. Cyllarus would not bring this ruin down upon him, upon Hippodamia, and survive.

"My lord, wait!" Melanthos called. How he had stayed at his side, Pirithous was not certain. "They will swarm you!"

"They will try." He jerked his chin to the other men, struggling against the tide. These centaurs were well armed, but they did not know how to use the swords they swung, not as well as his men. Even Kotullon managed to deflect their blades, though he was still grim, muscles trembling, and raining sweat. "Keep them together. And if some of the centaurs follow me, all to the good. Keep them safe, Melanthos. As safe as they can be kept."

"Pirithous—"

"That is my command!"

Melanthos clasped his arm, squeezing tightly. "May Zeus protect you."

Pirithous bared his teeth, not quite a smile, and left him behind.

CHAPTER THIRTY-NINE

HIPPODAMIA

Hippodamia did not understand what she saw at first. The centaurs charging, the clash of swords and the shouts of men. She did not understand the two men who broke through, hesitated together, and parted. Not until she realized it was Pirithous, and he was charging toward Cyllarus.

The centaur reared, sword high and flashing with reflected fire. There was so much fire. So many flames, and so much smoke, and yet, somehow, she could see them so clearly. As if the gods had parted the haze to watch from above. As if they meant for her to see it, too.

"Oh, Pirithous," she breathed. "Oh, Pirithous, please. Please, Poseidon, protect him."

Antiope grabbed her by the arm, jerking her down just as an arrow flew past her head. "Keep your head, Mia, or you will lose it."

"He cannot think this will finish anything. He cannot think it will do any good!"

The Amazon craned her neck, peering over the stone, and then slumped back again. "Fool man. They are all fools, every one. No Amazon would have left the shelter of the walls. Not to fight against beasts. There is no honor in it. No purpose at all."

Hippodamia closed her eyes, letting her head thump against the stone. Beasts without honor. She could not even argue against the words. The way they had attacked the women at the feast. The things Cyllarus had said since. Everything he had done. To forge an alliance with Peleus and betray the Lapiths so completely. Centaurus would have killed him for it. Everything the centaurs had done, and all because Peleus had whispered in Eurytion's ear and poured him more wine.

She drew an arrow, fitted it to her bow, and glanced over the wall, searching for Pirithous, for Cyllarus, for Hylonome, who would not be far from his side. Never far. And after this, it would be only a matter of time. Days, perhaps months, but she would die. They would all die in payment for this destruction. They would be torn from their mountain, from the trees, with only their rotting corpses left behind.

Cyllarus swung, and Pirithous raised his sword, catching the blade and spinning out from beneath it, looking to reach the centaur's flank. Cyllarus was too fast, dancing back before he could strike. She lifted her bow, waiting for the right moment, for Cyllarus to forget about the danger of the archers upon the walls. Cyllarus had taken her peace. He had destroyed everything she had worked for. She would not let him take her husband, as well.

She would not let him destroy her.

"Mia…"

"He betrayed everything, Antiope. Everything I was raised to do, he ruined. And now my people will die because of him."

"He was your friend, Mia," she said. "Leave him to Pirithous, and he will give you justice. Or even let it be my arrow, my aim. It need not be done by your hand."

"He is Ixion's madness made flesh. Pirithous has faced enough of it, suffered enough of his father's nightmares. I brought this madness down upon him again, and I will finish it."

Pirithous and Cyllarus danced, blades flashing as they tested one another, and the other centaurs, those not facing his men, had begun to take notice. Hylonome had come down the mountain, a bow in her hands, and Hippodamia cursed at the sight of it. "Can you disarm her?"

Antiope let an arrow fly, and Hylonome reared with a shout. Cyllarus glanced back and Pirithous brought his blade down, catching him at the hairline and slicing across his nose, his face, his chest. Enraging, but not mortal, and Cyllarus struck at him with his hooves, catching him square in the chest. Pirithous stumbled back, tripped over a rock and nearly fell. Cyllarus was at his heels, stamping and kicking as if he were a snake to be cut to pieces in the dirt.

Hippodamia loosed her arrow and watched it sink into his loin. Too high and too far back to slow him by much.

"Down!" Antiope snapped, and Hippodamia dropped. Hylonome's arrow clattered against the stone, and Antiope was up again, taking aim. Her arrow struck true, through the shoulder, and Hylonome twisted, the arrow in her hand slipping through her fingers.

But Pirithous had recovered, and Hippodamia fitted another arrow to her bow. Another centaur galloped past, swinging his club, and Pirithous ducked, driving his sword up between his ribs, stabbing straight into the heart. Cyllarus howled. Howled and charged.

"No," she said, aimed, and loosed. The arrow struck his barrel, lodging deep, but not near enough to the heart. He only stumbled, but it gave Pirithous time to act. His sword flashed, down and then up, cleaving the centaur's shoulder before entering through his horse's breast. Cyllarus's cry of rage caught in his throat, and as Pirithous leapt back, the centaur's legs gave out, forcing him to his knees.

Pirithous looked up, and she knew he had found her on the wall. He pressed his fist to his forehead in salute. As if he had won. As if there were not a dozen centaurs charging toward him where he stood, his sword dripping with Cyllarus's blood.

She raised her bow, and beside her Antiope took aim as well, calling to the other men upon the wall. "Protect your king! Shoot the beast, aim for the horse's breast, not the man's!"

It seemed to Mia that they released as one, their arrows flying in a cloud. Pirithous spun to face his enemies, crouched and ready, and Hippodamia counted them as they slowed, stumbled, and fell. Three, four, six, eight. A ninth tripped by his brother, falling face first into the earth.

It left three.

Three, armed with clubs and fury, determined to run him down. To run straight through him and trample him beneath their hooves until his blood watered the ground.

She loosed another arrow, a second, a third, but she was too late now. Too late, and the first centaur's club clipped Pirithous's shoulder, the second hard across his back. But it was the third centaur, bowling him over, knocking him flat to the ground that made her cry out, so loud and desperate and broken that her throat closed.

Arrows could not save him now. Not anymore. He rolled, then stilled, his limbs limp, the sword knocked from his hand. And Hippodamia all but flew, racing down the stairs toward the mountain gate, ignoring Antiope's shouts. She had to get to him. She had to get to him before the centaurs tore him apart.

Theseus caught her, his arms as unyielding as bronze, but she could not hear his words over her own sobs, her own cries. "Let me go! Let me out! Open the gate and let me out!"

The men wouldn't meet her eyes, wouldn't look at her, and Theseus dragged her back.

"Pirithous! PIRITHOUS!"

"You must stay," she heard him say, at last. "You must stay inside!"

"You have to let me out. I can stop them. I can get him back."

"It's too late, Mia," Theseus said. "It's too late. And I promised him I would keep you safe."

But he didn't understand. How could he when he was only a man? He did not understand that if Pirithous was gone, her husband, her mate, she must follow. She was still centaur enough to know that.

***

Theseus gave her over to Antiope, and Antiope half-dragged, half-carried her through the palace and into her rooms, calling for a maid to ready a bath. But Hippodamia did not want a bath. She did not want the warm water washing away her tears, soothing her grief. She did not want to forget, even for a moment, that Pirithous was lost. Did not want to expect him to push open the door to the baths at any moment and tease her. She wanted salt water, poured burning over the rawness of her pain. She wanted to rend her garments and claw her way out of her skin.

"Dia ruled alone, and perhaps if we are lucky, you will be given that right, too," Antiope was saying, as she pulled the tunic over her head. "You more than proved yourself upon the walls, and even your grief serves to show your loyalty to the Lapiths, to Pirithous."

Hippodamia stared at her blankly, unsure of her meaning, her words.

"You can still be queen, Hippodamia. You can still rule these people, and perhaps protect your own."

"There is no protecting the centaurs now," she said. The same thought she'd been spinning since she went to meet Cyllarus before the battle began. "There is no saving them, and even if there were, the Lapiths would not listen to me. And I am not so sure they should."

"Then rule for yourself, for Pirithous's sake," Antiope said, twisting a shoulder in half a shrug. "But rule as queen. Do not let them take it from you."

"You think I would stay?" Hippodamia asked, her words sounding hollow in her ears. "That I could go on as if nothing had changed? Live a full life when half of me is dead? Pirithous was all I had left."

Antiope straightened, her eyes narrowing. "You cannot mean that, Mia. Whatever bond you shared, it is nothing now. A blink, a heartbeat of your life, nothing more. Hardly *half* of you, no matter how much you thought yourself in love."

"Centaurs mate for life," she said through her teeth. "For *life*."

"Yes," Antiope said, her forehead furrowed. "And if Pirithous is not dead already, he soon will be. You will be free of him. You will be queen in your own right."

"I will be dead," Hippodamia said coolly. Never free. Never free again. "Just as Hylonome will be, before long. After she has seen to Cyllarus's body, and performed the proper rites, she will follow him. It is our way."

Antiope's hand closed hard around her arm, squeezing too tight, so tight she could feel the pulse of her own blood. "The centaur way, but not the way of the Lapiths. The way of beasts, not men. And you are Lapith now, Mia. You are a woman, not an animal."

"I am Centaurus's daughter."

"You are Pirithous's wife!" she snapped. "And what do you think he would say to this, if he heard you now? After he kept Theseus back to guard you? Made him swear to protect you, to support you, if he failed!"

"Let him curse my shade in the Underworld, if he desires, then. But I will do my duty to him. I will honor him as my husband. That is all that is left for me now. He was all I had left."

"You would *waste* your life. Throw away everything he's given you! You would be no better than the centaurs outside these very walls!"

"I *am* Centaur, Antiope!"

"No," she said, her hand squeezing tighter. "Not in this. Not this way. I forbid it. If I must watch you night and day, guard your body, your life, to stop you, I will. You are meant to be queen. You are meant to rule—here, now, these people, in Pirithous's absence.

That is your duty. *That* is the honor you can do your husband. The rest is only a lie. A cheat!"

"If you install me as queen of the Lapiths, leave me here to rule, I will follow him, Antiope. Before you have even cleared the gates."

"You stupid girl," Antiope sneered. "You stupid fool of a girl. You do not understand at all. Cannot see outside your own needs, your own wants and desires. Men are not worth this! No man is worth your life! If Theseus asked it of me, I would spit upon his grave."

"And why should Theseus ask it, when it would not be a sevenday after your death before he found another woman to warm his bed? He is just. He would ask nothing from you that he would not give himself."

Antiope slapped her. Hippodamia stumbled back, falling onto her bed. The bed where Pirithous had shown her passion beyond anything she had ever imagined. Pleasures she had never dreamed of. But they had never made love in it. She had been too stubborn, too angry, too slow to forgive. And now they would never make love again. She would never have his child, never see him bounce their babe upon his knee...

"Theseus would not give up his life for me because I would not wish it. Because I would want him to live on, guided by his memories of me. Because the highest honor he could give me would be to remember all I had taught him. All the ways he had learned to be a better man, a better king for his people, for the women of Athens. And Pirithous? He would live the same way for you. To honor you!"

"He is not Centaur," she said, tears stinging her eyes. Pirithous would still have had his people, his friends, his brothers-in-arms to live for. She had nothing. Not anymore. "I do not expect him to understand. Nor you. I only know what I must do."

"It is the coward's way, Mia. And I pray the gods curse you for it."

And then Antiope was gone, leaving her alone in the room. Hippodamia let out a breath. There was nothing to do now but wait. For the centaurs to give up their rampage or be repulsed. For Pirithous's body to be collected and brought to her, to be anointed. She would paint his wounds upon her body and see him entombed with all the proper rites and honors of his people, in peacetime. Buried beside Dia in the domed chambers, heaped over with earth, that the Lapiths built for their kings.

And with or without Antiope's help, she would follow her husband to the House of Hades.

Chapter Forty

Hippodamia

She did not know how she found her way into his room, did not remember clothing herself in his tunic. But she woke, wrapped in the lavender and musk of his bed linens, to shouting and pounding against the doors, Pirithous's final command loud in her mind.

…If Peleus comes before we finish, do not stay atop the wall. Go to the palace. To the storeroom.

Peleus. She had forgotten Peleus and his Myrmidons, in her grief. She had forgotten and now he had come, and she had not even honored Pirithous's last request—

"—lives! The king lives! The centaurs are repulsed, and my lord Pirithous survives!"

She threw the linens off and launched herself at the door, tearing it open. It was one of the servants, running through the halls, banging on every door and shouting himself raw. The same words, over and over.

"He lives! The king lives! The centaurs are repulsed and my lord Pirithous survives! Praise Zeus and thank the gods, the king lives!"

Hippodamia raced through the halls, down the stairs and into the inner yard, where men clogged the way. She pushed through them, careless of their swords and spears and shields, undisturbed even by the pong of sweat and smoke and the bronze flavor of blood choking the air. And then they began to part before her, stepping back to allow her through before she reached their backs, making way with a murmur of her name upon their lips.

"Let the queen through!" one of the men called out. She had seen him speaking with Pirithous, and now he touched his fist to his forehead, offering her the same salute Pirithous had, before… Before.

"My lady," he said, bowing. "My lady, we forced them to retreat with a storm of arrows and spears after he fell. I heard your screams even through the walls and knew—I brought him back to you, my lady. I brought him back."

She swallowed, nodding absently as he stepped aside, and her eyes fell upon her husband, bruised and swollen, beaten and bloody and pale. But breathing. Hard and laboring, the sound of fluid rattling in his chest, but breathing still. She let out a sob then, more relief than sorrow, and dropped to her knees at his side.

They had laid him upon the table, and he clutched his sword again, his fingers white-knuckled on its hilt. She covered them with her own, pressed her forehead to his hand, and let her tears spill down her cheeks.

He was alive. He was alive, thank all the gods. Thank Zeus, and Poseidon Horse-Lord. He was alive, alive, alive.

"Mouse."

It was less than a breath, a rasp and gargled cough, but she lifted her head and met his heavy-lidded eyes in the lamplight. His fingers gave up the sword, twisting through hers instead.

"My brave mouse."

She smiled, then laughed, and kissed his knuckles, his hand. How it had escaped injury, she did not know, did not care, only too glad to feel his strength, still, somewhere. "Do not waste your breath," she said. "You must rest and heal."

He gave a jerk of his head, struggling up, as if he meant to sit, and Theseus pushed him down again. "You have broken ribs, you fool, and likely a cracked skull, though your head is so thick, I do not wonder that you haven't noticed. Lie back."

"Peleus," he gasped.

Theseus pressed his lips together, his gaze meeting hers. Pirithous could not fight. Likely could not even walk, as difficult as it was for him to breathe. And they faced still another battle. A greater one.

"They will not come until sunrise," Theseus said. "And I will do what I can to prepare your men. But you must rest, if you are to survive this night. And you must survive, Pirithous." He met her eyes again, his jaw tight, his gaze knowing. Antiope had told him. "For your queen's sake."

He let out a breath, rattling again, and closed his eyes. "My brave mouse. I'll be well enough—" he coughed, rough and wheezing, "—by morning."

"Melanthos," Theseus said, and the man who had brought Pirithous, who had heard her cries, stepped forward again. "Take him to his rooms. Your queen will no doubt wish to care for him there."

Melanthos nodded, and three other men joined him as he advanced. Hippodamia squeezed Pirithous's hand and moved back. The four men, all broad-shouldered and bloodied, lifted the table itself rather than their king, and Melanthos murmured something to Pirithous that she did not quite hear. She hesitated, glancing at Theseus again, his face grim as he watched them shoulder their burden through the doors and then the crowd of men in the yard.

"He cannot fight against Peleus," she said to him, her voice low enough that they would not be overheard. "Son of Zeus or not, he will be fortunate to heal from his wounds at all, never mind by morning."

"He promised to let me lead his men against the Myrmidons when he asked me to remain inside the walls. I think he knew—or at least, he feared he would not be able to do so himself."

"It will not be enough," she said. "With Pirithous half-dead, defeated already, his men will lose confidence. Even if you lead them."

"And what would you suggest, Lady?" Theseus asked, his voice hoarse. "Would you have me do nothing? Would you rather let Peleus kill you both, sparing you the trouble of arranging your own death later?"

She lifted her chin. "Pirithous lives. As long as there is breath in his body, I will fight for everything that is his."

"Then fight," Theseus growled. "As long as his people survive, you must fight. Not just for him, but for them too. That is what it means to be a queen. What it means to be their queen. And no matter how you were raised, as centaur or woman, that is what you are now. Queen of the Lapiths even more than you are Pirithous's wife!"

He did not wait for her response. Did not give her the chance to answer at all.

***

She stayed at Pirithous's side, her eyes scratchy and dry with exhaustion, but awake, watching his every breath. Pirithous, her Pirithous, her king now, with Centaurus's death. And he had made her his queen. Expected her to rule in his absence, to protect his people while he went raiding. To rule, as Dia had after Ixion's death.

Queen of the Lapiths, even more than you are Pirithous's wife.

The sky shifted from the deep black of the smoky night to the purple of false dawn, the haze of burning fields still lingering in the valley. Pirithous stirred, his hand tightening around hers, and she stroked his hair, careful of his bruised flesh.

"Atukhos," he mumbled, not truly awake. He had spoken of him before. Spoken of Melanthos, too, and his ships. Called out for Antiope to take the women and children below. All the things he could not do, all the things that must be done to preserve his people, haunting his dreams. "The horses."

"Sleep, Pirithous," she murmured. "Theseus cares for your people."

She did not know if he heard her, but he quieted, falling into a deeper slumber. Hippodamia drew her hand from his, leaning down to press a kiss to his forehead. Too warm with fever, now. She hated to leave him. Hated to walk away from the reassuring rise of his chest, the sound of his rattled breaths.

But Theseus had been right. She was queen. The only woman Pirithous thought worthy of the role. The only woman he trusted to rule in his place. She was *his* queen.

And she must fight.

***

Pirithous's armor, bronze and leather both, was far too large, but she was not so much smaller than Antiope that the Amazon's leather breastplate would not fit. Finding her, however, was not so easy. She was not in the room she shared with Theseus, nor in the megaron with the women. Hippodamia should have expected to find her upon the walls, at her husband's side, with her bow strung and her quiver full, but she had thought perhaps she might have taken some sort of rest…

"Pirithous has not taken a turn?" Antiope demanded, catching sight of her before she could speak.

She shook her head. "He sleeps. But uneasily. He worries for his ships and his horses, and I promised him before to see to the women and children—Pirithous wishes them sent below, into one of the storerooms."

Theseus grunted, though she had not realized he'd been listening. "I will go now and shift the stone, but I would not close them in until there is real threat. It is bleak and black beneath the palace."

"I remember," Hippodamia said. "And I agree."

Theseus gave her a nod, murmured something to one of the other men upon the wall—Melanthos, she thought—and left them at a jog.

"Antiope, I must beg a favor from you."

The Amazon gave her a hard look, her lips pressed thin. "Must you?"

"I have need of a breastplate at least, if not greaves and bracers as well. Pirithous's will not fit me, but I thought perhaps you might know where I could find something that would."

She had more than Antiope's attention now, for Melanthos stared at her with eyes just as narrowed, if far more lined with exhaustion. He had already fought once this night, and by the look of him, he had not even taken the time to wash the dust, smoke, and blood from his skin. "What need does the queen have for armor?" he asked.

Hippodamia stiffened. "It is the queen's right and duty to defend the palace in the king's absence. I mean to ride out to meet Peleus and his men, as I rode out to meet Cyllarus."

"You have even less a chance of swaying Peleus than you did Cyllarus," Antiope said. "None at all, in fact."

"Perhaps that is so, but just as I did then, I must try now."

"If you intend this only to get yourself killed—"

"I intend to lead Pirithous's people as their queen. As Dia would have, before me. As Pirithous wished me to do, in his place. Whether he is off raiding or lying bloodied in his bed, it is my duty, and I *intend* to see it through."

"And I will ride with you," Melanthos said, his lips curving. "My lord Pirithous would want me at your side. King Theseus, as well, if he is willing."

Antiope glowered at him, tugging Hippodamia a step farther away and lowering her voice. "You have said yourself you know little more than how to hunt with a bow, that you were taught no other weapon. If that is so, and you wish to fight, you are better off upon the walls, as before. Safer."

"And I will take my place there, after I have done what I am able to do for the Lapiths. After Peleus sees that we do not cower, afraid, behind the walls. You wanted me to be queen, Antiope, and you were not wrong. As queen, this is my responsibility. Not Theseus's. Not yours. Will you lend me the armor, lend me your support and aid, or not?"

"You are still a fool," Antiope said, her jaw tight. "A brave fool, but still a fool. I have only leather, and we must dress you in bronze, at the least, but I am certain we can find you something. Theseus will know where to look. I'll speak to him, and we will meet you at the stables with armor of some kind."

"My thanks, Antiope."

Antiope embraced her, hard and tight. "Just live, Mia. That will be thanks enough."

"Pirithous spoke of Atukhos, with the herd," Hippodamia said, addressing Melanthos after Antiope had gone. He had obviously been listening from his place at the wall. "If Peleus has come for the horses, should we not send men to defend them?"

Melanthos shrugged. "You are queen, my lady. If you believe we should send men to protect the horses, command it."

"A queen who commands without first learning all she can does not deserve to be obeyed. I would know your thoughts, and anything Pirithous might have mentioned."

He grinned as if she had passed some test, and offered her a bow. "Pirithous sent a dozen men to the herd when the centaurs came. King Peleus is the greater threat, to be sure, and another dozen fresh men sent out would not be amiss. But we dare not send many more than that. Better to lose horses who will find their way back than to see our women and children taken as slaves. And we will need all the men we have to defend the palace."

"Choose the twelve you think most capable of the task, and tell them it is their queen's command," she decided, staring out from the wall. Smoke still rose from the smoldering remains of the village, and she could not see the river or the ships grounded upon its bank. "Was everything burned? Even the ships?"

"What wasn't destroyed by the centaurs will surely be burned by the Myrmidons," Melanthos said grimly.

"No," Hippodamia said. "The twelve men you send to the horses will take the best remaining ship upstream, out of sight, then go to join the others with the horses. It will slow them, I know, but I will not give Peleus the satisfaction of crippling us. See it done, now."

"As you wish, my queen."

She let out a breath after he had gone, and hid her hands by crossing her arms, the better to keep the others from seeing how she shook. The sun had not quite risen yet, and she could only hope the men Melanthos chose would slip away before Peleus came. *Poseidon, protect us!* One more long look from the walls, her gaze sweeping from the village to the mountain, and she forced herself not to hesitate over the bodies of the centaurs still dotting the ground. She had given them every opportunity to save themselves. They had made their choice. They had chosen Peleus, and there was nothing more she could do for them now.

She had made her choice, too. To be queen. To be Lapith.

Lord Poseidon, protect us all.

Chapter Forty-One

Hippodamia

She felt steadier atop Podarkes's back, though the gold oval plate over her chest felt awkward and heavy as she rode. At least the rest of her armor was leather and bronze, but Antiope had insisted she should look the part of queen if she meant to act as one. And she must. Peleus's ships had been sighted, and if she meant to ride out to meet him, to show him the Lapiths were not afraid, not broken, she must go now.

"Are you ready, my lady?" Melanthos asked.

Hippodamia clutched the reins all the harder, her knuckles white, and Podarkes tossed his head in response. Perhaps she was not feeling so much steadier after all.

"You need not do this, Mia," Theseus said, at her other side. "It was never my intention to suggest you should endanger yourself, and Pirithous will hardly forgive me if Peleus takes you captive while he lies injured in his bed."

"There will be nothing for Pirithous to forgive," she said, lifting her chin. "We will ride out, prove our strength, and with the blessing of the gods, take the heart out of some of Peleus's men."

"Even better if we water the river with their blood," Melanthos said. "We are ready at your word, my queen."

"Open the gate!" she called out, before she lost her nerve.

The bar was removed and the wooden doors groaned on their hinges. A touch of her heels to Podarkes's flanks, and he broke into an eager gallop, bursting through the gate to the other side. The thunder in her ears told her the other men followed. Every horse in the palace stables had been turned out, and men with spears and bows rode at her back, following her to the riverbank.

The Myrmidons did not fight on horseback, and in truth, the Lapiths did not either, outside of the hunt. But why should Peleus not think them more skilled than they were? Why should they not show themselves to be a mightier force, when from birth they were set astride their horses?

She raced with them through the scorched embers of the village, Melanthos and Theseus no more than a nose behind Podarkes. At the edge of the once-lush bank, just before the land sloped down into silt and sand and loose rock, she drew her horse to a halt and raised her arm, signaling the others to do the same. The men formed a line, their horses steady beneath them, and spread out along the bank, forming a wall of horseflesh between the river and the palace. Bronze and gold glinted in the sunlight, an advantage now that they no longer fought in shadow. Hippodamia hoped it blinded Peleus's men, visible on their three ships as they heaved upon the oars. She curled her fingers into a fist, and the Lapiths fitted arrows to their bows. Flame passed from arrowhead to arrowhead, for if Pirithous's ships could burn, why not Peleus's as well?

"I am Hippodamia, Tamer of Horses, Queen of the Lapiths and Daughter of Centaurus," she called out. "If you land upon our shores, you will meet death by our swords!"

"And where is King Pirithous, that his queen addresses us so boldly?" a voice called back. "A queen who could not even save the Lapiths from the violence of her own people!"

She dropped her hand and her men loosed their arrows in answer to his taunt. A ripple of heat and fire raining down upon their Myrmidon heads. Shouts broke out. Shields, hastily thrown up for protection, caught fire. A few arrows lodged into the hulls and the decks, flame licking at the wood. Her men had already drawn their bows again.

She lifted her arm to hold them, narrowing her eyes. The Myrmidons were armored. More bronze than the Lapiths had ever dreamed of wearing, covering their chests and backs completely. But not all of them had donned their helmets yet, and their heads and necks were exposed, along with their arms and legs. She would simply have to hope the gods were on their side, and in the meantime, she waited until they put down their shields and began to scramble—

"Now!" she said, dropping her arm, and another wave of arrows broke and arced up and over, striking the Myrmidons as they rushed to put out the fires on their decks, their shields only half-remembered, and their heads still bare.

She thought she could identify Peleus now, his sword drawn as he leaned out from the mast, using the blade to direct his men as they stamped out the fires. He wore a helm of bronze and gold, plumed with a long tail of horse hair, likely stolen from one of the raided horses of the Lapiths. Hippodamia wished she could reach out and tear it from his head. Instead, she lifted her own bow, pulled an arrow from her quiver, and took aim.

"Leave these lands or you will only suffer worse," Hippodamia called over the sounds his men made, some shallowly wounded and others merely angry.

Peleus sheathed his sword, and even from this distance, she felt his eyes upon her. Knew he had found her as she had found him. "If Pirithous is so desperate as to send his wife to meet us, the only people who will suffer are yours!"

She let her arrow fly, grinning wildly at Peleus's shout as it speared the plume of his helm against the mast. Beside her, Melanthos laughed aloud, and a few of the other men chuckled with him. Her men, sitting upon their horses like kings. The Myrmidons might as well have been the ants they were named for.

"He cannot turn back, or he will be shamed by his men, now," Theseus said, though even he smiled. "You should not linger, Lady.

Peleus has marked you, and he will want your head for that trick. We will pick off his men as they come ashore, if we can, but most will make it through, and you will be in grave danger then."

"If I retreat now, it will only encourage his men."

"Let them have their courage, leaping from their ships. They'll be that much easier to kill," Melanthos said. "And we have our horses. Once they're off their ships, we'll run them down one by one if need be, but after the line breaks, it will be that much harder to guard you."

"Then I will be more difficult to guard," Hippodamia said, resolved. Let Peleus mark her. Let him wish to do her harm. "If Peleus will come for me, we will know how to find him. And besides, as long as I ride Podarkes, he will never catch me. Not even upon another horse. I will stay and watch, to give our men heart."

Melanthos touched his fist to his forehead in respect, and she leaned forward upon her horse, watching Peleus order his ships to beach. The first men who leapt over the side of his ship fell to well-aimed Lapith arrows, but the next did not forget their shields, covering themselves more carefully, and once the ship was grounded, they spilled over the deck too quickly and too numerous to be struck down at all.

The horses began to dance beneath their riders, and even Hippodamia had to tighten her hold upon the reins as Podarkes caught the excitement of the others. Theseus raised his arm, taking command of the men now that she had done her part. The Myrmidons had begun taking aim at them now, and Hippodamia threw her bow across her back, taking up the light shield instead. Leather wrapped over wood with a thin sheet of gold atop it, which offered no protection at all, no matter how fine it looked with Medusa's snake-haired head glaring at her enemies.

She worried more for Podarkes than herself, for he presented the larger target by far. He sidled back a step, and she let him, holding the shield up high over both of them and doing her best not to flinch at the arrows raining down around them.

"Hippodamia!" Peleus roared, drawing her attention back to the bank. He held a spear, his arm cocked back, and at her glance, he let it fly.

She ignored the wrench of fear as it arced up, aimed so finely she had no doubt he meant it for her breast, and dug a heel into Podarkes's ribs, shifting him just enough that the spear missed its mark, the tip sinking deep into the earth beside her. She swallowed hard, forcing herself not to give it more than a dismissive glance, and holding her head up high.

If he had hoped for her to break and run, she would not give him the satisfaction of even a glimmer of unease.

Theseus cursed, circling with his horse to tear the spear from the ground. "If you do not retreat now, I cannot guarantee you will be able to at all. Do not make me tell Pirithous he lost his new wife to Peleus's men. He wanted you in the storeroom, safe."

"He wanted me off the walls," Hippodamia said, keeping her voice even with an effort. "And I have done as he asked. Antiope will see to the women and children should the worst come to pass."

Theseus grimaced, glancing down the line of men. "She would if she had remained behind the walls."

Hippodamia followed his gaze, fixed upon a too-slender rider at the end of the line, bow in hand and lips peeled back in a feral grin as she loosed her arrows with an easy grace. There was no question in her mind that it was Antiope, just as Theseus said. And that left the palace walls without leadership of any kind, beyond the handful of Pirithous's host who had promised to guard the gates. She would simply have to trust the men Melanthos and Theseus had left behind.

"Antiope to me!" Hippodamia called out, and then she lowered her voice, meeting Theseus's eyes. "Set fire to the bank if they are fool enough to leave their ships grounded upon it. I only wish I had thought of torching the whole of it before now, that they might have leapt from their ships into flame from the start."

"You are certain you will not turn back?" Theseus asked, lines of worry fanning from his eyes, as he watched his wife gallop toward them. "Take Antiope with you and return to the walls?"

She shook her head. "I will not deny her, as I beg you not to deny me now. But I will keep her as my guard, along with Melanthos. For your sake and mine. Just try not to ruin Pirithous's horses, or he will never forgive me."

Theseus barked a rough laugh. "I will do my best to keep the men and horses in one piece, if you will promise to do the same for yourself."

"You needn't fear for her, Theseus," Antiope said, having joined them. "I'll be at her side."

He pressed his lips together, as if his wife's words offered no reassurance at all, but he put his heels to his horse, turning it neatly in place as he called to the men to follow, and Hippodamia let herself believe they would win.

They had to win.

CHAPTER FORTY-TWO

PIRITHOUS

It was the shouting that woke him, the far-off cries slipping through his dreams and reminding him there was more yet to do, another battle to win before he could lie in his bed. Peleus. Peleus and those thrice-cursed Myrmidons, come to steal his horses.

"Mia?" he called, his voice far too thin.

Pirithous sat up slowly, stabbing pain in his chest with every movement and the rattling sound of his breathing too loud in his ears. She was not at his bedside, where he dimly remembered she had been, offering him words of comfort and soft touches. She was not in his room at all.

"Hippodamia?" he called again, still wheezing but louder. Stronger, in spite of the pain. He used one of the bed posts to climb to his feet, wincing only once at the shattering flame that coursed through his leg when he put his weight upon it. He did not have time for fractured bones, nor cracked and broken ribs, and he had rested enough now that the ichor in his blood would have done some of the work of knitting them.

Even so, he felt light-headed, and had to close his eyes, leaning heavily upon the doorframe to gather his strength. He could not breathe deeply yet. Could barely breathe at all. But he had to rise. Had to fight.

Father, grant me a measure of your strength. I have need of it now.

If Zeus heard his plea, there was no answer, and every breath was as belabored as the last. Every beat of his heart just as loud, just as throbbing. He had the strength. He had always had the strength to rise. But to fight?

"Mia," he murmured again, opening his eyes. He must find Mia, and learn what had happened. And he was a fool to think she would be waiting at his bedside with the clash of swords ringing in the distance. She would be upon the walls, with Antiope, or in the megaron with the women and children. She would be where she was needed most.

Pirithous managed to dress, even tying his sword belt around his waist—though lifting it up cost him his breath for a time—then he went in search of his wife.

Lord Zeus, my father, grant me your strength, I beg of you.

The farther he walked, the less he ached, and the more he burned instead. Fire in his blood, lightning lacing his bones. The ichor in his blood answering his prayers, as it often did when he called upon his father for aid. He would have the strength to stand, even perhaps to fight, but tomorrow he would be more than worthless for anything at all.

In the megaron, the women busied the children with small games, but he saw no sign of Hippodamia or Antiope among them.

"She went with the men," Karpathia said, when he found the servant Antiope had gifted his wife.

"Not Antiope," he said. "Hippodamia, your queen."

Karpathia smiled. "Yes, my lord. The queen went with the men in your place. She led them out on horseback, as many as she could mount, with bows and spears and swords. My lady Antiope was meant to stay upon the wall to guard us, but I doubt she has remained behind. She would not let my lord Theseus go into battle alone."

"But surely if Theseus led the men, there was no need for Hippodamia to join them?"

"She is queen, my lord," Karpathia said simply. "Who has the right to stop her?"

He shook his head, staring blankly at the hearth. She must have been still upon the wall. He could not imagine she would enter battle when she knew nothing of defense. Nothing of war, truly, at all. To risk herself so foolishly…

His brave fool of a mouse.

"Perhaps Erithia will know more, upon the wall," Karpathia suggested.

He gave Karpathia a smile and nodded to the rest of the women as he left, before he made more of a spectacle of himself. A king should not have to go in search of his wife, and learn from the servants that she had gone to battle in his stead. Hippodamia should have told him what she intended. She should have woken him, at the least.

His blood burned all the hotter by the time he reached the wall and climbed it. He was not quite wheezing when he reached the top, and he closed his hands into fists to keep from pressing a palm against his ribs. he dared not show weakness, and it would not ease the pain besides.

Glaukos, one of his raiders, spotted him before he got far, and grinned widely to see him. "My lord! I knew you would not stay in bed for long with a battle to be fought, no matter how grievous your wounds."

"Yes," Pirithous said absently, for he could see them now. The Lapiths on their horses, wheeling about, raising dust and ash beneath their hooves as they charged the Myrmidons, all flashing sunlight from the bronze and gold and silver of their armor. He searched for Hippodamia among them, or even Antiope, but it was impossible to tell one figure from another at such a distance. "Hippodamia fights?"

"She would not hear any objection, and even King Theseus was worn thin. I think he hoped she would ride back to the safety of the walls when the fighting broke out, but we've seen no sign of her. Melanthos acts as her guard, you need not fear."

Pirithous snorted, unable to tear his eyes from the battle upon the plane. He was too far away. Too far to know for certain how much fear should tighten around his heart. As it was, he could not breathe, thinking of Hippodamia among the horsemen, risking herself for him.

"I require a horse, Glaukos. Or perhaps a chariot would be better."

"I fear there are no suitable horses, my lord. Just Fire, left behind, too old to be trusted in battle."

"Then I will ride Fire," Pirithous said, turning from the wall and setting off down the stairs again. It jarred his ribs, but the lightning burned away the pain before he was forced to stop, and he did not care besides. Fire was his horse, after all. She had been his first horse, and it seemed only fair to give her the honor of being his last, should the Fates demand it.

"My lord, be reasonable," Glaukos said, following after him toward the stables. "You are injured, and while Fire might run herself to death for you, I cannot imagine that is what you want for her end. Stay upon the wall with us, and leave the fighting to Theseus and Antiope."

"I will not leave my queen to face Peleus alone," Pirithous said. "If I must sacrifice Fire to the gods for her safety, to stand at her side or die with her, so be it."

"You must at least wear your armor, my lord," Glaukos said, catching hold of his arm at the stable door. "Please at least do that, or the Myrmidons will spear you through the heart before the queen has even caught sight of you."

Pirithous bared his teeth, closing his hands into fists and letting the lightning in his veins spark and crackle over his skin. Glaukos leapt back, a prayer to Zeus upon his lips.

"Tell the men to be ready to open the gate," Pirithous said. "And find me a spear and a shield. I'll need nothing more beyond that."

***

He charged through the gate with Fire, the cheers of his men upon the walls filling his ears and his gaze fixed on the river bank, upon the horses and the glinting of arms and armor. What had possessed her to mount his men, he did not know, could not understand, but he promised himself he would find out soon enough. That he would find her, alive.

Glaukos had given him a shield of bronze, still begging him to armor himself. But lightning crackled through his blood, over his skin, and that would serve him well enough. Let Peleus see what he had woken, let him understand fully what he had done. For years, the Lapiths had ignored his small raids upon their horses, but no longer. Peleus would not escape this day unscathed.

"Peleus!" Pirithous roared. "Cowardly swine. Hiding behind centaurs, bronze, and gold! Face me, Peleus! FACE ME!"

He did not even see the men who came at him, simply struck them down as he rode through the fighting. His own men parted before him, making way. Pirithous caught a spear out of the air when it came hurtling toward him, and threw it back at the Myrmidon who had sent it. Arrows bounced off his shield, even his skin, leaving the scent of burning wood and scorched metal in the air. None of it mattered. He had his father's protection, his father's power, and none of their weapons would reach him.

"You come late to your own defense, Pirithous!" Peleus called out, and Pirithous found him at last, sitting atop Podarkes. And Mia nowhere to be found. "Your wife was kind enough to bring me the horses I desired directly. Such a generous gift, do you not think?"

"Where is she?" Pirithous demanded.

"Who?" Peleus asked, smiling.

"My wife!" he snarled. "You sit atop her horse and profess to know nothing of her fate?"

"This horse?" Peleus jerked on the reins, making Podarkes spin in a tight circle, but even from this distance, Pirithous could see the wildness of the stallion's eyes. Podarkes had always required a soft touch, and if Peleus was not careful, he would not sit atop him for long. "I believe I'll keep him for myself when this is over."

Pirithous growled, tightening his grip upon his sword and digging his heels into Fire. She reared and launched herself forward, unafraid. Peleus grinned, lifting his sword to meet the swing, but at the last moment Pirithous brought up his shield instead, causing Peleus's blade to slide instead of catch and his balance to shift. Fire snapped at Podarkes's flank, making him kick. Peleus fell. As quickly and as easily as that, he was unseated, and Podarkes did not wait to be mounted again, but fled.

"You never were much of a horseman," Pirithous taunted, swinging a leg over Fire's neck and sliding off her back. He landed lightly, sword and shield held loosely in his hands. "No matter how many horses you steal, you cannot keep them. You cannot break them. You cannot stay upon their backs. And Podarkes of all horses, to think you had the skill to ride him? Why? Because Hippodamia had tamed him? A mere woman? My wife has more skill in her smallest finger than you have in your whole body."

He could not kill Peleus until he confessed what had become of Hippodamia, but Pirithous could hurt him. On horseback or off it, he had the advantage, and Peleus was still scrambling to find his feet. His sword had slipped from his hand when he struck the ground, but Pirithous could see in his eyes the realization that he could not risk turning away to look for it.

Peleus bared his teeth. "That wife of yours is just another prize I'll steal from you. And all the more reason if she is so skilled. She can keep your horses in my stables, instead of yours. And at night, I'll give her to my men to do with as they please."

"You cannot steal my wife if you are dead," Pirithous said, brandishing his sword.

"And how do you know I haven't taken her already?" Peleus asked. "While you were sleeping off your wounds, I've been fighting your men, cutting them down one by one, and sending your precious horses back to my ships. You and Theseus both are fools to think we would not take your women, too, simply because they dressed themselves in armor."

"Antiope would die before she gave herself up to you," Pirithous said, advancing. Upon the rise, he could see down the bank to Peleus's ships and the men who had remained there as guards. The horses they'd rounded up in makeshift pens. Mia could never have lost Podarkes by accident. Would never have been caught so long as she was atop his back. She was too smart, too quick. "And if Hippodamia is taken, it is only because she allowed it for her own ends. Because fool that you are, you think to hold her hostage in a sea of horses. Horses she has tamed to her hand, to her voice, with the Horse Lord's own skill."

Peleus's face paled, his gaze darting toward his ships, then back to Pirithous again. He licked his lips, standing, straight-backed and proud. "You only wish to rattle me. As if I would ever fear a woman. Even the Amazons are nothing to the might of the Myrmidons."

Pirithous grinned, then caught Peleus's sword by the hilt with the tip of his blade and flipped it up at him. All the better to keep him distracted, to keep his back to his ships and his men and his prizes, and give Hippodamia the time she needed. He could see her, now, a small figure moving among the horses. "Give up your armor, call off your men, and face me, man to man. Let us settle this, you and I."

Peleus's eyes narrowed. "If I win?"

They circled one another, Pirithous careful to keep Peleus's back to the bank. "Keep the horses and plunder already aboard your ships as my gift to you."

"You'll be dead," Peleus said, "and your queen will be mine, as well. Your people will have nothing left."

"That is none of your concern, surely," Pirithous said. "And at least they will live freely."

"And if you win?" Peleus asked.

"I take back my horses and my queen, and your men leave my lands, never to return."

Peleus smiled slowly. "Are you truly so confident in your father's favors, Pirithous?"

He twitched a shoulder. "I wish to put an end to this fighting, once and for all. If the cost is my life, so be it."

"Perhaps I do not wish for so quick an end. Perhaps I would prefer you to suffer."

"Then may the gods have mercy upon you," Pirithous said. "For I will surely show you none."

"Myrmidons!" Peleus called out. "To me!"

Pirithous grinned, though he could feel himself weakening. Exhaustion so deep it ached in his bones. He grinned because even if Peleus won, he would sail away with nothing. From what he could see over the fool's shoulder, Hippodamia would see to that.

Chapter Forty-Three

Hippodamia

She hadn't planned on being captured. Antiope and Melanthos had fought for her fiercely, but the Myrmidons had surrounded them, leveling their spears at the horses' breasts, and Hippodamia, fool that she was, had not been willing to sacrifice Podarkes for her freedom. She had made them swear to let Melanthos and Antiope go free, and given herself up to them as a prize, along with their three horses, to be kept alive.

But it had not only been that, either. She had seen the Lapith horses taken. Watched as, after their riders were unseated or killed, the Myrmidons rounded them up into a makeshift pen to be loaded on their ships. And she had cursed herself for her foolishness in bringing the accursed Myrmidons all the plunder they had hoped for—the finest of the Lapith horses, theirs for the taking. The king's own stables, turned into prizes, without even having to breach the palace walls.

Peleus had been right. She was no threat to his Myrmidons.

Or at least, she had not been much of one, even upon Podarkes's back. Among the penned herd of horses, however, whispering in one ear after another, seeing the spark of Poseidon's rage lit in their rolling eyes and stamping hooves, perhaps she was not entirely without worth. These horses knew her, trusted her words, and with the Horse Lord's favor, she would set them free.

The horses stamped and whinnied as she moved through them, now, and the Myrmidons laughed, just as they had laughed when she had asked to be penned with the horses and thrown her into their midst.

"Had enough, yet, centaur-girl? Or do you prefer the favors of beasts to men?"

"No wonder King Pirithous let her ride out to meet us," another said. "After being pleasured by those horse-men, she can't have been satisfied even by a son of Zeus. Maybe he hopes to be rid of her to save his pride."

"Look at her, half-wild, worse than an Amazon—perhaps she unmanned him altogether," said the first.

"She's so skilled at horse riding, it can't be too hard to teach her to ride a man instead," said a third.

Hippodamia ignored them. Whatever they believed, whatever rumors had been spread about her desires, natural or unnatural, hardly mattered. She stroked the neck of the horse she had chosen to ride in Podarkes's place and smiled to herself. She would see them soundly thrashed soon enough. Trampled until they were nothing but bruised, broken flesh. And let them speak spitefully of her behavior then. If they could speak at all.

"You'll lead them," she said to her horse, named Aithon for the brilliant flame-chestnut of his hide and the fiery temper to match. One of the ten Pirithous had gifted her, and Fire's get, besides. He had the heart for it, the size and strength and speed, even if her Podarkes was finer—deeper in the chest, and sturdier in the leg. Aithon threw back his head, nostrils flaring wide as he snorted and stamped, and the other horses responded.

She trailed her hands over his back, circling him with a careful eye for any wounds he might have been given, anything that might slow him, but he was unmarked, unbloodied, and eager. Hippodamia caught him by the bridle, pulling his head down until they shared the same breath. She inhaled his, warm and grassy, and gave it back again from her own lungs, binding him to her body, to her will.

"You'll lead us all to freedom, and destroy any Myrmidon in your path. They are ants and snakes, to be stamped and cut to pieces beneath your hooves. Do you hear me?"

He sighed, going still in her hold, and she pressed her forehead against his, breathing with him again and finding her own steadiness. And then she swung up onto his back, feeling his body as an extension of her own, all muscle and power and effortless grace.

She had always felt stronger on the back of a horse. As if she belonged there. And among the centaurs, as a child, it had been the one place where she had always been safe, where she'd never had to worry about being stepped on or trampled. She could sit upon a horse's back and never be lost. And upon Aithon's back, she could see more clearly now. The horses, their own fury fed by her determination, her outrage; and the guards, turned away, never thinking for a moment that the herd behind them might be the greater danger.

Hippodamia twisted her fingers through Aithon's mane and pressed her heels to his ribs, urging him forward. Slowly at first, forcing their way gently through the other horses to the front of the pen. The only way out, unless she meant them to swim against the river's current, for the horses were trapped between two ships and the river itself, the final barrier of the pen made of broken spears and pikes, any makeshift wood that the Myrmidons had found. Pirithous's horses were too well-trained to force their way out alone, but wild and angry and led—that was another matter altogether.

"Now," she breathed. And Aithon surged forward, kicking out with his hooves to break through the pen as the other horses reared and whinnied, following in his wake. The broken spears, the pikes, the driftwood turned to splinters, ground into sand and soot, and the guards turned too late, swords still sheathed.

Aithon reared and the first man fell, trampled beneath the horse's strength. Another man freed his sword, but one of the mares landed a kick square upon his chest, and he stumbled back. Aithon used his teeth, then, snapping at his hands until there was nothing but blood staining the hilt of his sword. Hippodamia slithered from his back, taking up the blade and stabbing it into the man's neck. The bronze was strong and sharp, and his flesh offered no more resistance than the soft goat cheese their guests had spread upon the bread at the wedding feast. Three more men fell beneath the horses, moaning and rolling in the dust, but she wasted no more time on foot.

Mia ran to catch Aithon, not waiting for him to slow before vaulting up on his back again, and they were flying over the sooty bank, the burned grasses and the scorched earth. She raised her stolen sword, wet with blood, and loosed her own frenzied cry, matching the furious screams of the horses around her. The thunder of their hooves echoed in her heart, throbbed through her veins, and she kicked Aithon faster. Up the hillside and onto the plain, into the field above.

But the fighting she had expected was stilled, the men gathered all together, the clang and clash of swords ringing clear from inside the loose circle they'd formed. The horses slowed, sensing her confusion, her hesitation, and she slid from Aithon's back once more, the sword in her hand just a weight, falling to her side.

"Go," she told him, absent-mindedly. She could not drag her eyes from the men, her stomach twisting, her heart too tight. "Back to the palace. To your stable and your grain. Go."

Aithon snorted, tossing his head in defiance, but the others turned away, the fury draining from them as quickly as it had leached from her. She let the sword drop, felt Aithon's breath upon her shoulder as he followed in her wake. Her legs were so much stone, her mind whirling. There was Theseus, among the men, his jaw tight, his body stiff. And Antiope beside him, bloodied but whole. And if it was not Theseus in the center, fighting, if it was not Antiope, who else? Who else could it be?

Hippodamia picked up her pace, stumbling over the uneven ground. Aithon bit at her tunic, impatient, but she only swatted him away. She did not want to see. She did not want to see, but she knew she must, and she broke into a run.

"Pirithous." Her lips shaped his name without thought. Her body knowing what she could not yet see with her own eyes. What her mind refused to believe. "Pirithous, you fool, you fool!"

And then she was shoving her way through the men, past Melanthos and the other raiders, bunched together in the mob. Past Theseus and Antiope, leaving Aithon, at last, behind.

"Pirithous."

Bruised and beaten, eyes blazing white and lightning crackling over his skin. How he even stood upright, she did not understand, but it was Pirithous, his sword crossed against Peleus's blade, both men bleeding from shallow cuts on arms and legs. Both men bloodied.

Pirithous swayed, losing half a step to the force of Peleus's blade upon his. She could see the exhaustion in every line of his face, every shift of his weight. And she did not dare call out to him. Could not risk distracting him, even for a moment, weak as he was. Too weak for this.

"Mia?" Antiope touched her shoulder. "Mia, he knows what he is about. And Zeus is with him, do you not see?"

She shook her head, pulling away. "He'll get himself killed."

"He won't," Antiope said. "Not so long as his father protects him."

Peleus grinned, feral now, as if he sensed he was near victory. Pirithous stumbled back another step, breaking away. He listed to one side, his shield hand dragging him down. He wore nothing but his kilt and his sword belt. No armor of any kind, beyond the lightning licking at his skin. And now that he had turned, she could see another long, shallow cut, across his bare chest.

But Pirithous's gaze searched beyond Peleus, and then the men surrounding them, ever so briefly. He straightened, pressing his lips together into a thin line, and she made a soft noise, half-strangled, for his distraction. He was looking for her. She was almost certain of it. Looking for her below, and now—

Hippodamia stepped forward. "Here!"

Peleus and Pirithous both turned at her voice, the Myrmidon king wide-eyed and disbelieving. But Pirithous only laughed, the lightning in his eyes fading to the storm-gray she knew so well, and lit with fierce joy instead of Zeus's fire.

"Please," she said, hoping he understood all the rest. All her worries, all her fears for his safety, all her hopes for their future—lost if he did not win, if he did not end this. "Please, Pirithous."

Peleus growled and charged. "You planned all of this! You knew!"

Too slow, Pirithous turned, and Peleus's sword slipped between his ribs, where his shield no longer guarded him. Lowered just too far when he had seen her, when he had realized what it meant that she stood in the circle of his men.

Pirithous grunted, his eyes closing for just a moment, and his face going white. So white. And then he lifted his shield and brought it down hard on Peleus's sword arm. Something cracked between them, but she could not tell what, until Peleus screamed, stumbling back, cradling his arm to his chest.

The sword still stuck from between Pirithous's ribs, and he grasped the hilt, drawing it slowly from his body, jaw tight, teeth clenched. How he made no sound, Hippodamia did not know, and it was only Antiope's hiss in her ear that kept her from running to his side.

Pirithous threw the blade away as he stalked forward, far more menacing now, even so gravely injured. Perhaps because of it. He no longer listed. No longer swayed, but stood straight and tall and strong, though she could not imagine he would remain upright much longer.

"You should not take what you cannot keep, Peleus," he growled. "You should have learned that lesson long ago, instead of coming here now. You should have given up before it came to this. While peace was still possible between our peoples."

"You swore to let us leave," Peleus said, backing away still. "You swore if you won you would take nothing but the horses and your wife."

"I did not promise to let you live. Why should I?" Pirithous said. "To let you betray us again? You came as a guest to my hall, sowed the seeds of war while you drank my wine, and you expect me to let you walk away now, to trust that you will keep your side of the bargain we struck?"

Peleus bared his teeth. "In all honor, you have no other choice."

"There is always a choice, Peleus. The same choice you made when you gave Eurytion my wine and whispered treachery in his ear."

"And bring Ixion's curse back down upon your people?" Peleus taunted. "The gods are with you now, that much is clear. But if you kill me, what of tomorrow? Is that not why your father was cursed, in the end, for abusing their love and favor? Would you take so great a risk when you are so newly made king? And what will become of your wife, then, when the Lapiths have driven you out?"

Pirithous's jaw tightened, Peleus's words no doubt cutting just as deeply as his sword had. She could see the pain in the lines fanning out from the corners of his eyes.

"Pirithous, he has lost everything he came for. And if he ever dares return, we will defeat him again."

"And what of all you have lost?" Pirithous asked, though he did not take his eyes off the Myrmidon king. "What of all he has cost you?"

"Centaurus would not want more blood spilled. It will not bring him back. It will not give us peace with the centaurs, whether Peleus lives or dies. But do not let him take your honor, too. Let him go, shamed before his men."

Pirithous grunted, lifting his sword and pointing it at Peleus's throat. "You are fortunate that my queen has a merciful heart." Then he raised his voice, loud enough to carry even to the river's edge. "Swear now, before all your men, never to return here again, and I will let you go."

Peleus sneered, his gaze upon her hot with hate, but Hippodamia only lifted her chin, ignoring the threat. Let him hate her. He was in her debt now, and if he tried to harm her in the future, the gods would not forget what was owed. And she was owed much.

"By the Styx, I swear never to return," Peleus spat. "But I will never promise you peace, Pirithous. Not so long as we both live."

"I could not stomach it, if you did," Pirithous replied through his teeth. "Take your men and go, and be glad my wife did not burn your ships when she stole back her horses."

Chapter Forty-Four

Pirithous

He managed to keep himself upright until Peleus turned his back, leading his men down the slope to the riverbank and their ships, but only just. He dropped his shield, and tried to sheath his sword, only to find his hands shook too fiercely to allow him to slide the blade into the leather scabbard.

Hippodamia's hand covered his, steadying him. But she could not stop the cold which had replaced the burning pain in his side. She could not stop death if it came for him this day, and he knew he had pushed himself too far, drawn too much on his father's blood. The lightning gave strength, but it came at a cost, and he was scorched through and through.

"Melanthos!" he called, unable to tear his gaze from Hippodamia's face. Those warm brown eyes and the white light of her love almost drowning him.

"My lord?"

"See that Peleus leaves none of his ants behind."

"Of course, my lord," Melanthos said. And he heard him call out to the others—his raiders—passing along the command. He heard, but he did not look away, because the only thing keeping him standing was Hippodamia, and he did not think even her presence, her love, her courage, could hold him up much longer.

"Pirithous," she said, lifting her hand to his cheek. Stroking his face. Likely the only part of him which did not bleed, though not for lack of trying on Peleus's part. "I suppose it was too much to hope you would stay in your bed."

He sank to his knees, buried his face in the softness of her body, nestling his head beneath her breasts. He was so cold. And she was so warm. "Forgive me."

Her breath hitched, her fingers curling into his hair. "What is there to forgive?"

But even if she did not remember, he did. Her voice hoarse with fear and pain and desperation. How small and broken she had looked when she confessed she had nothing left but him. He had promised to return to her whole and unbloodied, and he had known even then it was a lie. But he had not quite expected to fail her so utterly. He had not expected to die. Not truly. Not yet.

"Forgive me," he said again, though he did not know if she heard.

He did not know, because even the bright light of her love could no longer hold the darkness back.

CHAPTER FORTY-FIVE

HIPPODAMIA

Pirithous!" He was so heavy, too heavy for her to lift alone. Hippodamia dropped to her knees, struggling to keep him upright. He'd gone completely slack, his eyes rolled back in his head, and she swallowed a sob at the sight of his face, so pale, so wan. "Pirithous! Please! Antiope—Antiope, help me. Find Podarkes, or Aithon."

Theseus reached her side before his wife could, cursing under his breath. "Thrice-cursed fool!"

"King Theseus, my lord, there must be something—he cannot die, not after all this. He cannot die!"

"What Zeus gives he can take just as easily, even from his son." Theseus grunted, lifting him up. Pirithous's head lolled, his arm hanging limp. She folded it back neatly over his waist, her eyes blurring, her throat too thick for words.

"Your horse, my lady," Theseus said. "The sooner he is back in his bed, the better, though I can promise you nothing. If he has spilled too much blood…"

"No," she said. "He must live, Theseus. And if Zeus will not save him, Poseidon will. If I must sacrifice every horse I have been given, I will see it done for Pirithous's sake."

"Here," Antiope said, having returned atop Aithon with Podarkes not far behind, both horses and rider breathing hard. "Give him to me. I will return him to the palace. Mia can follow on Podarkes."

"Quickly," Hippodamia urged, though she knew it was needless. If there were any two people who loved Pirithous more than she did, it was Antiope and Theseus. She watched Antiope take Pirithous in her arms, cradling him like a child across her legs, and mounted Podarkes, who snapped and pawed with frustration and impatience when she did not give him his head at once to race Aithon to the walls. She liked it even less than he did, but she could not see to her husband until she had done what she could for the rest of his men. "Theseus—I fear I must beg a favor more, though you have done so much already."

"Anything, my lady."

"Help Melanthos and the others. I would not have Peleus turn back at some rumor of Pirithous's collapse."

Theseus gave her a grim nod. "Go, my lady. I will do what must be done here. And happily, for Pirithous's sake and yours. He will need your strength now more than these men."

She did not need him to tell her twice. With the barest touch of her heel against Podarkes's flank, they took flight.

***

Old Machaon had the rest of the palace horses well in hand when they rode through the gate, though he grumbled about the cuts and scrapes and sweat stains on their hides. Hippodamia ignored his complaints, leaving Podarkes in the horsemaster's hands, and shouting for men to help Antiope carry Pirithous up the stairs to his rooms.

"Good man, Glaukos," Antiope said, when the scarred and tow-headed raider lent his aid. How she knew so many of Pirithous's men, Hippodamia did not know. Particularly when she thought them so beneath her. But she was grateful for the

Amazon's memory for names and faces, for she could see nothing beyond Pirithous's pale, waxy skin.

Lord Poseidon, protect him. Guard him. Only tell me what I must do to see him saved.

"To his bed, I beg of you. And send for the physician," Hippodamia called out, not even glancing up from his face to be sure her orders were followed.

She went ahead of them through the hall, clearing the way, and then ran up the stairs to push open his bedroom door and roll the excess bedding out of the way. Antiope and Glaukos half-carried and half-dragged him between them, one of his arms draped over each of their shoulders, and she helped them to ease him down on the bed, pulling first one leg, then the other over the side.

She searched him over carefully then, counting the cuts and bruises, every nick and scrape. There were so many. But she must know where he needed the physician's attention most, and Theseus had said Pirithous needed her strength. Perhaps if she stayed near to him, kept her hands upon him, somehow, some way, he might borrow what he needed for his own ends, the way he had lent her so much of his love, his desire, his sympathy.

"You must come back to me," she said, smoothing the hair from his brow. "You must live, do you hear me? Whatever you need from me, whatever I can offer—I am yours, Pirithous. I am yours, and you are mine, and you cannot leave me behind."

She rested her forehead against his, breathing him in, all blood and dust and sweat and scorched earth. Dia had born such a fine son. Maybe that was how she had survived, how she had found the strength to continue on, after Ixion. Because she had not truly been alone so long as Pirithous lived.

Zeus, Lord of All, I beg of you, do not let this be the end of your son! Send Paeon to heal his wounds.

"The physician, Mia," Antiope said, startling her from her thoughts with a touch upon her shoulder. "You must give him room."

Hippodamia nodded, slipping from the bedside, but keeping her hand upon his head, her fingers knotted in his damp hair. "The worst is between his ribs," she told the man. Nikostratos was old and gray, but his hands were steady as they hovered over Pirithous's wounds, just as they had been steady and strong in setting the bones Pirithous had likely displaced again with his foolishness. "And the slice across his chest next, from what I can tell."

Niko grunted, packing the wound at Pirithous's ribs with poppy-milk soaked wool. He muttered to himself with the rhythm of an incantation, applying perfumed oils to the other cuts and scrapes as he went. Hippodamia bit her tongue to quiet her own impatience with his slow, careful movements, and turned her attention back to Pirithous's face. The stillness of his expression wrenched her—even his eyelids did not so much as twitch.

"He'll need stitching," Niko said after a moment. "And I will have to reset some of his bones, and splint them properly this time to keep him in his bed. I fear my lord will not like it, if he wakes."

If. The word cut through her, sharper than a Myrmidon blade, and she lifted her gaze to the old physician, her eyes hard. "You will do everything you can to be sure that he *will* wake. Do you understand me?"

"I helped Dia bring him into this world, my lady. I don't intend to outlive him, now. But it is in the hands of the gods more than mine. May Paeon have mercy upon him, and Lord Apollo grant his blessings as well."

She let out a breath, closing her eyes against the despair which threatened to overtake her. Pirithous would not die. She would not let him. If she had to remain at his side in vigil, fasting, while the gods feasted upon her very blood, she would suffer it to keep him alive.

"Send for the priests, Antiope. If it is in the hands of the gods, I would know what they demand of us, and see their needs fulfilled."

"Of course," Antiope said, squeezing her shoulder gently in farewell before she left.

Mia only wished Theseus had returned with the rest of the men as well. She might have begged him to appeal to his father or to his uncle, Zeus. And it would mean Peleus had gone, and they need not fear. Not for a time, at least. It would be decades before Peleus ever dared to turn his greedy eyes back to the lands of the Lapiths and their horses. Because she and Pirithous had shamed him. Together.

Together, as they would go on.

"My queen," Nikostratos said, forcing her from her thoughts, "there is much for me to do. Perhaps you would rather retire to your own bed? Or attend to your other business while I work?"

Her eyes narrowed. "I do not intend to abandon my husband and my king when he has the greatest need of me. Do what you must. I am not afraid of blood."

"As you wish, my lady," the physician said.

She paid him no mind after that, keeping her eyes upon Pirithous's face, her hand wrapped around his.

My strength is yours, Pirithous, if you will only take it.

But he did not so much as twitch beneath the physician's ministrations. He barely breathed.

Lord Poseidon, please. If you grant me no other favor ever again, give me this. Give me Pirithous, strong and whole and living. I will give you anything of mine, if you will only save him.

Hold his hand and pray. It was all she could do.

And she had no intention of stopping.

***

She gave Aithon to the gods, sending him up the mountain to the shrine of Zeus and the priest who had begged Pirithous to delay their wedding—the only one she trusted to see the truth in the blood. She would have sent Podarkes, but Antiope and Machaon had refused to let her.

"Let the priest read the signs, and if a larger sacrifice is needed, you will have Podarkes still to give," Antiope had said. "Aithon is brave and strong. A fit offering for any god."

Antiope was not wrong. If Zeus refused to grant his son any favors, at least she would still have Podarkes to offer to Poseidon. The finest stallion for the Lord of Horses. And she had to believe that Poseidon would be swayed, even if Zeus could not be. She had to believe that the Horse Lord would hear her. And if not her, then his own son.

She studied Pirithous's face, still a pale mask of the man she had married. The physician had done all he could, closing the worst of his wounds, and smearing honey over the rest. Hippodamia had trickled broth and water between his lips, but there was little else for her to do. Little else to be done at all, if the gods would not help him.

Mia laced her fingers through his and held tighter.

"My lady?"

She did not have to turn to know it was Theseus. The compassion in his voice would have been telling enough, even if she had not grown so used to his presence in the palace. It would feel so much emptier when Antiope and Theseus left. And how much longer could they truly stay, when Theseus had his own lands to rule? Pirithous would not have a quick recovery, if he recovered at all.

"Peleus and his men are gone. Melanthos follows them down the river with a handful of the blooded raiders, to be sure they do not turn back before they reach the sea, but I do not think we need worry. Peleus is well beaten, and his Myrmidons are not likely to risk the wrath of the gods by returning armed to your banks."

"I wish Peleus would try, that I might see his blood spilled by my own hand," she said softly. "To have secured our safety at the cost of our king—it seems too great a sacrifice."

"If a king is not willing to sacrifice himself for his people, he is not worthy of the throne. Pirithous has proven himself, as you have, and when he wakes there will be no question of his rights.

You will both be safer for it, and I do not believe Pirithous will think his sacrifice too great if it means you are protected."

She turned then, searching his face. Dusty and blood-smeared still from battle, but sincere. "*When.*"

Theseus's jaw tightened. "If he survived being trampled, he will survive this. He must survive this."

His words echoed her thoughts so closely. As if he knew her mind. As if his happiness, too, depended upon Pirithous's survival.

"He has been a brother to me, if not in body and blood, certainly in spirit. He has been more than a brother to me," Theseus said. "Until he stops breathing, I will not give up hope. I will never give up."

"Might you appeal to your father?" she asked. "For his sake? For mine?"

Theseus shook his head. "I dare not without offending Zeus. Not yet. Perhaps not at all. But Antiope says you have offered a generous sacrifice, and I do not believe for a moment that Zeus will abandon his son now. Not wholly. Not while Pirithous has no heir."

She touched her stomach, flat as ever. But it was far too soon to know if his seed had caught. Too soon for anyone but the gods to know.

"Let us hope your bleeding comes as it ought," Theseus said.

She swallowed, unsure. Because if Theseus was wrong, and Pirithous died, still—

Dia hadn't been alone. And if Hippodamia was meant to take her place, to rule as queen after Pirithous was gone, she did not want to be alone, either.

CHAPTER FORTY-SIX

HIPPODAMIA

Antiope and Theseus stayed.

"As long as you have need of me," Antiope said. "I will send Theseus back to Athens alone if necessary, but I do not think he will go until he knows Pirithous's fate. And even then, he would not abandon you."

Hippodamia was still at Pirithous's bedside. She'd slept beside him, careful not to touch his body beyond her hand upon his, that he might take what strength he needed from her, should he wake at all. The physician had come again at sunrise, smearing more honey over his wounds and checking his sutured side before leaving, and then she had been alone. She sat upon a stool, near his head, and watched him breathe.

"Thank you, Antiope." It was all she could think to say. All she had in her. Everything else was focused wholly upon Pirithous.

"I'm certain you will hear from the priest today," Antiope said, resting a hand on her shoulder. "Theseus believes Pirithous will live, Mia. He says he is too strong to be killed so easily as that."

She wanted to laugh. So easily. Trampled by centaurs first, and then stabbed by Peleus, after he had tried to fight with a broken leg, broken ribs, to say nothing of all the lesser injuries he'd sustained before that. There was nothing easy about the wounds Pirithous had suffered. Nothing small.

"Theseus believes Zeus will spare his son because he has no heir yet," Mia said. "Am I to wish now, when he lies dying, that he has given me no child? That nothing of his body will survive him? I cannot hope to lose him so completely as that. But am I then praying for his death, if I hope for his son?"

Antiope sighed. "No, of course not, Mia. And Theseus, wise as he is, does not understand all. He has never known anything but confidence. In himself. In his friend. He has never allowed the thought of failure to enter his mind, be it by death or otherwise. Everything he has ever set out to accomplish, he has succeeded in. To him, this is no different. Pirithous will live because he cannot fail. Because they are both too strong, too young, too blessed by the gods to be brought so low."

"It is hubris," Mia said, the realization sinking like so much stone inside her, weighting down all her hopes. "And all the more reason that Pirithous could be left to die, heir or no heir. That he might be punished for his pride."

"Theseus's hubris, perhaps. But I am not so certain Pirithous is so afflicted. He has had a different life—a harder life. And in his youth, he failed more often than he succeeded. For all that Pirithous lives fearlessly, I think it is because he does not forget how quickly his fortunes might change."

"They have certainly changed now. Ever since we were wed, it has been nothing but disaster. I have been the source of his suffering at every turn, and still he has clung to me, protected me, desired me…"

"Because he loves you, Mia. And if there is anything in this world that will serve him now, it is that. No matter how still he lies, I am certain he fights for life. For you. And Hades himself will have to drag him from your side."

Mia smiled, brushing his hair from his forehead. Antiope was not wrong about him. From the moment she'd told him she could not love him, he had pursued her with a single-minded intensity.

She could not imagine he would let even death stand in his way now that he had won her.

"He is a fool," she said softly, but she could not keep the affection from her voice.

"All men are," Antiope agreed. "But Theseus and Pirithous are the better sort, thanks to their mothers. Certainly Aethra is the finest of women. She would have been a queen had she been born Amazon. And Dia—Dia would have survived the world falling down around her. She had the strength and the stubbornness of Atlas."

"Let us hope she passed that same stubbornness on to her son, along with the rest," Hippodamia said. "And in the meantime, I hope you will not let Theseus tempt the gods with his speech."

She could not bear it, otherwise. Much as she appreciated his confidence, she had only to look at the last sevenday to see what punishments the gods might see fit to inflict. And she could not lose Pirithous, too.

"You needn't fear, Mia. Theseus would never knowingly risk his friend. And if the worst comes to pass, I will stay with you for as long as you require it. Or perhaps Aethra will come to support you instead, if it serves the Lapiths better."

She said nothing. It would do her no good to tell Antiope she did not care what served the Lapiths. She did not care for anything beyond Pirithous's next breath. Not right now. Even though she recognized her duty as queen, had chosen to be bound by it, she was still Centaur enough not to desire life beyond the loss of her mate. And perhaps that was barbaric of her. Perhaps it did not match this strange notion of honor that the Lapiths and the Athenians prized so much, but it honored Pirithous, all the same.

She could not be what she was not. And while Pirithous had been raised by Dia, had been granted her strength along with Zeus's, Mia had only what Centaurus had given her. What kind of queen would she be if she was not true to herself above all? What kind of woman, for that matter?

As long as Pirithous lived, she would fight for him, for his people, for everything they dreamed of building together. But beyond that?

Beyond that she was not certain she had the strength. Not if she must face it all alone.

Even Dia had not had to do that.

***

"Zeus remains silent," the priest said, not meeting her gaze. He had arrived as the sun set, shoulders bowed and back hunched beneath a cloak.

Mia narrowed her eyes, wishing Pirithous were awake to give her his counsel. He knew this man, knew his motivations, what he desired. He would know if the priest lied, hoping for more horseflesh, more gold, more offerings for himself rather than the gods.

"Aithon would not betray me so," she said. "His shade would not rest until he had charged through the gates of Olympus and appealed to Zeus himself. If the sign of the god is not clear, perhaps it is your eyes which fail you."

"My queen, I swear to you, the fault is not mine," he said, wringing his hands. "My lord Pirithous would tell you, I am loyal to my king and my gods, above all."

"A shame then that King Pirithous does not wake. But the physician tells me it is in the hands of the gods now, and as such, his life depends upon you." She had not moved from Pirithous's side when the priest had entered, nor even risen from her stool, and now she grasped her husband's hand all the more tightly. "Do not tell me you have wasted my horse. That the sacrifice was for naught!"

"Perhaps it is only that Lord Zeus has not made up his mind as to his son's fate," the priest said, his eyes darting about the room, not daring to rest for even a moment upon his king. She resented that even more than she hated how he refused to meet her eyes.

"Until he is decided, there is nothing to be seen. But of course the sacrifice is not wasted. Lord Zeus can only be pleased by the honor you've shown him with such a fine animal! Perhaps… perhaps another sacrifice would help persuade him to our cause?"

"Another horse?" she demanded.

"No, my lady, of course not! I would not ask the Lapiths to sacrifice another horse so soon. A bull would be better, for Lord Zeus."

She closed her eyes, inhaling deeply through her nose in order to keep her temper. A bull. Just as valuable at the moment as a horse, with so much livestock lost to the centaurs. The Lapiths did not keep an excess of cows and bulls even at the best of times, preferring to focus upon their horses instead. But if Zeus would prefer a bull, she would give him one. She must.

"I will send a bull up the mountain with the dawn," she said, opening her eyes. She struggled to unclench her jaw, to keep her tone polite, though she resented his uselessness. At least it had been Aithon and not Podarkes lost. "And if you desire it, you will have our hospitality tonight."

"My thanks, Lady," he said, bowing. "As you must know, it is not safe to climb the mountain after dark. The centaurs were defeated but not expelled…"

She looked away, focusing on her hand wrapped around Pirithous's. It was something she would have to see to, it seemed. The fates were cruel to place this burden upon her shoulders. Truly twisted to ask it of her.

"Glaukos!" she called out.

Pirithous's men had been taking it in turns to stand outside his door, awaiting her commands, in service to their king. Melanthos had not yet returned, but she had begun to know the others a little better, and they were all respectful toward her, even solicitous. Whether it was because they saw her pain, or because they loved their king, she was not certain.

Glaukos opened the door from the hall, stepping inside and offering an abbreviated salute with a touch of his fist to his forehead. "My queen?"

"Glaukos, please escort our priest to the steward and see that he is given a room. And I would speak to Theseus, if you can find him. Will you ask your brothers to send word directly when Melanthos returns, as well?"

"It will be as you say, my queen," Glaukos said, inclining his head. "And I will do even better, and send you Melanthos himself, if you do not mind him still covered in the filth of the road. He has only just arrived."

She let out a breath, relief making her lightheaded. She had half-feared he would not return at all, and she had known that, whatever came, she would need him. "Give him time to bathe then, and send him up a meal. He deserves that much."

"Of course, my queen." He bowed again and then extended his arm, directing the priest to the door. "After you."

The priest hesitated for just a moment, as if he wished to say something more, perhaps to press her for some action, but another glance at Glaukos's fierce features and he only bowed instead, and left the room.

Useless man. To think she had hoped for some kind of answer from him, some solution. To think she had trusted him at all. She was likely better off making the sacrifice herself. And perhaps she would, if the bull she had promised him came to nothing. It was only that she did not like the thought of leaving Pirithous. Even for so short a time as to wash and relieve herself, though she had done that much.

She sighed, leaning forward to press her forehead against the back of his hand. "What will I do?" she asked him. "What would you have me do?"

But she knew the answer. The only thing which had checked Pirithous's own response to the centaurs had been his concern for her. He had held back, and as a result his men had died, their village burned to the ground along with their crops. The centaurs had proven themselves faithless, now that Centaurus was dead, and any hope of reconciliation was lost utterly.

Which meant she had only one choice, even if it shattered her to see it through.

The centaurs must be driven off. Hunted into exile.

As queen of the Lapiths, she must let them die.

CHAPTER FORTY-SEVEN

HIPPODAMIA

"You're certain this is what you wish?" Theseus said, searching her face.

He had arrived with Melanthos, and between the two of them, they had brought enough food for ten men and insisted she eat with them at the small table in the corner of the room. She had not had much of an appetite these last days, but they had both argued that she must keep up her strength. After all, she would do Pirithous no good if she did not care for herself. She had choked down the relish of cooked greens and nibbled at the lamb, but it was the wine she needed, to strengthen her resolve and dull the pain of what she must do.

"I see no other way forward," she said. "I will not have the Lapiths live in fear of attack when they step outside the palace walls. The centaurs—they have brought this upon themselves, Theseus. I have tried to reason with them, as have you, but if they would not hear us before, they certainly will not now. Too many will be deranged with anger and pain for the deaths of their loved ones. They must be driven off."

"She is right, my lord," Melanthos said, picking at the bread on his plate. He pinched pieces from the softer interior of the heel and rolled them into balls between his fingers before tossing them into his mouth. "And if she means to rule in Pirithous's place, this is where she must begin. To prove her loyalty to the Lapiths above all other ties, even in Pirithous's absence."

"Few will survive this, Mia," Theseus said, his voice gentled with compassion. "You will see your people wiped out. Destroyed."

"I know," she said, unable to meet his eyes. She would not let him see the tears that stood in her own. "I know, and believe me, I do not desire it. I do not like it. I do not know, even, if the pain of it all will not destroy me. But what else is there to be done? I feel certain it is what Pirithous would wish, were it not for me. And perhaps we would be better off if he had not tempered his response for my sake to begin with."

Theseus shook his head. "If you think to blame yourself for what has happened, I can promise you Pirithous would not stand for it were he awake, and I do not intend to allow it either. Pirithous would not have allowed rage and bloodlust to rule his decision, regardless of your marriage. And knowing what Peleus had done, caution was the wiser choice, besides. If you must blame yourself for anything, know that Pirithous's choices, were they colored by his love for you at all, saved any number of lives, men and women both!"

"You cannot know it," she said.

"King Peleus would have attacked while the men were gone to fight the centaurs, my lady," Melanthos said. "It was the opportunity he hoped for from the start, though I am certain he was happy enough to see us weakened by Cyllarus's charge. Even if Antiope had remained upon the wall to guard the women against the Myrmidons, you would have had little hope of success in keeping him at bay while we were away. The women and children would have been taken as slaves, Pirithous's palace sacked, and the horses taken or killed as well. If my king delayed his attack against the centaurs for your sake, as you believe, then we all owe you a debt."

She fell silent, brushing the moisture from her eyes before it spilled down her cheeks. Melanthos had been loyal to her from the moment she had chosen to defend the Lapiths, for her own character, not only for the sake of his king. She was all the more grateful for it, now, and she knew if she chose to rule in Pirithous's place, he would support her. Stand at her side and offer her his strength.

Even so, she feared it would not be enough.

"Give the men time to rest and recover, a sevenday, perhaps," she said. "I will not offer them gold, as Pirithous thought to, for I would rather the centaurs be given the opportunity to flee, but they must be driven from the mountain all the same. With any luck, perhaps they will go all the way south to Phthia."

"I would not wish that, if you desire them to live," Theseus said. "But all the same, we will see them gone. Melanthos and I can each lead a small party of men hand-picked for the task. None who desire blood over the safety of the Lapiths themselves."

"That will leave you with a large number of men, still, to protect the palace and the horses," Melanthos agreed. "I do not think King Peleus will return, but there are plenty of others who, having heard of our misfortunes, might seek to take advantage, and I would not leave you or Pirithous without defense."

She lifted her head, meeting both their gazes in turn. "You both have my thanks for everything you have done already. I am sorry to ask more of you."

"Pirithous is my brother in every way but blood," Theseus said, offering her a small smile. "I would not turn from him now no matter what he demanded of me. Nor will I abandon his wife. We will always be an ally to the Lapiths."

"And we Lapiths will not forget what we owe to the King of Athens," Melanthos said. "If that is all, my queen? I fear I am in desperate need of rest, and there is much to be done tomorrow."

"Yes, of course," she said. "Thank you, Melanthos. And thank Pirithous's men, particularly, on my behalf as well."

He rose, touching his fist to his brow. "They are proud to serve their queen, my lady. As am I."

Theseus made no move to rise with him, but watched Melanthos leave before turning his gaze back to her. Too thoughtfully, she felt. Sometimes, she wondered if King Theseus did not see into her very heart.

"The priest offered nothing of help?" he asked, but she was certain he knew the answer already, even before she shook her head. "What guidance did he give?"

"He asked for a bull, a second sacrifice, since Zeus was so unmoved by the first."

Theseus grunted, his gaze growing distant. "You agreed?"

"I do not see how I could refuse," she said, rising from the table. "If there is even the smallest hope that Zeus might smile upon us, I must pursue it. But…" She pressed her lips together on the rest of her words, thinking better of them. Theseus had made his feelings clear, after all.

"But what?" he asked.

She forced herself to smile, and presented a different concern instead. "But I am not certain I trust him."

"He knew the banquet would end in blood," Theseus said. "He warned us. Is that not proof that he hears the gods?"

"He serves his king, I have no doubt. But I am not so certain he serves his queen as loyally, that is all. And why should he, when I have brought his king nothing but trouble?"

"I will speak with him," Theseus promised. "If he lies, I will know it. And in the meantime, perhaps I should send for my own physician. Ariston has served me well, and perhaps he will know some potion or invocation that Pirithous's man does not. At the very least, you will know you can trust him."

"And the priest?"

Theseus grimaced. "Even I cannot remove a priest of Zeus from his position, or cast him aside without risking some curse of the gods. But if there is anything that can be done for Pirithous, you can be certain I will discover it."

She gave him a stiff nod, rubbing her wrist. And if the bull did not serve, she would find more worthy blood to spill. Make her own sacrifice, without the priest's intercession.

It was a queen's duty, was it not?

***

Pirithous slept on.

The bull had resulted in the same silence as Aithon's sacrifice, and the priest had asked again for more. A matched pair of snow white lambs this time, to be delivered to him on the seventh day after Peleus's raid. The day Theseus and Melanthos meant to lead their men up the mountain against those centaurs that remained.

Theseus had spoken to the priest, and while he was not wholly convinced, neither did he think he lied outright. "The gods are known for their fickle natures, after all," he'd told her later, "and it is possible the priest's vision is simply clouded by their capriciousness, rather than any particular malice or dishonesty."

She'd accepted his suggestion, for she had no proof that the priest did not serve them properly. Only her knowledge of Aithon's spirit, and how strange it seemed for the gods to fall so silent, when they had been more than happy to warn them of bloodshed and fire not a sevenday earlier.

"You see treachery where there is none," Antiope had said. "It is the strain of all this waiting, all your worry for Pirithous and the pain of your decision to sever the bonds between yourself and your people so completely. It would distress Theseus in the same manner if he were made to war upon the people of Troezen, and his grandfather the king. And I cannot imagine bearing arms against my sisters. Even the thought of it rends my heart."

"May the gods spare you such a fate," Mia said, for she doubted that even Antiope, strong as she was, would survive it whole.

In body she might triumph, but in spirit, she would be scarred forever. Just as Hippodamia feared she would be, as well. Even for Pirithous—no. The only choice she would have made differently in all of this would have been to keep to her room on the eve of her wedding banquet. Pirithous would have had no reason to doubt her, and perhaps he might have listened to the warning of the priest. Then again, as determined as he had been to bed her, he might have disregarded the warnings with a laugh just as easily as he had with a scowl.

"You are better off sending more sacrifices than fewer," Antiope said. "It is not as though the gods will resent the gift, and Pirithous can well afford to replace any livestock you give up for his sake. He would not begrudge it. Not when it is given to his father."

It seemed it was an argument Hippodamia would not win. Not that she desired to. She only wanted Pirithous to wake—and whatever the gods demanded, she would gladly give. If they would only tell her! If the priest could only discover the price!

"Perhaps we appeal to the wrong god," she said. "Perhaps it is Poseidon who desires our obedience, not Zeus. Surely he takes a special interest in the Lapiths, or their horses would not be half so fine. Were they not bred, too, from the Mares of Magnesia? A gift from Poseidon Horse-Lord, himself?"

"Surely the priest would know if Poseidon was not appeased," Antiope said.

"I am not so certain." Hippodamia poured herself a cup of the mint water Pirithous liked so much. She'd dribbled a measure of it down his throat already, along with broth, and smeared his lips with honey. How much good it did him, she did not know. Only that she must continue to try. It had been nearly five days, now, and he still did not stir. "But it might easily account for the silence of Zeus, and I cannot continue to sit here doing nothing, waiting for a priest or a physician to tell me nothing has changed, or worse, that there is no hope at all. Theseus says he does not dare appeal to his father for fear of offending Zeus, but Poseidon is *my* god, too. Honored above all by the centaurs. It is my right to offer him sacrifice—and I would know I had done everything I could!"

Antiope frowned. "And if it offends Zeus, what then?"

"At least he might send some message, one way or another. At least we might know if he means to abandon his son to death."

The Amazon's lips pressed thin, her eyes narrowing. "And what do you intend to offer the Earth Shaker?"

Mia stared into her water cup. "There is no worthier gift than blood."

But she did not think even an Amazon would understand if she admitted she meant to offer her own.

Chapter Forty-Eight

Hippodamia

The sacrifice of the lambs had provided them with nothing but more silence, though at least this time she'd had the satisfaction of watching the priest sweat with fear and distress when he delivered the news. He had not dared to ask for another victim, not with Theseus and Antiope both scowling beside her.

Melanthos had left already with his party of men, and Theseus had only awaited the outcome of the sacrifice before he followed. Antiope and Glaukos would remain behind as guards and war-leaders, should trouble come in search of them while the other men were gone.

"Ariston will arrive before long," Theseus said in farewell. "Perhaps there will be something he can do."

But even he did not look as though he believed it. His forehead was grooved with troubled lines more often than not, and he spent nearly as much time as she did at Pirithous's side during the days, leaving his bedside only reluctantly at night. If Antiope had not been there to draw him away, Hippodamia did not think he would go at all.

Antiope followed her husband from the room, then, to say her own farewells and watch him ride out from the walls. And when they returned successful, and the mountain was safe, Hippodamia would ride out herself, alone, to the shrine of her people. She could not wait any longer. Would not wait, not when Theseus's words echoed in her ears.

Let us hope your bleeding comes as it ought.

She pressed her hand to her belly, atop her womb. The priest had promised them a fertile marriage. Promised Pirithous his heir. And while it could simply be distress which delayed her woman's blood, she dared not wait for certainty. Not when Pirithous's life might depend upon it.

"Are you ill, my queen?" Glaukos asked, startling her from her thoughts. Of course he would come, knowing Antiope had gone to the wall.

She made herself smile and shook her head. "I am only concerned for the men. I cannot stand for more blood to be spilled so soon."

"You need not fear for them. Melanthos is more than capable, and even the sight of King Theseus is likely to set the centaurs fleeing." He hesitated for a moment, then met her eyes directly, knowingly. "There will be little fighting on either side, my queen."

She flushed. "The centaurs have abandoned and betrayed me. It is not for them I worry."

But saying it aloud did not make it true, and she did not think it fooled Glaukos in the slightest. She did worry for them. She hated herself for the choice she'd made, but what else was there to do? At least Theseus and Melanthos both understood. And they had promised her it would not be a slaughter. They meant only to drive them off. To send them into exile.

"There is no shame in caring for the people you have no choice but to leave behind, my queen. And those who would tell you otherwise—they are blind fools who cannot see beyond their own pain. If you did not ache for the loss, it would be stranger. King Pirithous would say the same, himself, were he able."

"Maybe so." She turned her face to the window, staring out at the mountain without seeing it. How she wished Pirithous were able to say anything at all. That this choice had been his instead of hers. But giving up her people made her all the more determined. She would do what she must, whatever the gods asked, if only he would live. All her sacrifice, all her people's suffering, would not be for nothing.

"Thank you, Glaukos."

She did not have to look to know he touched his fist to his forehead before he left the room, closing the door with a soft thump behind him.

***

She did not join Antiope upon the wall, but stayed at Pirithous's bedside while the sun sank lower and lower, thickening the shadows between the trees on the mountain slope. She had hoped the men would have returned by now. Some small part of her prepared to make her trip to the shrine that very night.

She had hoped, because the longer Pirithous lay motionless in this unnatural sleep, the more she feared he would not wake at all. And the more time passed, the more worn she felt, the title of queen weighing heavily upon her shoulders.

"You should not stay locked up in this room," Glaukos said when he allowed a servant in with her evening meal.

Warm bread and honey, roasted goat, and more of the relished greens she detested. Pirithous had promised her she could have them however she liked, but she had not had time yet, or energy, to face the kitchens and request her greens served uncooked. It seemed such a worthless thing to concern herself with, after all that had happened.

"King Pirithous would not want you tied to his bed day after day, and truly, you look too pale. Sickly."

"I will see to my own health, thank you," she replied. The servant had brought broth, too, for Pirithous, and she took up the small bowl, moving to his side. "But if it will reassure you, I mean to climb the mountain once the men return and it is safe. To pray for my husband's recovery."

"Melanthos will wish you to take a guard, if that is your intent."

She shook her head. "I will ride Podarkes and go alone."

"My queen, it is not safe. Even with the centaurs driven off, there are other dangers—wolves, bears, even wild boar. If you fell—"

Fury burned through her veins, and the glare she gave him stopped his words. "Do you think I am not familiar with the hazards of the mountain? I, who was raised upon it, even within its very heart, while you Lapiths cowered behind your walls?"

Glaukos stiffened. "You have seen for yourself the need for our walls, and it has little to do with the beasts in the wood."

"And you have seen my skill upon a horse, yet you suggest I might *fall*?"

He lowered his eyes, a flush suffusing his cheeks. "Even the most talented horsemen can be caught off-balance when their horse rears or kicks. If any harm were to come to you, for any reason, King Pirithous would never forgive us. And you must understand, my queen, that if my lord Pirithous does not wake, the Lapiths depend upon you."

"Perhaps they shouldn't."

His gaze flashed up again, alarm written in every line of his face. "Who else, if not the woman chosen by Queen Dia and King Pirithous, both?"

She pressed her lips together, busying herself by spooning a trickle of broth into Pirithous's mouth. It was excuse enough to look away. To turn her eyes from such earnestness, such painful loyalty. She deserved none of it. Not the way Dia had, or Pirithous after her.

"I will climb the mountain alone," she said, careful to keep her voice steady. "And with the blessing of the gods, Pirithous will wake. You need not worry about the rest."

And neither would she.

CHAPTER FORTY-NINE

HIPPODAMIA

Hippodamia!" Antiope burst through the door, gasping. She must have sprinted all the way from the palace wall. "They've returned. Theseus and Melanthos and the rest of the men!"

Mia's stomach lurched, like snakes coiling around her lungs, her heart, squeezing too tight. "All of them?"

Antiope twisted a shoulder in dismissal. "I hardly counted them when they left, but they look in good spirits. Theseus is whole and unharmed, and Melanthos does not look injured, either. Beyond that, I can tell you nothing. But they will both be here to tell you everything you might wish to know before long."

Two days they'd been gone, and Mia knew Antiope had hated the waiting. Glaukos had told her that the Amazon paced the palace walls, strung taut as a bow, and liable to snap at anyone who approached her. She would not admit it, but Mia thought it was fear which had put her so deeply on edge, and her exultation now was proof enough of the truth. If she had not worried for Theseus, she would not be so ecstatic at his return, safe and sound.

And Hippodamia was more familiar with fear of that kind than she liked to be, at the moment.

"I know you will wish to take Theseus straight to your bed, but I must speak to him first," she said. "I promise it will not take long."

Antiope rolled her eyes, but she smiled still, going to the window, no doubt to catch another glimpse of her husband. "Theseus would not let me drag him off until he'd spoken with you, regardless. His pleasure never comes before his duty."

Hippodamia wasn't certain she believed that, for if she had learned one thing from her own marriage, Theseus's decision to take Antiope as his bride had been far from dutiful. That the Athenians had stood for it at all was a testament to their love for their hero, but if things had gone just the slightest bit differently…

She shivered, pushing the thought of the war Athens had escaped from her mind. Surely if the Amazons meant to reclaim their queen, they'd have done so before now. And she would not borrow trouble for her friends when she had enough already for herself.

"You needn't wait here with me," she said, forcing a smile. "Go to your husband."

Antiope sniffed. "I am not so foolish that I cannot spend two days apart from Theseus without falling all over myself to reach his side again."

"And I never believed I would be so loyal to Pirithous that the thought of leaving his bedside would make me ache, yet here I am. There is no shame in your joy, Antiope. Go. Pretend I sent you, if you wish."

She smiled over her shoulder. "When did you become so wise?"

Hippodamia's gaze slid back to Pirithous, lying far too still. "It is not wisdom, Antiope."

"Then what would you call it?"

"Grief."

Antiope was silent when she wished to be, but the rustle of her tunic and the soft scuff of her sandals warned Mia before the Amazon's arms wrapped around her shoulders. "Do not give up all hope, my friend. Not yet. And even if the worst comes to pass, you will not be alone. Not in your sorrow, and not in your duty."

But Hippodamia was alone already. She had sent Theseus and Melanthos to make it so.

***

The two men entered the room to stand grim-faced before her, still clothed in dust and dirt from their journey. She sank to her stool at their expressions, her heart constricting before they'd even spoken. She did not need them to. Their faces said it all.

"How many?" she asked, the words half-broken.

"More than could be persuaded to flee," Theseus said. "You were right that there would be no reasoning with them. Most were too crazed by grief to think of anything but striking at us. I am only grateful we lost so few of our own men in the fighting."

She closed her eyes, struggling to breathe. "How many escaped?"

"It was the widows with their foals," Melanthos said. "They were consumed—"

"How many, Melanthos?" she demanded, before he could paint the horror any more clearly behind her eyelids.

He cleared his throat. "A dozen, perhaps." He hesitated, and her stomach sank, sour and roiling and heavy as rock. "They were all too young, my queen."

Too young. Foals, only, and too young to survive on their own in a strange land, without the safety of their caves, without food, without the means to hunt. She had murdered her people. Was that not sacrifice enough for the gods? For Zeus? She had watered the mountain with the blood of the centaurs, and still Pirithous lay all but dead.

"I must go to the shrine of Poseidon upon the mountain, and make offerings to the Horse Lord." How her voice remained steady, even cool, she did not know, for she wanted to scream at the pain inside her. As if she had been torn apart slowly by despair, and a dull, thick needle was piercing through her body with the heaviest of strings to sew her back together again. "I would ask that Pirithous not be left alone while I am away."

"My queen, you mustn't go—"

"Alone?" she opened her eyes to meet Melanthos's pitying gaze. "Alone is what I am, Melanthos. Alone is what I will always be. But I will not betray my people any further by allowing a stranger to set foot in our most sacred grove. No. I will go with Podarkes, and trust in the Horse Lord to keep me safe upon the journey. You and the rest of the men will remain here and see to your king."

"Will you not even accept my company?" Theseus asked.

She knew by his voice he did not expect her to say yes. "If you wish to make sacrifice to your father I will not stop you, but you will not do so with me, upon the mountain."

"Pirithous would not want you to go unguarded, Hippodamia."

"Pirithous would trust that I know my way through the woods. He would not like it, but he would let me go. And so will you. He is all I have left, Theseus. I will not do less than everything in my power to protect him now."

Theseus pressed his lips together. "And if he wakes, what would you have me tell him?"

"That I have gone for his sake, and I will return before nightfall, two days hence."

"My queen—" Melanthos began, but she stopped him with one uplifted hand.

"I have made my decision. You may go." Her gaze shifted to Theseus, then away again, before she weakened. Before he saw through her utterly, and argued in Pirithous's name with words she couldn't refute. "Both of you."

***

She did not even wait until morning. The supplies she needed were already gathered by Glaukos, though he had not liked it, and Podarkes, bridled by Machaon, was waiting ready at the stable door. The horsemaster did not question her, and she was glad at least for that. He merely gave a sniff after she'd swung herself up onto Podarkes's broad back.

"Keep your bow handy," he said. "The scent of so much blood is bound to have drawn beasts by now." Then he gave Podarkes a pat on the rump and turned away, disappearing inside the cavernous mouth of the stable doors.

Hippodamia touched her heels to Podarkes's flanks, and rode out the gate into moonlight and shadow.

She only hoped that Pirithous would forgive her.

Chapter Fifty

Hippodamia

She did not dare tie Podarkes, but let his reins fall to the ground and whispered in his ear to keep close. Machaon was not wrong about the blood, and while dawn's first fingers were crawling over the earth, it was still night enough for the wolves to think themselves stronger. She tried not to look at the darker puddles and stains on the ground as she walked past the cluster of caves she had once called home. In the dusky light, she could see hoof prints in the packed earth, the only sign that her people had ever lived, now. The only sign of life.

She touched the stone arch of Centaurus's cave, which she had shared for so long, and ached for her father's presence, his reassurance and love. If she failed today, perhaps she might join him before long. But she could not imagine what he must think of her, of the choices she had made. Of all this blood, spilled and rotting, filling her mouth with the taste of bronze and mildew.

Hippodamia straightened and continued on, averting her eyes from the splintered wood and shattered crockery, and following the lonely hard-packed path away from the settlement itself. Upward, weaving through clumps of stone and boulders, so well-trodden that she had to watch her feet carefully to keep from tripping on the exposed roots of the old, stunted drys trees, planted by

Centaurus in his youth for their acorns. She climbed on until she reached the pines, planted on either side of two immense stones.

The path wound between them, and so did she, stepping out onto a wide slab of exposed limestone, worn into a shallow bowl by wind and rain. An altar stood at its heart, built of the same pinewood, sacred to Poseidon, and holding a small stone bowl, stained with blood from countless sacrifices. Hippodamia drew the knife from her belt and crossed to the altar before she lost her nerve. None of the animals she had sent in sacrifice to Zeus had been worthy of his response, but Poseidon would have no such complaint. With one swift stroke of the blade, she opened her arm and let the blood of her own body pour into the bowl before dropping to her knees before the altar.

"Lord Poseidon, hear me. Forgive my failures, and accept this blood in sacrifice. Protect my husband. Guard him from death, and give him the strength to rise again, to live. This much, I beg of you, and nothing more."

She wrapped a bandage tightly around her arm, to stop the bleeding, but remained upon her knees. She would stay until nightfall, if she must. Even through the night, if the god demanded it, letting her blood flow until it spilled over onto the altar and, from the altar, soaked the stone beneath her knees, but she would not be ignored. She would not leave without some sign, some answer from the gods.

"Lord Poseidon, hear me," she began again. "I beg you to spare my husband, to keep Pirithous from death, to grant him life. He has lost so much. We have both lost so much."

***

She continued that way, upon her knees, leaning forward every so often to spill more blood into the bowl, repeating her prayers and singing hymns to the god until her voice grew hoarse and her head too light. And even then, she still gave more blood, her lips moving, shaping the words her voice could no longer carry.

Hear my prayers, and save him. Lord Poseidon, father of horses, protect us both.

Her body slumped until her head rested upon the altar.

Lord Poseidon, accept my blood in sacrifice. Bring Pirithous back to true life. Let him live, let him live, let him live.

When the sun began to sink beyond the rise of stone, she closed her eyes to stop the mountain's rocking, sure it was only the result of too much blood lost, and the long fast while she waited for the god's response. But the darkness only intensified the sensation, and the whinny of a horse brought her head up, her eyes narrowing against the glare of the sunset. The horse whinnied again, shrill and nervous.

Podarkes. She had left Podarkes below. She looked toward the entrance, considered rising, but she was so unsteady, even upon her knees, with the stone rocking beneath her—

The stone, rocking.

She sat back upon her heels, her mind suddenly sharp and her gaze fixed upon the stone bowl which shuddered along with the rest of the mountain, splashing and spilling her blood upon the altar.

Lord Poseidon Earth-Shaker, hear me! Spare Pirithous's life!

The altar itself jumped and toppled, along with the stones bracing the entrance to the shrine, and the limestone beneath her cracked, fissures flowing out like the branches of a river, spiraling around her where she knelt, and circling once, twice, three times, before disappearing into a pool of her blood. The earth went still, and all she could hear was the thunder of hoofbeats. Podarkes's whinny, high and anxious and near.

She touched the cracks, feeling the pulse of heat, of life, in the stone. Three circles, ending in a pool of blood. Her blood. She touched it, too, dipping her fingers into the puddle, cold and hollow. She shuddered, jerking her hand back just as quickly again. Death. The circles were life, and the blood was death. Three lives? Or…

She swallowed hard and scrambled up, lurching to her feet. Podarkes was pacing, whinnying and rearing, on the other side of the toppled boulders. When she reached them, pressed her hand against the cold stone in search of some small leverage in order to climb, the boulders cracked, the sound so loud, so near, it made her ears ring.

Three pieces. Two large, one small. A child's face, she thought. A child's face in the raw, broken rock. And hers. And Pirithous's. A laughing, living, Pirithous, so clear and joyous it made her eyes prick with tears.

She touched the second boulder and it turned to dust, falling in a spiral around her body, circling three times. Three times. Three circles.

Three years.

Podarkes charged through the dust, scattering the spirals, and she grasped the base of his mane, vaulting up on his back. Her body was covered in fine, white powder, blood staining the bottom of her tunic above the knees, and when she looked at her arm, meaning to wrap her wounds, the cuts were closed—leaving three long, white scars in their place.

Poseidon had answered.

He had accepted her sacrifice.

He had accepted *her* in sacrifice.

Poseidon, through Centaurus, had spared her life as a child. And in three years, he would take it back.

Chapter Fifty-One

Pirithous

Hippodamia was gone. Climbed the mountain alone, like a fool, to make sacrifice to the Earth Shaker, as if she could not do so just as easily within sight of his walls, and from the moment Theseus had told him what she'd done, he could not stand to lie in his bed a moment longer. Could not imagine a moment's rest.

"Take me to the wall, I beg of you," he rasped, his voice rough with disuse. Theseus had claimed he'd slept a sevenday through, and then some, and Pirithous cursed himself for pushing his body too far. For provoking Hippodamia to such foolishness. As if seeing her caught by Peleus was not agony enough. "Or better yet, get me a horse, and I will ride after her."

"No horse would have the patience to carry you in the state you're in," Theseus said, pushing him back down when he tried to sit up. "How you have the strength even to fight with me, I cannot guess."

"You never should have let her go," he accused. "You ought to have stopped her. What good are you if you cannot even keep my wife safe while I lie ill?"

Theseus had the gall to roll his eyes, shoving him back again, more forcefully this time. "There is no stopping your wife when she has made up her mind. Surely you must realize that by now. Or do you think I would have let her lead the charge against Peleus, to start?"

Pirithous closed his eyes, not wanting to admit that the room still spun. "I felt the ground shake beneath me, the bed shudder…"

"If Poseidon spoke to her, then that is some assurance she has come to no harm. And it means she had reason to go, Pirithous. It was Poseidon himself who woke you from your fell sleep."

He let out a breath. "Am I to raise a son of Poseidon as my own, the way Ixion was forced to raise me?"

Dia had never taken another man to her bed after Zeus had come to her. Not even after Ixion's death. To be given back his life, only to lose Hippodamia's love—he could not bear the thought. He could not bear to think that bright, burning light of her love might never touch him again, when he had only just realized how desperately he needed her, wanted her, loved her.

Gods above, how he loved her. The fierce heart that sent her up the mountain to bargain with a god for his life. The brave spirit that had ridden out against Peleus in his place. The queen who had known precisely what words to use to end the slaughter at their wedding feast.

"The centaurs?" he asked suddenly. "You did not let her ride out with the centaurs still roaming the mountain!"

"No," Theseus said, the word far too soft. And he would not meet his eyes. "Hippodamia—she is as strong as an Amazon, Pirithous. Even Antiope is in awe of her."

But the sentiment brought him little reassurance. "What happened while I slept, Theseus?"

He grunted, sinking to the stool beside the bed. "For good or ill, that wild child Centaurus gave you as a bride has become a queen, my friend. Your queen."

"She was never wild," Pirithous murmured, his gaze going to the window. "Or a child."

He could see nothing from this angle, and he wanted desperately to find her upon the mountain. To see her returning to his side. To see her. Particularly when Theseus refused to speak in anything but riddles.

"Help me to the wall, Theseus. I beg of you."

His friend sighed. "It could be half a day, yet, before she returns."

"And when she does, she will see me waiting for her, whole and awake. Whatever price she paid, she will know it was not for nothing."

"You risk your health, you know."

Pirithous snorted. "As if it ever stopped you."

"Glaukos!" Theseus called out, and the man opened the door almost at once. No doubt he'd been waiting with his ear to the panel. But Theseus was already half-lifting him, and he had not the breath to speak sharply. "Your fool king insists upon a better view of the mountain. Support his other side, will you? Perhaps if we make him walk, he'll give up before we make the stairs."

Pirithous gritted his teeth, ignoring the stab of pain in his leg, set and splinted properly. Even plastered, this time, though his physician knew he hated to be so confined. He could look forward to a long lecture about walking on an unhealed limb, later, he was certain. But so long as Mia sat beside him while he endured it, he did not care.

"If I collapse, you'll simply have to haul me the rest of the way," he managed to spit out. "But under no circumstances will I be returning to that bed without my wife."

Glaukos steadied him, and he hung half-suspended between the two men, his arms across their shoulders. "I tried to talk her out of it, my lord, I promise you."

"Yes, yes," Pirithous said, unable to focus on much more than the awkward hop of one leg after another. "And if she'd listened, I'd still be flat on my back, waiting to cross the River Styx. Just get me to the wall, the both of you, and leave me in peace."

"Forgive me, my lord, but the queen said you weren't to be left alone while she was away," Glaukos said.

Pirithous stared at him. "The queen said, did she?"

Theseus turned a laugh into a cough. "You certainly can't say you weren't warned. And it's hardly fair to Glaukos to make him choose which one of you he'll disobey."

The queen said she didn't want him left alone.

He'd never let her out of his sight again.

***

He was half-dozing against the stonework when he heard a shout from the guards a ways down. Dawn painted the sky in shades of orange and pink, washing out the deep purples of night. It had been long and dark and cold, and his muscles ached from keeping upright when he had lain so still for so long. Ached, but did not betray him. He'd even managed to drink down a healthy cup of broth, which was all his thrice-cursed physician would allow him.

Glaukos stirred, then rose stiffly from his stool to look out over the top of the wall.

"The queen!" the same guard called out. "Open the gate for the queen!"

"Glaukos, your arm." Pirithous managed to rise, leaning heavily on his friend, but his stomach turned to ice at the sight that greeted him.

Mia, moon-white and slumped over Podarkes's neck, barely kept herself upon the horse's back, and Podarkes himself moved far too gingerly, as if afraid she might fall. As if she had fallen already.

"Get me to the gate," he demanded. "Quickly!"

Glaukos cursed, and then called for another man—Leukos. Pirithous had never been so glad for his raiders as he was in that moment. He could only imagine the huffing and hemming a man like Plouteus would make when he asked for aid. Leukos and Glaukos had him braced between them in a handful of heartbeats, and Pirithous did not even bother to pretend to hop down the stairs, but let them carry his weight completely. If reaching

Hippodamia cost him a little pride, so be it. The thought of Mia falling from a horse…

She would have to be gravely ill, that much was certain. And if Poseidon had done her harm, or taken her by violence, Pirithous would climb Olympus to make the god pay, if he must! He would dive beneath the depths of the sea and tear the god's palace apart stone by stone to reach him. He would—

"Mia." He shoved free of his men and stumbled toward her, clutching at Podarkes's mane with one hand to keep upright, and the other cupping her cheek, stroking her hair, her face. She was covered in the finest dust. Like the silky powder in a sculptor's room, and it streaked beneath his fingers. "Little mouse, open your eyes. Look at me, please. Just a glance. Just a word!"

Her eyelashes fluttered, followed by a soft groan. She was breathing, stirring at his touch, and some of the tightness in his chest eased.

"My brave mouse," he murmured, pressing his forehead to hers. "My brave, foolish mouse."

She opened her eyes, then, and a strangled noise rose from her throat, her whole body going tense, first with surprise, and then cool, blue relief. One arm wrapped around his neck, weakly, and she slithered slowly from Podarkes's back, nearly over-balancing him with her weight. But he didn't care. He didn't care if she toppled him to the ground, so long as she lay in his arms, safe and whole.

Her lips moved without sound, shaping his name, and then she hid her face against his throat, shuddering in his hold. Hot tears spilled against his skin. Thank the gods for Podarkes, standing solid beside him, or he'd never have kept himself upright, and he had no intention of letting Mia go, not then, when she gripped him with all that was left of her strength and wept.

"It's all right, now, mouse," he mumbled into her hair. "We're both all right."

At least he hoped so. But from the way she cried all the harder at his assurance, he was beginning to doubt the truth of his own words.

Chapter Fifty-Two

Hippodamia

Somehow they had managed to make it to his bed. How exactly, with his broken bones and her weakness, she was not so certain, but when she woke, it was daylight and she was wrapped in Pirithous's arms, surrounded by the lavender of his bedding and the spice of his skin. Maybe it had all been a dream. One long nightmare, to be forgotten in the sunlight streaming through his window, warm and bright and caressing.

"I worried you would never wake," he murmured, pressing a kiss against her temple. "You were so still, so limp, and so deeply asleep for so long."

"How long?" she asked, her voice rough. As if she had been screaming.

Or singing herself hoarse with hymns.

She buried her face in the curve of his shoulder, pushing the thought away. It had to have been a dream. Eurytion and Centaurus's death, Cyllarus's attack, Peleus… all that came after. She wanted to believe it was a dream, just a little bit longer.

"The night you returned, through the day following and straight through last night again, until morning," he said. "I feared we had only traded places. But Ariston had arrived, and he and Niko both pronounced you well, if exhausted, and I suppose Niko was pleased that I kept to my bed while you slept beside me. I'd be cautious of any drinks he offers you, now that he knows how to keep me off my feet. He's liable to dose you for my sake."

His voice was soft and teasing, filled with good humor to match the tickle of the sunlight along her limbs. Gods above, but she was glad of it. So glad to hear his voice again, to know his laughter brimmed just beneath. She burrowed deeper into his arms, beneath the linens, into her desire to forget everything else but this moment. Pirithous was well, and she was with him, and surely none of the rest mattered beyond that.

"Will you not tell me what happened, Mia?"

She tugged one of the furs over her head, his question squeezing her heart, twisting her stomach. Because it wasn't a dream. It would never be a dream, and he did not know, yet, just what she had cost them. She didn't want him to know.

"Ah, mouse." He pulled the fur back, his fingers finding her chin, tipping her face up, until she met his eyes. So bright, and warm as the sun at her back. "Whatever passed between you and the god—you needn't fear I will turn from you. If a child comes, I'll raise him as my own, I swear to you. He'll never know he isn't mine, unless you wish it otherwise."

She blinked, her forehead furrowing. "What on earth are you talking about, Pirithous?"

"Theseus said—" He cleared his throat. "That is, I worried, when he said you had gone up the mountain to make sacrifice…"

It must have been her expression that stopped him, or the absolute befuddlement he felt from her heart, because he trailed off, then, and she was more than glad of it. "You think Poseidon took me as his lover? That I offered my womb to the god?"

His face flushed. "My mother—"

"I gave him my blood," she said, before he could go on. She couldn't bear it, for him to dwell upon the thought a moment longer. And never mind what else the god had taken. It was not a lie. She did not need to lie to reassure him of this. "Only my blood.

Though I cannot say for certain that I do not carry a child. *Your* child."

He let out a breath, and then laughed, thick and throaty and delighted, as he drew her in all the more tightly, burying his face in her hair as his hand found her waist beneath the bedding, slid over her stomach. She could feel his joy leaching into her skin with the contact, bubbling in her throat.

"I suspect you have Zeus to thank for it," she said, trying not to think of the child's face in the rock. It was promise and curse, and she did not know how he might respond—she did not want Pirithous to blame the boy for the choice she had made. "Theseus was right about his wanting your heir. But Poseidon took pity upon me, after I'd bled myself half to death. Or else Zeus feared for the babe in my belly. It hardly matters, now. Whatever their reasons, Poseidon gave you back to me."

"I ought to have known that Dia would choose me a bride strong enough to stand against the gods," he said, lifting his head enough to search her face. "I never should have doubted. Not for a moment."

She stroked his cheek. "I loved you too much to let you die. After all you had done for me, I could not sit by."

He caught her hand, pressing a kiss to her palm. "It's all behind us now. We've nothing left to fear."

She would let him believe it, she decided. To repay him for everything he'd done, all that he'd given her. For the precious days she had wasted in blame and hurt and anger.

If they had only three years, she meant to fill them with love enough to last for the rest of his life.

For Pirithous.

For their son.

For herself.

She would not let the gods take anything more.

Epilogue

Pirithous

Polypoetes, at two years old, rode with all the skill of his mother. Just watching him atop Podarkes's back made Pirithous ache with grief still too fresh to ignore. The funeral banquet was tonight, but he had not wanted their son to steep in the palace, listening to the weeping and mourning as the women prepared the feast. And he had wanted him to know where Hippodamia had been laid to rest, that he might know she was at peace in the caves of her people.

Theseus had helped him find them. Just as he rode with them now, behind the cart where her body lay shrouded in gossamer silk. The finest, lightest fabric he had ever seen. Pirithous had made the proper sacrifices, going all the way to Mount Pelion to speak to Chiron, the half-horse son of Cronus, about the proper rites for Mia's funeral. He'd marked himself with blood at the throat and the heart, since Hippodamia's body carried no visible wounds.

Apollo's arrows did not always leave marks, no matter how deadly their aim.

"Papa, look!" Polypoetes leaned forward on Podarkes's back. His legs, too short to fit the stallion properly, were tucked up beneath his bottom, allowing him to rise up on his knees. Pirithous swore he was more at home on the back of his mother's horse than he was walking on two legs.

He followed his son's gaze to the peak of the mountain. The end of another path, long overgrown with wiry scrub oaks and pines, but still visible as a trace of packed earth. Looming at the top were three stones. Perhaps it had been one large boulder once, cracked by lightning, or wind or water over time. Two large stones and one small, huddled together like a family.

Pirithous glanced back at Hippodamia's shrouded figure, then slid down from his horse. "Stay with Theseus," he told the boy, patting Podarkes's neck absently as he passed.

But of course he didn't. Polypoetes was his mother's son, after all, and it wasn't long before he heard Podarkes's hooves on the path behind him, the horse's world-weary sigh blowing against the back of his neck. Pirithous shook his head and pushed his way through the brush and trees, grateful the path was not too terribly steep for the horse. It wouldn't be, he supposed, if the centaurs had made use of it.

And then he reached the rocks, stopping so abruptly that Podarkes huffed, startled and annoyed.

"What is it?" Theseus called up from below.

Pirithous reached out, letting his fingers trace the features in the stone. Roughly carved, but distinct, with two bright smudges of brown quartz where the eyes should have been. Hippodamia's eyes. Her lips. Her face.

He lifted his gaze, searching beyond the rocks. The shallow depression, the broken and rotted wood at its heart, and the stone, somehow still clear of windblown debris, but stained black with spilled blood. He could even see where she had knelt. The impression of her knees and her toes in the center of a spiraled crack in the rock.

"It's Mama. An' you, Papa," Polypoetes said.

Pirithous brought his attention back to the stones. Carved with their images. Small Polypoetes just as he stood today. Their little family. And he knew what he was seeing now. The sign of

Poseidon. The Earth Shaker had touched these grounds, hallowed them with his power.

And Hippodamia.

Gods above.

All these years, she'd known. She'd seen it in the stone, and when she had come back down the mountain, she'd known their time was short. Known what was coming.

It explained so much. Her peace when she had fallen ill. Her bravery. The love she'd lavished upon both of them.

She'd traded her life for his, for their son's. For three years of joy.

He would have laughed if he had not wanted to weep.

"My brave, foolish mouse," he whispered, touching her face in the rock. "My bride, my queen. My love. Enjoy your days in Elysium, for it is impossible the gods would find you undeserving."

"Pirithous?" Theseus called again, from below.

"Come, Polypoetes. Let us see to your mother's body, that her shade might find the peace in death she has earned by her life."

For the first time since Mia had fallen ill, he felt some small measure of comfort. She had not died for nothing. It was not some greater cruelty of the gods, sent to punish them both. Hippodamia had bargained with the gods for his sake. For love. She had bargained and she had won them three years of glory.

And Pirithous did not mean to waste her sacrifice.

ACKNOWLEDGMENTS

Huge thanks to the usual suspects: Diana Paz, Zachary Tringali, Valerie Valdes, L.T. Host, and particularly Nick Mohoric, who demanded *a* Pirithous book and ended up getting a lot more than he bargained for. Extra special thanks to Libbie Hawker, who gave me a shove when I otherwise might have despaired of ever getting this book into the world. And a million thank yous to Lane Brown for his fantastic work bringing Hippodamia to life for the cover.

And of course I would be terribly remiss if I did not thank my family: Adam, naturally, but also Mattias and Emilia who both read early versions of this manuscript and provided valuable insights and opinions. I can't tell you how much I appreciate those early reads!

And last but not least, thank you so much to all of you who read and reviewed and spread the word about *Helen of Sparta*, because without *Helen*'s success, I would never have been brave enough to publish *Tamer of Horses*. I hope you'll find it a worthy installment of Greek Bronze Age heroics, despite the presence of so many centaurs. Hippodamia's story is one that is very close to my heart, and I hope you'll love her as much as you did Helen.

Author's Note

Pirithous's legend is incredibly fragmented, but his marriage to Hippodamia and the war with the centaurs that followed is one of the few larger pieces of his mythology that's survived. Ovid, Psuedo-Apollodorus, Diodorus, Plutarch, even Homer, among a great many others—there are so many accounts of the Centauromachy in ancient literature, as well as artwork appearing on vases, in friezes, and sculpted in marble and bronze from antiquity into the modern day. Hippodamia and Pirithous themselves, however, are more obscure. Of Pirithous, we have only the moments when his path crosses with Theseus in the myths, and of Hippodamia there is even less from which to draw her character. But one piece, one small line that's stuck with me, is her suggested kinship to the centaurs. I couldn't help but wonder what that might mean. If Hippodamia was, in some way, *kin* to the centaurs, what would that look like? How was it possible?

For the most part, *Tamer of Horses* is the end result of that thought experiment. Hippodamia as a foundling daughter of the centaur king would have made a perfect match for Pirithous, a convenient means to shore up the difficult relationship they must have had with the Lapith people, as the unnatural children and grandchildren of the former king, Ixion. Could she have been something else altogether? Absolutely. Sometimes she's a daughter of Atrax, himself a son of a river god. Or maybe a daughter of a man named Butes. Some accounts even give her a different name, Deidamia or Laodamia, or Hippoboteia, or even Dia or Ischomache. Such is the nature of Greek Myth, that it gives us so many variations—particularly when it comes to non-heroic women. But as a foundling with no notion of her true parentage, my Hippodamia could still be any of these things.

But also as a foundling, raised by centaurs instead of inside the incredible palace society of Mycenaean Greece, she gets to be a different kind of woman, with different expectations of what her life and her marriage should be. She is not bound by the same societal restrictions, and with the examples of Pirithous's mother, Dia, and Theseus's Amazon wife, Antiope, she's able to find even greater strength and agency. And to be frank, I couldn't imagine Pirithous taking just any woman as his wife. She had to have been exceptional and unique. Exceptional enough that decades later, he would accept nothing less than a daughter of Zeus for his second wife—a decision which would lead him into much the same ruin as Ixion, costing him his kingdom and his life when he is trapped in Hades for his hubris in thinking to steal Persephone herself as his bride.

As in *Helen of Sparta* and *By Helen's Hand*, to which this book can be considered a prequel and is certainly meant to be read as part of the same larger world and timeline, my imagining of Mycenaean Greece is influenced hugely both by the work of Dr. Dmitri Nakassis, who suggests a flourishing middle class outside the palaces, and M.I. Finley's *World of Odysseus*, which proposes that the kings of this period could not rule without the consent of their people. Interestingly, Thessaly, unlike the more southern regions of the Peloponnese and Attica, escaped much of the destruction we associate with the collapse of Mycenaean society. And we see this most clearly, perhaps, in their burial sites, where we can watch the slow progression from Tholos tombs and simple graves in the Bronze Age to cremation and funeral pyres, which don't appear at all in Thessaly until the early Iron Age—though they were certainly in evidence among the Hittites, their neighbors across the sea.

But because Homer is by far the greatest influence on our cultural consciousness regarding the disposal of the dead during this period, and Homer chooses to depict the fallen warriors and heroes of Greece set ablaze upon a pyre, I felt a small compromise might be in order. Both the Homeric pyres and the Mycenaean archaeological evidence point to the same basic rituals and superstitions, the same concern for the body and spirit pre-decomposition, and in contrast to such extreme consideration, a certain amount of carelessness for the remaining bones, after. This suggests that the spirit was no longer connected to the remains, but was considered to have completed its journey to the afterlife. Hippodamia and Pirithous both make mention of the use of tombs and graves, and note that the pyres they've chosen for the disposal of their dead are an exception, not the rule, but it isn't outside the realm of possibility, either, that faced with a large number of dead, and their potentially malicious spirits, a pyre might have been considered to speed up the natural processes of decomposition. And for the Lapiths, with the centaurs still a threat, time was certainly short.

As to the burial rituals and practices of the centaurs themselves, it made sense to me that they would follow similar traditions, utilizing natural caves instead of building complex tombs. Centaurus is, after all, more man than beast, and unquestionably a son of Ixion. His natural offspring, however, are something else altogether. And in this element of their culture, also, I followed mythic tradition—for as Nestor so frequently reminds us in the *Iliad*, it was natural to the Greeks for each successive generation to be considered less worthy than the one that came before. That this degeneration might have been hurried by Centaurus's mating with the Mares of Magnesia seemed a reasonable progression within the confines of that established mythic tradition. But it doesn't make Hippodamia's ultimate decision any more horrific, nor excuse what feels to my modern sensibilities like a genocidal solution, which ultimately all but wiped out an entire tribe, if not an entire species.

I've chosen to keep the fantastic element of the centaurs intact, to allow Pirithous to be an exceptional man with exceptional and god-given power, just as Heracles might have been. While these elements are not strictly historical, I do feel it's important to allow myth to still *be* myth and leave room for these elements of the supernatural. Because even today, in the modern world, with all our advantages, we are still *so* limited in our understanding of history, and I'm inclined to give the Ancient Greeks the benefit of the doubt when it comes to their own beliefs. Perhaps the centaurs were only a warring tribe of men with a gift for horsemanship that rivaled the Lapiths—who, for all their skill, did *not* yet realize that horses could be ridden into battle as cavalry, though I have allowed Hippodamia to mount her Lapith warriors as a show of strength. Perhaps the story of the Centauromachy was a metaphor explaining why these fantastic beast-men no longer lived in Archaic and Ancient Greece. But perhaps, too, they were something else altogether which we haven't yet uncovered in all our digging and reconstruction of the past.

We'll never know for certain whether Hippodamia and Pirithous lived, or what happened during their wedding feast. We'll never know for certain how Theseus came to marry his Amazon bride, or if they existed at all to marry. We'll never know what life was truly like in the Greek Bronze Age for those who lived within it. But the more I learn about this fascinating time, the more I think they weren't so different from you or me. Even during the Bronze Age, people were still just people, and if there is one thing the myths make more than clear, it's that even the greatest hero-kings and -queens often made mistakes—and maybe we only *want* to believe they aren't the same kind of mistakes we're still making today.

As always, if you're interested in learning more about my research and the myths that inspired the books you've read, there's plenty more on my website www.amaliacarosella.com, including links to sources and articles within a variety of blogposts.

And if you loved *Tamer of Horses*, or any of my other books, please do consider leaving a review, or subscribe to my newsletter, **The Amaliad**, to stay up to date on future works from Authors!Me.

ABOUT THE AUTHOR

photo © 2015 Thomas G. Hale

Amalia Carosella began as a biology major before taking Latin and falling in love with old heroes and older gods. After that, she couldn't stop writing about them, with the occasional break for more contemporary subjects. She graduated with a BA in Classical Studies as well as English from the University of North Dakota. A former bookseller and an avid reader, she is fascinated by the Age of Heroes and Bronze Age Greece, though anything Viking Age or earlier is likely to capture her attention. She maintains a blog relating to classical mythology and the Bronze Age at www.amaliacarosella.com and can also be found writing fantasy under the name Amalia Dillin at www.amaliadillin.com. Today, she lives with her husband in Upstate New York and dreams of the day she will own goats (and maybe even a horse, too).

More From Amalia Carosella

Helen of Sparta

More than two decades ***after*** *the events of* Tamer Of Horses...

Long before she ran away with Paris to Troy, Helen of Sparta was haunted by nightmares of a burning city under siege. These dreams foretold impending war—a war that only Helen has the power to avert. To do so, she must defy her family and betray her betrothed by fleeing the palace in the dead of night. In need of protection, she finds shelter and comfort in the arms of Theseus, son of Poseidon. With Theseus at her side, she believes she can escape her destiny. But at every turn, new dangers—violence, betrayal, extortion, threat of war—thwart Helen's plans and bar her path. Still, she refuses to bend to the will of the gods.

A new take on an ancient myth, Helen of Sparta is the story of one woman determined to decide her own fate.

***

Available for kindle from Amazon and in trade paperback wherever books are sold.

By Helen's Hand

Picking up directly where Helen of Sparta *left off,* By Helen's Hand ***completes*** *Helen's story...*

With divine beauty comes dangerous power.

Helen believed she could escape her destiny and save her people from utter destruction. After defying her family and betraying her intended husband, she found peace with her beloved Theseus, the king of Athens and son of Poseidon.

But peace did not last long. Cruelly separated from Theseus by the gods, and uncertain whether he will live or die, Helen is forced to return to Sparta. In order to avoid marriage to Menelaus, a powerful prince unhinged by desire, Helen assembles an array of suitors to compete for her hand. As the men circle like vultures, Helen dreams again of war—and of a strange prince, meant to steal her away. Every step she takes to protect herself and her people seems to bring destruction nearer. Without Theseus's strength to support her, can Helen thwart the gods and stop her nightmare from coming to pass?

***

And coming soon from Lake Union Publishing:

DAUGHTER OF A THOUSAND YEARS

Greenland, AD 1000

More than her fiery hair marks Freydís as the daughter of Erik the Red; her hot temper and fierce pride are as formidable as her Viking father's. And so, too, is her devotion to the god Thor, which puts her at odds with those in power—including her own brother, the zealous Leif Eriksson. Determined to forge her own path, she defies her family's fury and clings to her dream of sailing away to live on her own terms, with or without the support of her husband.

New Hampshire, 2016

Like her Icelandic ancestors, history professor Emma Moretti is a passionate defender of Norse mythology. But in a small town steeped in traditional values, her cultural beliefs could jeopardize both her academic career and her congressman father's reelection. Torn between public expectation and personal identity, family and faith, she must choose which to honor and which to abandon.

In a dramatic, sweeping dual narrative that spans a millennium, two women struggle against communities determined to silence them, but neither Freydís nor Emma intends to give up without a fight.

***

Available February 2017 for kindle from Amazon and in trade paperback wherever books are sold

CPSIA information can be obtained
at www.ICGtesting.com
Printed in the USA
FSHW011949300420
69818FS